KU-611-800

THE MARSHAL'S JUSTICE

BY
DELORES FOSSEN

MILLS
& BOON

All rights reserved including the right of reproduction in whole or in part in any form. This edition is published by arrangement with Harlequin Books S.A.

This is a work of fiction. Names, characters, places, locations and incidents are purely fictional and bear no relationship to any real life individuals, living or dead, or to any actual places, business establishments, locations, events or incidents. Any resemblance is entirely coincidental.

This book is sold subject to the condition that it shall not, by way of trade or otherwise, be lent, resold, hired out or otherwise circulated without the prior consent of the publisher in any form of binding or cover other than that in which it is published and without a similar condition including this condition being imposed on the subsequent purchaser.

® and ™ are trademarks owned and used by the trademark owner and/or its licensee. Trademarks marked with ® are registered with the United Kingdom Patent Office and/or the Office for Harmonisation in the Internal Market and in other countries.

First Published in Great Britain 2016
By Mills & Boon, an imprint of HarperCollins*Publishers*
1 London Bridge Street, London, SE1 9GF

© 2016 Delores Fossen

ISBN: 978-0-263-91903-5

46-0516

Our policy is to use papers that are natural, renewable and recyclable products and made from wood grown in sustainable forests. The logging and manufacturing processes conform to the legal environmental regulations of the country of origin.

Printed and bound in Spain
by CPI, Barcelona

Delores Fossen, a *USA TODAY* bestselling author, has sold over fifty novels with millions of copies of her books in print worldwide. She's received a Booksellers' Best Award and an RT Reviewers' Choice Best Book Award. She was also a finalist for a prestigious RITA® Award. You can contact the author through her web page at www.deloresfossen.com.

Chapter One

The shot cracked through the air. Mercy. That was definitely not what Marshal Chase Crockett wanted to hear.

Or see.

The bullet slammed into the woman he'd just spotted. Her gaze connected with Chase's a split second before she crumpled to the ground.

If she wasn't dead, she soon would be. Chase was sure of it.

He cursed when he couldn't go out in the clearing where she'd fallen and pull her out of the path of more gunfire. Cursed, too, that he hadn't been able to stop that bullet from hitting her in the first place.

How the devil had this happened?

He didn't have time to try to figure that out because the next bullet came right at him, and Chase had no choice but to dive behind a pile of rocks. Maybe he'd get a chance soon to return fire and make the shooter pay for what he had just done.

And what he'd done was shoot the criminal informant, Deanne McKinley, on the banks of Appaloosa Creek. A woman who had phoned Chase earlier and begged him to help her. If he'd just gotten her call a few minutes sooner, maybe he could have arrived in time to stop this.

Whatever *this* was.

Clearly, someone wanted Deanne dead, and now whoever had attacked her was shooting at Chase, too.

"If you want to get out of this alive, you might as well give up now," the gunman shouted.

Chase didn't recognize the voice, but he'd caught a glimpse of a guy wearing a ski mask before the man shot Deanne and then darted out of sight. He wasn't even sure if the idiot was yelling at him or Deanne. Chase didn't have nearly enough info, other than the call a half hour ago from Deanne to tell him she was in trouble. She said someone was trying to kill her, that she needed his help.

Help was exactly what Chase had intended to give her when he'd arrived.

So far, all he'd managed to do was dodge bullets, but if he had anything to say about that, things were about to change.

Chase heard Deanne's hoarse moan, and she moved her hand to her chest. *Alive.* He had to do something now to keep it that way.

He didn't know the exact location of the shooter, but Chase fired two shots in the guy's general direction. In the same motion, he scrambled toward Deanne to try to pull her away.

Basically, it was a high-risk move with little chance of succeeding.

Or at least it should have been.

But another set of shots blasted through the air. Definitely not ones that Chase or the gunman had fired. They'd come from a cluster of trees about thirty feet away, and the bullets had been aimed at the shooter.

Maybe backup had arrived a little sooner than Chase

had thought it would. Or it could be a hunter or nearby rancher who'd heard sounds of the attack and had come to help. Either way, he'd take it.

Chase grabbed hold of Deanne's arm and pulled her behind a tree. It wasn't much cover, but it was better than leaving her out in the open.

He fired off another shot to keep the gunman at bay and sent a quick text requesting an ambulance along with the backup. It would likely be one of his brothers who responded to his request since all three of them were in local law enforcement. Chase only hoped the backup and the ambulance arrived in time.

It'd be close.

Deanne was bleeding out from the gunshot she'd taken to the chest. Chase did his best to add some pressure to the wound, but it was hard to do that without constricting her breathing. He didn't want her to suffocate.

More shots came from the gunman.

The idiot was moving closer to them, no doubt coming in for the kill.

Deanne mumbled something, something that Chase didn't catch, and without taking his attention off the area where the shooter was positioned, he leaned in closer, hoping to hear what Deanne was trying to say.

"Help," Deanne whispered.

"Help is on the way," he assured her. Chase wanted to say how sorry he was for what had happened to her. Deanne had a criminal past, but she didn't deserve this.

Deanne shook her head. "No, help *her*." Her gaze drifted in the direction where those two other shots had been fired.

Each word she spoke was a struggle, and by the time

she was done, Deanne was gasping for air. Still, she managed to say one last thing.

Something that twisted his stomach into a tight, hard knot.

No more breaths from Deanne. Her chest just stopped moving, and Chase could only watch the life drain from her eyes. Watch and mentally repeat what Deanne had said to him with her dying breath.

April's in trouble.

His gaze whipped in the direction of the second shooter. The person was still hidden behind a tree, but Chase had the sickening feeling that he knew who'd fired those two shots at the gunman.

Was April really out there?

Just the thought of it twisted and tightened that knot even more. There was plenty of bad blood between April and him. But a different kind of connection, too. One that would last a lifetime.

Because April was pregnant with Chase's baby.

However, April shouldn't be here. *Couldn't* be here. She was in WITSEC, tucked away somewhere safe with a new name and a location that even Chase didn't know. A necessary precaution so that no one could trace her by following him.

April was also nine months pregnant, ready to deliver any day now.

He waited until the original shooter fired another shot, and he used that to help him pinpoint the guy's position. Chase fired. He also got moving right away, heading toward those trees where the second shooter had been. Maybe he wouldn't find April there after all.

But if she was, then that meant something had gone wrong.

He tried to recall every word of the short phone conversation he'd had earlier with Deanne. She'd been frantic, said she was in her car, somewhere near the Appaloosa Creek Bridge, and that she was being tailed by a gunman wearing a ski mask.

Had Deanne said anything else?

No.

Definitely nothing about April being with her.

So, maybe he was wrong about April, and Deanne's words were merely the mumblings of a dying woman. And maybe that was one of his brothers out there helping him with the shots.

Chase scrambled his way through the trees and the underbrush, cursing the wet spring weather that'd clogged this part of the woods with mud and briars. It slowed him down.

He ducked behind a tree, fired off another shot and then had to reload. It was his last magazine so he'd have to be careful with the shots now and make every one count.

Whoever was returning fire at Deanne's killer didn't seem to have the problem of not enough ammunition. The person continued to shoot, spacing out the shots several seconds apart.

"Jericho?" Chase whispered, hoping his brother, the sheriff, was the one returning fire behind the sprawling oak that was now just a few yards away.

No answer.

And if it'd been Jericho, or his other brothers, Levi or Jax, they would have responded somehow to let him know not to fire in their direction.

Chase kept moving, working his way through the muck, and he finally got in position to spot someone. It was late afternoon and some sunlight still hung in the sky, but the woods created deep shadows. There was nowhere near enough light for him to see the person's face, but whoever it was wore all black.

He risked lifting his head just a little, to see how this shadowy figure would respond, but he or she didn't even seem to acknowledge Chase.

"I'm coming closer," Chase warned the person, hoping this didn't turn out to be a big mistake, and he scurried toward the tree.

Thank God the person didn't shoot him, but this definitely wasn't one of his brothers.

Not April, either.

Because while he still couldn't make out much of the person's face, he could see the silhouette of the body. Whoever this was darn sure wasn't nine months pregnant.

Chase scrambled the last few feet to the tree and landed on the ground right next to the person who was kneeling. His heart skipped a beat or two though when he saw the ski mask. Identical to the one worn by the other shooter.

Hell.

He brought up his gun. Took aim. Just as the person shoved up the ski mask to reveal her face.

April.

Yes, it was her, all right. There was no mistaking her now. The black hair, the wide blue eyes. But she didn't have her attention fixed on him. It was on the other shooter.

"Is Deanne okay?" she asked on a rise of breath.

"No. She's dead."

April had no reaction to that. Well, none that he could pick out in the dusky light anyway. A surprise. Deanne and she weren't friends. Far from it after everything that'd happened, but still April had to be shocked by a woman's murder.

However, reactions and that ski mask weren't his only concern about this situation. Chase couldn't stop himself from looking in the direction of her stomach again. Definitely flat.

"The baby?" he managed to say.

His baby. The one April should have been giving birth to any day now. But she certainly didn't have a newborn with her, and she didn't look as if she'd just delivered, either.

"Play along," she whispered, a split second before she hooked her left arm around his neck, dragged him in front of her and put her gun to his head.

"I have Marshal Crockett," April called out to someone.

"What the devil's going on here?" Chase snarled, and he shoved her away from him.

"You have to play along," April repeated. Definitely not the tone of a terrified woman on the run. Nor was that a weak grip she put on him when she yanked him back against her.

Damn. Was April up to her old tricks again?

"Put down your gun," she added in a whisper. "And whatever you do, don't shoot him."

Chase didn't get a chance to ask her anything else because he heard the footsteps. Heavy, hurried ones. And he soon spotted the guy who'd been firing shots at him.

The very snake who'd killed Deanne.

Chase didn't put down his gun as April had demanded, but she shoved his hand by his side. Maybe so that his weapon would be out of sight. Or perhaps because this was some kind of sick game she was playing.

The killer came right toward them, and the moment he spotted April—and the gun she had to Chase's head—he lifted his ski mask.

And he smiled.

Chase didn't recognize him. The guy was a stranger, but judging from his sheer size and the hardened look on his scarred face, this was a hired thug. He certainly didn't look like a man ready to negotiate surrender, not with that Kevlar vest and multiple guns holstered on his bulky body.

"Good job," the guy told April. "Well, sorta good. That wasn't you shooting at me, now, was it?"

"I aimed over your head. I wanted Marshal Crockett to think I was trying to kill you so he'd come to me. It worked."

Oh, man. Was this really a trap? Possibly. But Chase kept going back to April's *play along* comment.

What kind of sick plan was this?

The man stared at her. A long time. As if he might challenge what she'd just told him. Then, he shrugged. "Guess it did work. Now take a hike so I can finish this. Unless you'd rather watch while I have a word with your ex-lover. It might involve a bullet or two."

Shaking her head, April stood. Slowly. "No, I'd rather skip that part. Just give me what you promised, and I'll leave."

Chase stood, too, hoping it wasn't a mistake that he hadn't already put an end to this hulking clown. Or that he'd semi-trusted April when she'd rattled off those whispered instructions about not shooting the guy.

"Give me what you promised," April demanded to the man.

Now Chase heard some emotion in her voice. She was scared. Which meant whatever the heck was going on here was possibly about to take an even worse turn than it already had.

"You'll have to wait a little longer," the man said. He motioned for her to leave. "I'll meet you at your car, and you'll get it then."

Chase still didn't have a clue what this conversation was about, but he had no doubts that this bozo was about to try to kill him.

"You promised." April's voice was trembling now.

The man smiled again. There was no friendliness or humor in it. "And it's a promise I'll keep, okay? Just not right now at this second. I need to have that little chat with this cowboy cop first while you hurry along."

April stayed put, and even though Chase kept his attention on the man and couldn't see her, he thought she might be glaring at Deanne's killer. Chase was certainly doing his own share of glaring at both of them.

"I need you to find somebody in WITSEC," the killer told Chase. "April claimed she wasn't able to help, but since you're a marshal, I'm betting you got access to stuff that she doesn't. I need to find Quentin Landis."

Chase groaned. He shouldn't have been surprised this was about Quentin. It usually was when April was involved.

Because Quentin was her brother.

Along with being a criminal. And the only reason Chase had met April to begin with was because he'd been investigating Quentin. At the time he had thought

April was innocent and had no knowledge of her brother's criminal activity. He'd been dead wrong about that.

"You expect me just to tell you where he is?" Chase asked, making sure he let this jerk know that wasn't going to happen.

Quentin might be scum, but he was in WITSEC after turning state's evidence in an upcoming murder trial, and it was part of Chase's job to make sure that even scum stayed protected. Whether they deserved it or not.

The gunman stared at him. "Yeah. I didn't figure you'd cooperate, but we had to try, didn't we? Maybe if I put a few bullets in your kneecaps, you'll recall something."

"We?" Chase spared April a glance, but she only shook her head. He had no idea what that head shake meant.

Nor did he have time to figure it out.

"No!" April shouted. Not at Chase but at the gunman.

The gunman lifted his Glock and aimed it at Chase. Chase was doing the same to the killer with his own Smith & Wesson.

Chase beat him to it.

He didn't fire into the Kevlar vest, but instead he double-tapped two shots to the gunman's head. And Chase didn't miss. The man dropped like a sack of rocks just as Chase had intended.

With that taken care of, Chase turned to April. "Now, what the hell's going on?" he demanded.

But she didn't answer. Probably because of the hoarse sob that tore from her mouth. "Oh, God." And she kept repeating it.

She dropped to her knees and she grabbed the dead man by the shoulders, lifting his torso off the ground. "Tell me where she is!" April yelled. "Tell me." The sobbing got worse when she put her fingers to his neck. "He's dead. He can't be dead."

It wasn't exactly the reaction Chase had expected since she knew this snake was a killer and had been prepared to kill again.

She looked up at him, tears shimmering in her eyes. "The baby."

All right. That got his attention. "*Our* baby?" Chase asked.

April nodded, and her breath shattered. "Someone took her. And that dead man was my best hope at finding our daughter."

Chapter Two

April felt the fresh wave of panic slam into her like a Mack truck.

First the baby. Then Deanne's death. Now this.

The emotions were too raw and strong, overpowering her so much that they were hard to fight. But April knew she had no choice except to keep fighting.

If she gave in to it, her baby might be lost forever.

Despite possibly destroying evidence, April rifled through the dead man's pockets. Looking for anything that would tell her where he was holding the baby.

No wallet. No ID. No photos. No scraps of paper with details of any kind.

Nothing.

Tamping down the panic, she forced herself to get to her feet. Chase helped by taking hold of her arm. April didn't have to look at his expression to know that he wanted answers. And he wanted them *now*.

However, April didn't have some of those answers, especially the ones Chase would want most.

Even though Chase still had hold of her, April started toward Deanne. Yes, she knew the woman was dead. April had seen her fall after taking the bullet. Had also seen her talking with Chase moments before it looked as if she took her last breath. April didn't know what, or how much, Deanne had told him, but she figured she'd soon find out.

"Who has the baby?" he snapped. "And when was she taken?"

April had to shake her head again, and she motioned toward the dead man. "Whoever he was working for took her. Around midnight two masked gunmen broke into my house, held me at gunpoint and demanded to know where Quentin was. When I said I didn't know, they kidnapped the baby."

A sound came deep from within his chest. Not a good sound, either. Pure anger. "And you didn't call me?"

She'd braced herself for the question, and the anger. Or so she'd thought. Hard to brace herself, though, for that kind of emotion.

"The kidnapper said if I contacted you, anyone in your family or anyone in law enforcement, I'd never see the baby again." She hadn't wanted to believe that, but April hadn't been able to dismiss it, either. "They said they'd be in touch soon and left."

"So, you called Deanne instead." Chase didn't sound happy about that at all. Of course, nothing about this situation was going to make him happy.

"Yes, I thought it would be safe for her to come. I figured no one would be trailing Deanne to get to me. Especially after things ended so badly between us."

Well, it'd ended badly between Deanne and April's brother anyway. Deanne had been the one to turn Quentin in. Of course, in doing so Deanne had turned in April, as well.

"As a CI, Deanne dealt with dangerous thugs like the

ones who took the baby," April explained. "And she did come right away when I called her."

"Because she felt guilty for what happened," Chase supplied. "She shouldn't have. Both Quentin and you made your own beds."

Since it was true and there was no way to make Chase see the legal shades of gray that had gotten her to that point, April just continued with her explanation. "I waited for a ransom demand, or any kind of communication from the kidnappers. And about an hour and a half ago, someone finally called and said for me to come to the Appaloosa Creek Bridge, that there'd be instructions for getting the baby back."

Chase didn't come out and tell her she'd been stupid, but what he felt was written all over his face.

A face that shared a lot of features with their daughter.

Same light brown hair. Same deep blue eyes. It both broke April's heart and warmed it to see those features on her precious baby.

"I guess Deanne got spooked and called me?" Chase asked.

Chase was not going to like this, either. "Not quite. When I got to the bridge, the kidnapper was waiting for me. The same one you just killed. But he said he wouldn't give me the baby unless you came to the bridge, too. I tried to talk him out of that, but he insisted it was the only way."

She'd been right. Chase didn't like that. Because it meant she had lured him there.

"So, you had Deanne make the call," Chase said.

April nodded. "I knew if I called, you'd have too many questions, and I wouldn't have had time to get into it. Like now." She paused. "Are your brothers on the way?"

Chase didn't jump to respond, but he did follow her as she approached Deanne's body. "Yeah. They should be here any minute. How safe are we out here?" He took out his phone and fired off a text. To one of his brothers, no doubt, so they could find them in these woods.

"I'm not sure if it's safe at all," she admitted. "I'm sorry. I hadn't wanted to get you involved in this, but I didn't have a choice."

"You had choices. Everybody does."

They weren't just talking about the baby now but her past. A past that Chase was probably sorry had included him.

"Now tell me what the hell happened here," he insisted.

She would. But where to start? The past sixteen hours had been one nightmare after another. Though Chase would want to know the details prior to that. Especially one detail.

The baby.

The one they'd conceived nine months ago when they'd had to face yet another nightmare. Landing in bed with him had been a lapse in judgment. Or Chase would consider it a lapse, anyway. Yes, they'd been attracted to each other since they first met, but Chase considered her a common criminal. And in many ways, he was right.

"I gave birth two months early," she said.

April tried to rein in her emotions. The fear. The hatred for the person who'd put all of this in motion. Hard to rein in anything, though, when she knelt beside Deanne and touched her.

Dead.

Of course, she already knew that, but it sickened her to confirm it for herself. The tears came. No way to stop them, but she tried to brush them away. Later, she'd grieve for the woman who'd lost her life way too soon and had died trying to help April.

Later, April would do a lot of things.

After she figured out how to untangle this mess that could cost her the baby.

Chase knelt, too. So they were face-to-face. And even though he tossed some glares at her, he continued to keep watch around them.

Always the lawman.

A good lawman, too. For all the good it'd done. It hadn't been good enough to help Deanne or their daughter today.

"Why didn't you have someone call me and tell me you'd had the baby?" he snapped.

Yet another long story, and she was already dealing with too much to bring those memories this close to the surface. "Bailey…that's what I named her…was a preemie, and at first she had trouble breathing on her own. She had to spend most of the time since her birth in a neonatal unit. It was touch-and-go there for a while, but she's fine now."

At least April prayed she was.

And the possibility that she wasn't fine brought on the tears again. Sweet heaven, she was so tired of crying. So tired of being terrified. So tired of not having her precious baby in her arms.

"That doesn't explain why you didn't tell me." Chase's tone didn't soften despite the tears, but he finally cursed and slid his hand over her back. For a very brief moment. Probably in an attempt to comfort her.

Too bad it didn't work.

April figured she could use some serious comforting right now, but comfort wasn't going to help her find the baby.

"I didn't tell you at first because I didn't want to risk anyone following you to the hospital," she said. "Because I delivered so early, we didn't have nearly enough security in place for you to come running to me."

It was the truth. But it wouldn't be a truth that Chase wanted to hear. Soon, he'd press her for a better explanation.

But that had to wait.

"The gunman and I left our cars by the Appaloosa Creek Bridge," April told him. So that's the direction she headed. "Maybe there's something inside his car that'll help me find Bailey."

"Not me. *Us.* You're not looking for Bailey alone."

He hesitated when saying their daughter's name, the way someone would hesitate when pronouncing a foreign word. Maybe because he was just getting accustomed to the idea of fatherhood.

An idea that he'd struggled with for months.

Now, here it was, slugging him in the face. Crushing him, too. Because it was certainly crushing her.

"Maybe the baby is in the kidnapper's car?" Chase suggested.

"No. Believe me, I checked. I even looked in the trunk when he opened it to take out an extra gun and some ammo." There'd been absolutely no sign of the baby.

Chase walked in step beside her. "What about Deanne—was she faking being afraid so she could lure me here? Or was the gunman actually threatening to kill her then?

"Deanne's fear was real. And warranted. The thug said the only way I could get Bailey back was for you to come, and that if I didn't agree, he'd kill Deanne. I thought we'd be able to overpower him or something. I also didn't think he'd want you dead. Not right off the bat like that anyway."

She'd been wrong about a lot of things. Definitely a stupid plan.

"The thug made me put on these clothes," she said, motioning at the all-black garb. "Deanne, too. I'm not sure why exactly, but I think he wanted to make you believe you were surrounded by hired guns."

And the thug knew that Deanne and April couldn't just shoot him. Because he was the only one who knew the baby's location.

Still glaring, Chase cursed. Not general profanity, either. Like the glare, it was aimed specifically at her. But this time, the glare didn't last as long as the others. That's because Chase stopped and, without warning, latched on to her and hauled her behind a tree.

Had he heard something? Because she certainly hadn't. Of course, with her heartbeat thumping in her ears, it was hard to hear much of anything.

The moments crawled by, but Chase still didn't budge. "Why did that goon want to find Quentin?" he whispered. Obviously, he intended to use this waiting time to fill in some of the blanks. But in this case, she had just as many blanks as Chase did.

April had to shake her head. "My guess is Tony Crossman wants to settle up things with Quentin and me."

Which wasn't much of a guess at all because Quentin and she were responsible for putting the king of thugs, Tony Crossman, behind bars. Their testimony, along with the testimony of Crossman's CPA, had put the CPA, Quentin and April into WITSEC, too.

However, even behind bars Crossman still had plenty of money and resources, and he'd apparently used both to come after her and take the baby. There was only one thing that could have gotten her to cooperate with one of Crossman's thugs.

And that was Bailey.

"I haven't seen my brother the entire six months I've been in WITSEC," she added when Chase got them moving again.

Something Chase probably already knew because that'd been the plan all along. It would make it hard for Crossman's henchmen to find Quentin and her if they were in different places leading separate lives.

Chase mumbled more profanity. "Someone probably hacked into WITSEC files to find Bailey and you. We thought we had a breach not long ago, but it turned out to be a false alarm."

April had heard about that possible breach, and it'd involved yet someone else connected to Crossman. A criminal named Marcos Culver, who'd been running one of Crossman's side businesses of money laundering. But that man had never been a threat to her. And besides, Culver was dead now.

"I need to find out who could have hacked into WIT-SEC," Chase continued, "and try to link that person back to Crossman. Or anyone else who might be involved."

Even though he didn't spell it out, April knew what he meant. Chase believed her brother could be involved in this.

And maybe Quentin was.

After all, April would have paid a huge ransom to get Bailey back. Chase would have as well once he'd learned what had happened, and the one thing her brother probably needed right now was cash since he'd blown through his trust fund that their grandparents had set up for both of them. Still, something like this seemed extreme even for Quentin.

"Stop," Chase said, and without warning he yanked her behind another tree.

Again, April hadn't heard anything, but clearly he had because Chase lifted his head, listening. Finally, she heard the footsteps. Someone was coming up on them fast.

"Your brothers?" she whispered.

Chase shook his head.

April leaned out just a little and spotted the man skulking his way toward them. Definitely not a Crockett lawman. This guy was dressed all in black and was wearing a ski mask.

Another hired gun.

She instantly felt fear, and hope. This man could try to kill them, but he also might know something about Bailey.

Chase handed her his phone. "Text Jericho and give him the guy's position," he whispered. "Also tell Jericho we need him alive."

April couldn't do that fast enough. She certainly didn't want the sheriff eliminating this hired gun before they got a chance to talk to him.

Jericho didn't respond to the text, but April soon realized why. She saw him, and he wasn't that far behind the guy in the ski mask.

Her heart went to her knees.

April nearly shouted out for Jericho not to shoot the man, something that would have almost certainly put

Jericho in danger because it would have alerted the gunman. But Chase glanced down at her, shook his head.

"If Jericho had wanted this guy dead, he already would be," Chase mouthed.

It took her a moment to fight through the panic going on in her head, and April realized he was right. The man obviously didn't know that Jericho was tracking him, and she was well aware that the sheriff had a deadly aim.

Chase eased her even farther behind the tree so that her face and body were pressed right against the rough bark. Chase pressed, too. His chest against her back. Touching her. Of course, he hadn't meant for this to be an intimate situation, but it always seemed to be just that when she was within a hundred feet of Chase.

Her mind tried to shut out the memories. But her body remembered every second she'd spent in Chase's arms.

In his bed, too.

She could no longer see the gunman or Jericho, but April could still hear the footsteps. The guy wasn't moving that fast, but he was definitely headed right for them.

Did he know Chase and she were there?

Or like them was he simply trying to make his way to the car?

April hadn't seen a second gunman in the car that'd been left by the bridge, but it was possible he came in another vehicle. Not exactly a comforting thought.

Because Chase was pressed against her, April felt his muscles tense even more than they already were. He was getting ready for something.

But what exactly?

She soon got an answer to that, too. Chase lunged out

from cover, tackling the gunman, and he slammed the guy to the ground.

The gunman cursed, and he tried to bring up his weapon, no doubt to shoot Chase. But Chase didn't give him a chance to do that. He knocked the gun from the thug's hand.

That wasn't the end of the fight, though.

The guy punched Chase. Hard enough to have knocked the breath out of him, but Chase managed to deliver a punch of his own.

And just like that, the guy stopped fighting.

It took her a couple of seconds to spot Jericho. He was moving in and had a Glock aimed right at the gunman's head. April prayed the man wouldn't give Jericho a reason to pull the trigger.

"Where's the baby?" Chase demanded, pointing his gun at the man, too.

Jericho didn't make a sound, but April knew he had to be confused about his brother's question. Then, Jericho's gaze dropped to her stomach for a split second, and that seemed to tell him all he needed to know. The baby had been born.

And had been taken.

Later, Jericho would have as many questions as Chase and the rest of the Crocketts would. For now, though, this ski-masked man might tell her what she needed to know.

"Where is she?" April repeated.

He didn't answer. Chase yanked off the guy's mask, and like their other attacker, he wasn't someone she recognized.

Chase got right in his face with the gun. "I won't kill

you, but I'll make you wish you were dead if you don't tell me where the baby is."

When the man still stayed silent, Chase bashed his gun against the side of the guy's head. "Tell me!" Chase demanded.

The man didn't open his mouth, not until Chase drew back the gun again to hit him. "I don't know where she is. Somewhere with the nanny."

So her baby wasn't alone in these woods. That was something at least. Well, it was if this snake was telling the truth.

"A nanny you hired?" Chase asked her.

"No." Which meant it was someone working for the same person as these hired thugs.

"And where's the nanny?" April pressed, moving even closer to the gunman.

"Don't know. I don't!" he shouted when Chase made a move to hit him again. "She was in a separate car with the kid. A black four-door, and she was supposed to follow us here."

Chase glanced at his brother. That was all it took, just a glance. "I'll tell Jax to look for the car," Jericho volunteered.

With that search started, Chase turned back to the man. "Who's *us*? Who else is here?"

The man tipped his head to the dead guy. "Just Hank and me."

April wished she had a lie detector to know if he was telling the truth about there being no other gunmen, but even if he wasn't, that wouldn't stop her. "I'm going to look for the nanny's car," she said to no one in particular.

But Chase clearly thought she'd been talking to him

because he stopped her. "Hold on a second and I'll go with you."

Chase turned his attention back to the man and he put his gun in the guy's face. "One more question, and trust me, a wrong answer will cause you a lot of pain. Who hired you to do this?"

The guy's eyes widened, filling with fear. "I don't know. I swear, that's the truth. I just had orders to find anything that would lead to Quentin Landis. And to get that info by any means necessary. That includes killing you."

"Tony Crossman hired him," Jericho spat out. "Unless somebody else is gunning for you and your idiot brother." He slid a glare at April.

"I can't speak for Quentin, but I think only Crossman and you hate me," she settled for saying.

However, she wasn't sure at all that it was the truth.

Chase glanced at her, too, but his attention quickly shifted back to the gunman on the ground. He stared at him, his gun still poised to do some damage, but after several long moments, Chase stepped back.

"Arrest him," Chase said to his brother. "Maybe he'll remember some things in interrogation."

Jericho didn't waste any time hauling the man to his feet, and he took out some plastic cuffs from his pocket to restrain him.

"Go ahead," Jericho said as he checked the guy for other weapons. "Look for the nanny. I'll take care of this piece of dirt and get someone out here for the woman's body and the dead guy."

The word *body* gave April another slam of grief. And guilt. But there wasn't anything she could do for

Deanne right now. Though she could do something to find her baby.

April turned and started in the direction of the Appaloosa Creek Bridge. She'd made it only a few steps when Chase's phone rang. He caught up with her, glancing down at the phone screen before he answered it.

"It's Jax," Chase relayed to her, and he put the call on speaker while they kept running.

"I found a black four-door car," Jax said. "It's on the east side of the road, less than a quarter mile from the bridge."

Good. The gunman had said the nanny was driving a vehicle like that. "Is the baby there?" April and Chase asked in unison.

Her stomach sank, though, when Jax hesitated.

"Chase," Jax finally said, "you need to get over here right now." And with that, Jax hung up.

Chapter Three

Chase batted aside some low-hanging tree branches and ran as fast as he could.

His thoughts and heart were racing, too. He wasn't sure what had put the alarm in Jax's voice or why his brother had hung up without an explanation, but with everything else that'd gone on the past hour, Chase figured it could be *bad*.

And it could involve his baby.

He hadn't had even a moment to come to terms with the fact that he was already a father. Of course, he'd known April's delivery date was approaching, but Chase had thought he had a little more time to deal with it.

Or rather more time to deal with his feelings for April.

His feelings for the baby were solid—he loved her, sight unseen, and would lay down his life to protect her.

April was a different matter.

Chase did indeed regret sleeping with her nine months ago. It'd been a mistake, one that had caused his family pain on top of pain.

Him, too.

However, he didn't regret the baby. Not for one second. His only regret when it came to Bailey was that he hadn't been there when she needed him to protect her.

He could partly blame April for that.

If April had just told him about Bailey, then maybe he could have put some more security measures in place.

Somehow, April kept up with his breakneck pace, and it occurred to him that he should at least ask her if it was okay for her to be doing this. After all, she'd had a baby two months ago. Maybe this was too much activity, too soon for her body. But since he figured he didn't stand a chance of talking her into slowing down, Chase just kept running.

Even though it was only a couple of minutes, it seemed to take a lifetime or two for them to reach the road. The bridge was just to their left, but Chase went right since that was the direction where Jax should be. He prayed his brother was okay and hadn't been hurt by yet another hired gun.

Maybe that wasn't the reason Jax had put such an abrupt end to the call. But something had certainly caused him to do that. Since Jax had just as much experience as Chase in law enforcement, it must have been something damn important.

"I don't see him," April said.

She sounded frantic. Looked it, too. Her eyes were wild. Her breath racing, and yet she didn't even pause. She kept running up the road until Chase pulled her back to the side.

"This could be an ambush of some kind," he reminded her.

Something he didn't want to consider, but his lawman's experience put it—and plenty of other bad possibilities—in the forefront of his mind. It could have been the reason Jax ended the call. Because Jax could have walked into a dangerous situation.

Chase didn't want April and him doing the same thing.

He made sure his gun was ready. Made sure April was behind him, too, and using the trees and brush for cover, Chase made his way east. About a quarter of a mile, Jax had said, and from Chase's calculations, that meant his brother and God knew who or what else were just around the curve ahead.

"This way," Chase told her, and he led April just a few yards off the road and back into the woods so they could thread their way to Jax without being out in the open.

Finally, he spotted his brother. Jax was literally in the middle of the road, his gun aimed at the car.

Oh, man.

Nothing could have held April back at that point. She raced out onto the road while Chase tried to keep himself between her and whatever had put Jax on full alert. Chase soon saw the cause.

A woman.

Tall, blonde and wearing a white maternity dress. She was mega pregnant with her back against the car.

And a .38 aimed at Jax.

His brother hadn't been harmed. For now. That was something at least, but this was definitely a volatile situation.

Was this the nanny? The car description certainly fit. But the baby was nowhere in sight.

"Don't come any closer," the pregnant woman warned them. Her hands were shaking. Not a good sign since she had her index finger on the trigger, and the way she was holding the gun told Chase that she didn't have a lot of experience with firearms. "I've already told the deputy here that if he shoots me, he won't find the baby."

April was trembling as well, and she lowered her gun

to her side. "Where is she? Where's Bailey?" The worry and fear practically drenched her voice.

"Safe, for now. Keep it that way and don't come closer."

Chase didn't move, but unlike April he didn't lower his gun. He couldn't shoot a pregnant woman, but she might not be so anxious to shoot Jax if she had two guns trained on her.

He craned his neck to try to get a look at the interior of the car, but with the tinted windows, he couldn't see much of anything. The engine was running, the windows all up, and since the woman was between them and the car, Chase figured he wasn't going to get a better look inside until he dealt with the situation right in front of him.

"What do you want from us?" Chase asked her.

"Money, a getaway vehicle," Jax provided. "And any information about Quentin's whereabouts."

"The last one is especially important," the woman said, tears springing to her eyes. "I have to find him." She slid her left hand over her belly. "He has to know he's about to be a father."

Good grief. So, she was connected to Quentin? And clearly this woman wasn't just any ordinary nanny.

"I'm Quentin's sister," April said, taking a step toward her. "He wouldn't want you to hurt his niece. He wouldn't want any of this to be happening."

That was probably true. Quentin could be scum, but to the best of Chase's knowledge, the man had never endangered a baby.

"Quentin would want *me* protected. He wants to be with me and our baby, but he can't be because of him." The woman pointed at Chase. "You're the marshal who put him in WITSEC. You're the one who took Quentin away from me."

Obviously, she had a skewed idea of what'd happened six months ago. "I did that for his own safety."

"Then you can put me there with him! Quentin loves me and wants to be with me."

Since Quentin hadn't requested that and since this was the first Chase was hearing about the man having a pregnant girlfriend, he glanced at April to see if she'd known.

April shook her head. "I've never met her. But maybe Quentin mentioned your name," she added to the woman.

"I'm Renée Edmunds," she volunteered.

"Quentin didn't always tell me the details of his personal life," April mumbled. "He certainly didn't tell me he was about to become a father."

"Because he doesn't trust you, that's why," Renée snapped. "He said I wasn't to trust you because you betrayed him by spying on him. You became a criminal informant to save your own skin."

April nodded, readily admitting that. "Quentin was involved in some bad things then. With a very bad man. I did what I had to do to put an end to it."

That was the sanitized version anyway, and that very bad man was none other than Tony Crossman. April had uncovered her brother's illegal activity but had sat on it for a while. Long enough for someone to get killed. Only afterward had April turned CI to help arrest Crossman.

"Were you doing what you had to do when you slept with Quentin's enemy, Marshal Crockett?" Renée asked.

Quentin would indeed consider him his enemy. Chase felt the same way about him.

"Is that why you took our daughter, because you

thought it would help you find Quentin?" April went another step closer to Renée.

"I didn't take her." A hoarse sob tore from Renée's mouth, and she repeated her denial. "But when I got the call to be involved in this, I didn't say no. I'd do anything to see Quentin again."

Anything, including putting an innocent baby in danger. It didn't matter if Renée had or hadn't been the person who kidnapped Bailey, she certainly hadn't turned the baby over to the authorities. And she darn sure wasn't cooperating now.

Somehow, he had to get that gun out of her shaky hands.

"Who hired you?" Chase asked her, and he made sure he sounded like the lawman that he was. Maybe he could intimidate her into surrendering the weapon.

"I don't know," Renée said.

Chase huffed, already tired of this ordeal. He wanted it to end so he could find his daughter and deal with the aftermath of everything else going on here.

"Who hired *you*?" he tried again.

"I don't know!" Renée's answer was louder this time. "I got a call from a man who said Quentin was in danger and that if I wanted to find him then he'd help me."

"Did this man have a name?" Jax asked. He, too, sounded like a lawman. A riled one. Probably because he was as fed up with Quentin and April as Chase was. Still, his brother would do whatever it took to get the baby back.

"His name is Jason Toth," Renée finally answered. "He said he was Quentin's friend."

It wasn't a name Chase recognized, and apparently neither did April or Jax. Of course, whoever had come up with this sick plan probably wouldn't have used a real name.

"Do you know Tony Crossman?" Chase asked the woman.

She gave a shaky nod. "He's the man Quentin helped send to jail. He wants to hurt Quentin."

"Crossman wants to *kill* him," Chase spelled out for her. "And he'd do anything—that includes using you—to find him."

Chase didn't add more. He just waited and let Renée fill in the blanks. It didn't take her long.

"Toth might be working for Crossman," Renée whispered, her mouth trembling now.

Bingo. "I don't know Quentin's location," Chase continued, "but if I did and I told you, then Crossman could get to Quentin before you do. Let me guess, you're wearing some kind of wire right now so Toth can hear whatever you're saying?"

Renée's gaze drifted down toward her stomach. And she nodded. It was a good thing Chase hadn't known Quentin's whereabouts and revealed it because assassins would have likely already been on their way to kill him.

April cursed and stormed toward Renée. "Where's my baby?" she yelled to the person on the other end of that listening device.

April probably would have latched on to Renée as well, but Chase held her back. After all, Renée still had the gun, and the woman was past the point of just being panicked and upset. There was no telling what she would do in her state of mind.

"You need to come with us to the Appaloosa Pass sheriff's office," Chase told Renée. "We can figure out where the baby is. And just how much Crossman's henchman has learned." If anything. "You might be able to save Quentin from being hurt."

Chase didn't care a flying fig if Quentin got hurt. The only thing he wanted right now was the location of the baby. Once Bailey was safe, then he could deal with Crossman, his hired guns and anyone else who had a part in this.

"Oh, God," Renée said, tears spilling down her cheek. "I was a fool to trust Toth."

Yeah, she was. But Chase kept that to himself. "Just put down the gun and come with us."

She volleyed glances at the .38, Chase and April. When Renée lifted her hand, Chase was certain that she was about to surrender.

He was wrong.

Renée made a feral sound that came deep from within her throat. Definitely not the sound of a woman who'd just realized she'd made a huge mistake. This was more the sound a trapped animal would make.

She turned, racing around the back of the car. Chase still wasn't sure what she had in mind, but he didn't want to risk firing a warning shot. He cursed and went after her.

Renée didn't stop at the back of the car. She kept running. She jumped the narrow ditch and headed for the woods. For a pregnant woman, she ran pretty darn fast.

"Don't hurt your baby," April shouted out to her.

It was a good thing to say. It should have gotten a concerned, expectant mother to slow down.

But Renée definitely didn't slow down.

"She can't get away," April said, following right along behind Chase and the woman.

"Go after her," Jax insisted. "I'll stay and search the car to make sure there's no other gunman inside."

Good plan. Too bad Chase didn't have time to talk April into staying with Jax because she, too, went after Renée. Thankfully, it didn't take them long to catch up with the woman, and when they did, Chase latched on to her shoulder and dragged her to a stop.

Renée didn't exactly cooperate.

"Let me go," she shouted, and she started to fight. Clawing and scratching at Chase while she tried to kick him.

Chase did something about that .38. He knocked it from her hand and April snatched it up before Renée could grab it.

That still didn't stop Renée.

She rammed into Chase and she didn't hold back. Renée off-balanced them, and Chase knew he couldn't stop them from falling to the ground. However, he did try to take the brunt of the fall so that Renée's unborn baby wouldn't be hurt.

But when he heard April gasp, Chase figured he hadn't succeeded in doing that.

Until he saw what'd captured April's attention.

Renée's dress had been shoved up during the scuffle. Way up. Chase saw a wire, but he also saw something strapped to her stomach.

A fake baby bump.

"She's not even pregnant," April mumbled.

That caused Renée to make another of those feral sounds, and she started fighting again. Not just scratching and shoving this time, but she punched Chase hard in the face.

Enough of this.

Since he was no longer dealing with a pregnant woman, Chase rammed her against the ground and pinned her in place.

"Tell Jax I need a pair of plastic cuffs," Chase told April.

April turned, no doubt to call out to Jax. But his brother responded before she could even get out a word.

"Get up here now," Jax shouted. "I found a baby."

Chapter Four

April ran as fast as she could, the horrible thoughts running right along with her. Jax had said he'd found a baby, but that didn't mean it was Bailey, and it didn't mean her precious daughter was safe.

After all, the men who'd taken Bailey were the same ones who'd murdered Deanne.

Chase ran, too, dragging Renée along with him. But Renée still wasn't cooperating, and that slowed Chase down.

April finally reached the road, but her heart sank when she didn't see Jax. She soon spotted him, though. He was sitting in the backseat of the car next to an infant seat.

And Bailey was in that seat.

"She's okay," Jax insisted. "Someone's obviously been taking good care of her."

April's breath whooshed out, and she practically crawled over Jax to get to the baby. He stepped out, hurrying toward Chase so he could take hold of Renée. But Jax did more than that. He clamped his hand over Renée's mouth.

"I don't want her calling out for help if she's got any other comrades in the area," Jax said.

Yes, and it was something that April should have

thought about already. Renée could still be dangerous, but before April could deal with her, she had to see to Bailey first.

Bailey didn't appear to have any injuries, but April had to check for herself. She took her from the seat, peeling back the blanket so she could check for any scrapes or bruises. None.

Jax had been right. Someone had been taking care of her. Bailey had on a fresh diaper, a clean pink gown, and judging from the bottles in the diaper bag next to the infant seat, she'd been well fed. Thank God. She was okay.

But Chase wasn't.

April had been so caught up in making sure Bailey was unharmed that she hadn't noticed Chase was right there by the door, and he had his attention fixed on the baby. He looked as if someone had slugged him, but the shock lasted for only a couple of seconds. Then, April saw something else she instantly recognized.

Love.

One look at his daughter and Chase was as smitten as April was.

"They didn't hurt her," Chase said, gulping in a long breath.

The love was mixed with a hefty dose of relief. Again, that love and relief didn't extend to April. Chase's gaze was practically icy when it landed on her.

"You should have told me when she was born," Chase snarled and likely would have said a whole lot more if Jax hadn't cleared his throat to get their attention.

"I hate to break up this family reunion, but it's not a good idea for us to be hanging around out here. There could be other gunmen."

Jax was right. Plus, he was still dealing with Renée.

He kept his hand clamped over her mouth so she couldn't yell, but she was struggling to break free.

Chase glanced around, probably trying to keep watch and figure out a solution to this. "Don't say anything about where we're going," April reminded him. "Renée's wearing that wire."

"I disconnected it, but it's still taped to her fake baby bump."

Good. Because April didn't want any more info relayed back to whoever had hired the woman or any other of those thugs.

"Where are you parked?" Chase asked Jax.

Jax tipped his head toward the road. "I left the cruiser about a quarter of a mile from here."

Not that far, but he would have to fight Renée every step of the way. Chase obviously figured that out right away because he opened the driver's side door of the black car and got in.

"I'll drive you to the cruiser, and I can come back later and get my own car," he told Jax. "You and Renée get in the front. April can ride with Bailey in the back."

Good, because April didn't want Bailey next to the woman. At best, Renée seemed unstable, but she could also be a hired killer. How the heck had Quentin gotten involved with her?

Or maybe he hadn't.

April wasn't sure anything coming out of Renée's mouth had been the truth, but maybe they could sort it all out at the sheriff's office. It was possible they'd also get some info from the wire she was wearing. First, though, April needed to try to sort out things with Chase. Or rather make peace with him.

"Let me go!" Renée snarled again when Jax put her in the cruiser. "I want to talk to Quentin."

"Take a number," Chase muttered under his breath.

April wanted to talk to her brother as well, but she wasn't sure if he'd actually played a role in this. This had Crossman written all over it.

"Crossman must have hired someone to hack into WITSEC files to find me," April said, thinking out loud.

Chase met her gaze in the rearview mirror. "Then why didn't the hacking include Quentin? If Crossman found you yesterday, he could have found your brother, too, and he wouldn't have needed to use Renée."

True, and she definitely hadn't heard anything from the marshals about Quentin being injured or killed. Of course, perhaps they didn't know yet. That didn't help the throbbing in her chest.

April forced herself to think this through. "Maybe the hacker did get Quentin's file, but it's possible he's not staying at the place the marshals arranged for him. He's not exactly a rule follower."

Since Chase had known Quentin for two years, as long as he'd known her, there was no way he could argue with that. Plus, Chase and plenty of other lawmen had investigated Quentin. For a good reason, too. The bar her brother owned was a hangout for all sorts of criminals.

At one time, that included Tony Crossman himself.

And yes, Quentin had gotten involved with Crossman's schemes and had in turn gotten her involved since April handled the finances for him. Worse, Quentin had tricked her into helping Crossma n with some money laundering. Chase would never believe it was a dupe, though. No. He would always think she'd done it willingly.

In a way, she had.

Chase pulled to a stop behind the cruiser, and Jax didn't waste any time getting Renée out of the car. "Tell Quentin I need to see him right away," the woman shouted.

"Oh, I will," Chase assured her. He glanced back at April. "I'll deal with your brother soon."

April had no trouble hearing the implied threat— Chase would do that after he dealt with her. He didn't use the rearview mirror this time. Chase turned and looked at her. Despite the horrible circumstances, April still wasn't immune to that face. *Hot* seemed like much too mild a word when it came to Chase. He'd gotten to her from the first time they met. Was still getting to her.

But she forced that heat aside.

It was easy to do when his gaze went from her to Bailey. He couldn't actually see Bailey's face because of the rear-facing infant seat, but his expression softened a bit. Well, for a few seconds anyway. It would no doubt take him a while to come to terms with the realization that he was the father of a two-month-old baby.

"I need to call the marshals first," he said, taking out his phone. "They should check on Crossman's former CPA to make sure her identity hasn't been compromised, too."

That was a good idea, especially since it'd been the CPA, Jasmine Bronson, who'd been the one who'd actually witnessed Crossman talking about the murder he'd committed.

"After I'm done with the call," Chase added, "I want to hear everything. And I mean *everything*."

"Just be careful what you say when you make that call. The breach in security could have happened right there in that office."

He didn't dispute that, though it looked as if that's exactly what he wanted to do. Chase made the call to his boss, and he asked him to check to see if April's identity, or anyone else's, had been compromised.

"Start talking," Chase insisted the moment he finished the call. He didn't have his attention on April now. He was watching as Jax maneuvered Renée into the backseat of the cruiser. "You'd better have a darn good reason for keeping Bailey from me for even a minute much less two months. And I'm not buying your excuse that you gave me earlier about those thugs finding you through me."

"It wasn't an excuse." April took a deep breath before she continued. "The morning I went into labor, I got a call from Deanne, and she said she'd heard on the streets that someone was watching you with the hopes of finding me. Needless to say, I believe the person behind that was Crossman."

Chase immediately shook his head, and he drove away once Jax had everything under control with Renée. "I didn't see anyone watching me, and I would have noticed something like that."

Yes, he would have. Especially in the past couple of months. He would have been on high alert because of Bailey's impending birth and because he'd also been recently attacked by a serial killer. April didn't know the details of the attack, but she was betting Chase had been looking over his shoulder a lot.

"Deanne said she'd heard the watching was being done through cameras," April explained, "that someone had managed to set them up in or near your house and by the marshals' office. The CI also told her that there was an informant in the marshals' office, too.

"And you believed Deanne?" he snapped. He took the road toward the town of Appaloosa Pass.

"Why wouldn't I? Deanne's never lied to me. She was trying to help me tonight, and that's why she's dead." That caused her chest to tighten, and April had to fight back a fresh batch of tears.

"Jericho has the guy who was working with Deanne's killer in custody. We'll get justice for her," Chase reminded her. No doubt to get her mind back on their conversation.

"Yes, but justice won't bring her back."

"No," Chase quietly agreed. Maybe he was grieving some, too. After all, Deanne had been one of his own criminal informants for several years. "Who told Deanne I was being watched?"

"I have no idea. As you know, Deanne didn't like to share the names of her sources. She said it kept them cooperating so she could use them to get info to help the cops."

Chase made a grunt of agreement, and while continuing to keep watch, he pulled out his phone. "I need a big favor," he said to the person who answered. "When you get a chance, go to my place and see if anyone has put any surveillance cameras around the house. Call me if you find anything."

As he put his phone away, he said, "That was Teddy McQueen, one of the ranch hands. If he doesn't find anything, I'll have him go through the house itself."

A place she remembered well since it was where Bailey had been conceived.

April didn't have to tap too deeply into her memories to guess where someone would have planted a camera. There were several large shade trees in his yard, a detached garage and even a small barn. But with the hours that Chase put in as a marshal, it was indeed possible that someone had gotten inside the house.

"I couldn't be sure the person hadn't planted listening devices along with cameras," April explained.

That didn't soothe the glare Chase shot her. "So what? You weren't going to tell me at all?"

"I was, but Bailey didn't get out of the hospital until three days ago. I didn't want to call the marshals because of the possible informant."

"You could have sent Deanne to tell me."

"That was the plan. She didn't want to call you because she wasn't sure if the informant or one of Crossman's thugs had managed to tap your phone. And she did try to speak to you in person, but you weren't at the office."

"The Moonlight Strangler investigation," he grumbled several moments later.

Yes, *that*. A cause very close to home. Since Chase and his family had recently learned that a vicious serial killer, the Moonlight Strangler, was the biological father of Chase's adopted sister. The Moonlight Strangler had murdered Jax's wife and had even attacked Chase.

"I was out of the office a lot," Chase added along with some profanity. Probably beating himself up for not being there. But this wasn't his fault.

Again, it was Crossman's.

And that led April to her next concern when Chase took the final turn into town, and she spotted the sheriff's office.

"Is it safe for us to be here?" she asked.

Chase didn't exactly jump to answer that. "We won't be here long. I'll arrange for a safe house. Not through the marshals just in case Deanne was right about an informant. And we won't go to the ranch house or my place, either, just in case there are cameras set up."

Good. Chase's house was at the far edge of the ranch property, and with the threat of the cameras, she'd figured going there was out. However, she was glad he'd dismissed taking her to his family's home on the ranch. For one thing, it might not be safe there, either, and for another, she didn't want to have to face the rest of his family just yet.

Chase didn't pull into the parking lot. He stopped directly in front of the door of the sheriff's office and glanced around. Since it was only about six-thirty, there were still people out and about, and there were diners in the café across the street. Chase studied each one of them and made another call.

"Come to the front door," Chase said.

A moment later, Deputy Mack Parkman appeared in the doorway of the office. He was sporting a very concerned look, no doubt because he'd gotten updates from Jericho and knew they had a murder on their hands.

Mack's look of concern went up considerably when he saw the baby. Obviously, he'd known she was pregnant with Chase's child. Everyone in town knew. But like Chase, Mack hadn't known that she'd delivered.

"Don't bring in the infant seat," Chase warned her. He drew his gun and stepped out. "It could have a tracking device on it. Just take the baby and get out on the side near Mack. Once we're inside we can dispose of anything the baby's wearing in case it's bugged, too."

She hadn't even considered something like that, but thankfully Chase had. April eased the baby into her arms, bundling her in the blanket, and as Chase had instructed, she hurried inside. Chase followed, but they didn't stay in the reception area. He rushed her toward the hall and into Jericho's office.

"Jericho will be here any minute with the prisoner," Mack told them. "The ME is on the way to the woods for the bodies."

"Jax is on his way, too," Chase said. "He was right behind us and he'll have a prisoner with him, as well."

Mack nodded. "What do you need me to do?"

"We need baby supplies. Formula, bottles, clothes and a blanket. Have one of the clerks from the drugstore bring whatever they have. Also, the car outside and everything in it should be processed. I doubt there'll be anything inside to link it to Crossman, but we might get lucky."

"Crossman?" Mack's concern went up yet another notch. He belted out some profanity under his breath, then blushed when he glanced at the baby. "Sorry."

She waved off the apology because it wasn't necessary. Crossman was a killer. Worse, a cop killer.

And it was that murder that had put some blood on April's hands.

Mack stepped away, undoubtedly to take care of getting the CSIs out to examine the car and arrange for those supplies. Leaving Chase and her alone with the baby. The first moments they'd been together alone with Bailey.

Chase walked closer, staring down at her, and he touched his finger to Bailey's cheek. Bailey was half-asleep, but that got her attention, and she turned her head, studying Chase as hard as he was studying her.

The corner of Bailey's mouth lifted, and even though April figured it wasn't a real smile, it still had a powerful effect. Chase groaned, the impact of fatherhood no doubt hitting him hard. And hitting him in the exact same way it'd hit April. Because he smiled, too.

A rarity.

Chase Crockett wasn't exactly the smiling type—especially since things had fallen apart between them. Too bad because that smile stirred the too familiar heat inside April.

Heat she pushed aside again.

That was something she always had to do around Chase. Because he'd spent the past two years trying to put her brother behind bars, April and Chase had never dated. But that hadn't stopped them from landing in bed together. For one glorious night, Chase had been hers for the taking, but then his friend had been murdered. Crossman—and Quentin—had been implicated in that. And anything she'd ever hoped to have with Chase had vanished in the blink of an eye.

Well, everything except Bailey.

That would give them a connection that she was certain Chase would rather have with someone else. *Anyone* else.

"Check her for tracking devices," Chase prompted.

April hurried to do that, causing Bailey to fuss, but thankfully she didn't see anything on her gown, blanket or diaper. That was something at least.

She heard the front door open, and Chase stepped back into the hall. Even though she couldn't see who'd come in, she did notice the alarm on Chase's face.

"What's wrong?" Chase immediately asked.

April hurried to the door and looked out to see Jericho. He had the gunman in cuffs and handed him off to Mack, but his attention stayed on Chase.

"We've got trouble," Jericho answered. "Jax was attacked on the road. He's okay, but the woman he was bringing in just escaped."

Chapter Five

Chase so didn't want to have to deal with anything else right now. What he wanted to do was hold his daughter and get to know her. Instead, he was neck deep in making sure Crossman, or whoever was behind the kidnapping and attacks, didn't get to Bailey and April again.

That meant going to a safe house. Something he was still working on, but for now, his baby was stuck sleeping on the cot in the break room at the sheriff's office. Hardly premium accommodations, but Bailey didn't seem to mind. She was sacked out, not a care in the world. Unlike April.

Chase saw plenty of those *cares* in her eyes.

"Anything?" she asked the moment Chase stepped into the doorway of the break room. She moved away from the cot and came closer to him.

Chase figured that one-word question encompassed a lot because there were plenty of cogs moving in the investigation. What wasn't moving was a solution to put an end to this.

"Renée's still missing." Thanks to the help from a gunman who'd run Jax off the road and taken her.

April's mouth tightened, clearly not pleased about that. *Welcome to the club.*

Renée could have given them some answers, and now the woman was missing.

"And what about Jax? Is he really okay?" Not displeasure now but rather concern in April's voice.

Chase nodded. "A few cuts and bruises. He's pissed off more than anything." An emotion that Chase completely understood.

He should have made sure Jax wasn't being followed. Should have done more to protect his brother. But Chase had had so many things on his mind that he hadn't taken more precautions. That couldn't happen again. Because the next time, Jax or someone else could be killed.

April came even closer to him, glancing back at the baby. Probably to make sure their whispered conversation wasn't disturbing her. It wasn't. Now that Bailey had had a bottle, she was sleeping, well, like a baby. However, Chase was betting April and he wouldn't be getting much sleep, if any, tonight.

"I'm sorry," April said.

Not especially something Chase wanted to hear. Or feel. But he felt something all right.

Sympathy.

And he'd learned the hard way, that was never a good thing to feel when it came to April. Best to keep this conversation on a more business level. Easy to do since they had plenty of nonpersonal things to discuss.

Well, one huge thing anyway.

There was something he should probably tell her. Eventually. Something that was indeed personal. But it would have to wait.

"Someone did hack into WITSEC files," Chase confirmed. "We won't know the extent of what was compromised for a while, but it's obvious the hacker was able to find you."

"And my brother?" she asked.

"The marshals went to his house, but Quentin wasn't there. The place had been ransacked and there were signs of a struggle." Chase paused, trying to brace himself for how she was going to react to the next thing he had to tell her. "There was blood on the floor."

That caused her breath to shudder, and she staggered back. Maybe would have fallen if Chase hadn't caught her. He hooked his arm around her waist, putting them body to body again. Also giving him feelings he didn't want to have.

Lust.

Not an especially good time for it, but it always seemed to happen with April. Chase cursed it and wished there was some way in hell he could make himself immune to her.

Rather than stand there with her in his arms, Chase led her across the room and had her sit in one of the chairs at the dining table.

She shook her head. "Quentin doesn't even know how to get in touch with me if he needs help."

"No, but he knows how to contact me. If it's a real emergency, he'd call me."

April looked up at him, blinked. "You don't think the blood they found is real?"

Chase was 1,000 percent sure she wasn't going to like this. "I think it's real all right, but Quentin could have planted it so it would look as if he'd been injured. And he could have done that so we wouldn't believe he had any part in kidnapping Bailey."

There were holes in that particular theory, but Chase knew that Quentin was very good at doing criminal things.

"You think Quentin could have had Bailey kidnapped for ransom money," April said. She didn't exactly jump to deny that though it was no doubt what she wanted to do.

"It's possible. You have to admit your brother has been involved in some illegal moneymaking schemes before."

She didn't deny that, either. Couldn't. Because it'd been Quentin's dirty dealings with Crossman that had set this entire mess in motion.

"I don't think Quentin would work with Crossman," April said. "Not again. Not after what happened the last time."

And what'd happened the last time was murder. Specifically, the murder of a cop, Tina Murdock. Tina had gone to question Quentin, had found Crossman instead, and some kind of argument had ensued. Crossman had shot and killed her.

"You trust your brother a lot more than I do," Chase reminded her.

"I know. And I also know you don't trust me. That's all right. I deserve it."

She did. But there was no need for him to spell that out to her. April had known about her brother's illegal activity. If she had reported it sooner instead of trying to get Quentin out of hot water, Tina wouldn't have walked into the bar where she'd been murdered.

Of course, April hadn't mentioned anything about knowing of Tina's visit or her brother's criminal activity when she'd gone to Chase that night. Even though Chase hadn't known it at the time, she'd been looking for a shoulder to cry on because she was about to turn in her brother. And during the *consoling*, they'd landed in bed. Only afterward did Chase learn the truth, and he was still dealing with it.

"I need some good news," she said, groaning. "*Any* good news."

"The safe house will be ready soon. I didn't go through the marshals for it, just in case. Dexter Conway and one of the other deputies are setting up a place in the local area. They're stocking it now and making sure there's plenty of security. After we're settled there, I can work on getting you a new identity."

Just thinking about that put a knot in his gut. A knot that'd been there since he'd known April was pregnant with his child.

Basically, as long as Crossman was a threat, April and Bailey would have to live in hiding. And if he wanted to be part of his baby's life—which he absolutely did—Chase would have to go in hiding with them. It'd mean giving up everything he knew. His family. His job. His life.

But that's exactly what was going to happen.

Of course, Chase had thought he'd have a few more days to come to terms with it. However, the little girl sleeping on the cot was the ultimate reminder that his time as a marshal was nearly up.

And that crushed him.

Since April looked very tuned in to his thoughts and appeared to be on the verge of another apology, Chase nipped it in the bud and continued giving her the update on their situation.

"Teddy hasn't found any cameras or anything else suspicious at my place, but he'll keep looking," Chase explained. "And the marshals haven't discovered anyone in the office who could be a mole."

April kept staring at him. "You don't sound as if you think they'll actually find anything."

Chase shrugged. "Deanne could have been wrong."

"Maybe." April took a deep breath and repeated her noncommittal response. "But she believed she was right. Believed it enough to risk her life to help me find Bailey."

That put some tears back in her eyes, and this time April didn't succeed in blinking them away. "God, Chase, I got Deanne killed. That's more blood on my hands."

The tears came faster. Sobs, too. And he would have had to be a heartless jerk to just stand there and watch her fall apart. Chase sank down in the chair next to her and pulled her into his arms.

"You might have saved Tina, but Deanne's a different matter," he said. It wasn't exactly a full dose of comfort he was offering, but he hated the tears. Hated even more that there was reason for the crying. "It was Deanne's choice to try to help you. She was by the creek because she chose to be there."

And Chase was thankful for it. He hadn't wanted Deanne to die, but at least the woman had given up her life while trying to save Bailey.

"Please tell me the man who was working with Deanne's killer is talking," April said through the tears.

"Not talking exactly, but Jericho did learn some info about him when he took his prints. His name is Gene Rooks, and he's a career criminal. He lawyered up or rather a lawyer showed up here shortly after Jericho arrested Rooks."

She stayed quiet a moment, probably giving that some thought. "Someone must have been watching. That's how Crossman knew Rooks was in custody." Another pause. "If it's Crossman. Renée isn't off my suspect list just yet."

Nor his. It was obvious that Renée was desperate to find Quentin. Why exactly, Chase didn't know, but desperate people did stupid things.

"Is Renée Edmunds even her real name?" April asked.

Chase nodded. "I pulled up her DMV photo and it's a match. Unlike Rooks, Renée doesn't have a record. No family for us to contact, either. I've put out feelers to see if she has a genuine connection to your brother. She could be just a nutcase or a groupie."

There'd been plenty of publicity following Tina's murder and Crossman's arrest, and Quentin's photo had been plastered in the newspapers. Quentin was a rich, good-looking guy. A bad-boy criminal. He was the type who could have attracted a nut job. Including one who could have faked a pregnancy. Of course, it was just as possible that Renée had indeed had a relationship with Quentin, and that was something Chase would ask her.

If they found her, that is.

It was going to be hard to track her down. No job. Renée lived off a trust fund, and her neighbors said they hadn't seen her in weeks.

Chase's phone rang, and even though he'd lowered the sound, it still caused Bailey to stir. April sprang out of the chair to go to her while Chase glanced at the screen. It was Teddy McQueen, the ranch hand.

"I found something," Teddy said the moment Chase answered. "Two cameras. One on your front porch. The other on the back."

Chase choked back a groan because he didn't want to wake the baby, but that was not the news he wanted to hear. "You're sure?" he asked, stepping out into the hall.

However, he'd already gotten April's attention. Despite her having picked up the baby, she had her gaze fixed on Chase.

"Yeah, I'm sure," Teddy answered. "I didn't see them at first because someone had hidden them in the eaves. And that's not all I found. There are little black box–looking things—one underneath the windowsill in your office. There's a second one outside your bedroom."

Hell. Eavesdropping devices no doubt. It sickened him to think someone had trespassed onto Crockett land to do something like that. It sickened Chase even more that if April had indeed called him, then Crossman or whoever was behind this could have learned her and Bailey's whereabouts.

Of course, the person had learned it and kidnapped Bailey, but at least Chase hadn't been the one to spill that info.

But who had?

Chase intended to find out soon.

"You want me to take this stuff down?" Teddy asked.

"No. I'll need to call in the CSIs and have them do a clean sweep of the place." Because if the person had gotten close enough to install the cameras and bugs, the individual could have gotten inside, as well.

Chase thanked Teddy, ended the call and made another one to the CSI lab. The conversation was important, but Bailey snagged his attention. The baby was wide awake now and was smiling at April. Chase made the request for the sweep as quickly as he could and then joined them on the cot.

"Deanne was right," April said. Not exactly an *I told you so* tone. More like one of frustration. They were dealing with someone who was thorough and well connected. Definitely not a good combination.

Chase nodded and made a mental note to have the marshals look even harder for the possible mole in the office. Until then, he wouldn't make any calls to the marshals or share any information about April with them. Not exactly ideal because he would miss using their resources to help him figure out what was going on. But the mental note he was making flew right out his head when Bailey looked at him.

And she smiled.

Oh, man. That little smile packed a wallop.

"You okay?" April asked him.

He managed a nod but then got another wallop when April eased the baby into his arms. Chase had heard Jericho and Jax talk about what it felt like to be a father, but nothing had prepared him for this overwhelming love. It was instant and so strong that he was glad he was sitting or it would have brought him to his knees.

"I held my nephew when he was this age," Chase said. "This is different."

"Yes. And scary."

It was. Chase knew exactly what April meant. The stakes suddenly seemed sky-high. Because they were. Someone had already kidnapped Bailey once, and Chase had to make sure that his baby wasn't put in the path of any more danger.

"I didn't know if I could do this," he admitted. "If I could be a father," Chase clarified.

She nodded and most likely did understand. He'd made it clear to April so many times that he didn't consider himself daddy material. Chase had always thought he'd missed that particular Crockett gene.

Heck, maybe he had.

Just because he loved this baby, it didn't mean he'd be

a good father to her. Though he would try. Too bad trying might not be nearly enough. Suddenly, nothing seemed as if it'd be nearly enough.

Chase's gaze came to April's, and even though she didn't say a word, he saw the doubts in her eyes, too. Of course, she'd been telling him right from the start that his giving up his badge for fatherhood was a bad idea. That he would resent it. Maybe not this year. Or next. But eventually.

April wasn't completely wrong about that.

He wouldn't resent Bailey. Not ever. But Chase couldn't be sure that he would ever be able to get past what April had done. Not good. Because Bailey would eventually pick up on that.

"I want Bailey in my life," he said. "We'll just have to work out the rest as we go along."

April didn't get a chance to say anything about that because the footsteps got their attention. Jericho was walking up the hall toward them, and he had his phone pressed to his ear.

Chase put the baby back in April's arms and stood. Waiting for Jericho to finish his call. Thankfully, he didn't have to wait too long.

"That was Houston PD. A uniform was responding to a call in Quentin's neighborhood and spotted your brother near his house," Jericho explained.

April slowly got to her feet. "Is he okay?"

Jericho shook his head. "Quentin appeared to be bleeding, but he ran. The cop's in pursuit now."

Chapter Six

April held Bailey even though the baby was sound asleep and would likely stay that way for hours. Her head was spinning with too many bad thoughts and images. Ones that would be there for a lifetime no doubt.

Images of Deanne dead.

And of Bailey being ripped from April's arms during the kidnapping.

Having Bailey so close to her now helped stave off some of those nightmares. Being at the safe house helped some, too. But April still couldn't fight off all of those bad thoughts. Now she had her brother to worry about. The police had yet to find Quentin, and he was out there somewhere, on the run. Maybe injured.

Maybe dead.

Plus, there was the additional worry of being in the safe house itself. The place wasn't that big, only one living area, two bedrooms and two baths, and while it was better than staying at the sheriff's office, it meant close quarters. With Chase.

Chase finished up his latest round of calls. All whispered conversations he'd had in the kitchen. And while looking over the notes he'd taken during those calls, he made his way back into the living room. He checked

Bailey first, but it was obvious from Chase's bunched-up forehead that he'd learned some things in those conversations that hadn't pleased him.

"The CSIs gathered up all the cameras and bugs from my house," Chase explained, keeping his voice low probably so that he wouldn't wake the baby. "There were eight in all, and they'll be analyzed for prints and trace. We might get lucky."

She doubted Crossman's lackeys would be that careless, especially after they'd done such a thorough job of installing them. After all, Chase hadn't had a clue they were there until April had pointed out the possibility.

Chase scowled again, something he'd been doing all night, and despite what he'd just said to her, he looked at her as if she'd screwed up yet once again.

And in his eyes she had.

But since Deanne had been right about those cameras at Chase's place, the woman had probably been right about the mole in the marshals' office, as well. It'd been too big of a risk for April to call him when Bailey was born. Of course, in hindsight that hadn't kept Bailey safe. Maybe nothing would, and that broke April's heart.

"What about the man you killed, the one who murdered Deanne," she said. She kept her voice at a whisper, too. "Anything more on him?"

"Nothing. Especially nothing to connect us to Crossman or Deanne. I thought maybe Deanne knew him. Maybe they had somehow been involved."

He didn't need to spell that out. Chase had been looking to see if Deanne had been hired to lure Chase and her to that creek. "Deanne was just as afraid of Crossman as I am," April pointed out.

"Maybe. But Deanne had been living her normal life.

Well, normal for a CI anyway. If Crossman hadn't gone after her in these past six months, then I figured he didn't want to pay her back for the part she'd played in his arrest."

And Deanne had indeed played a part. But the difference was Deanne hadn't agreed to testify against Crossman. Instead, the cops had made a deal with April and Quentin because they thought their lack of a police record would make them more credible. They'd turned informant, and in exchange they wouldn't be prosecuted for the crimes that'd gone on in the bar that Quentin owned.

In Crossman's eyes, that no doubt made them traitors. Along with his CPA, who was also scheduled to testify at his upcoming trial.

"I want to pay for Deanne's funeral," April offered. "It's the least I can do for her."

Chase nodded. "I'll let Jericho know, but it'll be a while before the ME will release the body."

Yes, because it was a murder.

"Still no sign of Quentin," Chase continued a moment later, "but the blood found in his house is being tested to see if it's really his."

April had been in worst-case-scenario mode for a while now, and she hadn't figured the blood belonged to anyone but Quentin. However, maybe it belonged to one of Crossman's thugs. She hoped it did. Maybe Quentin had managed to hurt one of them before he'd escaped.

Chase looked over his notes. "I found out more about Renée. The local cops interviewed some of her neighbors, and according to several of them, she's mentally ill. Has been for years."

April groaned softly. This was the woman who'd had Bailey for hours. Thank God Renée hadn't done anything to harm her. "Did Renée's neighbors believe she was actually pregnant?"

"Yeah. With Quentin's baby." Chase paused. "I think we have to consider that Renée, not Crossman, was behind the kidnapping. It's possible she hired someone to hack into WITSEC to find you because she was planning to pass off Bailey as her and Quentin's child."

April's stomach twisted and turned to the point where she had to take several deep breaths to steady herself. "If that's true, then she hired those gunmen. She's the one responsible for Deanne's death."

Chase nodded. "And it could have been her plan to kill us once she found out where Quentin was."

What sickened April even more was that it could have worked. If Renée and Quentin had been actual lovers, that is. Since Quentin had many lovers, she figured Renée could be telling the truth about that.

"If Renée hired those two gunmen, then she could have hired others," April said, thinking out loud. "Or at least one other one who helped her escape."

He nodded. "That's what I was thinking, too. Even though Jax said Renée seemed scared when the gunman took her. Of course, she could have been faking that or maybe she decided hired thugs weren't so trustworthy after all."

True. The thugs could have turned on Renée.

"Renée has an estranged husband we're trying to track down," Chase added. "His name is Shane Hackett, and one of the neighbors said whenever Renée's in trouble, she always turns to Shane for help."

Well, that was a start. The woman was definitely in trouble now so maybe she was with her husband. Though

April couldn't imagine Shane or anyone else staying with a woman who was so obsessed with another man.

"Any indications that Shane knows about Renée's possible affair with Quentin?" she asked.

"He knows. That's the reason Renée and he separated. He hasn't filed for a divorce yet, though, and at least one neighbor thought that was because Shane was still in love with her."

Heaven help him. Of course, it was possible Shane was off his rocker, too.

"I can't get started on a more permanent safe house and a new WITSEC identity for the three of us," Chase continued a moment later. "Not until I'm sure it's okay to deal with the marshals. But we can stay here until I figure out a better solution."

Chase walked closer, eased down on the arm of the sofa next to her. No scowl this time because he looked at Bailey instead of her. He smiled, something he had been doing every time he looked at their daughter.

That smile could be trouble.

Not just because it stirred the heat inside April but because the love he had for Bailey might make it harder for her to talk him out of making one of the biggest mistakes of his life.

"You told me once you had no plans for fatherhood," April tossed out there. Obviously, not very subtle.

His eyebrow lifted, and Chase gave her a *where's this going?* look. "I didn't. That was then. This is now."

Yes, but his *now* was colored by the love he had for his daughter. "You said the badge would always be your first priority. What you loved most."

Oh, that got her another scowl. "What I love most is my family. That includes Bailey." He huffed. "What's this about? Are you trying to talk me out of going into WITSEC with you?"

"Yes," she readily answered. "Just hear me out," April added before he could dismiss her. "You do love being a marshal. You and your brothers have that whole need-to-get-justice thing. Nothing wrong with that, but it's not just a job. It's a way of life. It's *you*."

The scowl got worse. "If you think I'll just walk away from my daughter—"

"No, but I believe there's another way of being a father without giving up what you are. *Who* you are," April corrected. "It wouldn't be easy, but we could set up secure locations for you to visit Bailey on a regular basis."

"Visitation rights." Chase said that as if it were profanity. Somehow, though, despite the intense conversation, he managed to keep his voice soft. "I don't want to just visit my daughter. I want to be her father."

"I know. But I'm trying to look down the road. We might be in WITSEC for the rest of our lives. What will you do? Because you certainly can't be in law enforcement again. That'd make you too easy to track."

"So, I'll find something else."

She groaned. "And at some point, you could start to resent giving up your badge. You might not want to resent it, but you will."

"And you won't?" he fired back.

"It's different for me. I wasn't exactly looking to hang on to the life I had. Not after what happened."

April saw the moment that Chase shut down. The subject was straying too close to something he didn't want to discuss with her. Not now. Maybe not ever. The murder of the cop.

The one she could have prevented.

"Just think about it," April suggested.

Chase didn't have time to think about that though or anything else she'd said because his phone rang. It woke Bailey, and the baby started to fuss. However, even the fussing didn't stop April from seeing the puzzled look on Chase's face.

"You know anyone by the name of Melody Sutterfield?" he asked, glancing at his phone screen.

April had to shake her head, but she instantly had a bad thought about all of this. "Is there any way someone could use your phone to trace our location?"

"No." But Chase didn't answer the call until she had the bottle in Bailey's mouth to quiet her. He put the call on speaker, but he didn't say anything.

"Marshal Crockett," April heard the caller say. Not a woman as the caller ID had indicated. It was a man. One whose voice April instantly recognized.

The chill slammed through her. Head to toe. Chase mumbled some profanity. Because he obviously recognized the caller, too.

It was Tony Crossman.

"Cat got your tongue, Marshal?" Crossman taunted. "Or have you defriended me?"

"I seriously doubt you got permission for this call," Chase said. No taunting for him. His eyes narrowed. "Let me guess—you're using your lawyer's phone."

"Guilty. But I needed to talk to you, and this was the only way. I heard Deanne was dead."

"Who told you that?" Chase countered.

"I'm in jail, not deaf. It's on the news. And someone hacked into WITSEC files." It wasn't a question. "You've had a rough night, Marshal. April and her scumbag brother, too."

"Did you do something to my brother?" April snapped.

Obviously, Chase hadn't wanted her to say anything, but if Crossman was talking, she needed to hear what he had to say. Besides, Crossman had probably already figured out that Bailey and she would be with Chase.

"How could I do anything to Quentin?" Crossman challenged. "I'm behind bars. You know that better than anyone because you lied to put me here."

"No lies. In case you've developed selective amnesia, you should remember I found proof that you were using Quentin's bar to launder money."

"Yes, that. But yet you didn't go to the cops. Must not have thought I was doing anything so wrong if you didn't report it or confront me about it."

Despite the glare Chase was giving her, April continued. "I was trying to protect my brother. And gather more evidence against you. I didn't know you were going to gun down a cop."

Crossman made a noncommittal sound. "All that sneaking around on your part, trying to gather dirt on me. Then, you got distracted by the marshal. Things didn't work out so great between you, though, when he learned you knew all about a sister in blue being killed."

"A woman you killed," she pointed out.

"Allegedly."

"You're in jail, waiting to be tried for it," April reminded him. "Your CPA actually heard you talking about it. And I didn't know about the dead cop when I went to Chase."

"*Allegedly,*" Crossman repeated. "That's the rift between you two, isn't it? Chase says you knew. You said you didn't. So what's really true?"

"Did you call for a specific reason?" Chase demanded before April could say anything else.

Crossman took his time answering. "I did. I wanted April to know I'm not behind this. I didn't hack into WITSEC and I didn't kill Deanne."

April rolled her eyes. "I'm just supposed to take your word for that?"

"Of course. Why would I lie?"

She could think of a very good reason. "Because it wouldn't look good if we managed to tack on more charges to the ones you're already facing, that's why." April wished she could see his face to know if she'd struck a nerve.

"Maybe. And maybe I'm trying to help you. For instance, you need to watch out for Malcolm Knox."

Everything inside her went still, and Chase looked at her, obviously wanting an explanation. Well, she wanted some explaining done, too.

"How do you know Malcolm?" she asked.

"I know lots about you and your new life. Be careful, April. Malcolm has some pretty nasty secrets of his own. Bye for now." Crossman hung up before April could ask about those secrets.

"Who's Malcolm?" Chase immediately wanted to know.

"Someone I met when Bailey was in the hospital. He's supposedly a cattle baron and was regularly visiting a sick friend."

Chase's stare stayed on her. "Supposedly? Does that mean you didn't believe him?"

"I didn't trust him. But then, I didn't trust anyone I came in contact with." She paused. "Truth is, he gave me the creeps. He kept showing up outside Bailey's room."

His eyebrow lifted. "Stalking you?"

She shrugged. "I did a background check on him and he doesn't have a record or any history of that. But maybe I need to do another check if Crossman's warning me about him."

"Crossman could be lying or yanking your chain," Chase reminded her. But then he groaned, scrubbed his hand over his face. "Or there's another possibility. Malcolm could be working for Crossman."

Mercy, that didn't help the sickening chill she was trying to stave off. Just hearing Crossman's voice had been bad enough, but if Malcolm did indeed work for him, then that meant Crossman had had "eyes" on her for two months. And one of his thugs had been way too close to Bailey that whole time.

"I'll ask Jericho to see what he can find out about Malcolm." Chase fired off a text to his brother.

April thanked him and tried to rein in her fear. Hard to do, though, with Crossman still a threat. Maybe Malcolm was one, too. Having Bailey in her arms helped some, but once again, April found herself fighting back tears.

Tears that caused Chase to scowl again.

"Sorry." April wiped them away as fast as she could. "The last thing you need right now is a crying woman. Especially a woman who's caused you nothing but trouble."

His gaze stayed fixed on her, and by degrees the scowl softened. Chase gave a heavy sigh, reached out and touched her arm. Not a hug, but it still gave her far more comfort than it should have.

"You've caused trouble, yes," he said, "but you don't deserve what's happening to you. Neither does Bailey."

No, her baby didn't deserve it. "I'm afraid this will

be her life. Hiding out in safe houses. Having to learn to look over her shoulder and not trusting anyone."

He nodded. "And that's why I need to go into WITSEC with you. I want to be able to protect her."

April couldn't argue with the protection part, but she prayed there would be another way. After all, Bailey wasn't the only family Chase had, and leaving his life would mean leaving them, too. And being with her. Something that would never sit well with him.

"It was true what I said to Crossman," she tossed out there. "I didn't know the cop had been killed when I went to your house that night, and I didn't go there expecting to land in bed with you. I went because I was upset and wanted to talk to you."

A muscle flickered in his jaw, and his gaze slowly came back to hers. "You didn't seduce me. I willingly got into that bed with you."

True, but even now she could see that he still regretted it. Despite Bailey, Chase always would, and that put the ache right back in her chest.

His phone rang again, and for a moment April thought it was Crossman calling back for another round of taunting. But it wasn't Crossman this time. It was Jericho. Chase answered it and put it on speaker.

"We found Quentin," Jericho said the moment he was on the line.

April felt the jolt of relief. Followed by another jolt of fear. Because that wasn't a good news kind of tone from Jericho.

"Quentin's in the Appaloosa Pass Hospital," Jericho explained. "He walked in and admitted himself about fifteen minutes ago."

"Is he all right?" April asked.

"He's hurt, a gunshot wound to the arm, but he'll live. He wants to see you now, but I told him that's not going to happen. Not until we have plenty of security in place."

"Why does he want to see April?" There was plenty of mistrust and skepticism in Chase's expression and voice.

"I'll tell you what he told me. You can decide if it's the truth or not. He won't spill anything to me, but Quentin claims he knows who's trying to kill April and you."

Chapter Seven

Chase figured visiting Quentin in the hospital wasn't a smart thing to do, but he'd also known right from the start that he stood no chance of nixing the idea. Despite the kidnapping, attack and the mess that Quentin had caused, April had every intention of seeing her brother.

But that didn't mean Chase was going to allow Bailey to be put in danger.

His brother Levi and Deputy Mack Parkman had come to the safe house to stay with the baby while Chase and April ventured into Appaloosa Pass to see Quentin. And they wouldn't make that visit alone. Jax was meeting them there. As far as Chase was concerned, he was treating Quentin just as he would any other dangerous criminal who crossed his path.

"It's not too late to change your mind," Chase said to April as he took the final turn toward town. "You can always call your brother and demand to know what information he has."

"He won't tell me unless I'm there," April insisted.

And to her credit, she had tried to get that info from Quentin over the phone. But Quentin had only restated his demand that she come to see him in person. Still,

Quentin might change his tune if April flat out refused—especially if he did indeed want to save her life.

However, Chase wasn't so sure that was the case. Quentin might not care if his sister was in danger. Especially since he'd already been hurt. Chase still didn't know the details of how Quentin had been shot, but it was one of the questions Chase intended to ask the man.

"I don't trust Quentin," she said, surprising him. She'd always been so defensive when it came to her kid brother. "But I want to see his face when he tells me what he wants me to hear."

Chase gave that some thought. "You think Quentin could have been involved in the kidnapping?"

"I don't want to believe it." She sighed, leaned her head against the truck window. "But he goes through money like water and he has a penchant for getting involved with the worst kind of people. I believe he could have gotten himself into some kind of bind and needs money desperately enough to have possibly done something like this. *Possibly*," April emphasized.

Chase had to admit it was a *possibly* for him, too. Quentin was a scumbag, no doubt about that, but Crossman and Renée were still their top suspects, with Crossman occupying the number one slot on that very short list.

His phone rang, causing April to practically snap to attention. No doubt because she was worried about something going wrong at the safe house. But it wasn't Levi or Mack. It was Jericho.

"I just got the background check on Malcolm Knox," Jericho said the moment Chase answered. Chase put the call on speaker since he knew this was something April would want to hear. "He's rich. Worth millions. He's a cattleman and also owns a very high-end security com-

pany. Thirty-nine and never been married. No criminal
record, not even a parking ticket. So, you want to tell me
why you needed a check on him?"

"Because Crossman warned April about him," Chase
answered.

"And you believe Crossman?"

"No." Chase didn't even have to give that any thought.
"But I want to know if there's a connection. It's possible
Crossman used Malcolm to spy on April while she was
in WITSEC."

April didn't nod exactly, but he saw the agreement in
her eyes. And the chill that went through her. She'd said
she hadn't exactly trusted Malcolm, but it had to make
her sick to think that one of Crossman's henchmen could
have been so close to her at such a vulnerable time.

"I didn't find any obvious connection to Crossman,"
Jericho said. "But there's something about this guy that's
just not right. Perfect credit, perfect driving record. Hell,
he even had a perfect grade point average in college. Everything in his background lines up in *perfect* detail."

Normally, a good clean record didn't bother Chase,
but it did in this case. "You think he's living under a created identity?"

"Maybe. But if so, he's not in WITSEC, and he's not
an undercover cop or in any other form of law enforcement that I can find. That means if he's living under a
false identity, he's likely doing it for his own reasons."

And Chase figured those reasons probably weren't
good ones. "Were you able to get his financials?"

"Some. Lots of money in and out of his accounts. Hard
to tell if he's getting regular payouts from someone like
Crossman. But I'll do some more digging."

"Thanks," Chase told him, and he took the final turn

to the hospital. "Anything new with the prisoner this morning?" Not that he expected Gene Rooks to start blabbing, but Chase could hope the man had had a change of heart.

"Nothing yet, but Rooks is with his lawyer now. And no, I can't trace the lawyer back to Crossman or Renée. Already tried." Jericho paused. "The lab called on that blood they found in Quentin's house. It wasn't his, and it's not a match to anybody in the system."

April shook her head. "But Quentin was shot."

"Not there at his place. Or if it was there, he didn't leave any blood behind. I questioned Quentin about his injury, but he's being very vague. If you get answers from him, I want to hear them."

"Of course. Any news about Renée?"

"She's still at large. Still nothing on those bugs and cameras the CSIs gathered from your house. There were no prints or trace on them, but they're trying to find the location where the images and recordings were being sent."

"They can do that?" Chase asked.

"They can try. Don't get your hopes up. I think our best bet at finding out who's behind this is to get what you can from Quentin."

Chase believed that as well, and he ended the call when he pulled into the hospital parking lot. He spotted Jax right away under the awning at the drop-off area, and Jax motioned for him to park right by the door. Good. Because Chase didn't want April out in the open any longer than necessary.

"How's Quentin?" April immediately asked him.

Jax didn't answer right away and didn't waste any time near the door. Firing glances all around, he got them moving out of the reception area and up the hall. "He's fine. The doc said he'll be released this afternoon."

April didn't seem relieved about that, and Chase knew why. Being released could mean Quentin would be in even more danger since they weren't sure yet if they could trust the marshals.

"Who'll be protecting him?" April pressed.

Jax seemed annoyed, not with the question exactly but with the answer. "Me. The other deputies weren't exactly jumping to volunteer."

Chase didn't blame them. Quentin had been business partners with a cop killer. That wouldn't put the man on any popularity lists with law enforcement.

"Thank you," April said as they made their way down the hall.

"No need for thanks. I'm hoping Quentin will lead us to some information about who kidnapped Bailey." Which meant Jax thought Quentin might have played a part in that, too.

Chase didn't have to guess which room Quentin was in because the uniformed hospital security guard was posted outside the door. He opened it for them, and Jax went in ahead of April. Probably to make sure the area was still safe. It was. Only Quentin was there, and he was in the bed hooked up to an IV.

April didn't rush toward him, but Chase did get her inside the room so he could shut the door. He could have sworn the temperature in the room dropped with the frosty looks April and Quentin were giving each other. Seeing that was a first for Chase. April had always jumped to defend her brother and had always acted like a mother hen whenever she was around him.

"I'm glad you came," Quentin greeted, his attention going straight to her stomach. "I heard you had the baby."

"Who told you?" she snapped.

Quentin's frost intensified. "It doesn't matter. I'm sorry someone tried to kidnap her."

"They didn't try. They succeeded. Chase and I just got her back last night." She glanced away from him. "Deanne's dead."

"Yes, I found out about that, too." Something flickered through Quentin's eyes. Grief maybe? Or it could be fake grief. "Who killed her?"

"We don't have an ID on him yet, but he was working with a man named Gene Rooks," Chase answered. "Do you know him?"

The icy look he'd given his sister was a drop in the bucket compared with the one Quentin gave Chase. "Are you accusing me of something?"

"I'm only asking a question. You have a guilty conscience?"

Quentin growled out some profanity under his breath. "No, I just know how you are. You've been on a vendetta to get me for years."

Chase tapped his badge. "Just doing my job. I'm funny like that."

His attempt at smart-mouthed humor didn't soften Quentin's glare one bit. And it wasn't moving this conversation in a direction it needed to go. "Did you have anything to do with the kidnapping and attack on April and me that took place yesterday?"

"Of course not. Why would you think such a thing?" The denial was loud and intense enough. But that didn't mean Chase was buying it.

"Because you could be broke enough to be desperate."

Quentin dodged his gaze. Definitely not a good sign. "I do need money, but there's no way I'd kidnap my own niece to get it."

The room went completely silent for several moments.

"How'd you even know I'd had the baby?" April asked, taking the question right out of Chase's mouth. "And while you're explaining that, tell us how you found out about the kidnapping and that Deanne was dead."

Quentin huffed. Then, he sighed. "When I was attacked last night, the man said my niece had been taken and that if I didn't cooperate and pay up, I'd never see her."

Chase went through each word of that, but there were some huge gaps in the information. Chase tipped his head to Quentin's bandaged shoulder and went to April's side. "Who shot you?" he asked Quentin.

"I don't know. Maybe it was you?" Quentin countered.

That got Quentin a huff from not only just Chase but Jax and April, too. She went closer to the bed and stared down at her brother. "Tell us everything that happened so we can try to prevent any further attacks."

Quentin held the stare for several moments and then eased his head back onto his pillow. "Someone broke into my house yesterday. A man wearing a ski mask. He told me my niece had been kidnapped and that he would take me to her. I didn't believe him. We fought, and I'm pretty sure I managed to cut him with a kitchen knife. I couldn't get to my gun so I ran out the back, and that's when he shot me."

That explained the blood on the floor at his house. However, it didn't mean Quentin was telling the truth. "What happened then?" Chase asked.

"I kept running. I wasn't sure who to trust so I didn't

call the marshals. I haven't trusted them right from the start. So, I made my way here, figuring April would be with you." He paused, glancing at them. Or rather glancing at how close they were standing to each other. "I was right."

Quentin seemed to be implying there was something going on between April and him. Something more than just Bailey.

And he was right.

The old attraction was indeed still there, and anyone within a hundred yards of them could likely see it. Chase wanted to believe he could keep pushing it away, but it just kept coming back. That's why he needed to concentrate on the investigation. Because losing focus now could put Bailey right back in danger.

"Tell me about Renée," Chase insisted.

Quentin blinked as if surprised or just plain uncomfortable by the change in subject. "What does she have to do with this?"

"Maybe everything," April answered. "She was with Bailey when we found her."

More than a blink that time. Quentin's head came off the pillow. "You think she's the one who kidnapped your baby?"

April shook her head. "We're not sure what her role was in all this. Tell me about Renée," she repeated, sounding more like a cop than a sister.

Quentin took a deep breath. "I met her at the bar and we had an affair. A short one because she turned out to be a little too high maintenance for me. I'm talking dozens of calls and texts each day. I know she's in love with me, but I just don't feel the same way about her. I haven't heard from her, though, since I went into WITSEC."

"Does Renée know Crossman?" Chase asked.

If Quentin was faking the surprise from that question, then he was very good at it. "You don't believe she'd team up with Crossman?" He cursed, not waiting for the answer. "Renée knows him, all right. She met Crossman at the bar."

Of course. Crossman spent a lot of time at the bar Quentin owned so it was logical that Renée and he would run into each other. Chase hoped those encounters hadn't led to some unholy alliance.

Chase glanced at Jax, who was already taking out his phone. "I'm on it," Jax said, stepping back into the hall and shutting the door behind him.

"On what?" Quentin demanded. "Who's he calling?"

"The jail," Chase answered. "If Renée visited Crossman, we can maybe get access to their conversations. It's possible Crossman put her up to doing the kidnapping." But then, it was just as possible that Renée was acting on her own. "Was Renée ever pregnant with your child?"

Quentin's eyes widened. "She said she was. Did Renée have a baby?"

"No." But that was the only part of the explanation that Chase managed because the door opened again, and when Jax stuck in his head, Chase knew something was wrong.

"Quentin has a visitor," Jax explained. "The guard's already frisked him. No gun." His attention went to Quentin. Then to April. "The guy says his name is Malcolm Knox and that he's a close friend of yours. He wants to see both Quentin and you now."

APRIL SUCKED IN her breath and held it a moment. And yes, it was indeed Malcolm who came through the door. There wasn't a strand of his sandy-blond hair out of place, and he was wearing one of the pricey black suits that he favored. He was also carrying a huge bouquet of flowers.

"April," Malcolm said. He smiled at her as if this were a social visit.

Chase wasn't smiling, though. "Did you know he was coming here?" he asked her.

She shook her head, glancing back at her brother, but Quentin had a startled expression that was similar to her own. "You know Malcolm?" her brother asked her.

"Yes. And I take it so do you." She folded her arms over her chest and snapped toward Malcolm. "Why are you here?"

Malcolm didn't seem put off by her brusque tone. He went closer to Quentin and placed the flowers on the table next to the bed. "I came to check on you. I was sorry to hear of your injury. Are you all right?"

"I've been better." Quentin was still studying April's reaction. "What's this all about?"

Chase stepped between Malcolm and her. "Start talking. How did you even know Quentin and April were here?"

Malcolm certainly didn't extend a smile to Chase. "You're the marshal. Bailey's biological father." He didn't exactly add any endearment to that label.

"Bailey's *father*," Chase corrected. No endearment for him, either.

Part of April wanted to be flattered that Chase was jealous. After all, Malcolm was good-looking. But that wasn't a jealous look Chase was giving the man. He was a marshal looking at a potential suspect.

The very one Crossman had warned them about.

"Get started on answering those questions I just

asked," Chase demanded. "How did you even know they were here?"

"When I heard there was blood found at Quentin's house, I hired a team of private investigators to start checking the hospitals. I thought if he was seriously hurt, he would need some help."

Chase shook his head. "Quentin wasn't admitted here under his own name."

"I didn't figure he would be," Malcolm readily answered. "Not with April and him being in WITSEC. But I had the PIs check this particular hospital because I thought Quentin might try to come here. Because of your past connection to April."

Past? That was not the right thing to say.

Malcolm wasn't an idiot. At least she didn't think he was. So maybe he was just pushing Chase's buttons on purpose. And in Malcolm's case, April was fairly certain that jealousy was involved here. She hadn't done anything to lead Malcolm on. In fact, she'd been out and out rude to him on numerous occasions, but that hadn't caused him to back off.

"You knew I was in WITSEC?" she asked. "For how long?"

"Practically from the first day I met you." Malcolm paused, smiled again. But this time, there was discomfort in that smile. "I don't allow many people into my life. I've been burned by those who are only after my money. So, after we met at the hospital, I ran a background check on you."

April glared at him. Both Quentin and Chase groaned, but it was Chase who responded. "Nothing would have turned up about April in a normal background check."

"My staff was thorough," Malcolm said as if choosing his words carefully. "And soon they found Quentin."

Quentin didn't just groan that time. He cursed and looked at her. "I had no idea he knew you. He never said." Then, his gaze flew to Malcolm. "What the hell were you trying to do? Get information on April?"

"I was trying to figure out a way to keep Bailey and her safe," Malcolm said without hesitating.

"It wasn't your job to do that," Chase pointed out.

That put some fire in Malcolm's otherwise ice-blue eyes. "Well, you didn't do a very good job of it, did you?"

April had known Malcolm only two months and she'd never seen his temper flare. She was certainly seeing it now. But then, so was Chase's. She didn't want this to turn into a man contest, not when they were so short of answers. Still, Malcolm was giving her the creeps.

"Did you hack into WITSEC files to find me?" she asked, and April didn't bother to make it sound friendly.

Malcolm looked as if she had punched him. "Of course not. I wouldn't have endangered you that way. The PIs used facial recognition software and matched it to some old photos of you they found on the internet."

The marshals had deleted as many photos as they could find, but April had always known there might be some still floating around. That was the main reason the marshals had wanted to place her in a different state, but April had always figured if someone wanted to find her hard enough, they could.

And apparently Malcolm had.

"April," Malcolm said, coming closer to her. At least that's what he tried to do, but Chase blocked his way. Despite that, Malcolm snagged her gaze from over Chase's shoulder. "I know this all must seem strange to you, but what I felt for you was instant. Love at first sight."

She dropped back a step. "You don't even know me."

"That's not true. We spent all that time talking when Bailey was in the intensive care unit. You cried on my shoulder."

Chase glanced back at her.

"I would have cried on anyone's shoulder then," April explained. She huffed, tried to say this in a way that would make it crystal clear to Malcolm. "I don't have those kinds of feelings for you. And I never will."

If he was fazed by that, Malcolm didn't show it. "Forever's a long time. People change. *You* might change."

"Enough of this. Tell me how you know Tony Crossman," Chase came out and demanded.

Malcolm pulled back his shoulders. "I don't know him. Not personally anyway. I've read about what he did, of course, and with Quentin and April scheduled to testify against him at his upcoming trial, I figure that means he'd like to get back at them." He shifted his attention to April. "Is Crossman the one who kidnapped Bailey?"

She lifted her shoulder. "Crossman seems to think you're responsible. Or at least you know something about it."

"I don't!" There it was again. That temper. "I wouldn't hurt you or Bailey. Unlike him." Malcolm jabbed his index finger at Chase.

That put a hard, dangerous look in Chase's eyes. "What the hell do you mean by that?"

However, Malcolm didn't answer. His attention went back to April instead. "There's something you should know. After I found out who you were and that the marshal here was Bailey's father, I had a background check done on him."

"You what?" she snapped.

Chase didn't say a word, but April could practically see every muscle tightening in his body. Despite that, Malcolm still didn't even spare Chase a glance.

"Marshal Crockett didn't tell you?" Malcolm pressed.

April tried to tamp down the uneasiness that was racing through her. She failed. "Tell me what?"

She didn't like that smug look that Malcolm got. Now he looked at Chase, and the smug look intensified tenfold. "The marshal hired a lawyer, and he's planning to challenge you for custody of Bailey."

Chapter Eight

Oh, man. This was not something Chase wanted to discuss with April right now, but judging from how fast her expression went from shock to anger, he didn't have much of a choice.

"You did what?" she asked. Not a shout. No, this was barely a whisper. Probably because her throat had clamped shut.

"Come on. We need to talk," Chase said. It was stating the obvious, but he didn't want April to start an argument with him while they were still in the room with her brother and Malcolm.

Especially Malcolm.

Later, Chase would settle up with that idiot, but for now he had some explaining to do. The question was, would April actually listen? There was only a thin thread of trust between them, and this sure wouldn't help.

She didn't resist but didn't exactly cooperate, either, when Chase took hold of her arm. She slung off his grip but marched out into the hall with him. Since there was a stream of nurses, doctors and visitors, and the guard, too, Chase kept walking until he found a private waiting area.

"Did you hire a lawyer?" April asked the moment he shut the door.

Chase looked her straight in the eyes. "I did. But hear me out before you get more upset."

Too late. April pushed herself away from him and headed to the other side of the room.

"How could you?" She sounded angry. And worse, she sounded hurt.

"I only talked to a lawyer because I thought if I had custody, it would be better for Bailey. She'd have a real home with a large family. A grandmother, aunts, uncles and cousins. I thought she deserved that."

He could also see the anger and hurt evaporating from her body. Well, the anger anyway. And April certainly didn't jump to argue with him about the family part. She just stood there with tears shimmering in her eyes.

"You thought it was best for Bailey, and in a way, it is." April shook her head. "God, Chase. I'd miss her so much. It'd break my heart to lose her."

Cursing himself, cursing Malcolm, too, Chase went to her. "I didn't tell you about visiting the lawyer because I nixed the idea. Yes, Bailey would have a good home at the ranch, but it wouldn't necessarily be a safe one. Crossman's thugs could get to her there."

Of course, they'd gotten to her at the WITSEC house, too, but Chase figured the Crockett ranch was the first place Crossman would send his hired guns to look for her. Then, he could use Bailey to get to April.

April looked up at him. Maybe trying to decide if he was telling her the truth. He was. But after everything that'd gone on between them, Chase wasn't sure she'd believe him. So, he did something to prove it.

Something stupid.

Chase kissed her.

One touch of his mouth on hers and he got a fast reminder of why they'd landed in bed in the first place. This fire. Always there. *Always*. And the fire didn't seem to care that they weren't suited for each other.

After just a few seconds, Chase was ready to force himself away from her and give her permission to slap him into the next county. But when he went to pull away, April took hold of him and held on. She also made that silky sound of pleasure. Just a slight sound that came from deep within her throat, but it was yet another jolting reminder that he was playing with fire.

That didn't stop him.

In fact, it got worse. Because Chase deepened the kiss, dragged her closer until they were plastered against each other. With every part of her touching every part of him. Definitely not good, and thankfully that *not good* part finally made it through to his brain and he stepped back from her.

April stared at him, her breath gusting. "Wow," she muttered. "Was that your way of apologizing?"

"I wish." But unfortunately saying I'm sorry had nothing to do with that kiss.

She nodded as if she knew exactly what he meant. And she probably did. This wasn't a good time for the old attraction to fan these flames. It was a distraction. A nice one that he could still taste and feel. But a distraction nonetheless.

"Does this mean you'll hate me even more now?" she asked.

Chase opened his mouth to answer that and realized he didn't know quite what to say. "I don't hate you," he finally admitted. "I hate what you did." And he also hated he felt things for her he didn't want to feel.

She nodded, might have jumped deeper into this conversation that they shouldn't be having, but the door flew open. Chase automatically pulled his gun, and he didn't holster it when he saw their visitor.

Malcolm.

"I wanted to make sure you were okay," the man said to April.

He volleyed glances between Chase and her, maybe picking up on the vibes still in the room. Or maybe April and he just looked as if they'd kissed each other's brains out. Either way, Malcolm's sour expression said he didn't like it.

"I hope you didn't lie your way out of this," Malcolm snarled when his attention settled on Chase. "You went to see that lawyer and I can prove it."

Chase was about to set things straight with this clown, but April stepped in front of him. "Malcolm, it's time for you to leave."

Obviously, that wasn't the response Malcolm had been expecting. "You're taking his side?"

"Yes. He's Bailey's father. Chase was only thinking about her best interest when he saw the lawyer."

Malcolm threw his hands in the air. "He was trying to take your daughter away from you."

Chase was so tired of this. "*Our* daughter. Mine and April's. And in case you didn't hear her, April just asked you to leave. Now I'm telling you to get out of here."

The anger flared through Malcolm's eyes. "You're using your badge?"

"No. This isn't about a badge. This is about me telling you to leave, or I'll drag you out of here."

That didn't cool down any of Malcolm's anger. "I was there for April and Bailey when you weren't. I gave April comfort when you didn't. And I would have paid any amount of ransom to get Bailey back."

Chase was about to tell this jerk that he hadn't been there to comfort April only because she hadn't thought it was safe to let him know that Bailey had been born. But maybe Malcolm already knew that. Perhaps because Malcolm had been the one who'd planted those cameras and bugs at Chase's house.

Maybe he'd also been the one to kidnap Bailey.

The man's feelings for April seemed obsessive, and if he'd been able to "save" Bailey from the kidnappers, then Malcolm might have believed that would help him win over April.

Malcolm must have realized that his anger wasn't going to earn him any points with April because his expression softened. "Promise me you'll call me if you need anything," he said to her.

"I'll be fine," she answered. Which, of course, wasn't much of an answer in Malcolm's eyes, but the man must have decided that was the best he was going to get right now.

Malcolm nodded, and without giving Chase even another glance, he turned and walked out. Only then did April release the breath she'd been holding.

"I swear, Malcolm wasn't like this when I met him in the hospital," she insisted. "He was nice. Charming, even."

Chase believed her. That was classic stalker behavior, and he was betting if he dug a little deeper into Malcolm's past that he would find a pattern of this kind of behavior.

Well, unless Malcolm was faking it.

"I need to see if there's a connection between Crossman and Malcolm," Chase told her, and he holstered his gun.

She nodded without hesitation, which meant April had already come to the same conclusion. Crossman could have hired or coerced Malcolm into getting close to her so he could have the opportunity to do some very bad things to her.

Like kidnap Bailey.

"You said you didn't meet Malcolm until after Bailey was born," he continued, "but I saw that lawyer three months ago. So, how did Malcolm know that?"

He could almost see the thoughts racing through her head. "You're thinking Malcolm had me, and you, in his sights before he introduced himself to me."

Chase shrugged. "Either that or his PIs got very lucky. I only visited that lawyer once, and I didn't exactly share the news with anyone. In fact, I didn't even tell anyone in my family."

April closed her eyes a moment, shuddered. "If Malcolm's working for Crossman, then he could have found me right after I went into WITSEC. Maybe Crossman didn't want to kill a pregnant woman so he waited until after Bailey was born."

Maybe but that didn't explain why Malcolm or another of Crossman's hired guns hadn't killed April afterward. Unless Malcolm had developed feelings for her.

Not exactly a settling thought.

He really needed to find out if there was a connection between Malcolm and Crossman.

Chase heard the footsteps in the hall, and he reached for his gun again. False alarm this time because it was Jax.

"You're not going to believe who just called the hospital," Jax said. "Renée. And she's demanding to speak to Quentin. I've got her on hold for now, but I thought you might want to listen in on the conversation."

He did. "Did Renée say where she was?" Chase asked.

"Not yet. I'm hoping she'll let something slip." Jax sounded as if he had a score to settle with the woman. And in a way, he did. Because Jax could have been hurt or worse when Renée escaped. Plus, innocent people didn't usually try to run from the law. The trouble was, Chase wasn't exactly sure how Renée fit into this mess, but maybe he'd find out.

"I figure Renée might say more if she thinks she's just talking to Quentin," Jax explained. "But if the conversation doesn't go our direction, I'll let her know we're there."

Good plan. They hurried back to Quentin's room. Quentin was sitting up in his bed, the hospital phone already in his hand. Jax pressed the button to take the call off hold and then put it on speaker.

"Renée?" Quentin said.

"Thank God. It's so good to hear your voice." Renée's words rushed out with her breath. "How badly are you hurt?"

"I'll live. Where are you?" Quentin asked. A question that Jax had probably told him to ask.

"I'd rather not say over the phone, just in case someone's listening. But I need to see you. I've missed you so much, Quentin, and there are things I have to tell you."

"What things?" Quentin pressed.

"Can't get into that now. But later. How soon can we meet?"

Quentin looked at Jax, and Jax jotted something down on the notepad next to the phone. "Soon," Quentin read from the note. "Can you come here to the hospital? I'd love to see you."

Renée hesitated. "I doubt that would be safe. I mean, they're probably guarding your room, right?"

Quentin relayed the next part of what Jax wrote. "I can get rid of the guard. Just come here so we can talk."

More hesitation. "Promise me this isn't some kind of trap," Renée finally said.

The door opened, and a nurse pushing a wheelchair started to come in, but Jax motioned for her to wait.

"I swear it's not a trap," Quentin said to Renée before Jax could write down his next response. "I need to see you, but I also need to find out some other things. Like why my WITSEC identity was blown. April's, too. Any idea who's responsible for that?"

"I don't know," Renée answered right away. "I'm still working on that."

"Is that why you were with the men who kidnapped my niece?"

Renée let that question hang in the air for several moments. "We can talk about that when I see you. Quentin, I've been through so much." A hoarse sob tore from her mouth. "I have to tell you about the baby."

"Did you really have a baby?" Quentin snapped. "You told me you were pregnant, but I wasn't sure if it was a false alarm or not."

More hesitation. "We can talk about it when I see you. I can be there in an hour. Is that enough time for you to get rid of the guard?"

Quentin waited until Jax nodded. "That's enough time. Don't be late."

"I won't be. I love you, Quentin."

He didn't respond, and after several moments, Renée

ended the call. "I take it I won't be meeting her alone," Quentin immediately said to Jax.

"You won't be meeting her at all. In fact, she won't even make it into the hospital. I'll arrest her in the parking lot." Jax went to the door, opened it, and the nurse was still there.

"I have to take Mr. Taylor to have an MRI on his shoulder," she said. Taylor was the alias Quentin had used when he'd been admitted to the hospital.

"Hold on a sec," Chase insisted.

He checked her name tag. Kitty Gagnon, and the woman made a sound of surprise when he took her picture with his phone. Then, Chase made a call to confirm she was indeed a nurse. It took him several minutes to work his way through to the hospital chief, but he verified that the woman was indeed Kitty Gagnon and that she was a nurse assigned to this particular floor. Only then did Chase motion for her to get Quentin into the wheelchair.

However, before the nurse could take him out of the room, April caught Quentin's hand. "Did you have anything, and I mean *anything*, to do with what's been happening?"

Quentin cursed, shook his head, but it took him a long time to say the answer aloud. "No."

April let go of him, and the nurse wheeled him away with the guard following along behind them.

"Go ahead and get April out of here," Jax told Chase, and he took out his phone. No doubt to start getting backup in place so he could arrest Renée when she arrived. "I'll follow you out."

Chase didn't waste any time getting her out of the room and heading toward the exit. "You believe Quentin when he said he didn't have any part in this?" Chase asked her.

She huffed, pushed her hair from her face. "I wish I did. It'd help us narrow down our suspects."

Yes. Because three was too many. Or there were possibly even four if Renée, Malcolm or Quentin weren't working for Crossman.

What Chase needed to do was make a trip to the jail. Not to talk with Crossman. He wasn't sure the man would tell the truth. But maybe the visitors' logs and the guards would be able to give him some information that would link one of their suspects to Crossman. If he could just make that connection, then other charges could be filed against Crossman and his assets could be frozen.

Chase went ahead of her when they reached the door, but he'd barely made it a step outside when he saw something he didn't want to see.

Renée.

The woman was standing next to a black SUV, and she had binoculars pressed to her eyes.

"Get back inside," Chase told April.

It was already too late. The shot slammed through the air. And it hadn't come from outside.

It had come from behind them.

The shooter was in the hospital.

Chapter Nine

Before April even realized what was happening, Chase pulled her to the floor and to the side of a chair. Not a second too soon. Because another shot came their way and blasted into the glass surrounding the sliding doors.

Oh, God. Someone was trying to kill them again.

Bailey wasn't with them this time, but there were plenty of people in the hospital who could be hurt.

There were screams and shouts, people running and trying to get out of the path of those shots. The gunman didn't seem focused on any of them, though. The shots were coming in the direction of Chase, Jax and her.

"You see the shooter?" Jax asked. He, too, had dropped to the floor and was to the side of a display case. Not much cover at all.

Chase shook his head. "But I did see Renée in the parking lot."

April's heart was already pounding, and that only made it worse. She doubted this was a coincidence, especially since the woman had said it'd be an hour before she arrived for her meeting with Quentin. Maybe Renée knew that would spur Chase and her to leave so that Renée could have someone gun them down.

But the shots weren't outside. They were coming from the very hall that led to Quentin's room.

April wanted to believe a hired gun couldn't have gotten inside, but there was no metal detector in the small hospital, and the security guard was with Quentin.

"Keep an eye on the parking lot," Chase told her. "If you see Renée or anyone else coming closer, let me know."

She would. But she also doubted Renée would just come walking into the middle of this. Well, unless Renée planned on taking some shots at them, too.

While keeping his body in front of hers, Chase called for backup. Since the sheriff's office was just up the street, it wouldn't take Jericho and the other deputies long to get there. But it still might not be in time to stop someone from getting hurt.

Heavens, was this shooter after her? Or was this some kind of ploy to get to Quentin?

April didn't have time to think about that, though. There was another shot, followed by a woman's scream. "Help me," she shouted.

Chase glanced around the chair and cursed. So did Jax. Judging from the woman's frantic pleas, April figured the gunman had taken a hostage.

"Tell Jericho to approach through the back of the hospital," Chase whispered to Jax, and he leaned out.

A shot came right at him, and he ducked back behind cover.

"Let her go," Chase called out. "She has no part in this."

"She does if she'll get me out of here," the gunman shouted back.

April peered around the edge of the chair and spotted them. Like the other men who'd kidnapped Bailey, the gunman was wearing a ski mask, and he was using his hostage as a human shield. The woman was a nurse and couldn't have been more than twenty-five. And she looked terrified, her eyes pleading for someone to do something to save her.

"What do you want?" Chase asked the man. "Who sent you here?"

"I could answer that, but it'd get me killed in a really bad way. No thanks. So, here's how this is going to work. You're going to let me walk out of here, and once I'm sure I'm out of the line of fire, I'll let her go."

April replayed his words and shook her head. "Why would he come here without a plan to get out? A plan that didn't involve taking a random hostage? It's too risky. He could have just waited outside and gunned us down."

Chase agreed so quickly that it made her realize he'd already come to that same conclusion. And that meant maybe the gunman wasn't there to kill them but to create a diversion.

"Quentin," she said.

"Stay down," Chase warned her.

April had no intentions of running out there since she'd only be shot, but she prayed the security guard would be able to protect her brother if this attack was indeed aimed at him.

"Help me," the nurse begged again, and judging from the sound of her voice, her captor was moving her deeper into the hall. Where he would no doubt try to escape with her.

Unfortunately, there were too many ways for him to do just that.

There were clinics on one side of the hall, and most

of them had exits to the parking lot. If the thug made it that far, he could get away. That wouldn't be good for the nurse. Or for them. Because he wouldn't be able to give them answers as to why this was happening, and he might kill the nurse instead of letting her go.

"You have a clean shot?" Chase asked Jax.

Jax shook his head and checked his phone when it dinged. "Jericho's just now pulling into the parking lot. He spotted Renée, and she's armed."

No. That meant it might not be safe for Jericho to get out of his cruiser. Of course, that probably wouldn't stop him, but Renée could certainly slow him down if she started shooting.

The nurse screamed, and when April glanced at her, she saw something she definitely didn't want to see. The nurse was fighting to get loose, and her captor was fighting back. He bashed her against the head with his gun and then took aim at her. Ready to kill her.

Chase reacted fast. So fast that it was over before April even saw it coming. He leaned out from the chair and fired two shots, the sounds blasting through the hospital.

April held her breath, adding another prayer for the nurse. But it wasn't the nurse who'd been shot. It was the gunman. He crumpled into a heap on the floor.

"I need to get April away from this door," Chase told Jax. Probably because of Renée. The woman could come running in at any moment. "Stay behind me," Chase added to her.

April got to her feet, trailing along behind him as Chase made his way to the guy he'd just shot. The nurse was still screaming, but several of her coworkers rushed forward to pull her away.

When Chase made it to the man, he leaned down, retrieved his gun and stripped off the ski mask. April got just a glimpse of his face.

A stranger.

She supposed that was better than it being someone she knew, but this was the third armed thug who'd attacked them, and it made her wonder just how many assassins had been hired to come after them.

Or to come after her brother.

"Watch our backs," Chase called out to Jax.

Chase was watching all around them, too, as he made his way down the hall. No sign of the guard outside her brother's room, but then the man had gone with Quentin and the nurse to have the MRI done.

There were two nurses who were still cowering behind their station, and it probably didn't help their panic when they saw Chase's gun.

"Where's the patient who was in this room?" Chase asked them.

"Still in radiology," one of them answered and reached for the phone. "I'll call over there."

It seemed to take an eternity for her to do that. And while April waited, she tried to tamp down her fear. Hard to do that, though, with the adrenaline still pumping through her.

She couldn't hear the nurse's whispered conversation with whomever the woman had called, but April had no trouble figuring out that something was wrong. The nurse was trembling even harder when she finished the call.

"I called the receptionist at the check-in desk in radiology and she said no one's answering in the MRI room," the nurse finally said. "But that's where they took the patient and it's just at the end of the hall on the right."

That caused April's fear and adrenaline to soar, but she tried not to think the worst. Maybe the nurse and her brother had taken cover when they heard the shots.

Chase got them moving again. Kept looking around as well, and they made their way farther down the hall. When they reached the door for radiology, Chase eased it open.

And then he cursed.

April's heart went to her knees. Her brother wasn't there. The room was empty, but there were definite signs of a struggle. Equipment and a wheelchair had been toppled over.

"They took them," someone said.

With his gun ready, Chase pivoted in the direction of the voice. It was the nurse, Kitty Gagnon, and she was crying and hiding behind an examination curtain.

"They took the patient, Mr. Taylor," Kitty added.

"Who took them?" Chase snapped.

But she only shook her head. "Two armed men." A hoarse sob tore from her throat. "God, I think they killed him."

CHASE LOOKED OVER his notes from the phone calls he'd just made. Notes that he'd need to file an official report, but he didn't like much of what he'd jotted down. Quentin was missing.

Maybe dead.

And Renée was nowhere to be found. She'd managed to escape during all the gunfire.

He figured it wasn't a coincidence that Renée and those gunmen had been at the hospital at the same time. In fact he hoped it wasn't a coincidence. Because if Renée and her hired guns had kidnapped Quentin, then it likely meant the man was still alive. Renée hadn't seemed interested in killing Quentin, only renewing a romantic relationship with him. Of course, if Quentin wasn't willing to pretend he would do that, Renée might kill him anyway.

Chase made his way from the deputy's desk he'd been using and went to Jericho's office. April was there, right where he'd left her nearly an hour earlier. However, her expression had changed considerably. She no longer looked shell-shocked and ready to fall apart. She was smiling. And it took Chase a moment to realize she was smiling at something on the computer screen.

Bailey.

"Levi set up the computer so we'd be able to see Bailey at the safe house," April explained, turning the screen so Chase could see. "He said it was okay to do this, that no one could hack into the feed."

"Levi's right," Chase assured her, and it didn't take long before he, too, was smiling. Bailey was in her carry seat and she was grabbing her toes while making babbling sounds.

"I was just telling April that the baby's doing great," Levi said. "Big appetite, lots of diapers."

"Are you sure you know how to change a diaper?" Chase asked. It was a valid question since Levi was the only one of his siblings who didn't have a child.

"You're kidding, right? I got plenty of practice with Matthew," Levi reminded him.

Jax's son. Yeah, they'd all gotten plenty of practice with him since Jax was a widower, and they'd all pitched in to help from time to time.

"Gotta say, though," Levi went on, "I'm glad to have

a niece even if she is outnumbered by her nephews. I'll bet Mom can't wait to get her hands on her only grand-daughter."

Levi no doubt hadn't meant that to be anything other than lighthearted, but it caused April's smile to fade some. Probably because it was a reminder that there might not be any opportunities for Bailey to get to know her grandmother or the rest of the family. Of course, April's look could also have something to do with that visit Chase had made to the lawyer.

Or that kiss.

There'd been nothing to smile about in that particular department. It'd broken down walls between them that were best left standing. Chase didn't consider himself an emotional sort, but he wasn't sure he could handle another heart-stomping from April. Especially since he needed to be doing whatever it took to keep things amicable between them.

Bailey started fussing, and as if he were an old pro at tending babies, Levi scooped her up in his arms. "It's bottle time. I'll call you back after her nap." He paused. "Not that I mind babysitting duty, but when do you think you'll make it back here?"

"Soon," Chase answered.

That was wishful thinking on his part. More than anything, Chase wanted to be back at that safe house, giving his daughter a bottle and watching her for real, not via a computer screen.

But there was a huge problem.

Those two gunmen who'd taken Quentin. Chase couldn't be sure they weren't lurking around, prepared to attack the moment he stepped outside with April. Of course, eventually they'd have to leave the sheriff's office, but he was hoping those gunmen would be found, and jailed, before that happened.

Levi cut the video feed, the screen going blank, and the rest of April's smile went blank with it. Something Chase totally understood.

"I miss her, too," he said.

April nodded, blinked back tears that filled her eyes. "It's hard to believe how much you can love someone so much."

Yes, he got that, too. "It feels as if she's been in my life forever." But he figured most parents felt the same.

That didn't seem to do anything to put April in a better mood. "I don't suppose the nurse was able to describe the men who took Quentin?"

"Only that they were wearing ski masks. She said the two men stormed into radiology, grabbed Quentin and dragged him out the back exit of the hospital. She heard two shots fired."

April drew in a long breath. "The nurse didn't actually see, though, if Quentin was shot?"

"No. But there's more." And now here was the part Chase really didn't want to have to explain. However, he couldn't keep it from her. "Jericho interviewed an eyewitness in that back parking lot, and he said he saw one of the men fire shots into the air."

"Into the air?" April stayed quiet a moment, obviously giving that some thought. "You believe Quentin faked his own kidnapping?"

"I believe it's possible. Maybe he didn't want to have to answer any more questions about how he'd gotten injured." He paused again. "I found out through one of the CIs that your brother did indeed owe money to the wrong person. A loan shark. Word on the street is that he's the one who attacked Quentin and that it could get a whole lot worse for your brother if he doesn't pay back the money."

"And Quentin could have wanted to use the ransom money to do that," April finished for him. "Or he could have just been trying to escape before the loan shark got to him again."

Chase had come to the same conclusion. Too bad they couldn't find Quentin so they could ask him. Of course, that didn't mean he'd tell them what had actually happened. Honesty wasn't Quentin's strong suit.

April looked up at him. "Is it true—will we be going back to the safe house soon like you told Levi?"

"Hopefully. I'm just waiting on a call from Jericho." And hoping his brother had found those gunmen.

She nodded, probably reading between the lines on that. "Anything new on Renée?"

He had to shake his head. "The dead gunman is a wash for now, too. No ID, and his prints aren't in the system." And with Rooks still not talking, Chase was still way short on answers.

"Are you okay?" he asked her.

April's gaze met his, and he was pretty sure she knew he wasn't just asking about her in the general sense. "You mean that kiss."

Bingo. She zoomed right in on that.

"I thought you'd want to see it as a lapse in judgment," she said. "And nothing more."

That was indeed how he wanted to see it, all right. But parts of him were struggling to keep that view. "How did you see it?" he asked, despite the fact that it was stupid to continue this conversation on any level.

She stood, meeting him eye-to-eye. "You really want to know?" But she didn't wait for an answer. "I see it as a reminder of how things led to us getting Bailey. A reminder that's still there. Don't worry," April quickly added. "I know it's not what you want so it won't happen again."

Heck. For some reason that riled him. So much so that Chase took hold of her and kissed her again.

It wasn't the powerhouse kiss they'd had in the hospital. Just a quick brush of his mouth to hers to remind her that if they didn't put some distance between them, that it would indeed happen again. And it might have happened a lot sooner.

Like instantly.

If Chase hadn't heard someone come into the sheriff's office.

"Wait here," he told April, and he stepped into the hallway to see Jax ushering a dark-haired man through the metal detectors.

Chase didn't recognize the guy, but he was tall, thin. Late thirties. And while he was wearing jeans and a T-shirt, Chase was betting that both had designer labels on them.

"Marshal Crockett," the man said, his attention going straight to Chase. "I'm Shane Hackett, Renée's husband. I believe I know where you can find her."

Chapter Ten

April went into the hall when she heard their visitor. *Finally.* This could be the break they were looking for.

"Where's Renée?" April asked while hurrying into the squad room. Something that Chase obviously didn't want her to do. But if they could find Renée, they might be able to learn if she or someone else was behind the attack.

"You're Quentin's sister." Shane studied her for a moment, disapproval written all over his face. Disapproval maybe just for Quentin or perhaps because she happened to be the sister of the man who'd had an affair with his wife.

Shane slipped his hand in his jeans pocket, a move that sent both Jax and Chase reaching for their guns. Even though Shane had obviously cleared the metal detector, that didn't mean he still couldn't be dangerous. But it wasn't a weapon that he pulled out. It was a piece of paper, and he handed it to Chase.

"Those are the addresses of mine and Renée's properties. Some aren't in our names. My real estate company owns them. The first one is a cabin only about thirty miles from here. That's my best guess as to where she'd go, but the others are possibilities, too."

"I'm on it," Jax said. He took the paper and headed for

the phone. No doubt so he could get someone out there to check the place since it wasn't in the jurisdiction of the Appaloosa Pass Sheriff's Department.

"If you believe she could be there," April said, "why didn't you go out and check?"

Clearly, Shane wasn't comfortable with that, and he took his time answering. "Because Renée made it clear that she didn't want to see me. She said if I tried to find her, that she'd harm herself. I figured you'd do a better job protecting and restraining her than I could."

April thought about that a moment. It was possibly true. From everything they'd learned about Shane, he did still care for his wife. Though April had no idea why.

"Has Renée been in contact with you recently?" Chase asked the man.

Shane nodded without hesitation. "She called me yesterday, said she might have gotten into something over her head and wanted me to give her as much cash as I had on hand, that she'd have a courier pick up the money. She didn't want to take anything from her accounts because she said someone was after her."

Chase tapped his badge. "Someone is. She's a suspect in the kidnapping of a baby and two attacks."

Shane hadn't shown much emotion. Until hearing that. He didn't stagger back exactly, but he suddenly looked very unsteady on his feet. "Renée's off her meds. That's not good. Because she does impulsive things without her meds."

"Does that mean you believe she's responsible for the kidnapping?" Chase asked.

Now Shane paused, groaned and scrubbed his hand over his face. "Possibly." He looked at April again. "Does this have anything to do with your brother?"

"I honestly don't know but maybe. Renée was at the hospital earlier when my brother was kidnapped." Or when he faked a kidnapping, that is. April had no idea which—not yet.

Shane's jaw tightened. "Renée was with Quentin." Now there was another emotion, one that April had no trouble figuring out. Jealousy.

"I don't know if they were together or just happened to be there at the same time. As I said, my brother's missing, too."

Shane's next groan was louder. "He's bad news for her, you know."

Yes, April did know that. But she thought the relationship might have been toxic for both of them. "Was Renée ever pregnant?"

Shane's nod was slow in coming. "She was, but she miscarried about five months ago."

Only about a month after Quentin had gone into WIT-SEC. As emotionally invested as Renée was in Quentin, April wondered if that had triggered the miscarriage.

April stared at Shane. "Was it my brother's baby?"

"Renée said he was the father," Shane admitted almost hesitantly.

"Was he?" April pressed.

"Yes," Shane answered after another long pause. "Renée can be unstable when she's off her meds, but she didn't lie about being in love with your brother. After Quentin went into WITSEC and she lost the baby, she tried to kill herself."

That didn't sound so much like love, but April knew her brother didn't always bring out the best in people.

"Look, I just want you to find her," Shane continued,

"so she can get the help she needs. Just promise me you won't hurt her if you find her."

"I can't make a promise like that," Chase snapped. "But I can tell you if she's behind the kidnappings and the attacks, I will find her and I'll arrest her. Because there was a woman killed by one of those thugs. If Renée hired them, then she'll be charged with murder."

Of course, Shane must have known that, but it clearly bothered him to hear it spelled out. He reached in his pocket, took out a business card that he handed to Chase. "If you arrest her, call me so I can get her a lawyer. Am I free to go?"

"Not just yet. I need to ask you a few more questions." Chase looked back at Jax. "Why don't you go ahead and take April to Jericho's office?"

April was about to protest, but then Chase tipped his head to the windows. The blinds were all down, and the glass was reinforced and bullet resistant, but it was still risky for her to be out there. Risky for Chase, too, but April doubted she'd be able to get him to leave until he was certain he'd gotten everything he could from Shane.

Jax ushered her to Jericho's office, but he didn't leave once she was there. In fact, he checked the window to make sure it was secure. It was. And he positioned himself in the doorway. Guarding her and keeping watch over Chase.

"You think Shane could have brought hired guns with him?" she asked.

"No." And that's all Jax said for several moments. "I don't think Shane had anything to do with the stuff that happened. But if Renée wants to silence him so he can't help us find her, she might have her goons try to kill him."

April hadn't even considered that. Heck, she wasn't even positive the woman was an actual threat to anyone but herself, but Jax obviously felt she was capable of murder. And maybe she was.

Jax continued to look around the squad room. Continued to glance back at her, as well.

"Sorry you drew the short straw on guarding me," April said after one of Jax's glances looked more like a glare. "I know I'm not someone you actually want to protect."

No glare. But he did frown and seemed a little puzzled. "I don't hold a grudge against you."

"You should. I made a mistake."

"And it seems as if you've paid for it a couple times over," Jax countered.

Now she was the one who frowned. "You don't have to be nice to me."

"I know. But I don't want to stand in the way of Chase getting to raise his baby even if it means he's got to move and that we might not be able to see him for a long time. If ever. Plus, I also figure he's got feelings for you. After all, he slept with you, and Chase isn't the one-night stand sort."

No, he wasn't, but it hadn't been feelings that had caused him to take her to his bed. Well, not love-related kinds of feelings anyway.

"I think Chase started out just wanting to lend me a shoulder. I was upset." An understatement. And the shoulder he'd lent had turned to a heavy kissing session. Then more.

"You have feelings for him, too," Jax tossed out there. "Are you in love with him?"

April nearly choked on the quick breath she sucked

in. "No." She was almost certain of that. Almost. "What I feel for him is complicated."

"Yeah," Jax agreed.

She heard the voice of experience. No doubt because his relationship with his late wife, Paige, had fallen into that same *complicated* category. Despite having a young child, they'd divorced, only for Paige to be murdered by the Moonlight Strangler.

April heard the footsteps, and Jax stepped back from the doorway to let Chase into the room. "I didn't get anything more from Shane," he said. "But I believe he's genuinely worried about Renée."

So did April. Chase opened his mouth to add something else, but his phone rang before he could say anything.

He glanced at the screen, cursed. "What now?"

April hurried to his side to see Unknown Caller on the phone. Her heart sank. This couldn't be good. Chase hit the answer button and put it on speaker.

"Marshal Crockett," the caller said. Not a normal voice, either. The person was speaking through a scrambler, which made it impossible to know if this was any of their suspects. "We need to speak about Quentin Landis. And by *we*, I mean me, you and his sister, April."

Even though she was just a few inches from Chase, she moved even closer to him. "What about my brother?" she asked.

"Do you want to see him alive again?" But the caller continued without waiting for her to respond. "Then, you'll pay up. The ransom is a quarter of a million in cash. I'm giving you two hours to get the money."

She'd known right from the start that a ransom demand might come, but it knotted her stomach to hear it. "That's not enough time," April argued. "I'd need at least a day."

Chase motioned for her to stay quiet. "How do we even know for sure you have Quentin?" he pressed. "You could have heard about the kidnapping and be someone just trying to capitalize on it."

Sweet heaven. April hadn't even considered that. She'd gotten so caught up in her emotional reaction that she hadn't realized this could all be a hoax.

Maybe even one put together by Quentin himself.

"I want to speak to Quentin," Chase went on when the caller didn't say anything. "I want proof that he's actually with you and that he's still alive."

More silence. April heard some shuffling around, some whispers, and for a moment she thought the kidnapper was going to refuse. But finally she heard her brother's voice.

"April, I'm so sorry," Quentin said. "I didn't want to involve you in this."

More shuffling sounds. "There, you heard him," the kidnapper said. "Now get that money together. I'm not giving you a day, either. I want the cash within twelve hours. I'll call you back with the drop-off point." And with that, the kidnapper ended the call.

"You're sure that was Quentin?" Jax asked her.

April nodded. "But I'm not sure if this is a hoax or not. If Crossman had him kidnapped, he probably would have just killed Quentin. And I doubt Renée would be asking for a ransom."

"Shane said she asked him for cash," Jax pointed out.

"True. She might have done that just so she could pay off the hired gun who rescued her when you were bringing her into the sheriff's office," Chase answered. "Or she could want money so she could hide out for a while."

That made sense. "The loan shark could have kidnapped Quentin, though." April gave a heavy sigh. Because it might be true. And even if it wasn't, if Quentin had put all of this together, not getting the cash was still too big of a risk to take.

April reached for the phone. "I'll call the bank and start the process to get the money."

But Chase stopped her. "Think this through. This could be Crossman's work after all. He could be planning on having you make the ransom drop so he can kill both Quentin and you."

That caused her heart to skip a beat. Because it was exactly the sort of plan that Crossman would put together.

"That means if the kidnapper demands you do the drop, you have to refuse," Chase added.

And that kind of refusal could get Quentin killed.

April hated that her brother had gotten himself into hot water with the loan shark. It was possible this was all of his own making. Of course, it was just as possible that he was innocent. Of the kidnapping anyway.

"I won't do the ransom drop," she assured Chase. "I hope you won't, either."

He shrugged. "It'd be the best way to figure out who's really behind this."

But it would also put him right smack in the middle of danger. Of course, that was true of anyone who made that drop.

While April phoned the bank, both Chase and Jax stepped away to make their own calls. It took April several minutes to work her way through to the bank manager and to give him the security information that would allow him to access her savings and trust fund. Even though she was certain the manager was suspicious that she was withdrawing such a large amount, he didn't question it when she asked for it to be delivered to the sheriff's office.

By the time she was done, Jax had already finished his call, but Chase was still on the phone.

"The money will be here in about six hours," she relayed to Jax.

He nodded. "The sheriff over in Raymond Creek checked that cabin Shane told us about. Renée wasn't there, and there was no sign that anyone had been there in a while."

Too bad. In a best-case scenario, Renée would have been there with Quentin so that Renée could be arrested and April could have a long chat with her brother.

"Still no word back on the other addresses," Jax continued. "We might get lucky with one of them, though."

They certainly needed a huge dose of luck, but after glancing at Chase's expression, she doubted that's what they were going to get. "What's wrong?" she came out and asked.

"I had the Rangers do a thorough background check on Malcolm and there's a red flag. A couple of them, actually. Malcolm was a close friend of Tina Murdock."

That put her heart right in her throat. April shook her head. "Malcolm never said anything about knowing the cop who was killed." The cop whose blood was on her hands.

"I didn't think so. I also doubt Malcolm met you by accident at the hospital when Bailey was born. According to one of Malcolm's business associates, he was torn up when Tina was murdered."

The thoughts started to race through her head. "Torn up enough to want to get revenge on my brother and me?"

"Possibly," Chase admitted.

April tried to go back through all the conversations she'd ever had with Malcolm, including the most recent one in the hospital. He'd said nothing to indicate he was out to do her harm, but that didn't mean that wasn't exactly what he had in mind.

"Are you thinking Malcolm could have kidnapped Quentin?" Jax asked.

Chase cursed. "He could have, but there's more. I finally got the list of Crossman's visitors, and in the last three months, Malcolm has visited him four times."

April certainly hadn't seen that coming. Great day. "Why would Malcolm visit the man responsible for his friend's murder?"

"I'm not sure. The guards recorded all of Crossman's visitors, but those particular conversations have a lot of static, making it impossible to hear what they're saying."

April doubted that was a coincidence. "How could that have happened?" she asked Chase.

"Malcolm probably sneaked in some kind of jamming device."

Of course. But that didn't answer the big questions. "Why would Malcolm do that? What did he say to Crossman that he didn't want anyone else to know?"

Chase checked the time. "I'm not sure, but you can wait here with Jax while I find out. I'm going to the prison right now to have a chat with Crossman."

Chapter Eleven

Chase wasn't even sure this was worth the risk—visiting Crossman in jail. And he especially wasn't sure it was worth the risk to bring April with him. However, April had made a pretty convincing argument—that since she was Crossman's target, she wanted to be the one to confront him about the kidnapping and attacks.

And about those visits from Malcolm.

Chase wanted to confront the man, too, and considering that Crossman was a piece of slime, he just might spill everything about Malcolm. Well, if there was anything to spill, but it wasn't looking good for the man since Malcolm had a connection to both Crossman and a dead cop.

"I hope Bailey will be okay," April said while they waited for the guards to bring in Crossman. "Other than the kidnapping, this is the longest I've ever been away from her. When she was in the hospital, I slept there."

That didn't surprise him. But it did rile Chase a little that he hadn't had the opportunity to do the same thing. "Bailey will be fine, and once we're done here we can go back to the safe house." Where he hoped April would stay put until he had gotten their new WITSEC identities.

Of course, Chase was hoping that would be soon. Or at least part of him was hoping that. But the thought of turning in his badge for good made it feel as if someone was squeezing the life right out of him.

April fidgeted in the chair, glanced around, checked the time. "Nervous?" he asked.

"Impatient and ready for answers. I never got a sense that Malcolm hated me and wanted revenge."

"People don't always show you what's really going on in their heads," Chase reminded her.

She stared at him, as if looking for some deeper meaning in that remark. And there was one. It was aimed at Quentin, though April seemed to have gotten the big picture on her scummy brother.

"Are we talking about the kisses now?" she asked.

All right, so her train of thought hadn't exactly gone in the same direction as his. Not that his thoughts ever strayed too far from those kisses. Or from her.

"No," he answered.

April continued to stare at him, the corner of her mouth lifting. Almost a smile. Despite the cruddy situation they were in, it was nice to see she could manage even a half smile.

"It's always like this between us," she said. "I'm a criminal. A former one anyway. And you're a lawman. Not exactly a match made in heaven."

She was right. That kind of fire had a completely different origin than heaven.

"Maybe it was an opposites-attract thing," he suggested.

The slight smile returned for a moment, vanished, and it seemed as if she had something to say to him, that maybe it'd been a whole lot more than just opposites attracting. However, she didn't get a chance because at that very moment the guard ushered Crossman into the visiting area.

Despite having been in jail for the past six months, Crossman hadn't changed that much. Heavily muscled, bald and a nose that'd been broken a time or two. He looked exactly like the thug that he was.

Crossman's smile certainly wasn't a slight one. He flashed them a big grin when his gaze met Chase's. Then April's. The grin stayed in place as Crossman sat in the chair on the other side of the Plexiglas partition and picked up the phone.

Chase picked up the phone on his side, too, and he held it so that both April and he would be able to hear the conversation. Of course, that meant more close contact between them.

"April," Crossman greeted. "You're looking a little frazzled, like you haven't had much sleep. Something bothering you?"

"Yes," she readily admitted. "Tell me about your visits with Malcolm Knox."

For just a second, there was a flash of surprise in Crossman's mud-brown eyes. "They were just chitchat."

"That's a lie," Chase snapped. "You warned us about him. Why?"

The slight smile returned, and Crossman leaned back as far in the chair as he could. Which wasn't very far considering he was cuffed and wearing leg chains.

"Malcolm is somewhat of a mystery," Crossman finally said. "And I wasn't sure if he wanted to kill you for your part in that cop's death. They were good friends, you know."

Because April's arm was touching his, Chase felt her

tense. "Did Malcolm say anything about getting back at me for that?" she asked.

"Not specifically, but I got the feeling he wanted to do you and Quentin some harm. Especially Quentin."

"You also want to do us harm so we can't testify against you," April pointed out. "So, why warn us about Malcolm? Or were you afraid Malcolm would do the job you wanted your own thugs to do?"

"Interesting theory. But you're wrong. I don't want you or Quentin dead. Punished, yes, for turning traitor on me. Dead, no. I've known where you were for weeks. *Months*," Crossman corrected.

Chase tried not to look shocked and reminded himself that anything that came out of Crossman's mouth was probably a lie.

"If you found them that long ago, why didn't you do anything about it?" Chase asked.

"I didn't say I knew where Quentin was. Only April. Quentin has a strange habit of not being where he's supposed to be."

Chase shrugged. "Then why not just go after April?"

"Because as I said, I didn't want either Quentin or her dead. I wanted them to lead me to my former CPA. Jasmine Bronson. I need to…talk to her. Because you see, when my trial eventually starts, I'll need Jasmine to tell the truth, that it wasn't me she saw shooting that cop, that she was mistaken. In fact, I'd like for Jasmine to remember that it was either Quentin or someone else who pulled that trigger."

That was a not so subtle way of saying that Crossman wanted to intimidate the CPA into lying. And the problem was, Crossman might be able to do just that if he could find her. Apparently, he hadn't, yet.

According to the latest info Chase had gotten, Jasmine was safe but not at her WITSEC location. Like Quentin, Jasmine had struck out on her own. Considering the recent breach in WITSEC files, that had probably kept her alive. Because Crossman would definitely want her dead since she was the one who could testify about the worst of the charges against him—murder.

Too bad April hadn't been able to move around the way that Quentin and Jasmine had, but that would have been next to impossible to do with Bailey in the hospital for two months. Plus, April probably thought she was safe.

"How did you find April in WITSEC?" Chase pressed. "Did you hack into the files?"

"Hack? That's such an ugly word. One that carries more criminal charges. No, I didn't do anything like that. Let's just say a little bird told me."

Chase silently cursed. Because that little bird could be a mole in the marshals' office.

"Why should I believe any of this?" April asked the man.

Crossman smiled again. "The week before you had your daughter, you went to the store to buy some baby things. Clothes, diapers. And a white teddy bear. From what I've been told, it had a pink bow."

Judging from how fast the color drained from April's face, Crossman was telling the truth. About that anyway. That sickened Chase to know that April and his baby were so close to danger and he hadn't even known it.

"I want to find Jasmine." Crossman inched closer to the Plexiglas. He stared at Chase. "I need to talk to her. Now, if you can arrange for that to happen, I swear to you that April and your daughter will be safe."

Chase gave him a flat look. "Even if I believed that, which I don't, I wouldn't hand over a witness to you. Besides, murder isn't the only charge against you, and April can and will help convict you of money laundering and a whole list of other crimes."

Of course, that was backup. In case the murder charges didn't put Crossman away for life. Or if he managed to wiggle out of that charge altogether. He could possibly do that if he killed Jasmine.

"Money laundering," Crossman said, his tone dismissing it. "All a misunderstanding. My lawyers can work to fix that."

"Yes, by killing my brother and me," April challenged. "By any chance, are you the one who kidnapped Quentin?"

"Interesting." Crossman made it sound as if he was hearing this for the first time. "No. But this is a sweet turn of events, wouldn't you say? I suppose there's a ransom involved? One that involves milking you for a lot of cash to pay off that pesky loan shark your brother owes?"

April didn't respond. She sighed, maybe because it was the truth.

"Do you know anything else about the kidnapping?" Chase demanded.

"Maybe," Crossman admitted. "I got a lovely visitor about a week ago. She used the name Alisha Herrington, but her real name is Renée Edmunds. She's a *friend* of Quentin's."

Oh, man. Chase had checked that visitors' log but hadn't had time to figure out if anyone on the list had been using a fake ID. "What did Renée want?"

"She offered a very interesting deal. She said she'd tell me where April was if I'd agree to leave Quentin alone."

That kicked up April's breathing a significant notch. And tightened her muscles even more.

"I told Renée I wasn't interested, of course," Crossman continued. "No reason to bargain for information I already had."

True, but there were key bits of the info that were missing. "How did Renée know where April was?"

"Maybe from that same little bird," Crossman whispered as if telling a secret. "Sometimes birds chirp to more than one person feeding them. And sometimes people chirp for a whole different reason. Like sex," he said, turning that taunting stare in April's direction.

April ignored him, and she looked at Chase. "Are we done here?"

"Yeah." Though he wasn't sure they'd actually gotten much from Crossman. Still, he needed to mull over the conversation and figure out if Crossman had revealed something he hadn't intended to reveal.

"Leaving so soon?" Crossman asked when April and Chase stood. "And here we didn't get to chat about you two getting back together. You are back together, aren't you? Have you gotten him in bed again, April?"

April shot the man another glare but didn't respond verbally. With Crossman laughing, Chase and she walked out.

"I feel like I need a bath after talking to that piece of dirt," April mumbled.

Chase knew exactly how she felt. Except the image of her taking a bath flashed through his head. Not good. Because it was yet another reminder that he couldn't allow this attraction to make him lose focus.

The moment they were in the front waiting area of the prison, Chase took out his phone to call Jericho. "I want to see if there's anything that can be done to make sure Jasmine stays safe," he explained to April. "And I can't call the marshals until we find the mole."

She nodded. "After what Crossman just said, I think he definitely has some kind of insider in either that office or one of the others."

Chase agreed, but he didn't get a chance to make that call because he saw the man making his way toward the door.

Malcolm.

"I want to talk to him," April insisted. And it didn't sound as if it would be a friendly chat, either.

Chase slipped his arm around her waist to hold her back, waiting until Malcolm had gone through the metal detector and had been searched by the guard. Chase figured even if Malcolm was armed and gunning for April that he wouldn't risk an attack here in front of the prison guard and a marshal.

"Visiting Crossman again?" April demanded the moment Malcolm had cleared security and started toward them.

Malcolm nodded. "Why are you here?" He glanced at her, then at the way Chase had his arm around her. Chase got the feeling that what Malcolm was really itching to ask was, why are you here *together*?

"We wanted to know what you discussed with Crossman on your other visits," Chase informed him. "Crossman was more than happy to tell us."

Oh, Malcolm did not like that. Suddenly, there was no pretense of being in love with April. Or even liking her. The hatred was right there in his eyes.

April folded her arms over her chest. "Let me guess. You want me to pay for your friend's murder."

"I want anyone involved to pay," Malcolm answered. But then, he huffed and some of the anger was gone. "In the beginning, I wanted you to pay. That's why I found you, but then I couldn't go through with it."

Chase had already considered that's how things had played out. Still, it cut him to the core that this man had gotten so close to April and Bailey.

"How exactly did you find me?" she asked.

His mouth tightened, and at first Chase thought Malcolm might not answer. "Crossman," he finally said. "I'm not sure, but Crossman might have also told Renée how to find you so the woman could in turn locate Quentin."

Not according to Crossman, but Chase kept that to himself. Besides, Crossman could have been lying about that. He could have indeed given any and all info to Renée if it would have helped him find Quentin and Jasmine.

Malcolm huffed. "I know how this looks with me visiting Crossman again, but I'm here to tell him to back off, that I don't want April or the baby put in danger so he can satisfy the vendetta he has against Quentin and April."

Even if he hadn't been a lawman, a comment like that would have grabbed his attention. "You know for a fact that Crossman is behind the attacks?"

"Who else would it be?" Malcolm countered, and it seemed like a genuine question. "He needs April, Quentin and that CPA out of the way, or he'll spend the rest of his life in jail."

Actually, Crossman needed only Jasmine out of the way for the murder charges, and it didn't make sense he would go through all the trouble to find April to get to Jasmine. Because there was no way the marshals would put the two women in WITSEC together.

"How'd you scramble the recordings of the conversations you had with Crossman the other times you visited him here at the prison?" Chase came out and asked.

"I don't know what you're talking about. I didn't scramble anything. Maybe Crossman paid off a guard or something?"

That was always possible, but there were handheld devices that could interfere with a signal. Visitors would be checked for that sort of thing, but someone could have slipped something like that past the guards.

Someone like Malcolm, for instance.

"I'm sorry," Malcolm said, and he aimed that apology at April. "Tina and I were close, and when I found out you could have perhaps prevented her death, I wanted to confront you, face-to-face." He glanced away. "I couldn't do that, though, after I saw how torn up you were about your baby."

Chase stared at him a long time. "Are you sure all of this isn't just to cover your tracks? Because if you helped Crossman in any way get to Bailey or April, then you'll be charged with a couple of felonies."

That renewed some of the anger on Malcolm's face. "I didn't help him." Malcolm had to get his teeth unclenched before he could continue. "Crossman murdered Tina, and he *will* pay for that." It sounded like a threat and a promise.

Chase figured he should lecture Malcolm on not taking the law into his own hands, but he seriously doubted Malcolm would listen. Besides, he didn't want to hang around here with April next to the creep who'd basically stalked her for two months.

"Come on," Chase said, and he got April moving toward the exit. However, they'd made it only a few steps when Chase's phone rang, and he saw Jericho's name on the screen.

April and he stepped to the side, and because Malcolm was still in earshot, Chase didn't put the call on speaker.

"We got a visitor," Jericho said the moment Chase answered. "You and April need to get back here right now."

Chapter Twelve

April hadn't been sure what to expect when she stepped into the Appaloosa Pass sheriff's office. All Jericho had told them on the phone was that someone had just showed up out of the blue.

That someone was Quentin.

Her brother had refused to answer any questions until she got there.

April figured that wasn't a good sign, but the fact he was there proved he hadn't faked his own kidnapping. Well, maybe it meant that.

Knowing her brother, this could be part of a sick plan, too. But at least Quentin was alive, and she got proof of that the moment Chase and she arrived. Her brother was indeed there, sitting in a chair next to one of the deputy's desks.

Quentin stood when he spotted her, but he didn't move toward her. She didn't move toward him, either. Not because she wasn't glad to see him. She was, and she was thankful he was alive. But there were so many questions, and April started with the easiest one first.

"Shouldn't you be at the hospital?" she asked.

"Trust me," Jericho said, not looking especially pleased with this development, "I tried to talk him into it."

"I'm not going back there," Quentin insisted. "But a medic came and checked my incision. I'm okay. And he left me some pain meds to take. I'll do that after we've talked."

But he sure didn't look okay. Quentin was pale and didn't seem too steady on his feet.

Chase walked to him, meeting him eye-to-eye. "Tell us about the kidnapping and how you got away."

Quentin nodded, but he didn't look at Chase. He kept his attention on April. "When I was in radiology waiting for the MRI, two armed men stormed into the room. They were both wearing ski masks so I couldn't see their faces. They forced me out of the hospital and into a van, and then they took me to a house on the edge of town."

Chase jumped right on that. He took a notepad from the deputy's desk and dropped it next to Quentin. "Write down the address of that house."

Quentin nodded, eventually. He scrawled it down and handed it to Chase. That's when she noticed Quentin was shaking. Likely caused from a combination of pain and fear.

She tried not to give in to the old tug in her heart. The one that'd coddled and protected her kid brother way too many times. The bottom line was April wasn't sure she could trust Quentin.

Jericho glanced at the address, took out his phone and stepped into his office to make the call. No doubt to get someone out there to check it out. That probably meant calling in one of the night or reserve deputies, but April was glad he wasn't going himself because it would have left just Jax, Chase and her in the office. And if her brother's kidnapping had been the real thing, then those ski mask-wearing men could come after him again.

"How did you escape?" she asked her brother.

"They had some pain meds for me there, and I spiked their coffee with them. When they fell asleep, I got out and walked here."

Chase and she exchanged glances, and he was clearly bothered by one part of that explanation, too. "The kidnappers gave you pain meds?"

Quentin nodded. "I didn't take them, though, because I knew they'd make me sleepy."

Her brother had missed the point, and April clarified it for him. "You really think Crossman or the loan shark would have cared if you were in pain?"

His eyes widened. "You believe Renée was behind the kidnapping? If she was, she didn't come to the house and the men didn't mention her."

"Did they mention anyone?" Chase snapped.

Quentin eased back down into the chair. "No. The only thing they said to me had to deal with the ransom. They said once they had the money, they'd release me."

April had no idea if that was true or not. This could still have been a ploy to draw her out. Except for those pain meds. But then, as devious as Crossman was, that might be something he'd do just to throw them off his trail.

"Renée wouldn't have put me in danger like that," Quentin added several moments later. "She's crazy, but she loves me."

"She's crazy, period," Chase corrected. "And yes, she could have put you in that kind of trouble. She could have done the same to Bailey, April, Jax and me."

Quentin made a sound as if he didn't quite buy that, and it made April wonder if Renée and her brother had indeed partnered up on this. But if so, then why had Quentin escaped?

Or had he?

"Did you get the ransom money?" Quentin asked her. "Because if you did, I need to borrow some of it."

April didn't even bother trying to choke back a groan. Chase groaned right along with her. "Did you fake all of this?" Chase came right out and asked.

That got Quentin right back on his feet. "No. Absolutely not." But the burst of energy didn't last long. "If I don't pay the money I owe, they'll kill me."

Again, April tried not to give in to the emotion that caused inside her. "How much?"

"A hundred thousand," Quentin answered after a long pause.

Less than half of what the kidnappers had demanded. Still, it was a lot of money. "How the heck did you get involved with a loan shark?" But April waved off any answer he might give her.

And he would have had an answer, all right. One that she likely wouldn't want to hear. Her brother always seemed to be involved in something messy, and criminal, like this.

"It's not like you think," Quentin insisted. "The money wasn't…" He stopped and shook his head. "You've always taken care of me. Ever since Mom and Dad were killed, you've been the one person I can rely on."

He was playing with her heartstrings now. Or maybe he was dodging the truth about why he'd borrowed that money. The ploy was something April recognized. She had indeed taken care of him, but that was about to end.

"I'll give you the money," April said. "But there are conditions attached. You'll take a polygraph, and during that test, I intend to ask you a lot of questions. If you've lied to me, about anything, then you won't get another dime of my money."

The surprise, then the anger, flared in Quentin's eyes. "How could you not trust me? I'm your brother and you claim to love me."

That was probably meant to hurt her. It didn't work. "I do love you, but I don't trust you." She didn't linger on Quentin but instead turned to Chase. "How soon can you set up a lie detector?"

"Soon," Chase assured her.

Jax made a sound of agreement. "I'll get started on that right now. I can probably have the examiner in here within an hour."

"The test could be wrong," Quentin argued. "I mean, there's a reason the results from a polygraph aren't admissible in court."

April ignored him and headed for the break room at the end of the hall. Chase followed her. She wasn't sure what his reaction would be to her demand, but he gave her a nod of approval.

"You think he'll go through with the polygraph?" Chase asked.

"He'll probably try to worm his way out of it. It won't work. Without the test, the loan shark won't get the money, and Quentin will just have to deal with the consequences himself."

Chase took her by the arm and led her to a chair. It took April a moment to realize why he'd done that. She was trembling. It wasn't just because she'd finally stood up to her brother, but an avalanche of all the things that'd happened.

"I know that wasn't easy for you," he said, handing her a cup of water.

"Quentin made it easier." She looked up at him. "He's not telling the truth about something. I just hope that something doesn't have anything to do with Bailey's kidnapping."

Judging from the hard look that put in his eyes, Chase felt the same way.

April looked up when she heard the footsteps. Not Quentin, thank goodness. It was Jericho.

"The place where Quentin claims he was held is a rental house that's supposed to be unoccupied according to the owner," Jericho explained. "I'm short on help right now so two Texas Rangers are headed out there. If they see anything, they'll bring in the CSIs to go through the place."

April figured there wouldn't be anything to find since the hired guns wouldn't have left anything incriminating behind. Still, it was all necessary since any and every little thing could perhaps help them untangle this dangerous situation.

Jericho glanced over his shoulder into the squad room, and April saw what'd gotten his attention. Quentin. He was making his way toward them. But Jericho put a stop to that.

"You can wait in the interview room," Jericho said, and he shut the door to the break room.

April made a mental note to thank Jericho for that later. "I wasn't ready to go a second round with my brother," she told Chase. "I just want to go back to the safe house so I can see Bailey."

Chase made a weary sound of agreement. "Soon."

She thought there might be a *maybe* attached to that.

And there probably was. There were hired guns on the loose, and it was highly likely there could be another attack.

"I've forgotten what normal feels like," April continued. "What with WITSEC, Bailey being premature. And all the rest of it," she added.

The next sound Chase made was a weary sigh. "Sorry, but I can't give you normal."

No. He couldn't give it to himself, either. Because soon he'd have to surrender that badge and quit being himself.

"I'm sorry," April added.

He frowned. "You've been telling me that a lot lately."

"There's no telling how many apologies I'll owe you. Unlike me, you actually have a good life you'll have to give up. I think we can both agree that my old life was a mess."

Chase didn't argue with that, but he did move closer. And he stared at her. "Your new life's also a mess."

Considering it was the truth, April was surprised that she managed a smile. Surprised, too, when Chase slipped his hand around the back of her neck and eased her to him.

No kiss, but he brushed his mouth against her temple. His arms were so warm. His breath, as well, and April just slid right into him, taking everything he was offering. Despite the consequences.

Getting close to Chase always came with a high price.

Maybe not immediately. But he'd regret this. Soon, there'd be the resentment in his eyes. Soon, the bad blood would resurface, eating away at him and making him remember all the reasons he should have never gotten involved with her in the first place.

But no high price right now. Just the warmth. Then,

the heat. Always the heat. Even though he didn't tighten his grip, she felt the attraction tug at her. Urging her to get closer and take even more from him.

He cursed, a really bad word that had her looking up at him to see if something had prompted it. Something had. *Her. This.*

April started to move away from him, but Chase held on, pinning her against the wall with his body. Now, the kiss came. The full slam of heat, too. She was certain Chase didn't actually want this, but he was just as powerless as she was when it came to this attraction.

He deepened the kiss. Mercy, did he. His mouth knew hers way too well and knew just how to coax the fire from her. Not that he had to do much coaxing. The kiss and being so close to him had already accomplished that. He robbed her of her breath, any shred of common sense, and he just kept on robbing until soon the kisses weren't enough.

April wanted more.

She wanted Chase.

And she got him. Well, more of that body-to-body contact anyway. She hooked her arms around him, pulling him closer. Not that he had far to go. They were already pressed against each other, but the slight adjustment aligned them in just the right way to have sex. It was out of the question, of course.

Still, her body got the notion that it was a done deal.

In that moment April understood why people did such stupid things. Because this was stupid. But it was also what she wanted more than anything. More than sanity. More than her next breath. The problem was she could feel the same need in Chase. Which meant they were in a boatload of trouble if one of them didn't stop.

Chase was the one to do that. Thank goodness, since April couldn't force herself away from him. But Chase let go of her and stepped back.

He didn't look at her right off. He stared at the ceiling while he mumbled profanity. And in this case, the profanity wasn't directed at her but rather at himself. Something April totally understood.

"I'm not apologizing," he finally said. He might have added more to that. Especially some more profanity, but his phone rang.

Timing was a strange thing. Because if the call had happened just a couple of minutes earlier, that kiss wouldn't have happened. Nor that non-apology. And despite the fact April knew she should regret it, she didn't. For those minutes, she'd had Chase, and even though it was only temporary, it was better than the scowls and the painful reminders of what she'd done.

"Unknown caller," Chase said when he glanced at the screen.

That took care of any of the remaining fire in her blood. April held her breath, waiting for him to answer the call and put it on speaker.

"Marshal Crockett," the woman said. "It's Renée."

Chase moved quickly, heading out of the break room and down the hall until he reached Jericho in the squad room. April was right behind him.

"Where are you, Renée?" Chase asked her. The question got Jericho's attention as it was probably meant to do.

"You know I can't tell you that because you'll arrest me." It sounded as if Renée was crying. "I can't go to jail and I can't live without Quentin." Yes, definitely crying because she made a hoarse sob. "April turned him against me."

Chase gestured for April to stay quiet before she could say anything. Probably because he thought Renée might say more if the woman believed she was talking to only him. Or maybe he just didn't want Renée to know April was with him.

"Why do you think April's turned him against you?" Chase asked Renée. "Have you spoken to Quentin?"

Silence, punctuated by more sobs. "Because why else would Quentin have left me?"

April could think of several reasons. Well, one big one anyway. Renée was crazy.

"How and when did Quentin leave you?" Chase pressed.

The next round of crying was considerably louder. "He ran away."

April heard the movement behind her, and whirled around to see her brother standing in the doorway of the interview room. Quentin had no doubt heard Renée's every word, but Chase also motioned for him to stay quiet.

"You're the one who had Quentin kidnapped?" Chase asked the woman.

"No. I didn't. I had him brought to me. But he agreed to it. He said it was a way of keeping him safe from Crossman. A way of getting the money he needed, too. And I would get to be with him."

The anger roared through April, followed by a sickening feeling in the pit of her stomach. She hadn't believed Quentin was telling her the truth, but it hurt to hear it spelled out.

Chase lifted his gaze, slowly, and he glared at Quentin. "Quentin was the one who came up with this plan?"

"I came up with it," Renée quickly volunteered. "After I made him understand all the advantages, he agreed to it."

"So, what changed?" Chase demanded. "Why did Quentin stop agreeing?"

"April must have gotten to him. Because Quentin left when I was out taking care of some things. Do you know where he is? I have to see him now. I have to convince him his sister's wrong, that I really do love him."

Part of her wanted to feel sorry for Renée, but April didn't feel anything but hatred for the woman.

"I can't stay on the line any longer," Renée said. "I don't want you tracing this and finding out where I am. Call me if you hear from Quentin."

The moment Renée hung up, April turned and faced her brother. "You lied. Again."

He nodded, his breath already gusting. "I was desperate."

"That doesn't make it all right." She wanted to scream. Or slap him. But the truth was, April should have expected exactly this from her brother. He'd done similar things time and time again.

Chase stepped closer to Quentin, and April hadn't thought it possible, but he looked just as enraged as she felt. "Why'd you *escape* from Renée? And this time everything you tell me—*everything*—had better be the truth."

Quentin nodded, swallowed hard. "I needed money so I called Renée. She was thrilled to hear from me in that stalker, obsessive kind of way. But like I said, I was desperate for the money and thought I could get it from her. She said she was into something and didn't have access to her funds."

"Into something?" April snapped. "What exactly?"

"I don't know, but after everything I've learned, maybe she was indeed behind Bailey's kidnapping. Renée might have thought she could use Bailey to find me."

April didn't doubt that, and the woman had said as much when they'd been by the creek. Plus, Renée had asked Shane for money, which meant she likely wasn't lying about not having access to her funds.

"So, Renée and you concocted that idiotic plan to have you taken from the hospital," Chase tossed out there.

Quentin's eyes widened. "Yes, but I had no idea she was going to use real gunmen. I certainly hadn't thought there'd be shots fired."

"A man died," April reminded him. "True, the guy was a hired gun and deserved it, but innocent bystanders could have been hurt. *We* could have been hurt." She motioned at Jericho, Jax and Chase.

"I didn't know until after the fact. I swear," Quentin insisted.

"What happened then?" Chase went on. "Did you have a so-called change of heart and escape from the very people who kidnapped you?"

"The gunmen were going to turn on Renée," Quentin explained. "I heard them talking after she left, and they were going to kill her, and me, once they had the ransom money."

April didn't say I told you so, but she wanted to badly. "You were a fool to trust hired guns."

Quentin nodded again, but it wasn't just regret that she saw in his eyes when their gazes met. It was something else. Determination, maybe?

"I can fix this," Quentin said to her before turning to Chase. "You want Renée and those men she hired? Then, I'll help you get them."

Chapter Thirteen

Chase was second-guessing this plan.

Yes, he wanted Renée and her thugs. Wanted answers that would put an end to the danger. But this plan put Jax and Jericho right on a collision with a crazy woman and Quentin, a man they couldn't trust.

"I should have been the one to meet with Renée," Chase said under his breath. Obviously, though, he didn't say it softly enough because April glanced at him and scowled.

"You and I have huge targets on us," she reminded him.

Something she'd mentioned several times during the planning stage of what could turn out to be a deadly trap. Because after all, if Quentin could try to turn the tables on Renée, then she could do the same to them.

It didn't help that Renée had picked a really lousy meeting place. And she'd been adamant about it, too. She had insisted on meeting Quentin at a public place with lots of people around. In other words, there was no way Jax or Jericho could control the security.

That's why Chase had wanted to nix it. His brothers and Quentin had disagreed just as adamantly. He was outnumbered, so the plan had been tweaked, then finalized, and now Jax, Jericho and Quentin were on their way to the fairgrounds, where crews were setting up for tomorrow's rodeo.

Thankfully, the tweaking had involved a slight change of venue. Instead of at the rodeo arena itself, the meeting would take place in the concession area, where there was less chance of having people wander onto the scene.

Of course, Jericho had put some of his own security in place, as well. Two Rangers and a reserve deputy had gone out ahead of them and were scoping out the fairgrounds to make sure this wasn't an ambush waiting to happen. If they got lucky, the precaution would just be overkill.

Because maybe Renée's only goal was to get her hands on Quentin.

If so, perhaps Jericho could arrest the woman and her armed *employees* before they managed to do any damage.

Chase had also made sure April was safe, too. He'd called in two of the deputies, Dexter Conway and Carlos Jimenez, to man the sheriff's office and provide backup if needed. He'd also locked the front door and set the security alarm to cover all the windows and exits. Chase hoped like the devil all of that was overkill, too.

"You look ready to jump out of your skin," Carlos said, glancing at April. "And you didn't eat hardly a bite of your dinner."

"I'm not hungry," April answered. But Carlos was right about the jumping-out-of-her-skin part. April alternated between pacing, checking the time and nibbling on her bottom lip.

Chase started to give her a mini-lecture on how she should indeed eat some of the sandwich and fries he'd ordered for her from the diner across the street. But then, he didn't have much of an appetite, either.

What had helped both of them was another quick video "chat" with Bailey. The baby had been sound asleep, but it'd been good just to see her face and to know that everything was still all right at the safe house.

"You could try to rest in the break room," Chase suggested. But he wanted to kick himself. Because judging from the surprise that flashed across her face, April was remembering those kisses they'd shared there just a few hours earlier.

Not especially what he wanted on her mind, or his, but at least she no longer looked to be on the verge of a panic attack. Too bad it didn't last. His phone rang, and April's nerves jumped right back to the surface.

He halfway expected to see Unknown Caller on the screen, but it was a name he actually recognized. Marshal Harlan McKinney. He'd not only worked with Harlan on several cases, but Chase also trusted the man.

Chase didn't put the call on speaker. Just in case this was another dose of bad news, he didn't want to send April over the edge. Still, she moved closer, where she would undoubtedly be able to hear at least some of the conversation.

"We found something," Harlan said the moment he came on the line. "There was a mole. Not a marshal, though. It was a computer tech working out of the Austin office. Her name's Janette Heller. Ring any bells?"

He had to think about it a few seconds. "No. Should it?"

"Maybe. She does background checks and such so I thought maybe you'd crossed paths with her."

"It's possible. I've had a lot on my mind lately." A huge understatement. "Has she been arrested?"

"Yeah, she's in custody. Lawyered up right away, of course, but we have what we need to set her bail sky-high. The FBI techs went through her computers, and they found enough to prove she's hacked into some WITSEC files."

"Any idea who hired her to do that?" Chase immediately asked.

"Following the advice of her lawyer, she hasn't said a word. Her lawyer's a bigwig, too. One who costs way over her standard of living."

"Maybe because she's using the money she got from hacking to pay for it?"

"Maybe." But Harlan didn't sound entirely convinced of that. "This is the kind of lawyer who has a waiting list of clients, but he dropped everything and came when she called."

So, obviously this Janette had some kind of clout or a backer who hadn't come up yet in the investigation. "You think she'll eventually talk and tell us who she's working for?"

"Not without some kind of incentive. It's my guess she won't be giving up that info unless we offer her some kind of deal. Are you okay with that, especially since it was her hack job that put April and your baby in danger?"

No, he wasn't okay with it. But Chase also wasn't okay with letting the person behind this go free, either. If it was Crossman and Janette was his "little bird," they could use this to freeze his assets and stop future attacks.

"Offer Janette the deal," Chase finally answered. "Call me if you get a name from her."

Harlan assured him he would and ended the call. Chase immediately turned to April to tell her the news.

"Thank God," she said. Obviously, she'd heard more than bits and pieces of the conversation.

Finally, he saw some of that tension drain from her, and April slipped her arms around him as if it was something she did all the time. This was a by-product of all that kissing. It'd broken down barriers.

Chase didn't go stiff, exactly, but April must have picked up on his hesitation because she pulled back. Or at least that's what she was in the process of doing, but Chase eased her right back to him. It didn't last because the movement behind him snagged Chase's attention.

Dexter walked toward the window and looked out.

"What's wrong?" Chase immediately asked the deputy.

Dexter shook his head. "I just thought I saw someone in the alley next to the diner."

Normally, that wouldn't have put Chase on edge, but there was nothing normal about this situation.

"Wait in Jericho's office," Chase told April, and he went to the front to have a look for himself.

Nothing.

"Maybe it was a shadow," Dexter added.

Maybe. But with everything else that'd happened, Chase wasn't taking any chances. He kept looking, searching for anything that was out of place.

There were people in the diner. People milling around some of the shops, too, but it would have been unusual for someone to be in that particular alley unless it was one of the diner workers on a smoke break.

The minutes crawled by, and Chase glanced over his shoulder to make sure April had gone into Jericho's office. She had, but she was peering out the doorway. When he shifted his gaze back to the alley, he saw it then.

Someone was at the back of the diner and darted out of sight. Someone dressed all in black.

Chase and Dexter drew their weapons.

"Who's out there?" April asked.

But Chase didn't get a chance to answer because he saw more movement in the alley. Not a person dressed in black, either. This was a woman, and someone he instantly recognized.

Renée.

Hell. What was she doing here?

APRIL COULDN'T SEE what'd caused Chase and Dexter's reaction. But both of them snapped back their shoulders. Chase and Dexter had already pulled their guns, but the other deputy did the same.

She tried to tamp down the fear. Tried to remind herself that this could all be just a precaution. However, it didn't feel like one.

Without taking his attention from the window, Chase took out his phone. April had no idea who he was calling, but she had no trouble hearing what he said once the person answered.

"Renée is here."

That put April's heart in her throat. Certainly the woman must have known Quentin wouldn't be here, that he was at the meeting that Renée herself had helped set up. So, what did she want?

April figured Renée hadn't come here just to chat.

Maybe they'd been wrong about Renée's obsession with Quentin. Maybe April was the woman's target.

Or...

April's stomach twisted. This could have something to do with the ransom money that would soon be delivered. April had slashed the amount to only what Quentin needed to pay off the loan shark, but what if Renée intended to take that money and use it to try to get Quentin back in her good graces?

But there was another possibility. One that April didn't like.

What if Renée and her brother were working together on this?

Chase ended his call, and with his gaze firing all around, he glanced back at her. He probably tried to give her a reassuring look. But he failed. April could practically feel the danger and his concern about it.

"Keep an eye on the roof," Chase told the deputies.

Though that order had no sooner left his mouth when April heard a sound she definitely didn't want to hear.

The alarm from the security system.

It started to scream through the building. It screamed through her, too. Because it meant someone had just broken in.

Chase ran to her, pushing her deeper into Jericho's office. "Take the gun from the top right desk drawer," he instructed. "And keep watch on the window behind you."

Her heart was already racing, but that caused it to race even more. April hurried to the desk and took out the gun. After going into WITSEC, she'd taken firearms training and knew how to shoot. She prayed, though, that it wouldn't come down to her doing that.

"The alarm was triggered from the break room," Dexter called out to them.

So close, just up the hall. There was a back door and windows in the room, but Renée must have known the sheriff's office would be wired for security.

Was it some kind of diversion?

Several moments later, the alarm stopped. No doubt because Dexter had turned it off so they could hear if anyone was actually in the building.

It was hard for April to hear much of anything with her pulse throbbing in her ears, but both Chase and Dexter had their guns aimed at the break room. She figured Carlos was watching the front in case one of Renée's hired thugs came crashing through the door. If that happened, it would be a gutsy move, an attack in broad daylight. But then, Renée hadn't exactly been predictable.

"Do you see anyone?" April risked asking.

Chase shook his head. "If someone opened the break room door, then they closed it."

The relief came. But didn't last. Because that could mean the someone had gotten inside before closing the door.

Carlos cursed, and that sent Dexter pivoting in the direction of his fellow deputy. Chase glanced at Carlos, too, and while he didn't curse, he certainly wasn't pleased about whatever he saw.

"Get down on the floor," Chase ordered her, and he stepped out. "A gunman's in the alley."

That was the only thing he managed to say before there was another sound that April didn't want to hear.

Gunshots.

Thick blasts that crashed into the front of the building.

"The windows are bullet resistant," Chase reminded her.

But he didn't return fire. Chase didn't spare more than a glance at the front. Instead, he kept his attention nailed to the break room.

And then he took aim.

Fired.

The shot rocketed through the hall, but since April was on the floor she couldn't see who Chase had shot at or if he'd hit his target.

More of those thick blasts sounded from the front. Chase fired another shot at the break room.

Then, nothing.

Everything went quiet. While April was glad the shots had stopped, she doubted that was a good thing.

"Renée's getting away," Dexter shouted. The deputy started toward the front, probably to go after her, but Chase stopped him.

"It could be a ruse to lure you out," Chase warned.

A ruse where more attackers could start pouring into the building as soon as the deputy was gone. Or else Dexter could be just gunned down by one of them.

"What about the shooter in the break room?" April asked.

"Gone, too." And Chase headed in that direction.

April wanted to shout for him to stop, that it could also be part of a ruse, but anything she said right now might be just a distraction. One that could get Chase shot. So, she waited. Breath held and praying.

It seemed to take an eternity for Chase to make his way back to her. He immediately checked on her, helping her to her feet, and he brushed a kiss on her forehead. A kiss of relief, no doubt.

"The shooter broke through the window in the break room," he explained. "But there's no sign of him or anyone else back there."

That didn't mean they wouldn't be back. Renée seemed determined to get to her.

"Why would Renée do this?" Dexter asked as Chase stepped back and took out his phone.

"Maybe for the ransom money," Chase answered, stepping back into the doorway. "Or maybe so she could kidnap April and use her to bargain with Quentin."

April hadn't even considered the last possibilities. But if Renée had thought something like that would work, she would almost certainly do it.

"Renée and her henchmen got away," Chase said to the person who answered the call he made.

It was Jericho. She recognized his voice when Chase put the call on speaker and she heard Jericho curse. "Renée must have figured out the meeting was a trap. There's not a sign of any gunmen here. We're heading back to the station now."

"Good. Because the window in the break room is broken, and I don't want to keep April here any longer than necessary."

"As soon as we get there, I'll have Jax drive with you to the safe house," Jericho assured him before he ended the call.

Finally, she'd get to be with the baby. But just as important, Chase and she would be away from another possible attack. That, in turn, might keep Jericho and the other deputies safe while they were at the office. There'd be no reason for anyone to fire into the building if she wasn't there.

"Before we leave, I'll have to check the vehicle for a tracking device," Chase reminded her. It was also a reminder that no matter how careful they were, the danger could still make its way to the safe house.

"Once Jericho makes it here, I'll do that for you," Dexter insisted. "Best if you're not out there any longer than necessary."

She agreed. Of course, that meant Dexter and anyone who went after Renée and those men were in just as much danger. It was Dexter's job, of course, but it didn't make her feel any better about it.

April just wanted all of this to end.

Chase didn't move from the doorway of Jericho's office, obviously still guarding her and still keeping watch, but he did glance back at her. He didn't try to assure her that everything would be okay. Maybe because she knew an assurance like that would be a lie. Still, she saw the shared emotions in his eyes.

The fear for their daughter.

Chase's phone rang again, and just like that her heart was right back in her throat. She prayed nothing else had gone wrong. Prayed even more when Chase didn't put the call on speaker. The only time he did that was when he wanted to shelter her from possible bad news.

Again, she waited and tried to figure out who had called and what was going on, but Chase wasn't doing any talking, only listening.

"How did that happen?" Chase asked. She couldn't hear the response, but she saw the muscles in his shoulder tighten. "You can tell me about it when you get here."

Thankfully, the conversation didn't last long. "What happened?" April asked the second he ended the call.

It took Chase a moment to gather his breath. "Quentin's missing."

Chapter Fourteen

April shook her head and continued pacing. "How could Quentin possibly go missing?" she mumbled. It wasn't really a question directed at Chase, but it was something April had been asking herself since Jericho had delivered the news fifteen minutes earlier.

Chase didn't have an answer yet.

However, the person who might have answers—Jericho—pulled to a stop in front of the sheriff's office and got out. Dexter unlocked the door for him, but Jericho paused only long enough to examine the damage to the front windows.

"Is all of this Renée's doing?" Jericho asked. Jax followed him inside.

"She was nearby," Chase settled for saying. "If we'd managed to catch her, she probably would have claimed she was in the wrong place at the wrong time."

Heck, maybe she was. There was a lot of crazy stuff going on, though, and Renée always seemed to be at the center of it.

Along with Quentin.

April went closer to Jericho as soon as he was inside. Dexter didn't come in, though. He headed toward the parking lot, probably to check to make sure no one had planted a tracking device on the vehicle they were driving back to the safe house.

"What happened to my brother?" April wanted to know.

Jericho huffed. "As we were leaving the rodeo, someone let out the bulls into the arena and then set off some firecrackers. That didn't please the bulls, and they started running around. In the chaos, Quentin disappeared."

"You didn't hear him yell for help or anything?" she pressed.

"No. But we did hear a vehicle speeding away shortly after we lost sight of him. That probably means someone was waiting for the right moment to grab him. Or else he was waiting for the right moment to escape."

Chase glanced at her, expecting to see more worry and fear on her face. But all he saw was the same frustration no doubt mirrored on his.

"Quentin knew he was going to have to face charges for faking his kidnapping," she admitted. "It's possible he set up this meeting just so he could escape."

"Yes," Chase readily agreed. "But then why did he come to the sheriff's office in the first place?"

"Maybe to make sure I was here. Or maybe he thought I'd jump to protect him."

And April certainly hadn't done that. She'd said she would give him the money, but she had also made it clear that it was the last of the funds he'd ever see from her.

"I hate to be the one to cut Quentin any slack," Jax spoke up, "but Renée could have arranged all of this. Quentin might not have called out for help because one of her henchmen might have put a gag on him or something."

That, too, was possible, but without Quentin or Renée, it was hard to know what the truth was.

Since the breach in WITSEC, Chase had given so much thought to Quentin that his head was aching. And all that thought and guessing was probably useless anyway. He'd been investigating Quentin for years and still hadn't figured out the man. It was the same for Renée, though he'd known her only a short period of time.

"Why don't you sit down," Chase said, leading April to one of the chairs. "As soon as Dexter's done, we can leave." Something they both clearly wanted to do.

But he saw something from the corner of his eye that not only had him wondering if that was going to happen, it also put him on full alert. Chase drew his gun.

That's because he saw Malcolm making a beeline toward the sheriff's office.

Great. Chase was so not in the mood to deal with that rat, and the rat wasn't alone. Shane was walking next to him. An odd couple, for sure, and it made Chase wonder what the heck they were doing there together.

"I'll frisk them," Jax volunteered, and he was ready when the two men stepped inside. Neither seemed pleased about that, and Shane especially wasn't happy when Jax took a gun from him.

"I have a permit for that," Shane insisted.

"You don't have a permit to carry it inside here," Jax insisted right back. He went to his desk to put the gun away and to make a phone call.

Malcolm's attention went to April. Then, it snapped to Chase. "I want you to call off your dogs."

Chase just gave him a flat look. "Am I supposed to know what that means?"

Judging from the sour expression on Malcolm's face, he did expect it. "Someone's been following me since I left the prison. Following Shane, too. We figured it was some of your law enforcement buddies."

"Well, you figured wrong," Chase set them straight. He pointed to each of them. "How do you two know each other?"

"I'm trying to clear my name since you're treating me like a suspect," Malcolm snarled. "To do that, I contacted Shane to see if I could speak with Renée. But he doesn't know where she is."

Chase turned to Shane to see what he had to say about that, and Shane nodded. "I haven't found her yet, and if I had, I would have turned her in to you. She needs to be back on her meds. She needs to be in a psychiatric hospital. If she doesn't get help, she could be killed."

He couldn't argue with that. Renée needed both. But first, they had to find her.

"We spotted her here in town less than a half hour ago," Chase explained. "Either of you know anything about that?"

Both men shook their heads, but Malcolm looked considerably more alarmed by that than Shane. Was that because he'd manipulated Renée in some way, maybe to get revenge against Quentin, and the plan had backfired? Too bad Chase couldn't hook all of them up to a lie detector.

Dexter came back in, but he didn't go far once he spotted their visitors. He stayed in the doorway, his attention volleying between them and the parking lot. No doubt so he could keep an eye on the vehicle he'd just checked out for them.

Chase turned to Jericho. "Can you handle these two? I want to get April out of here."

Jericho nodded, snagged Malcolm and Shane's attention. "You two, go to the interview room. We'll finish up there."

Shane readily complied, but for a moment Chase thought Malcolm was going to come up with an excuse to leave. He didn't, though. After saying something under his breath that Chase didn't bother to hear, Malcolm went up the hall toward the interview room.

Jericho waited until they were inside before he turned to Dexter. "Did you check the unmarked squad car?" he asked.

Dexter nodded. "The truck, too. There's nothing on either of them."

"Then go ahead and drive the car to the front of the building." Jericho gave Jax, April and Chase each a glance. "You ready to go?"

Chase was more than ready, but he kept April back when Dexter hurried back to the parking lot. He didn't want April outside any longer than necessary.

"I'll be back after I drop them off," Jax told Jericho. "We can search for Quentin and Renée then."

Chase wished he could help with that. Wished even more that he could find them. But this wasn't a safe place for April to be. The shot-up windows were proof of that.

Finally, Dexter brought the black four-door car to a stop directly behind Jericho's cruiser, and Chase was ready to get April moving.

But his phone rang.

Since any and all calls could be critical, he took out his phone and saw Marshal Harlan McKinney's name on the screen. Maybe the mole, Janette Heller, had spilled her guts after getting that plea deal.

"Please tell me you have the name of the person who hired Janette," Chase greeted when he took the call.

"No. She's still negotiating the plea deal. But that's not why I'm calling." Harlan paused. "Chase, there's been a murder."

APRIL HAD SEEN Harlan's name on Chase's phone screen, but she hadn't been able to hear any of what the marshal had said that could put the thunderstruck expression on Chase's face.

"A murder?" Chase asked. "Who?"

No. Her thoughts automatically went in a bad direction. Was her brother dead? She tried to brace herself, but that was impossible. As bad as things were between Quentin and her, she hated to think of someone murdering him.

"Call me back the second you know anything," Chase said several moments later. He hung up and looked at her. "It's not Quentin. It's Tony Crossman."

Of all the names she expected to hear Chase say, that wasn't one of them. "Crossman?" Jericho and she said in unison.

Chase nodded. "He's dead."

April sank down into the nearest chair. For months, Crossman had been a bogeyman for her. A killer who wanted Quentin and her dead. And he was the reason they were in WITSEC.

Now someone had killed the killer.

"This changes everything," she said, looking up at Chase.

Another nod from Chase, and he helped her back to her feet. "We should go. It'll be getting dark soon, and it'll be harder to see if anyone tries to follow us to the safe house."

He was right, of course, and somehow April managed to get her feet moving. Hard to do, though. She felt numb. Relieved, too.

At least April felt that way until Chase ushered her out. Both Jax and he drew their weapons before they hurried her to the unmarked cruiser. Dexter and Jericho kept watch—just in case they were attacked again. That's when a big chunk of her relief vanished. Because while Crossman's death did indeed change everything, it didn't necessarily put an end to the danger.

Chase maneuvered her in the backseat of the car with him. Jax got behind the wheel, and he didn't waste any time driving them away from there.

"What happened to Crossman?" she asked, though April wasn't sure she actually wanted to hear the details. She already had way too many memories and details of murder and violence.

"He was shanked in a prison fight about an hour ago," Chase explained. "Crossman died before the medic even got to him."

"They're sure he's dead?" she pressed. "Because this could be another of his sick games." However, she couldn't imagine what Crossman would hope to gain from something like this.

She must have started to look a little panicked because Chase slipped his arm around her. "He's dead. The guards are questioning the other inmates now, but no one is jumping to take credit for it. Harlan did say the guards were surprised, though, because the other inmates actually seemed to like Crossman."

Hard to believe that he was well liked by anyone, but Crossman was a rich man, so maybe he was buying protection and favors from his fellow prisoners. After all,

Crossman had been behind bars for six months, and there hadn't been even a hint of violence directed at him.

That reminder caused everything inside her to go still.

"Malcolm was at the jail earlier today," April said. "Maybe he's the one who arranged the murder. And Crossman did hint that Malcolm had something to do with the attacks against us and Bailey's kidnapping."

"The guards will look into that." Since Chase didn't hesitate with his answer, it meant he'd already given it some thought. "They'll look into the other suspects, too," he added.

That hung in the air for several seconds. "You mean my brother."

Chase lifted his shoulder. "Quentin had reason to want Crossman dead. Renée, too, since she knew Crossman was a potential threat to Quentin."

"True, and Renée did visit Crossman at the prison, but Quentin doesn't have the money to pay for an attack like that."

"He would have if he'd gotten the money from a loan shark," Chase quickly pointed out.

April touched her fingers to her throat. Then nodded. "Quentin was evasive about why he'd borrowed that money. But why wouldn't he have just told me if he'd done that?"

Chase gave her a flat look that she had no trouble seeing even in the dim light. "It'd be like confessing to murder. And it wouldn't matter that Crossman is scum. Murder is still murder."

Yes. It sickened her to think that Quentin might have gone this far. Crossman had been a genuine threat, but he would have been convicted. Would have ended up behind bars for the rest of his life. Of course, his conviction wouldn't have ended Quentin's and her life sentences. Because they would have had to remain in WITSEC as long as Crossman was alive.

"Don't focus just on your brother," Chase said to her a moment later. "There also might have been a dispute the guards didn't know about. In other words, this might not be connected to what's happening with us."

April hoped he was right. Having Crossman dead wasn't any big loss, but she didn't want his murder on her brother's hands.

Chase maneuvered her into the crook of his arm. "Why don't you try to get some rest? It'll take us hours to get to the safe house because Jax will have to drive around a long time to make sure we aren't being followed."

April was certain that rest was the last thing she'd get, but it was no hardship to be in Chase's arms. Of course, he wasn't resting, either. His gaze was firing all around them, probably looking for more of those hired thugs.

"What if all the gunmen were working for Crossman?" she asked. If so, that meant the danger was really over.

"We'll know soon enough." Chase idly brushed a kiss on the top of her head. That, too, was no hardship, and April wondered if Chase even realized the effect he had on her.

She didn't want to hope too much that Bailey and the rest of them would all finally be safe. But the hope came anyway. No danger. No WITSEC. She could live a normal life, and Chase wouldn't have to give up his badge and family.

The thought stopped in her head.

But that would mean things would change between Chase and her. They weren't exactly riding off into the sunset together, but they had eased some of that bad blood. Being in his arms proved that. So did all those hot kisses. However, if there was no reason for them to be in hiding together, that might also give Chase a reason for them not to be together at all.

Get a grip.

If the danger had already ended, that's all that mattered. And she couldn't lose Chase because he wasn't hers to lose. Though it did feel as if someone had just crushed her heart.

Chase's phone rang, getting everyone's attention in the car, and when April saw that it was Harlan calling again, she braced herself in case he was about to name her brother as Crossman's killer.

Thankfully, Chase put the call on speaker. "Did you find out anything else about Crossman?" Chase asked.

"Not yet, but there are a few inmates who seem to want to talk. In exchange for lighter sentences, of course. Something might pan out with that, but it's not the reason I'm calling. It's about Janette."

It took April a moment to remember that was the name of the mole they'd found in the marshals' office.

"Janette took the plea deal," Harlan continued a moment later. "And she gave us the name of the person who hired her to hack into WITSEC files."

Chapter Fifteen

Renée.

Chase wasn't exactly surprised that Renée had been the one to pay off Janette, the hacker. It'd been clear from the start that the woman would do anything to find Quentin. What was surprising though was that she hadn't covered her tracks better.

Most criminals would have used a middleman to broker the deal and added layer after layer of cover so that nothing could be traced back to them. Renée hadn't done that. Why?

That'd been the question on Chase's mind during the entire drive to the safe house. And it was still on his mind now.

The safe house was quiet with Levi and Mack asleep in the living room and Jax's return to the sheriff's office. Bailey was also sleeping in the makeshift nursery they'd made out of the second bedroom, and April was in the only other bedroom across the hall. Probably to give him some alone time with Bailey.

Alone time with his thoughts, too.

So much had gone on what with the attacks, Crossman's murder and now the news about Renée hiring Janette. All of it was twisted into a tangled mess, and even the quiet didn't help Chase sort through it.

What did help was knowing that Bailey and April were safe. For now, anyway. With Crossman out of the picture, Chase had to work on keeping it that way. That started with figuring out how Renée played into all of this. Whoever was behind this wanted April hurt.

Or dead.

If it was Quentin, it could be for whatever part of April's estate he'd inherit. If it was Malcolm, it could be simple revenge. Revenge that he'd perhaps already started by having Crossman murdered. But what would Renée possibly hope to gain by killing April?

Unless…

"What's bothering you?" April asked, snapping him right out of his thoughts.

Chase looked up at her. She was in the doorway, her hands bracketed on each side of the jamb, and she was watching him watch a sleeping Bailey.

He did a double take. Because April wasn't wearing any clothes. Well, she had on a bathrobe, but that was it. Judging from the towel she had draped over her arm, she was headed to the shower.

April did her own double take when she noticed where his attention had drifted. To her body. He quickly fixed that and turned back to the baby.

"Is something wrong?" April pressed.

Because something might indeed be wrong and since he didn't want to wake Bailey, Chase stepped away from the crib and joined April in the hall so they could talk. He reminded certain parts of himself that this was just for a chat. And not so he could keep gawking at her in that bathrobe.

"I'm thinking it's possible Janette was paid to say that Renée had been the one to hire her," Chase tossed out there.

April stayed quiet a moment, obviously processing that. "Is there anything specific that makes you think that?"

"Harlan said Janette got a top-notch lawyer, one that she wouldn't normally be able to afford."

She shrugged. "Maybe Renée paid for that, too."

"That's what I thought at first, but why wouldn't Renée just spend that money to better cover up what she'd done? There doesn't appear to be a personal connection between Renée and Janette, so I'm surprised Renée didn't just put up a front man to hire her and then let Janette hang if she got caught."

April made a sound of agreement. "Especially since Renée got the information she wanted—my location so she could use Bailey and me to help her find Quentin." She paused. "So, you're thinking Malcolm could be behind this?"

"Or Quentin." Chase didn't have to wait long for the surprise to appear on April's face.

"Quentin might have needed to find you so he could get the money to pay off his debts. After all, you had a do-not-contact order on him when you entered WITSEC, and he had no way of getting in touch with you."

"Only because I thought it was too risky for us to try to communicate with each other."

Chase nodded. "So, this might have been Quentin's only way of finding you. And then he could get rid of Renée by having Janette say that Renée was the one who hired her."

"You really think so?" she asked.

Obviously, he hadn't convinced her. Chase hadn't actually convinced himself, either, but he wanted to tell her what was on his mind and hope that she could see any flaws in his theory. Because it would be a lot better for April if her brother didn't want her dead.

"Think it through," Chase continued. "Yes, Renée resents you because she believes you turned Quentin against her, but Quentin could be manipulating that. He could be baiting Renée to go after you."

April groaned, leaned against the wall. And she blinked back some tears. "I know I shouldn't be shocked by anything he's capable of doing, but it still hurts."

Now he had convinced her. But maybe he was wrong.

"I know. I'm sorry. And this is all just a theory. Quentin might be innocent." Of this, anyway.

Even though it was a different kind of dangerous to get closer to her, Chase did it anyway. He pulled her to him. And he had to give those parts of his body yet another reminder that this was a hug of comfort. Too bad those parts couldn't tell the difference.

And April felt the difference.

She eased back, looked up at him, and he saw the questions—and the heat—in her eyes.

Not good. Chase moved away from her. It didn't help. He could still feel her in his arms. Still had the taste of her in his mouth.

Still wanted her more than his next breath.

"All right." April sounded disappointed that he hadn't acted on the heat crackling between them. She fluttered her fingers toward the bathroom just up the hall. "I won't be long, and then I'll probably spend the night in here with Bailey."

Chase wanted to remind her there was a baby monitor so she could sleep in the room set up for her and still hear Bailey. Heck, he also wanted to follow April and…

Well, he wanted to have sex with her.

That was the down and dirty, but considering everything that'd gone on between them, she might turn him down flat.

His stupid body seemed to take that as a challenge. Chase grabbed the baby monitor and headed for the bathroom. She'd already turned on the shower. He could hear the water running, which meant she'd likely already stripped down.

His body took that as a challenge, too.

He knocked once, just a sharp rap, and April opened the door. He stepped inside with her and set the baby monitor on the vanity.

April stared at him. Frozen. Well, except for her breath. It was gusting.

Chase had a big reason to keep his hands off her. April was a criminal. He was a marshal. Opposites. But that didn't seem to matter when it came to this attraction between them.

It sure didn't matter now.

There were times when he wished he'd never met her. Other times when he knew he'd never have this feeling with anyone else. Despite that whole opposite thing, his feelings for her ran hot and deep. And not just sex, either.

It would have been so much simpler if this were just about sex.

"I'm never sure what I should do when it comes to

you," she said, her voice all mixed up with that gusting breath.

"I know exactly what to do with you."

And he did. Chase proved it by sliding his hand around the back of her neck and hauling her to him. His brain sent up a red flag warning. Which he ignored and kissed her.

There it was. That slam of fire that he always got whenever he was near her. He put her body right against his. Her breasts against his chest. The rest of them aligned just right, too.

She tasted like something forbidden. Probably not too far off the mark. But there was something else, as well. Something familiar that whispered of home. And family. That was brief, though, because soon the fire had its way, and his body urged him to do more than just kiss her.

So, Chase did.

He pushed the robe off her, and he lowered his mouth to her breasts. She was curvier than she had been before the pregnancy. He approved and savored every inch of her breasts until she was breathless and clutching onto him.

And kissing him in return.

April sank to the floor, pulling him down with her. It was warm and steamy like the rest of the room, and they landed on the thick bath mat. She located his mouth again and did some damage there while she went after his shirt. Once it was off, he felt her bare skin against his. Not just her breasts, either.

She was naked.

And beautiful.

Man, she knew how to take away his breath, too.

Chase considered scooping her up and taking her into

the bedroom. *Briefly* considered it. But the bedroom suddenly seemed miles away.

Their other time together had been crazy and rushed. This time was no different, and even though he wanted to slow down, to savor her a while, he knew that was a pipe dream. The need pushed aside the foreplay.

Without breaking the kiss, she fought with his jeans and would have lost that battle on her own if Chase hadn't helped. His boots, holster and the rest of his clothes went flying over the small bathroom. At the last second, he remembered to take a condom from his wallet.

And then it was his turn to freeze.

"Is it okay if we do this?" Something he should have asked before he even started this.

She blinked, and then he saw the realization hit her. "You mean because I had a baby?" Relief washed over her face, and she pulled him right back to her. "It's been two months. This is fine. Better than fine," she added in a rough whisper.

Chase had to agree with that. It was much, much better than just fine.

Despite her assurance that all was well, Chase forced himself to be gentle when he entered her. The gentleness didn't last, though. April hooked her legs around him and forced him in deeper. Harder.

Then, faster.

Even though the need was in control now, Chase still looked at her. Savoring as much of this as he could. Hanging on to every second with her.

But it didn't last.

He knew it wouldn't. The thrusts inside her took them to the exact place that fire demanded they go. April made a soft sound of pure pleasure as the climax rippled through her. It was the sound, that look on her face, the way her body gripped his. All of that took hold of him. And didn't let go.

Chase gave in to it, in to her and finished what April and he had started.

Chapter Sixteen

April figured this was as close to perfect as her life could get. Sex with Chase. Great sex at that. They had a healthy baby girl. And Crossman was dead. But even with all the semiperfectness, something big was missing.

Chase himself.

He was there physically in bed with her at the safe house, but somewhere between the time they'd made love on the bathroom floor and then come into the bedroom after Bailey's late-night feeding, he'd taken a mental hike. And it wasn't just because he'd been asleep, either. He'd likely dozed through the night, but every time April had checked, he was awake, staring up at the ceiling.

Did he regret what they'd done?

No doubt. April was pretty sure he trusted her now, but there'd always be that divide between them. A divide that even the danger, Bailey and the sex hadn't been able to erase.

Of course, it might also have something to do with the two phone calls Chase had made during the night. From what she'd been able to gather, they'd been updates from Jericho. Or rather lack of updates since there'd been no new information about the investigation.

"Want to talk about it?" she risked asking.

Even though he was still wide awake, her question seemed to startle him, and it took a moment for him to turn his head and look at her. There wasn't regret in his eyes, but there was something.

"I'm not going to apologize for what happened," he said.

All right, so maybe he wasn't as distant as she'd originally thought. "I don't want an apology. If you hadn't come into that bathroom after me, I would have made my way back to you."

In fact, she had indeed been reaching for the doorknob when she'd heard Chase's well-timed knock.

"So, what's bothering you?" she pressed even though April wasn't sure she wanted to hear what had caused his forehead to bunch up like that.

"Today is Deanne's funeral," he tossed out there.

Oh. That. She certainly hadn't forgotten about it and felt a pang of a different kind. Grief. It was so senseless that Deanne had died. Even more senseless that they still didn't know who had hired the man who'd murdered her.

"Deanne didn't have a next of kin," Chase went on, "so Jericho arranged to have her buried at the church near the ranch. We have lots of family graves there that we maintain. We'll do the same for Deanne."

April had to tamp down the lump in her throat before she could speak. "Thank you for that."

"It was all Jericho's doing. He might act like a badass, but he's got a couple of soft spots."

She'd yet to see those soft spots, but Jericho had done his best to keep Bailey and her safe, and that was plenty enough for April.

There was a sound from the baby monitor. Not a cry exactly, but Bailey was stirring. She'd had a bottle only three hours earlier so probably wouldn't be hungry yet, but she might want some attention.

"I'll get her," Chase said, dropping a kiss on her mouth before he climbed out of bed.

He was already wearing his jeans. He'd put them back on shortly after returning to the bedroom and had slept in them. With his gun and boots nearby. Reminders that even though they were in the safe house, Chase was still on alert.

With good reason.

It was entirely possible the danger wasn't over.

Also entirely possible the danger wasn't going away anytime soon. Well, unless they did something to bring things to a head.

Chase came back in the room, holding Bailey and smiling at her. For a couple of moments, the thoughts of danger and fear vanished, and April went back into that near-perfect state. This was what normal couples had.

Not that their relationship was anywhere near normal.

Still, it was nice to think of what could be.

Chase sat on the bed, easing Bailey between them. The baby volleyed glances between them as if trying to figure out what was going on. April was trying to do the same thing. However, any plans or thoughts for their future meant getting rid of one big obstacle: the person who'd set all this danger in motion.

April wanted to believe Crossman had been the one to do that, but her gut was telling her otherwise. They had to know for sure.

"We could set a trap," April tossed out there, hoping Chase didn't nix the idea before she could even explain it.

He didn't.

"I know a trap might not even be necessary," she continued. "Maybe Crossman was the only one behind all of this, but if he wasn't, then the person responsible will still want to come after me."

And that person could be Renée, Malcolm or, yes, Quentin.

Chase nodded. "I was thinking about going to Deanne's funeral in the hopes of drawing out Quentin or Renée."

She shook her head. "You're not the target. I am. The only way it would work is for me to be there."

Now he shook his head. "Too dangerous."

"It's too dangerous not to do anything. And think of what it would mean to bring this all to an end. No WITSEC. You wouldn't have to leave your family or give up your badge. Bailey could have a normal life."

Chase wasn't surprised with any part of her argument. He'd likely gone over this too many times during the sleepless night he'd just had. But he still didn't jump to agree with her that this was the fastest way.

Bailey smiled, getting their attention. The conversation was way too dark, considering they had their precious baby next to them. But it was because of Bailey that something had to be done.

"You said the funeral would be at a church near the ranch," April went on. "How hard would it be to secure the location?"

"Hard." Chase lifted his head, his gaze meeting hers. "But not impossible. The church and adjacent cemetery are in a clearing with a road in front and pastures on the back and east side. It's the west side that would pose the biggest risk. There are plenty of trees where snipers could hide."

Obviously, he'd already given this some thought.

"Even if we caught a sniper, he might not talk and tell us who hired him," she admitted.

"Yeah, and that's why I don't think this is a good idea. Too big of a risk with little chance of a payoff."

"What if the culprit thinks he or she can personally get to me?" April suggested. "Just hear me out," she added when he started shaking his head again. "We put out the word that I found something to ID the person. No specifics, only that Crossman gave me some information when we visited him right before he died."

At least Chase didn't shake his head at that. "What kind of info?"

She shrugged. "Bank routing numbers maybe that could be traced back to the person who hired those gunmen. We could say that I'm not willing to share the info with the cops yet because I want to use it as a bargaining tool to get Quentin out of hot water."

Something she'd done with the last plea deal. And she'd been getting Quentin out of hot water most of his life.

"Then what?" Chase asked. "The person responsible tries to gun you down when a sniper can't?"

The thought of that required her to take a deep breath. "Maybe no guns will be involved at all. I could stay inside the church the whole time. Both Quentin and Renée are fugitives. If they try to get inside to see me, you can arrest them. Interrogate them. And maybe get them to crack."

Which shouldn't be hard in Renée's case. Her short fuse and mental instability might be enough to get a confession.

"What if it's Malcolm?" Chase snapped. "I don't have any grounds to arrest him—yet."

"No. But if he shows up, I can tell him Crossman gave me proof that he's the one behind the attacks. If Malcolm is indeed the one behind this, I think he'll have some kind of reaction to that."

"A bad reaction," Chase pointed out.

"And if it is, you'll arrest him."

"What if he attacks first?" he pressed.

"Then you'll stop him. We can add some urgency to all of this by saying after the funeral I'll be heading back to WITSEC. And meeting with the marshals to tell them everything I supposedly learned from Crossman because I've worked out the plea deal for Quentin to take his false kidnapping and extortion charges off the table."

Chase looked as if he wanted to curse. Hard to do that with a still-smiling baby between them. "I don't want you in that kind of danger."

"I'm already in that kind of danger," she reminded him. "And if the suspects don't show up, at least I get to say my goodbyes to Deanne."

Still, no response from Chase.

"Please," April pressed. "Call Jericho and let's set this up. Levi and Mack could stay here with Bailey, and in just a few hours this could all be over."

He didn't exactly jump to take out his phone, and she could see the wheels practically turning in his head. It wasn't a perfect plan. Far from it. However, she felt in her gut that one way or another it would bring all of this to a close.

"I won't make you regret this," she added.

"I already do," he said.

But Chase reached for his phone to make the call.

EVERYTHING WAS QUIET. Too quiet, maybe. Of course, if it hadn't been quiet, Chase would have still felt the same uneasiness.

And had the same doubts about this so-called plan.

Having April out in public like this could turn out to be deadly. But then again, having her anywhere could have the same consequences. After all, someone—maybe Renée—had tried to kidnap April from the sheriff's office in broad daylight. The woman certainly wouldn't have any trouble showing up at a country church.

Nor would any thugs she might have hired to finish off April.

That's why Chase had insisted on April wearing a Kevlar vest under her shirt. She could still be injured in an attack, but the vest was something at least. The church had also been searched from top to bottom.

Of course, there were plenty of places for an attacker to hide a bomb or some other kind of device in an old church like this, especially since Deanne's funeral arrangements had been made before this plan had been put into motion. Someone could have easily gotten into the church. Still, they'd done all they could in that particular area of security.

As a final part of this plan, April was also armed. Everyone in or near the church was since, with the exception of April, they were all lawmen.

Jericho, Jax, Carlos and Dexter.

No minister. Chase hadn't wanted to bring Reverend Marcum into the middle of this. And the burial crew wouldn't show up until April was away from the grounds. That would ensure the crew's and minister's safety.

Too bad Chase couldn't do much of anything else to give April that same kind of assurance.

Or comfort.

April had started crying the moment they'd stepped into the church for the closed-casket funeral. And she was still fighting the tears now while they stood in the back corner. Where they would stay to see how this plan played out.

The corner wasn't ideal since the walls of the church were wood, but it was away from any doors and windows, and it gave Chase the vantage point of being able to see both the front and rear exits while keeping April right next to him.

She was still looking shaky and had a death grip on the small bouquet of flowers she was holding. Flowers that Jax had remembered to pick up for her so April would have something to put on Deanne's coffin. Chase hadn't expected his brothers to be so accommodating to April, but he was thankful for it. Thankful, too, that they were putting their lives on the line for this.

"Deanne's death wasn't your fault, you know," Chase told her when the tears started again. But he was repeating himself, and April didn't look as if she believed him any more now than the first time he'd said it.

"If it hadn't been for Deanne, we might not have gotten Bailey back." She whispered it as if it were too frightening to say it aloud.

Chase shared that same frightening realization with her. Thank God they'd managed to get to Bailey because as bad as this all was—and it was *bad*—at least their baby was safe.

The challenge would be to keep it that way.

There was some movement near the front door, and Chase automatically stepped in front of April. But it was only Jericho, and his brother made a sweeping glance around before he made his way to them.

"Anything yet?" Chase asked.

Jericho shook his head. "No sign of snipers or anyone

else for that matter. But then, I wasn't convinced any of our three suspects or their hired guns would just come waltzing up to the place."

"They might if they believe this is their last chance to get to me," April reminded him. "Did the word get out that I'm about to leave for good?"

"It did. We used Janette for that."

Chase pulled back his shoulders. "The hacker who broke into WITSEC files? You trust her to do something like that?"

"I don't trust her one bit, but trust has nothing to do with this. As part of her plea deal, she told us that she communicated with Renée or whoever hired her by transferring the info she hacked into an encrypted file that she then put in an online chat room."

April jumped right on that. "You're not sure it was actually Renée who hired her?"

"Not sure of much of anything, and I don't think Janette is, either. It's fairly easy to pretend to be someone else on the internet. And I have to wonder—why would Renée let this be traced back to her?"

Chase had asked himself the same thing, and he didn't like the answer any more than the uneasy feeling in the pit of his stomach. Yes, Renée could have just screwed up. She was crazy after all. But it would have been just as easy for someone to frame her.

Either Malcolm or Quentin.

"Anyway," Jericho continued, "the marshals used the same encryption code and put out the news about April heading back to WITSEC today."

"But won't our suspects know the info didn't come from Janette?" Chase asked.

Jericho gave him a half smile. "It did come from her.

That was another part of the plea deal we worked out with Janette. They allowed her to log on to a computer but watched everything she was doing to make sure she didn't try to double-cross us."

April didn't seem that relieved. "What if Janette found a way around that? What if she figured out a way to tell her boss that this was a trap?"

"Then the bad guy or woman doesn't show up," Jericho explained, looking at Chase. "Which might turn out to be a good thing. If we don't catch him or her today, we'll keep looking, and maybe you won't have to be in WITSEC that long."

Maybe. But any amount of time was too long to be without his badge. Still, it was better than any other alternative Chase had managed to come up with.

Jericho checked his watch. "How much time are we going to give this to play out?"

Chase wanted to say not much time at all, but the look in April's eyes begged him to wait. "Let's give it another ten minutes."

That didn't please either Jericho or April. His brother wanted to wrap this up now, and April had probably been ready to stand there for the rest of the day despite only the thin possibility of ending all of this.

"I'll tell the others," Jericho said, heading back out the door.

April turned to him the moment Jericho was gone. "I'm sorry. I really hoped this would work."

Chase didn't tell her that no apology was needed. Instead, he brushed a kiss on her cheek.

She glanced at the casket at the front of the church. "Deanne deserved better than this."

Yes, she did. Despite the fact they'd put out the word

in the town newspaper about the funeral service, there'd been no visitors. Too bad.

"I think Deanne would have been pleased, though, that we're using her funeral to draw out the person responsible for her murder," Chase added.

April nodded. Gave a heavy sigh. And looked at the casket again. "I want to say goodbye to her, and then we can get ready to leave."

Chase was relieved about the leaving part, but he wasn't too happy about her being in the front of the church. It put her way too close to the windows and back exit. Still, he couldn't deny her this.

"Just make it fast," he insisted.

He drew his gun and kept watch all around them, though he knew if a gunman tried to get past Jericho and the others that he'd hear the commotion before anyone actually made it into the church.

That left the windows.

There were lots of them. A dozen, but they were all stained glass, making it impossible to see through them. However, if a sniper had indeed managed to get close enough, he could use an infrared device to pinpoint April's exact location. That was the main reason Chase had to keep her away from them.

Thankfully, April did hurry. She went to the front of the church, Chase was right by her side, and she placed the flowers on Deanne's coffin.

"Thank you," April whispered to the woman. "I swear, I'll do everything I can to make this right."

Chase didn't especially like that promise. He'd hoped this would be the last of April sticking her neck out there. That didn't mean he wouldn't be doing the same thing. He wanted this person caught and punished.

April paused, her mouth moving, but Chase couldn't tell what she was saying. A prayer, maybe. It lasted only a few moments before she turned to him, obviously ready to go.

Chase didn't waste any time. He got her moving toward the front entrance, where they'd left the unmarked cruiser. Of course, this was the most dangerous part.

With April out in the open.

There were only six steps leading down from the church and only about a dozen more steps to the car, but it would almost certainly feel like an eternity.

He stopped once they reached the door, and Chase looked out to get a signal from Jericho that it was okay to move April. His brother made a sweeping look around, gave him a nod, and he opened the door for them.

Chase took a deep breath, ready to move, but before he could do anything else, the worst happened.

A blast tore through the church.

Chapter Seventeen

The sound was deafening, and April wasn't sure what the heck had caused it.

Chase seemed to know what was going on, though, because he hooked his arm around her and bolted out of the building and onto the landing just outside the front door.

April saw Jericho and the others then. Jericho and Jax were scrambling around and taking cover on the side of the unmarked cruiser that Chase and she had used to get there. Dexter and Carlos hurried behind Dexter's truck. Thankfully, none of them seemed to be hurt.

Maybe it would stay that way.

She glanced over her shoulder and saw the damage inside. Someone had obviously set off some kind of explosive, and the blast had ripped through the center of the church, splintering the pews and scattering debris everywhere. Chunks of the ceiling were falling, some landing on Deanne's coffin.

Who had done this?

And how had they managed it?

The building had been checked and double-checked. And Jericho and the other deputies had patrolled the grounds the entire time Chase and she had been inside.

There was no way someone could have gotten past them to do this. Unless someone had managed to shoot a long-range explosive.

"We need to get in the car," Chase insisted.

With his body practically wrapped around hers and with his gun drawn, Chase started for the steps that led down to the flagstone walkway. But they didn't get far.

Before the shot rang out.

Quickly followed by a second and a third one.

Cursing, Chase yanked her back into the entry just as one of the bullets slammed into the doorjamb where they'd just been.

Her heart was going a mile a minute. The bad thoughts, too. Someone was shooting at them. Maybe someone who'd used the explosion as a distraction to get closer to fire those bullets.

April grabbed the gun from her purse and dropped the purse onto the floor. No need for it now, and she wanted to free up her hands in case she got the chance to return fire.

Or if she had to fight back.

That didn't help settle any of her nerves and fear.

There was a loud noise behind her, and for one terrifying moment, April thought maybe someone had sneaked in through the back and had shot at them. But it wasn't a bullet. Another piece of the ceiling had fallen. Worse, it looked as if the whole place was ready to collapse.

"We can't stay here," April managed to say.

Chase made a sound of agreement, his gaze zooming all around. The only other one of the lawmen whom she could actually see now was Jericho, and he was pinned down on the side of the cruiser, and someone was shooting at him.

That's when April realized there was more than one gunman.

Another part of the ceiling fell, crashing to the floor directly behind them. It was obvious they didn't have many options, but one of those options definitely wasn't to stay put.

"We'll jump off the side of the steps," Chase finally said, tipping his head in that direction. "Move fast and get down the second we're on the ground."

She nodded, but that was all April had time to do before Chase latched on to her arm and got them running. The bullets didn't stop coming, and she could have sworn it took hours for them to maneuver the short distance.

The steps were wide, at least ten feet across, and the moment they reached the side, Chase and she dropped to the ground, landing in the flower bed that stretched across the entire side of the church. All things considered, it wasn't the worst place to be since the steps were made of concrete and flagstone.

But Jericho and Jax didn't have that kind of protection.

They and the other deputies were pinned down, and the bulk of the bullets seemed to be aimed at them.

"Do you see the shooters?" Chase called out to them.

"They sped up in a black car the same time as the explosion," Jericho answered. "They're blocking the road. Two of them. Maybe more."

April thought her heart had skipped a beat. Maybe more wasn't good, and with the explosive and the gunfire, it was possible other shooters were getting in place to come at them from all angles.

Chase glanced back at her, probably to make sure she

hadn't been hurt by any of the falling debris or bullets. She hadn't been, but there was a cut above Chase's left eyebrow. Not serious. However, it was a reminder that this could have been a whole lot worse.

And still might be.

"I'll get in the car and will pull it over to you," Jericho said.

It was a possible way out. But it wasn't without risks.

When Jericho levered himself up to open the door, the shots came even faster, tearing into the vehicle. It was bullet resistant, but that didn't mean the bullets wouldn't get through. And the shooters were doing their best to tear through the engine. No doubt so they could disable it since it was the nearest vehicle to Chase and her.

April watched, her breath stalled in her throat, as Jericho opened the driver's side door. Jax did the same to the back. Jericho didn't have the keys, Chase did, but she was hoping once he got inside, it wouldn't take him long to hotwire the car and drive to them.

Of course, that wouldn't solve their problem of the road being blocked, but it was a start.

Behind her, April heard another sound she didn't want to hear. The old church seemed to groan, and the roof gave way. All of it. And it came crashing down.

Oh, God.

It was falling on them. If they didn't do something fast, they'd be crushed.

Chase latched on to her and started running. Not toward the cruiser since it would mean literally running out in the open where there was heavy gunfire. Still using the steps for cover, he took her toward the side of the church.

To the cemetery.

And he pulled her behind the first headstone they

reached. Chase didn't stop there. He pushed her to the ground and crawled on top of her, protecting her with his body.

None of the headstones in the cemetery were that large, but at least this one was marble, and she prayed it would be enough to stop bullets.

Especially since the bullets started to come right at them.

April couldn't see much because of her position, but she had no trouble hearing the crash. The church had collapsed. No doubt what their attackers had intended right from the beginning. This hadn't been a kidnapping attempt. But rather an attempt to murder them.

They'd nearly succeeded, and they weren't out of the woods yet. Neither were Chase's brothers and the other deputies. It sickened her to think they could all be killed because of her. Especially since April still didn't know who wanted her dead.

Or why.

"The engine won't start," Jericho called out, adding plenty of profanity to that.

Definitely not good. The unmarked cruiser was their best bet at escaping. Now they'd have to use one of the other vehicles. If they could get to them, that is.

Chase cursed, too, and it took April a moment to figure out he hadn't done that because of what Jericho had said. The angle of the shots had changed. Some were still going into the cruiser and toward the deputy's truck, but the bullets were also coming at Chase and her.

Not going into the front of the headstone, either. But rather to the side.

Where they could easily be shot.

"We have to get away from here," Chase warned her a split second before he got them moving again.

They darted behind another headstone, one that was positioned so that it would give them better cover. She hoped.

"The shooters moved the car on the road," Chase said. "They're tracking us."

It took a moment for that to sink in, and it didn't sink in well. The gunmen were closing in on them.

Chase tipped his head to the gravestone behind them. It was by far the largest one in the cemetery. "We're going there. Stay as low as you can."

She wanted to remind him to do the same, but there wasn't any time. Chase took hold of her hand again, and as he fired off a shot in the direction of the gunmen, they ran, diving behind the large headstone.

But before April even hit the ground, she screamed.

Because she tripped over something.

A body.

CHASE HADN'T SEEN the body before April and he had scrambled behind the large tombstone. But he certainly saw it now.

A man on the ground.

Every drop of color vanished from April's face, and she clamped her hand over her mouth, no doubt to stop herself from screaming again. She scurried away from the body, backing up against the marble headstone.

It took April a couple of seconds to lower her hand. "Is it Quentin?" she asked, her breath gusting.

Hell, Chase hoped not.

But it was a valid question and hard to tell since it appeared the guy had been shot at point-blank range in the head. There was blood. Lots of it. It had covered much of his hair, and since the man was facedown, the only way Chase could be sure was to turn the body.

Chase reached to do that, but the shots came at them again. Thankfully, the bullets were all slamming into the marble, and this particular headstone was wide enough that it should be able to stop April and him from being shot.

Not the same for his brothers and the deputies, though.

Jericho and the others were still out there in the line of fire with a disabled vehicle. Maybe they'd managed to find some kind of cover. Or better yet, perhaps they were close to ending this attack. There wasn't any backup to call, what with Levi and Mack at the safe house and the reserve deputy manning the sheriff's office, where they were still holding a prisoner. After all, this could be some kind of diversion to break out the man who'd killed Deanne.

But it didn't feel like a diversion.

April and he were almost certainly the targets.

He fired glances all around him. The car with the gunmen was obviously still out there on the road. No one was inside the collapsed church to his right, or if they were inside, they were dead and therefore no threat.

That left the pasture to his left and behind him. Both were dotted with a few trees and some high grass. Not the easiest way for an attacker to approach them, but it was possible. That's why he had to keep watch, and April would have to help him.

Chase motioned toward the left pasture. "Make sure no one comes at us from there."

She gave a shaky nod, pinned her attention in that

direction, with the occasional glances at the body. He hated she had to see that, but they had to stay put for now.

When the angle of the bullets didn't change and come at them, Chase risked turning the body. Again, not easy. Whoever it was, he was literally dead weight, and even after Chase maneuvered him to his back, it still took him a second to recognize the guy. Not Quentin.

Shane.

April's breath rushed out again, but this time he thought maybe there was some relief in it. He was relieved, too. He wasn't a fan of Quentin's, but Chase hadn't wanted April to see him like this, either.

"Why was Shane here?" she asked.

Chase didn't have an answer for that. This was the last place he'd expected to see Renée's estranged husband, and judging from the pool of blood around him, he'd been dead for at least a couple of hours.

Dexter had checked the cemetery earlier, but Chase doubted he'd gone from grave to grave since it would have been easy to see something lurking behind a tombstone. But then, Dexter wouldn't have been looking for someone lying flat on the ground.

His phone rang, and since Chase didn't want to take his attention off their surroundings, he passed the phone to April. "It's Jericho," she relayed to him when she glanced at the screen.

"Don't put it on speaker," Chase warned her. "There could be a listening device planted on Shane's body."

Judging from the way her eyes widened, she hadn't thought of that. Considering everything else their attacker had done to get to them, Chase figured anything was a possibility, including more explosives.

April put the phone next to his ear so they both could hear, and she hit the answer button.

"Where are you?" Jericho immediately asked.

"Behind the Millers' tombstone. We found a body here. It's Shane, and it looks as if he's been dead for a while."

Jericho cursed. "Please tell me it was suicide."

"No, he was shot in the back of the head. I'm guessing he knew his killer because the person managed to get close to him."

Of course, that meant it could be any of their suspects since Shane knew all three of them. Renée would have been the one who could get the nearest to him, but Shane also knew Quentin and Malcolm.

"We haven't been able to shoot any of the gunmen," Jericho went on. "They're using rifles with scopes and are out of range. I called the Rangers, but it'll take them too long to get here. The gunmen keep moving closer."

Chase made a quick glance to verify that. His heart slammed against his chest. Because it was true. It wouldn't be long before they were in position to blast April and him to smithereens.

"We can't wait for the Rangers," Jericho explained. "We'll have to use the truck to get April and you out of there."

"I'm listening." And he hoped Jericho had a workable plan because Chase certainly didn't.

"Dexter's going to try to get the truck out to you. I'll run some interference."

"How?" Because Chase didn't want his brother rushing out in the line of fire to create a diversion.

"There are some flares in the disabled cruiser. I'll

fire them at the gunmen when Dexter's driving the truck to you."

Chase doubted the flares would do any actual damage, but they could be a distraction. Plus, flares had been known to catch fire from time to time. Maybe they'd get a lucky break and that would happen now.

"There's no easy path for Dexter to get to you," Jericho went on. He was right. The tombstones were staggered, and there definitely wasn't enough room for a truck to drive around them. "So Dexter will get as close as he can, and you'll need to make a run for it. All right?"

Chase looked at April, and he could see the fear in her eyes. Not just fear for the gunmen, but also because this plan was risky. A lot of people could be hurt or killed. But that could happen if they stayed put, too.

She nodded.

"Go for it," Chase relayed to his brother. "When the truck's in place, we'll be ready to move."

April pressed the end call button and slipped the phone back into his pocket. Now all they could do was wait, and thankfully it didn't take long for Chase to hear the truck engine.

And the shots that were now going right at the truck.

He figured Dexter was staying as low in the seat as possible, but it might not be low enough.

The truck soon came into view, and though he couldn't actually see Dexter because of the cracked side window, the deputy stopped in between the fallen church and the edge of the cemetery. There was no fence, just the distance they'd have to cover since there were three tombstones between them and the truck.

Dexter eased open the truck door, and because this plan would mean April and Chase literally diving inside, Dexter got out from behind the wheel, dropping to the floor in front of the passenger's seat to give them as much room as possible. The trick would be to get April in there first without either of them getting shot. Then, Chase could drive away, provided the gunmen hadn't disabled the tires by then.

That's where they were aiming now.

There was a swooshing sound, and Chase saw the flare shoot through the air. Jericho had a good aim because it crashed directly into the gunmen's car.

"Let's go," Chase told April.

He took hold of her hand and hauled her to her feet. However, she didn't stay there.

There was another sound. The sickening thud of a bullet hitting something. Or rather someone.

The shot slammed right into April.

Chapter Eighteen

April froze.

The scream wedged there in her throat, cutting off the air. Strangling her. She couldn't move, couldn't run, but she could feel the pain radiate from her chest and knife through her entire body. She slumped to the ground, unable to break her fall.

God, she'd been shot.

"April's been hit!" Chase yelled to someone. Maybe to his brother or Dexter.

The pain made it hard to focus, but she heard another round of gunfire. Closer than the other shots. These were coming from Chase. And from someone else. Those shots stopped after just a few seconds, but the other ones, the ones aimed at the truck, continued.

Chase dropped to his knees next to her. He ripped open her shirt. Right where the pain was the worst.

"You're okay," he said. Though his expression said otherwise. "The bullet hit the Kevlar vest."

Only then did April remember she was even wearing the vest. It'd saved her, but it certainly hadn't stopped the pain. It felt as if a heavyweight had punched her in the chest and then burned her.

"Just try to breathe," Chase instructed, his gaze firing all around them.

Easier said than done. The pain from a real gunshot wound had to be much, much worse, but April couldn't imagine it.

"Who shot me?" she managed to ask.

"A guy who sneaked into the back pasture. I got a look at his face but didn't recognize him." He flicked away the hot slug that was imbedded into the vest. "Don't worry about him, though. He's dead."

No doubt because Chase had shot him.

Good. Considering there was another body just inches from her, it should have turned her stomach to know someone else was dead, but one less hired thug increased their chances of getting out of this.

Chase's phone rang again, and he answered it without taking his attention off their surroundings. Even though he was hovering right over her, she couldn't hear what the caller said, but she could tell it wasn't good news because Chase's forehead bunched up.

"Let me see if I can move her," Chase finally said.

"What happened?" April asked the moment he finished the call.

"The gunmen shot out the truck tires. And Jericho spotted another vehicle on the road. Maybe an innocent bystander, but it could be more gunmen."

Or the person behind all of this.

All of their suspects had reasons for wanting her dead, and that might mean the person wanted to personally kill her. Of course, the shot to the vest had come darn close to doing that. If it'd been just a few inches higher, the bullet would have hit her in the neck.

"Jericho lost sight of the second car so it could be anywhere by now," Chase added.

That didn't help her regain any of her breath. "So, what do we do?" But April was almost afraid to hear the answer.

"When I give Jericho a signal that you can move, he'll shoot off more of those flares while we run to the front of the truck. We can use it for cover, and then Dexter will maneuver the truck as best he can so that you and I can head behind the rubble of the church."

April lifted her head to get an idea of how much time it would take to do that. Just a few seconds. But they'd no doubt be long, dangerous seconds. At least the rubble pile was high enough to give them some protection, and they could maybe even use the debris for cover if the gunmen changed positions again.

"What about the other car on the road?" she asked. "What if the driver comes to the back of the church, too?"

"It's a chance we have to take." He paused. "The gunmen in that black car are moving closer to the cemetery."

And closer to Chase and her.

"The Rangers are about twenty minutes out," Chase added. "We won't have to hold up much longer. Can you run?" he pressed.

April nodded, prayed it was true, and she fought the pain to get into a crouching position.

"Stay by my side," Chase instructed. "Run as fast as you can."

She gave him another nod, and Chase tossed out a rock. Probably his cue for Jericho to set off the flare because almost immediately she heard the same swooshing sound. Not one but two.

And Chase and she ran.

Even though April was nowhere near 100 percent, Chase made up for that by hooking his arm around her waist. They barreled past the trio of headstones that were between them and the truck.

The shots came at them, of course, but they pelted into the ground, kicking up dirt. That's when April got a glimpse of the reddish-colored smoke from the flare. It had created a filmy curtain between them and the shooters.

When they reached the front of the truck, Chase pulled her to the ground. They wouldn't be able to stay there long because once the smoke cleared, the gunmen would be able to shoot under the truck.

"You ready?" Dexter called out.

"Do it," Chase answered.

Dexter threw the truck into Reverse, and even though all four tires were indeed completely flat, he somehow managed to back up a couple of inches. Then forward again. Angling the truck to give them the most cover before he scrambled out of the cab and joined them on the ground.

Another flare went off.

Chase didn't waste a second. He got her moving to the debris with Dexter racing along behind them.

Thankfully, there'd been no fire from the explosion, and with the roof fully collapsed, there was nothing to fall on them. However, the debris didn't look that steady, but maybe it would hold up until they could get out of there.

They ducked behind the first pile of rubble. It was mainly what was left of an office. Books, chairs and a broken desk stuck out from the chunks of the roof that had demolished it.

"Damn," Chase said. He leaned out and fired a shot.

"The men moved the car right by the truck," Dexter explained to her since she couldn't see. She was on Chase's left side with Dexter behind her.

April soon got proof that the gunmen were closing in because the shots came right at them. Again. She glanced at Chase to see if he was about to tell them to move, but he was focused on returning fire.

There was a thudding sound behind her, and April whirled around to see what had happened.

No!

Dexter was on the ground.

Before April could even react, someone knocked her gun from her hand and grabbed her.

CHASE SAW THE movement from the corner of his eye and pivoted toward April and Dexter.

His heart went to his knees.

Dexter was down. Not shot. It appeared that someone had clubbed him on the head and he was unconscious. The someone was wearing a ski mask like the other gunmen and now had April. She was fighting to get loose.

And the person—a man—was trying to shoot her.

Chase lunged at them, sending all three of them to the ground. The man slung his elbow into Chase's jaw, hitting him so hard that the pain exploded in his head. He fought off the pain and tried to latch on to April to pull her away. It was the only option he had right now because Chase didn't have a clean shot.

April was no doubt still reeling from taking a slug to the chest, but that didn't stop her from fighting. She clawed and kicked at him. Chase tossed his gun aside so he could go after the guy's own weapon. Because of all the flailing around, he only managed to take hold of the man's right wrist, but maybe that would be enough to stop him from aiming at April again.

Something he was clearly trying to do.

"Move away if you can," Chase told her.

She tried to do just that, but the man hooked his arm around her neck and put her in a choke hold. Not good. Because as long as April was in the middle of this, there was a chance she could be shot. Or strangled to death. Her attacker was trying to do both.

Chase tried to bash the man's hand against the ground and managed a few hits. Not enough, though, to dislodge the gun from his grip. Whoever this was, he was fighting like a wild animal.

April made a strangled sound and tried to pry his grip off her throat. The guy held on. Tightening the choke hold.

He was killing her right in front of Chase.

It was a risk, but Chase took one of his hands off the man's shooting wrist so he could punch him. Hard. Not easy to do, though, with April in the way. Still, he managed one good hit.

But then the shot blasted from the gun.

The man had managed to pull the trigger.

So many bad thoughts went through Chase's head. Had April been shot? She stopped struggling, her hands going to her ears, and for several terrifying seconds, Chase thought maybe the bullet had gone into her head.

But no blood, thank God.

The shot had been so close to her that it'd no doubt caused a jarring pain. The sound was clanging in Chase's ears, too, but he forced himself to keep fighting. Unfortunately, the guy did the same thing.

Chase pinned the man's right hand, and the gun, to the ground and tried to push April out of the way.

Another shot.

Hell.

Chase didn't know where the bullets were going, but Dexter was right there just a yard or so away, and the shots could hit him. Plus, they had an even bigger problem. He couldn't check to see where that black car was, but Chase figured the car, and all the gunmen inside it, were making their way to them so they could help their fellow thug. Once that happened, Chase would be seriously outgunned until Jericho and the others could get back, too.

April pulled her hands from her ears, and even though she was clearly still in pain, she started to fight back again. Both a blessing and a curse. He didn't want her just to give in to this, but he would have preferred that she get as far away from that gun as possible.

"Kill them both!" the man yelled.

Chase had no trouble recognizing that voice. And it wasn't the voice of just another hired gun.

It was Malcolm.

April froze for a second. They'd both known Malcolm was a suspect, of course, but Chase hadn't expected him to be directly involved in this since all the other attacks had come from hired guns.

More shots came, smacking into the ground all around them. Obviously, the men in that black car were now in a position to do some damage and to carry out their boss's order.

Kill them both.

Chase tried to make sure that didn't happen. He dropped onto his back, lifted Malcolm's wrist and gun, and he fired at the thugs who were shooting around them. He had no idea where the bullet went, but Chase hoped it would get them to back off so he could take care of this idiot who was trying to murder April.

Malcolm ripped off his mask and then yanked April back into his grip. Managed, too, to put her in another choke hold. More than ready to put an end to this, Chase punched him again. And again. He would have delivered a third punch if a bullet hadn't sliced across the top of shoulder.

The pain was searing and roared through him. Chase knew it wasn't a fatal shot, but it slowed him down just enough that Malcolm shoved Chase off him.

And Malcolm put the gun to April's head.

No. This couldn't be happening. After everything they'd been through, and survived, he couldn't let Malcolm kill her.

Chase snatched up his gun and scrambled to the side of some of the debris. He took aim. But like before, he didn't have a shot. Not with Malcolm holding April in front of him that way.

"You've been hit," April said, her attention not on fighting for her life but rather on his bloody shoulder.

"He'll be dead if he doesn't back off," Malcolm snarled. "April, if you want your boyfriend to live, tell him to stop and put down his gun. I hadn't planned on killing him, but if he gets in the way, I'll do just that."

"Please stop," she told Chase without hesitation.

Chase had no intention of stopping, but he wasn't sure how to get her out of this. He glanced over his shoulder. The black car was only about ten yards away, and even though Jericho and the others were shooting at it, the vehicle was inching closer, like a jungle cat ready to attack. Worse, it wouldn't be long before the men in that car would be able to use the debris for cover, too.

"I don't want you to die," April added to Chase. "So, please, just let Malcolm take me."

"Malcolm will kill you," he reminded her. "He wants to punish you for Tina's murder."

"Because she deserves to be punished," Malcolm readily admitted.

So, that was indeed his motive. Not that it did them any good to hear it spelled out. Still, he might be able to use it to bargain with Malcolm.

"Tina was a good cop," Chase reminded him. "She wouldn't have approved of any of this."

Malcolm's eyes narrowed. "You don't know that. She was gunned down trying to do her job. I doubt she'd shed any tears over the death of a lowlife like Crossman."

"You had him killed?" Chase asked.

Chase already knew the answer, but he got confirmation of it anyway when Malcolm nodded. But the man didn't just nod. He motioned toward his hired thugs in the car.

"And I figure Tina would be pleased that I'm avenging her death," Malcolm added.

It was hard to reason with a man obsessed with revenge, but Chase had to figure out something.

April's eyes widened, and even though Chase figured he wasn't going to like what he saw, he glanced over his shoulder again.

And, no, he didn't like it.

Two ski-masked gunmen were out of the car. Not alone.

They had a hostage.

Chapter Nineteen

Renée.

April certainly hadn't forgotten about the woman, but she was surprised to see that Renée was on the business end of a gun rather than the one who was pulling the trigger.

Maybe this was some kind of ruse.

Though April couldn't imagine why the woman would pretend to be a hostage. Still, it was hard to figure out the motives of someone so mentally unstable.

"You shot Shane!" Renée shouted, her attention zooming straight to Malcolm. "Is he dead?"

"He's dead," April confirmed.

Renée screamed and started struggling, trying to get away from her captors. It didn't work. The men held on to her, and when she didn't stop fighting to break free, one of them punched her right in the face. Hard. Renée's head flopped back, and blood splattered from what looked to be a broken nose.

Apparently, the woman wasn't a fake hostage after all. Or if she was, this was a convincing act.

One of the men continued to keep Renée in a fierce grip, and the other hurried to Dexter. The deputy was still unconscious, but the thug put some plastic cuffs on him and kicked Dexter's gun away.

While they were occupied with that, April tried to elbow Malcolm in the stomach so she could try to break free. She failed, and Malcolm tightened his grip on her even more.

Malcolm tipped his head to Dexter and then glanced at the thug who was hovering over him. "Shoot the deputy in the head if Chase doesn't drop his gun right now." His voice was ice cold.

April saw the debate in Chase's eyes. A very short one. Because they both knew the man would indeed murder Dexter.

Chase tossed his gun to the ground.

Her heart sank. Of course, April already knew they were in extreme danger, but now neither of them was armed. And they were outnumbered. Plus, Chase was hurt. The blood from the shot to his shoulder was now on the front of his shirt. It didn't look as if he would bleed out, but he needed medical attention. Fast. For that to happen, they had to get out of this.

"Go ahead and kill Renée if she doesn't stop fighting," Malcolm told his men. "I'd wanted them all together for this, but I can always change the plan."

What the heck was going on here?

"Why would you want Renée dead?" April asked.

"She's a loose end," Chase provided when Malcolm didn't say anything. "I figure Malcolm hired the hacker to get into WITSEC files but couldn't find Quentin because he wasn't where he was supposed to be. Malcolm then convinced Renée to kidnap Bailey so he could use the baby to draw Quentin out."

"The plan worked," Malcolm said. "Well, nearly. I'd

wanted Quentin to take the blame for all of this, but now that you've seen my face, that's not going to happen. Still, you can save your brothers and the other lawmen."

"How?" But Chase didn't wait for an answer. "By agreeing to let you leave with April, Renée and me?"

But they wouldn't be just leaving with Malcolm. He would kill them all when he had the rest of his so-called plan in place. That meant he wanted to get Quentin, too, and would likely use her—and possibly even Renée—to lure Quentin into a trap.

A trap that just might work.

"Come on," Malcolm said, and he started moving her.

Malcolm didn't take her toward the black car but to the other side of what remained of the church. Jericho had mentioned something about another vehicle, and it was possible Malcolm planned to use that to escape with them so he could finish out his plan.

"I'm not going anywhere with you," Renée shouted. "You killed Shane." A hoarse sob tore from her mouth, and she was obviously in pain from the punch to the face because she was wincing. "Why would you do that?"

"Sorry, but Shane was another loose end." That's the only explanation Malcolm gave them.

Though April could fill in the blanks. Shane loved Renée, and he had been a bulldog trying to track her down. Malcolm must have known Shane wouldn't give up. Something Malcolm would have totally understood since he was doing the same thing to get justice for Tina.

"Want to save your brothers?" Malcolm repeated to Chase. "If so, yell for them to put down their guns. They won't be hurt."

"And I'm supposed to believe that?" Chase challenged. "You've killed Shane, Crossman, Deanne—"

"Deanne was a mistake," Malcolm snapped. Not exactly an ice-cold voice now. There was some anger in it, too. "That was Renée's doing, wasn't it?"

There was more sobbing from Renée. "It was an accident. No one was supposed to die. The man I hired panicked when he spotted Chase."

"Well, someone did die." Malcolm sounded so angry that April thought he might shoot Renée then and there. "You had only one thing to do. Use the baby to draw out Quentin, and instead you got Deanne killed. She was Tina's CI, and they were close. You'll pay for that, bitch."

So, that explained why Renée's head was on the chopping block. Malcolm was trying to take care of anyone who'd wronged Tina or him.

April glanced back at Malcolm. "I can't believe you trusted Renée with my daughter."

"Nothing was supposed to happen to the baby. I warned Renée of that right from the start. I liked Bailey. In fact, the only reason I didn't gun you down when I first saw you in the hospital was because of her. I didn't want you shot in front of her."

Sweet heaven. He'd been planning to kill her even then. And April wouldn't have seen it coming. She'd been so torn up about Bailey's premature birth that she hadn't realized the danger was so close to her.

Too bad. Or maybe she could have ended it before it got this far.

There was more gunfire. All of it came from the front of what was left of the church. Probably more hired guns taking shots at Jericho and the others. She prayed they'd be able to stay out of harm's way, especially since she might not be able to save Chase.

That broke her heart.

He could die here. And all because of her. April wished she could go back and undo the damage, but instead more people, including Chase, could keep paying for the mistake she'd made. Malcolm would almost certainly kill both of them once he had this plan finalized.

And that meant Bailey would be an orphan.

April felt the tears spill onto her cheek. Then, she felt something else. Something much, much stronger.

The rage bubbling inside her.

She was letting Malcolm drag her to her death, and that was about to end. If she was going to die anyway, she'd do it fighting. April used that rage, pinpointing it into her fist. She whirled around and punched Malcolm as hard as she could.

Malcolm staggered back. Just a little. Just enough to off-balance him. She knocked the gun from his hand as Chase tackled the man. They both went crashing into the debris, some of it falling on them.

April knew she couldn't just stand there and watch. She snatched up Chase's gun, and she fired at the gunman standing over Dexter. She wasn't sure who was more surprised—him or her—when the bullet hit him right squarely in the chest. He collapsed onto the ground before he could even get off a shot.

Renée screamed again, and April pivoted in that direction, ready to stop the second gunman. But Renée was clawing at the man's face, and she kneed him in the groin. Again. And again.

The gunman fired, but his shot went into the dirt. So did he, and he howled in pain while Renée just kept kicking him.

"Get his gun," April told the woman.

Renée did that, after she kicked him again. She ripped

the gun from his hand, shot him in the stomach before she whirled around, her gaze landing on Malcolm. No scream this time. Just a low feral sound fueled by her rage. Considering that her face was streaked with blood and her nostrils were flaring, April doubted the woman had any control left.

And that meant Renée could possibly shoot Chase while she was gunning for Malcolm.

She raced toward Renée, to try to latch on to the gun. But again, she was too late. Screaming, Renée pulled the trigger.

April could have sworn her heart stopped. Her breath certainly did. It stalled there in her lungs, and it seemed to take an eternity for her to get to Chase and pull him away from Malcolm.

There was so much blood.

Too much.

"Chase," she managed to say. "Don't die. Please don't."

He shook his head. "It's not my blood. Well, most of it anyway."

It took April a moment to fight through the panic and realize he was right. Chase's shoulder was still bleeding, but it was nothing compared with the blood on Malcolm's chest.

Renée had shot him.

Chase took April by the arm, maneuvering her away from Malcolm. In the same motion, he yanked the gun from Renée's hand.

"I hit him," Renée said. "I hope I killed him."

Not yet. Malcolm was still alive, his eyes open, but he wasn't moving, and he was losing way too much blood to stay alive for long.

April saw the movement from the corner of her eye

and pivoted in that direction. It was Jax and Jericho. Thank God. And they had their attention focused on that other car. The one that no doubt contained other gunmen ready to do Malcolm's bidding.

"I hope you burn in hell for murdering Shane," Renée said, spitting on Malcolm.

April held her back. Not because she thought Malcolm deserved to stay alive for even a second longer, but because he appeared to be trying to say something to Chase.

"Two out of three's not bad," Malcolm mumbled, his voice weak, and the life draining out of his eyes.

"What do you mean?" Chase asked.

"I got Crossman." Malcolm lifted his gaze to April. "And while you and Chase might walk away from this, your brother won't. Quentin's a dead man." He lifted his hand, the same gesture he'd used with the other gunmen. It stayed in the air just a second before it slumped to the ground.

Malcolm didn't draw another breath.

Almost instantly, the door to the other car opened, and Quentin stepped out. Alive. But she soon realized what Malcolm had meant when he said her brother was a dead man. There was another of Malcolm's hired killers behind Quentin, and he had a gun pointed at Quentin's head.

"Tell your brother goodbye," the man taunted. "Because you're about to see him die right before your eyes."

This wasn't a bluff. She felt that in every part of her body. Quentin obviously did, too. He wasn't fighting. He'd already surrendered.

"Give me the gun," Chase said to April.

She handed it to him, not sure what Chase had in mind. And she didn't have to wait long to find out, either.

Without warning, Chase lifted the gun and fired. Not

a head shot. Probably because he would have hit Quentin. Instead, Chase shot the gunman in the leg.

The guy howled in pain. Staggered back a step. Just enough for Chase to shoot him again. The bullet smacked into his shoulder and put the gunman on his knees.

Quentin didn't waste any time grabbing the man's gun, and he turned, aiming the weapon at him. For a moment, April thought Quentin would shoot the man in cold blood. But Quentin cursed, lowered the gun and started toward them.

The relief flooded through her. But it didn't last. Because she looked at Chase and saw something she didn't want to see. More blood. The front of his shirt was red now, and choking back a sound of pain, he leaned against her.

"Call an ambulance," April shouted, and she caught on to Chase a split second before he lost consciousness.

Chapter Twenty

Chase opened his eyes. And he groaned. What he wanted to do was curse, but the first person he saw was April, and she had worry written all over her face. It was on Jax's and Jericho's faces, too, and Chase was responsible for it being there.

"I'm all right," Chase insisted, and he sat up. Or rather that's what he tried to do, but that's when he realized he was in a hospital bed and hooked up to an IV. He also realized he was in pain.

What the heck?

He remembered getting shot, of course. Hard to forget that, especially now with the blistering pain. He also remembered being in an ambulance, but everything was a little fuzzy after that.

"You're not all right," April said. Oh, man. She'd been crying and was still blinking back tears. "You had surgery to remove the bullet from your shoulder, and lost a lot of blood."

Jericho looked down at him. "He's fine. Chase is used to getting shot and stabbed, aren't you, little brother?"

That was a bad joke. But also true. He had been shot and stabbed before. Chase appreciated his brother's attempt at humor because it lightened his mood a little. However, it didn't work for April.

She went closer, eased down on the edge of the bed next to him. "You could have been killed."

He hated seeing her cry or hearing her voice break. It crushed his heart six ways to Sunday. And that's why he pulled her down for a kiss. Chase figured they both could use it, and he was right, though he wasn't sure how his brothers would react to the kiss.

Nor did he care.

There was a cut on April's head, and he moved away her hair so he could see it better. That set off a new wave of rage inside him. Malcolm had been responsible for that. Responsible, too, for nearly getting them all killed.

"Where's Bailey?" he asked.

"In the hall. Levi and Mack brought her from the safe house and your mother has her. Your mom will bring her in to see you in a few minutes. I just wanted to make sure you were up to it first."

Chase didn't even have to think about that. "I'm definitely up to it."

Like the kiss, seeing Bailey was something he needed, though he was certain his mom was enjoying every second of holding her first and only granddaughter.

"How's everyone else?" Chase asked. "Was Dexter or Quentin hurt?"

All three of them shook their heads. "Shaken up but okay," Jax continued. "Dexter's got a concussion from the blow to the head, but he'll be fine." He paused, his gaze drifting to April.

"Quentin's in a holding cell," April finished for him. "He'll be charged with faking his kidnapping."

"Jail time?" Chase added.

Jericho shrugged. "Some. If he had a clean record, maybe not, but this isn't his first rodeo."

"Jail time might do him some good," April snarled. "Even Quentin agrees with that, and if he hadn't, it wouldn't have mattered. I'm not bailing him out."

Good. Because Quentin had to grow up eventually, and even if he didn't, it was obvious that April was going to make her brother stand on his own two feet.

"Please tell me Malcolm's really dead." Because Chase hoped that wasn't something he'd dreamed.

"He's dead," Jax verified. "And Gene Rooks has decided that now that his boss is dead, he'll talk to get a few of the charges off the table. Rooks told us that Malcolm had explosives planted under the church when he found out that's where Deanne's funeral would be. Malcolm was guessing April might show up."

And she had. All because they'd wanted to set a trap. A trap that backfired big-time.

"When the explosives didn't work," Chase said, "then he turned his hired guns on all of us."

Chase cursed again, and April leaned in, stared at him. "This wasn't your fault. Or even mine. I know that now. If Malcolm hadn't come after us at the church, he would have found another way. Maybe a way that would have involved Bailey."

She was right. Malcolm was rich and willing to do anything to get revenge for Tina's murder. Since he'd found someone willing to hack into WITSEC files before, he likely would have tried it again and again until he found April and him. And Bailey would have indeed been with them.

"You're being logical about this," Chase pointed out to her.

April shook her head, blinked back more tears. "Not logical. Just thankful we're all alive."

Yeah, he was right there with her, and Chase wished he could have a moment alone, to tell her things. And kiss her.

Mercy, he wanted to kiss her.

But judging from Jax's and Jericho's expressions, there was still more they had to say. "Renée didn't escape again, did she?" Chase asked.

"No," Jericho jumped to answer. Now there was something more than concern for him on his brother's face. There was relief. "She's in custody, and after her hearing she'll be taken to the mental hospital. With all the charges against her, she'll be there a long time."

More good news. Not that Chase thought Renée would come after them, but she needed some serious help. "Did Renée say how she knew that Malcolm had shot Shane?"

Jax nodded. "Renée's been as chatty as Rooks. Malcolm lured her to a meeting near the church. He told her that Quentin wanted to see her. She didn't trust Malcolm so she called Shane to go with her. Malcolm shot Shane and then kidnapped Renée."

So Malcolm could no doubt set her up to take the blame for April's and Quentin's murders. And his plan might have worked if April and he had been killed in the explosion. Then, the gunmen could have picked off Quentin, too. That would have left a mentally unstable Renée holding the bag.

"I don't suppose Rooks or Renée knew anything about Crossman's murder?" Chase asked.

"No," Jericho verified. "The prison warden will investigate, of course, but I'm betting he won't get any confessions."

Probably not. Malcolm had paid someone to murder Crossman, but he'd also probably covered the money trail so that it couldn't be traced back to him. Since Malcolm had been at the prison that same day, it was even possible he'd managed to slip someone cash to shank Crossman.

"With Crossman dead and Malcolm dead, there's no reason for us to go to WITSEC," April said, caution in her voice. "Right?"

"Right," Chase assured her. Of course, that left them both with a really big question.

What next?

Chase didn't have much time to consider that because there was a light tap on the door, and when it opened a few inches, his mom peeked in. Smiling. At first, but then she got that worried look everyone had when he'd first woken up.

"I must look pretty bad," Chase told her, "but it's okay. I'm fine."

And he was, and that fine part went up a significant notch when his mother stepped into the room and Chase saw she had Bailey in her arms. The baby was wide awake and looking very content to have her grandmother holding her.

"I brought you a visitor," his mother said, coming closer to the bed.

April kissed Bailey, and his mom leaned in to put Bailey into the crook of his good arm. Bailey looked up at him, and she smiled.

Now, that was a cure for pain and just about anything else.

"She's such a good baby," his mother announced. "I hope I get to spend lots of time with her after you move April and her to the ranch." She paused, froze as if she'd said the wrong thing. "Sorry, I guess that's something you two probably need to talk about."

It was, and his brothers picked up on that right away. Jericho took out his phone and mumbled something about needing to check on a few things. Jax suddenly wanted to get home to see his son.

"Why don't I wait in the hall for a little while," his mother added. "Want me to take the baby with me?"

Something else Chase didn't have to think about. "No. Leave her here." He wasn't ready to let go of Bailey just yet, even though it would be harder to kiss April with the baby in his arms.

Or not.

April proved him wrong because the moment his mother stepped out of the room, April kissed him. No logistics problems at all, and it wasn't as if he was in any shape to haul April off to bed anyway.

Soon, though, maybe he could remedy that. Maybe he could remedy a lot of things.

"I want Bailey and you to move in with me," he tossed out there. Not that it was a surprise offer since his mom had already suggested it. And Chase waited. Breath held. Because what April said next would be some of the most important words he'd ever hear.

"Are you sure you want that?" she asked.

Well, it wasn't the enthusiastic response Chase had hoped for, but he was certain of the answer. "Absolutely. The danger's over, and there's no reason you two can't be there. Is there?" he added when April's forehead bunched up.

She didn't say anything for several really long moments. "But are you sure it's what *you* want?" It was nearly the same words, but he picked up on the under-current of her question.

"I want you there." Chase managed to maneuver her closer so he could kiss her again. "I want *you*."

When he eased back from her, he saw relief, but it wasn't relief he was going for. "We have a beautiful daughter," he reminded her. "She's perfect, but I think we can build on perfect."

Again, he waited, but April's forehead only bunched up even more. "I'm in love with you," she blurted out. "There, I said it, and I don't want to unsay it, either. I love you and I don't want to just move in with you, I want—"

He kissed her again. Hard and long. Hopefully enough for her to realize it wasn't necessary for her to defend her love for him or the life she wanted together with Bailey and him.

Because Chase wanted the same thing.

The kiss left her a little breathless, Him, too. And it left him wanting a whole lot more.

"I want it all, too," he told her. "You, the baby…the home. Together. Oh, and I want you to marry me."

He hadn't meant to make that sound like an after-thought. It wasn't. It was something he'd been think-ing about since he'd come too darn close to losing April today. That ordeal hadn't made him fall in love with her, but it'd been the knock upside his head to make him re-alize it.

Tears came back to her eyes. Then, a smile. "You're proposing?"

"You bet I am. I would get down on one knee, but I'm not exactly in any shape to do that. Just use your imagi-nation and imagine that I'm on one knee."

April smiled. "I'm imagining a lot of things when it comes to you."

So was Chase. And he couldn't wait to get started on all of it.

Bailey squirmed, kicked at him as if reminding him she was a part of this, too. "I just asked your mom to marry me. What do you think she'll say?"

Bailey smiled.

"That's the right answer," April said, kissing Bailey. Then, Chase. And then April made the moment perfect with just one word.

"Yes."

* * * * *

"Do me a favor?"

"I'd do anything for you."

In that instant, she believed he meant those words. Her heart ached. "Kiss me."

There was just enough room between those bars. He could kiss her once more. It would be a kiss goodbye.

Sullivan instantly leaned toward her. His lips brushed against hers, and then that kiss deepened.

She hated the bars. If only she could touch him fully. Savor him.

Why had fate been working against them from the very beginning?

She gave herself fully to that kiss, trying to forget everything else in that moment but him. She'd always loved his taste. Loved the way his lips pressed to hers. Her heart galloped in her chest and she pressed ever closer to him.

She'd never wanted anyone more.

ALLEGIANCES

BY
CYNTHIA EDEN

All rights reserved including the right of reproduction in whole or in part in any form. This edition is published by arrangement with Harlequin Books S.A.

This is a work of fiction. Names, characters, places, locations and incidents are purely fictional and bear no relationship to any real life individuals, living or dead, or to any actual places, business establishments, locations, events or incidents. Any resemblance is entirely coincidental.

This book is sold subject to the condition that it shall not, by way of trade or otherwise, be lent, resold, hired out or otherwise circulated without the prior consent of the publisher in any form of binding or cover other than that in which it is published and without a similar condition including this condition being imposed on the subsequent purchaser.

® and ™ are trademarks owned and used by the trademark owner and/or its licensee. Trademarks marked with ® are registered with the United Kingdom Patent Office and/or the Office for Harmonisation in the Internal Market and in other countries.

First Published in Great Britain 2016
By Mills & Boon, an imprint of HarperCollins*Publishers*
1 London Bridge Street, London, SE1 9GF

© 2016 by Cindy Roussos

ISBN: 978-0-263-91903-5

46-0516

Our policy is to use papers that are natural, renewable and recyclable products and made from wood grown in sustainable forests. The logging and manufacturing processes conform to the legal environmental regulations of the country of origin.

Printed and bound in Spain
by CPI, Barcelona

Cynthia Eden, a *New York Times* bestselling author, writes tales of romantic suspense and paranormal romance. Her books have received starred reviews from *Publishers Weekly* and she has received a RITA® Award nomination for best romantic suspense novel. Cynthia lives in the Deep South, loves horror movies and has an addiction to chocolate. More information about Cynthia may be found at www.cynthiaeden.com, or you can follow her on Twitter, @cynthiaeden.

Thank you, Denise Zaza and Shannon Barr!
It is truly a pleasure to work with you
two wonderful ladies.

Chapter One

"Hello, Sullivan."

At that low, husky voice—a voice Sullivan had heard far too many times in his dreams—his head whipped up. He blinked, sure that he had to be imagining the figure standing in his office doorway. He even shook his head, as if that small movement could somehow make the woman before him vanish.

Only she didn't vanish.

She laughed, and the small movement made her short red hair brush lightly against her delicate jaw. "No, sorry, you can't blink or even wish me away. I'm here." Celia James stepped inside and shut the door behind her.

He rose to his feet in a quick rush. "I wouldn't wish you away." Just the opposite. His voice had sounded too gruff, so he cleared his throat. He didn't want to scare her away, not when he had such plans for her. *And she's actually here. Close enough to touch.* "Should you… should you be here? You were hurt—"

Celia waved that injury away with a flick of her hand. "A flesh wound. I've had worse." Sadness flickered in her eyes. "It's Elizabeth who took the direct hit. I was afraid for a while…but I heard she's better now."

He nodded and crept closer to her. Elizabeth Snow

was the woman his brother Mac—MacKenzie—intended to marry as fast as humanly possible. Elizabeth was also the woman who'd been shot recently—when she faced off against a killer who'd been determined to put Elizabeth in the ground.

Only Elizabeth hadn't died, and in that particular case…it had brought Celia back into Sullivan's life.

Now I can't let her leave.

He schooled his expression as he said, "She's out at the ranch. And I'm sure Mac is about to drive her crazy." He was absolutely certain of that fact. His brother had broken apart when Elizabeth was shot. There was no denying the love Mac felt for her. "I think his protective instincts kicked into overdrive." *So did mine. When I saw you on the ground…*

Because Elizabeth hadn't been the only one hurt on that last case. Celia had also been caught in the cross fire.

But Celia didn't appear overly concerned with the injury she'd received. "I was knocked out for a few moments. My head hit the wall." Her calm expression dismissed the terrifying moment, but then, he knew it took a lot to terrify her. "The bullet just grazed me."

He hadn't realized that fact, not at first. He'd just known that she was limp in his arms.

A whole lot had sure come into crystal-clear perspective for him in those desperate moments.

"I came to make you a deal," Celia said as she took a step toward him.

His head tilted to the side as he studied her. "A deal?" Now he was curious. Celia wasn't exactly the type to make deals. She was the type to keep secrets. The type to always get the job done, no matter what.

During Sullivan's very brief stint with the CIA, he'd met the lovely Celia.

And he'd fallen hard for her.

Until I thought she'd betrayed me.

"I have information you want." She pulled a white envelope out of her purse. "I'll give it to you, but you have to promise me one favor."

Suspicious now, he asked, "And just what favor would that be?" She had plenty of government connections. She didn't need him now. Never had. He knew that now.

Her smile flashed. A smile that showed off her dimples. Those dimples were so innocently deceptive. So gorgeous.

So Celia.

They made her appear so delicate.

But the truth of the matter was…Celia James was a trained killer. One of the best to ever work for the CIA.

And she doesn't make deals.

Yet she was standing in his office, asking for one. The whole scene felt surreal to him.

"You have to agree *before* I tell you what I want." She shrugged. "Sorry, but it's one of those deal-in-the-dark situations. Promise me that you'll be there when I call in this debt. That you'll agree to what I need, and this information is yours." She waved the bulky envelope a bit, as if tempting him.

His gaze stayed locked on hers. He wanted to touch her. Needed to kiss her. Instead, he stood there and forced his body to be still. "Just what information is it that you *think* you have?" He didn't understand why Celia thought he'd be interested in any deal she had. He'd more than made it clear that he'd never work for the CIA again. He'd barely escaped before, when he'd been caught in a web of lies and death.

"I have your mother's real name." Her voice was soft, almost sympathetic.

But he wasn't impressed by her big reveal. He and his brothers had already uncovered his mother's real last name. They already knew—

"And I have the reason she was put in the Witness Protection Program."

Now, *that* information…he didn't know. And he was sure curious about why his mother had given up her previous life, adopted an entirely new name and wound up in Austin, Texas.

For years, Sullivan, his brothers and his sister had been working desperately to unmask the identity of the killers who had murdered their parents. One dark Texas night, two gunmen had broken into the McGuire ranch. They'd killed Sullivan's mother, then his father. Sullivan's sister, Ava, had managed to escape and get help, but that help hadn't arrived in time.

Years later, they were close—*finally* close—to unmasking the killers. They'd worked tirelessly on the case. When the local law enforcement authorities had given up the hunt, the family had formed a private agency, McGuire Securities. They'd kept working to solve a crime that would *never* be a cold case, not to them, and along the way they'd helped others with their investigation firm. McGuire Securities now had a topnotch reputation that drew in clients from the South and all along the East Coast.

Years ago, Sullivan had sworn he would never stop searching for the truth about that dark night, not until he'd given his parents the justice they deserved.

Celia offered the envelope to him. That white envelope looked so small and harmless in her hands, but it had the potential to change so much. "Do we have a deal?" Celia asked. "One favor, no questions asked… and you can have her past."

He stared at the envelope, and then he looked back up into Celia's blue eyes. "Deal." To learn more about his mother, he would have promised anything.

A faint sigh slipped from Celia's lips. She hurried toward him, closing the last of the distance between them.

His hand lifted and he took that envelope from her. Their fingers brushed, and the touch sent a hot, hard stab of need right through him. But that was the way it was for him when Celia was near. He saw her, he touched her and he just wanted. Some things couldn't be changed, no matter how much time passed.

"I'll be seeing you soon, Sully," she said as her fingers fell away from his. "And…good luck to you." Then she turned away and headed for the door.

That was it? She asked for a deal then just walked away? "Same old Celia," he murmured. "Secretive to the core, aren't you?" He put the envelope down on his desk.

She glanced back at him. Her red hair contrasted with her bright blue eyes—eyes that gave no hint to her emotions. "You know my life has to be about secrets."

Because she was an agent. CIA. Right. He got that. She was a real-life chameleon. When he'd known her before, her hair had been black. Her eyes…they'd been green. At first he'd thought he was seeing the real Celia back then. He hadn't known just how much of a mask she truly presented to the world. Then he'd gone to a team meeting a few days later, and she'd been blonde. With bright blue eyes.

The same eyes I see now.

She'd been able to change her appearance so quickly. She'd been able to *become* someone else with total ease, even adopting a new accent on command. She'd told him once that she could only be real with him.

With everyone else, she had an image to keep.

I should have believed her. But he hadn't. When the danger had closed in, he'd turned his back on her. "Would it matter," Sullivan asked her, aware that his voice had roughened, "if I told you that I was sorry?"

Something happened then. For just a moment, he saw a flash of emotion in her eyes.

Pain.

He hated that he'd hurt her. If he could, he'd take away any pain that she felt. He'd make sure she *never* felt pain again.

"Are you?" Celia asked him, cocking her head just a bit, as if it was now her turn to study him. "Are you sorry?"

He stared at her a moment, the past and present merging for him. He'd been drawn to Celia from the moment they first met. Without hesitation, he'd given in to his hunger for her. The passion had been hot, raging out of control, and when their world had imploded, he'd thought she'd been using him. Seducing him.

He hadn't realized—not until too late—that she'd loved him.

I lost her. "Yes," Sullivan said gruffly. "I am."

She smiled, and it was a smile that held bite. "Good. Then maybe when I come calling for that debt, you won't hesitate."

"I won't." He crossed the room and hurried to her side. He reached out to her.

But Celia put up her hand, stopping him. "Don't."

He wanted to touch her. Hold her. "Why can't we start again?" Did he sound desperate? Maybe. So what? When she'd been hurt on that last case, when she'd been lying so still on the ground, *everything* had changed for him. His priorities had shifted instantly.

Getting justice for his parents? Hell, yes, he would do that. He'd made a vow to himself, to his family, and he would keep it.

But getting Celia back in his life? Back in his bed? That was his immediate goal. Holding tightly to her and never letting go had become his obsession.

"We can't start again because you nearly destroyed me before," Celia said. "I needed you, and you left me."

He flinched at her soft words. Celia wasn't pulling any punches.

"But…" Celia shook her head. "You were always one fine marine, and you were incredible as a field agent."

Until he'd been taken. Because he'd been distracted…

By her. No, it hadn't been Celia's fault. None of it had been. Sullivan had been the one who wasn't on his game. He was the one who hadn't taken enough precautions. And he was the one who'd been afraid of what would come in the aftermath of his capture.

Even then, I didn't want her hurt. Even then, I was afraid of what could happen to her…because of me.

Her gaze was still on him. "I know that when you give your word," she added, "you mean it."

His hands fisted because the urge to reach out to her was too strong. He wanted to touch her. To see if her skin still felt like silk. Her scent—sweet, light—rose and wrapped around him.

"I'll see you again soon," she said. Then she opened the door. The heavy carpet swallowed her footsteps as she left him.

He stood there a moment, fighting the past and trying to figure out what the hell he should do in the present.

Go after her.

His head snapped up when he heard the ding of the elevator. And then Sullivan was racing down the hallway. The rest of McGuire Securities was deserted, so no one witnessed his frantic run. And it *was* frantic. But he couldn't just let her go, not like this. His hand flew out and he stopped the elevator, activating the sensors in the doors right before they closed.

Celia's eyes widened as she started. "Sullivan, what are you doing?"

What he should have done the first moment he looked up and saw her standing in his office.

"I gave you the envelope." She sounded dazed. "Have you even looked inside it?"

No, he'd left it on his desk, unopened. *Priorities.* He strode into the elevator.

She backed up against the wall. It was the first time he'd ever seen Celia retreat from anyone.

"I missed you," he gritted out.

Her lips parted.

"And you don't get to just vanish again."

Before she could respond, Sullivan leaned forward and he kissed her. His hands pushed against the elevator wall on either side of her head and he put his mouth on hers.

Her lips were still parted, just a bit, and his lips met

hers in a hot, openmouthed kiss. She tasted so sweet—even sweeter than he remembered—and Sullivan's heart drummed wildly in his ears. He held his body carefully away from hers, only touching her with his mouth. Touching her and trying like hell to seduce her with his lips and tongue. He kissed her a bit deeper, a bit harder, savoring her because it had been far too long since he'd been with her like this.

Far, far too long.

Dreams weren't enough for him. Memories weren't getting him through the long nights any longer. He needed her. Not a ghost. The real woman.

His Celia. But even as he deepened that kiss—

Her hands pressed to his chest and she shoved him back.

Sullivan's breath sawed out as he stared down at her.

"Do you like hurting me?" Celia demanded.

What? "No, hell, *no*."

"My life isn't some game. My emotions can't just be jerked around by you because you're in the mood to push my buttons." Her lips were red and plump from his kiss. Her eyes glittered with fury and passion.

"I wasn't—"

"In case you missed it before, Sullivan…" Her chin lifted. "Our marriage is *over*. You signed the divorce papers, remember?"

And he felt that shot, right in his heart. "Yes, I remember." He wished he could forget. *I thought I was doing the right thing. I was poison. She didn't need me.*

Though he'd always needed her.

"Get out of the elevator. When I need you, I'll be back."

He turned away from her. Exited that damn elevator. No one else was on the floor. It was way past operating hours. He wasn't even sure how she'd gotten up to his office.

Celia has her ways... Celia can do anything... Hadn't he heard folks say that about her time and again when he'd been working with the CIA?

Hell, most of his family didn't even know about the work he'd done for the government. Most of them didn't know a thing about Celia.

Mac knew.

And Sullivan…he'd tried so hard to forget her. An impossible task.

Before the elevator doors could shut, he lifted his hands, pushing against them. His gaze held hers. "What about when I need you?" It was a question torn from him.

She blinked in surprise. Or maybe in shock. A faint furrow appeared between her eyes.

"You said that…when you need *me*, you'd be back." Sullivan inclined his head toward her. "What about when I need you, C? What then?" Her old nickname rolled off his tongue. *C.* So simple, but…

It was our link. Only I called her that.

Back when she'd been his.

She laughed. It was a hollow, bitter sound. Not Celia's real laughter. He'd heard that light, musical sound once before. A lifetime ago. When would he hear her real laughter again?

"Oh, Sullivan," she said, her lips twisting in a cold smile. "We both know the truth. You've never really needed me. You wanted me for a time, but you never let me get close. When the chips were down, you turned on me."

Because he'd been told she betrayed him. Told again and again as his blood drained out in a dark, dank hell-hole.

"Don't do that again," she warned him. "Don't turn on me. I...I don't have a lot of options. I have to count on you."

"You can." He would *never* betray her again, and Sullivan would do whatever was necessary to prove that to her. He exhaled slowly and backed away. His hands fell back to his sides. The elevator doors began to close. "And just for the record...I think I need you more than I need anyone or anything else."

He saw the flash of surprise on her face.

Then the doors closed.

Breathe. Breathe. Breathe. Mentally, Celia James repeated her little mantra.

Only it was hard to breathe because she could still taste Sullivan. She could still feel his lips against hers. And when he'd dropped his last little bombshell on her, she was pretty sure her whole world had spun out of control.

She hurried across the darkened Austin street. She could hear the distant buzz of traffic. Random horns. Voices drifting on the wind. But...

Sullivan. Sexy Sullivan McGuire. *He* was what consumed her right then. And that was the problem with him—he always slipped past her guard. He always made her too nervous and aware. She couldn't afford the way he made her feel, not now. Not with all the other craziness happening in her life.

She was leaving the CIA. Leaving the agency that had been her life for far too long and...

I'm being hunted. She had enough going on without developing a new addiction to Sullivan.

Right…as if that were a *new* thing. She'd been craving him from the moment she looked into his green eyes. Then she'd heard the deep rumble of his voice. Seduction. Just straight-up seduction. She'd been lost before they'd even shaken hands and had been officially introduced.

She'd never looked up and just *wanted*. Until Sullivan, she'd always been so carefully controlled in all aspects of her life. But Sullivan had pretty much obliterated her control. He'd made her want to live for something other than the job.

When he'd left her, the job had been all she had left.

I won't make the same mistakes with him. Not this time. This time, she called the shots. He owed her.

Time had been kind to Sullivan. He was tall, fit, with powerful shoulders that had only gotten broader in the years they were apart. His dark hair was still thick, and her fingers had itched to slide through those heavy locks.

No, her fingers had just been itching to touch him. Sullivan had always attracted her. Like a moth to the flame, she'd been pulled right to him.

Not the same mistakes. Not!

Celia jumped into her car. She cranked the engine and drove away as fast as she could.

She'd only gone about four blocks before she realized she was being followed. That was four blocks too many. She should have spotted the tail instantly. But she'd been distracted…

By Sullivan.

Her hands tightened around the steering wheel.

She'd thought that she'd made a fairly clean escape when she'd sneaked down to Austin. She hadn't realized that the hunter on her trail had gotten so close.

And dammit, I led him straight to Sullivan.

Because if the guy on her trail had been waiting outside McGuire Securities...then he'd know about Sullivan and her connection to the McGuires. She'd gone to Sullivan for help. She hadn't intended to drag him straight into her nightmare. At least, not this fast.

She kept her left hand on the wheel even as her right activated the car's Bluetooth so she could call Sullivan. She'd memorized his cell number days ago—she had a knack for remembering pretty much everything. One of the reasons why she had been a good agent.

Had been.

He answered on the second ring. "Sullivan."

"It's me." She glanced in her rearview mirror. The headlights behind her were getting ever closer. Surely the guy wasn't going to hit her? Not on a public street.

"Celia, what—"

"Watch your back. I think I brought my trouble straight to your door. I—" The car behind rammed into her, and Celia's words ended in a sharp scream. Even as that cry escaped, she tightened her grip on the steering wheel and fought to keep her car steady.

"Celia? *Celia?*" Sullivan roared.

"Watch yourself," she said.

Her car had hurtled forward at the impact, but, thank goodness, she hadn't hit anyone or anything else. She shoved the gas pedal down as hard as she could. Her car shot forward, but the vehicle behind her, the one with the shining lights—

Killed the lights.

"Celia, what is happening?" Sullivan demanded.

She cut across the lanes, moving fast. She knew this city well, so she'd be able to disappear. Hopefully. But if that guy hit her again...

What is he thinking? Attacking in public?

"I've got company," she said as she fought to keep both her voice and the car steady. "The kind that isn't so friendly."

"Where are you?" he barked.

"Escaping," she told him honestly. And she was. She'd just turned down a dark side street. Celia turned off her own lights and whipped into the nearest parking garage. "Bye, Sullivan."

"No, Celia, wait—"

There was no time to wait. There was only time to survive. She was good at surviving. Celia jumped from her car and ran as fast as she could toward the shadows of the parking garage. She wouldn't have much time. She could already hear the engine of the other vehicle. An SUV waited a few feet away, and she rushed behind it, crouching down just as the squeal of tires reached her ears.

I knew my time was limited... I just didn't realize how close the hunter was to me.

Her heart slammed into her chest as the car braked just a few feet away. She reached into her boot and pulled out the knife she still kept strapped to her ankle.

Some habits sure did die hard.

She slipped around the SUV, keeping low and making certain not to make so much as a sound. The way she figured it, Celia had three options.

Option one...she could try to break into one of the parked cars and get a ride out of there. She would have to switch cars and temporarily *borrow* another if she went with the escape-in-a-vehicle option, because her car—with its busted bumper—wasn't going to get her far.

Option two…her eyes narrowed as she searched the garage's dim interior. Instead of stealing—um, borrowing—another car, she could rush for the nearest exit and escape on foot. Escaping on foot gave her a maneuverability advantage, but it sure wasn't the fastest option.

And, finally, she had option three.

She could fight.

Since she was armed with a knife and she had no idea what type of weapon the hunter had, fighting might not be—

"I know you're out there, Ms. James," a man's booming voice called. "So why don't you just save us both some time? Come out here…and let me put a bullet in your lovely head."

So he has a gun. Good to know.

"Because I have only one directive. Kill you. And I won't stop, not until you're dead."

That news was just rather unfortunate. Too bad for him, though. The unknown man wasn't going to achieve his directive any time soon—she had no intention of dying.

Her gaze slid to the red Exit sign she'd just spotted.

Knife versus gun wasn't such a good fighting option.

So I think I'll go with my second choice. Time to run…

"CELIA? CELIA?" SULLIVAN ROARED. But she wasn't answering him. The line had gone dead.

He shoved the phone back into his pocket, grabbed the white envelope she'd given him and then he rushed out of his office. He was in the elevator before he realized—hell, he had no idea where Celia was. He only knew she was in trouble. That she'd called him—telling him to watch his back.

And she'd screamed.

She could be hurt. And I don't know where she is. I can't help her.

The elevator took him to the ground floor. He rushed outside. Looked to the left. To the right. He didn't see anyone, but he wasn't going to stand there and keep making himself a target. He hurried to his car. Jumped inside.

"Celia…" Sullivan whispered her name as he cranked the vehicle and pulled away. "Where in the hell are you?"

Chapter Two

When he got home, Sullivan locked his door and reset his alarm. He'd driven around the damn city for far too long, searching in dark alleys, looking for any sign of Celia before he'd had to give up and head to his place.

He was sure that she'd been involved in some kind of accident. He'd heard what he *thought* was the crash and crunch of an impact when they'd been talking, but no accidents had been reported—he'd double-checked that with one of his contacts at the PD.

Celia had seemingly vanished.

Sighing, he turned on the lights. Tomorrow, he'd search for her again. He *would* find her.

"You're starting to go soft," Celia said, her voice calm and clear. "I mean, really, you didn't even know I was here?"

He spun around and found her sitting on his couch. She was leaning back against the cushions with her legs crossed in front of her, looking as if she didn't have a care in the world.

She's been here while I was searching the whole city for her? Frantic? He'd been imagining her broken body tossed away. And she'd been in his home.

"How long have you been here?" Sullivan asked

her. Her voice had been calm. His was tight with fury and fear.

Celia pursed her lips and glanced toward the clock near his TV. "About an hour. I was starting to think you must have been out with a hot date."

He stalked toward her. "I was out looking for *you*. I was tearing up the damn town because I thought you'd been hurt. I thought someone was after you and—"

"Someone was after me. Or rather, someone *is* after me." She didn't sound particularly worried. Her gaze held his. "A tail followed me from your office. He tried to take me. Or, actually, I think he was more interested in killing me than taking me. But that doesn't matter." She shrugged, moving her shoulders lightly against the leather of his couch. "He failed in his attempt."

Every muscle in his body locked down. "Take you?" Sullivan repeated. *"Kill you?"*

"Um…you know, the usual in our business. When forcing me off the road didn't work, he followed me into an old parking garage. I'd slipped inside there, thinking to use the place for shelter."

"Celia…"

"Like I said, he followed me. Jumped out of his vehicle. Gave me some nice line about how it would be easier if I just came out so he could put a bullet in my head."

His vision reddened as fury burned in his blood.

"I wasn't in the mood for that bullet, so I got away." Her words were said so simply. As if she hadn't just faced some life-or-death battle when he was far away and couldn't help her at all.

"How?" Sullivan demanded.

"The parking garage was dark, but it wasn't empty.

Other people approached from the elevator bank, so he had to put up his gun and act *not* killer-like. When I heard those folks approaching, I slipped away into the shadows and got out of there as fast as I could."

So the guy was still breathing. "He's a threat to you."

She just stared back at him.

"You saw him, though," Sullivan said, thinking quickly. "You got his description. With your contacts, you can find out who—"

"I didn't see him. I didn't stick around to get a full physical description. He had a gun, I had a knife, and with civilians in the area, I didn't want to risk them." Her fingers tapped along the arm of his couch. "So I left, without looking back. And as quickly as I could I…came here."

Her words gave him pause. "You came to me?" Sullivan stood about two feet away from her. He wanted to close that distance, scoop her up and hold her tight. Because he wanted that so badly, he kept his muscles locked and didn't move another step forward.

"I'm afraid I've brought you into this mess as a target. It's obvious that I went to McGuire Securities tonight, and if the guy after me has done any digging into my past, he'll know about you." She rose and came to stand right in front of him. "I'm sorry. I didn't mean to shine a bright target on you."

Sometimes, he forgot how delicate—physically—she was. She barely came to his shoulders as she stood there in her bare feet. He saw that she'd kicked her heels away, and they lay overturned next to his coffee table.

His hands lifted and his fingers curled around her shoulders. "You know I don't mind danger."

"That debt I was going to call in? It wasn't to protect me," she said. Had her eyes ever seemed bigger? Bluer? "I can protect myself. It was…I needed you to help me vanish."

He frowned at that bit of the news.

"I'm leaving the CIA. I've been compromised." She gave that bitter laugh again. The one that made him worry she'd changed—too much—since they were together. "Compromised again and again. I thought I could get away clean, but it sure seems my enemies aren't going to stop hunting me."

"You know who they are…"

"Actually, I don't. I've made a lot of enemies in my time at the agency. I joined right after college, was recruited straightaway. I was perfect for them, after all. No family. No close friends. No ties that would hold me back. I could become anyone they wanted me to be, and for a while, I did."

His hold tightened on her. "You have ties now."

"No, I don't. And that's why it was going to be so easy for me to leave."

But what had happened? Why was she quitting the agency? "The CIA was your life."

"Was it?" Her eyelashes flickered and then she seemed to notice that he was touching her. He felt her stiffen beneath his hands. "I'm sorry I broke into your place. After everything that went down tonight, I just needed to make sure you were all right."

She'd been worried…about him?

"But no one saw me enter your home. I was careful this time."

She pulled away. He let her go, but the temptation to hold her—it was far too strong.

"Maybe I will call in that debt you promised me

one day. My plans have changed now, so who knows?" She pushed back her hair, tucking a lock behind her left ear. "Remember what I said before, though. Watch your back."

She was walking away. Again. And he knew that if she slipped away, he wasn't going to see her again. Despite her words, she wouldn't be back to call in her debt. He suspected she wouldn't return to him at all. "Who is going to watch yours?" Sullivan wanted to know.

Celia tilted her head back as she gazed up at him. "Oh, Sully, be careful," she chided him. "It almost sounds as if you care about what happens to me."

I do. I never stopped caring, no matter how hard I tried. Some obsessions couldn't be conquered. "Stay here," he heard himself say, his voice way too gruff.

Celia shook her head. "What?"

He cleared his throat. "Stay the night. You said yourself that no one saw you come into my place. That means you're safe here. Stay the night. Get some sleep. Then you can make a new plan of attack or escape—or whatever the hell it is you want to do—in the morning."

She bit her lower lip. After a moment, voice strangely subdued, she said, "You know that's not a good idea."

"Do I?" It had sounded like one damn fine idea at the time.

"Yes." She sighed out that answer. "Sully, you know that—"

"I still want you." There. He'd said it. This time he wouldn't have lies or secrets between them. He'd tell her everything, because he wouldn't crash and burn again. Neither would she. Not on his watch.

"No." She put up her hand, as if to ward him off. "Stop it. Just…*stop it.*"

No way. He wasn't stopping. He could see her slipping away, and if she did—what would he do then? Go back to the bleak, empty world he'd been living in since he lost her before? Go back to looking at crowds—and always searching to see if he'd find her?

Mac had brought them back together on that last case. Sullivan had tried to warn his brother that he'd made a mistake. *How am I supposed to let her go again?* But Mac had been blind to the danger.

The simple truth was that Sullivan couldn't let Celia go. Not without losing too much of himself.

"I can't stop wanting you. Baby, I tried, but it just doesn't happen." He caught her hand in his and put it against his heart. A heart that always beat faster when she was near. "You think I don't know how much I screwed up before? I didn't trust you. I— Hell, I won't make the same mistake again. Give me a chance."

Her gaze searched his, but she shook her head. "I can't."

Those words—it felt as if she'd just driven her knife into his heart when she said them. The knife he knew she liked to keep strapped to her ankle.

"I can't go down this road with you again, Sully."

"I'm not talking about forever." He had asked for that, once. And he'd gotten it, with her. In a Vegas chapel, on one wild weekend. He'd promised forever to her.

I want it again.

But he knew he had to take small steps this time. "I'm talking one night. One night of safety for you. I have a guest room you can use. Just stay with me tonight. Tomorrow, we can make another plan together."

Maybe by tomorrow, he would have figured out a way to keep her with him.

"Hasn't your family been through enough?" Celia asked him. "Do you really want me and my danger close by?"

It wasn't about his family—and that alone told him just how far his obsession with her had gone. Family had always come first for him. The bond that he shared with his brothers and with his sister, Ava, was unbreakable, but...

But this isn't about them. It's about Celia.

"You have new evidence that can help you find your parents' killers," she said. "You should be sharing it with them and not—"

I haven't even opened the envelope. I was too worried about you. "It's almost midnight. Anything new I have can wait." Their parents had been waiting to receive justice for years. A few more hours wouldn't change anything. "Stay with me, Celia. I need to know you're safe tonight." And that was when he noticed the faint dark mark on her right cheek. His right hand lifted immediately and lightly touched that bruise. A bruise she *hadn't* possessed when she'd been in his office before.

"I think my cheek hit the steering wheel," she said, and Celia swallowed as his fingers lingered against her skin. "I got lucky—the air bag didn't deploy and I maintained control of my steering. If he'd hit me harder, the car could've died right there. He would've had me."

No one is getting you, Celia. I'm here now. "You saved my life once," he reminded her.

She gave a quick, hard shake of her head. "No, that's—"

"Did you think Mac didn't tell me? He did." *And as a thank-you, I signed divorce papers.* Dammit, could he have been more of a blind fool? He had so much to atone for with Celia. If he could just convince her to give him a chance…

"Your brother talks too much," she muttered darkly.

He laughed at those words. Sullivan just couldn't help it. Mac was pretty much the definition of the strong, silent type. The only guy more closemouthed than Mac?

That would be me.

Her face softened a bit as she stared up at him. "You should do that more, you know."

"What?"

"Laugh. Let go of that iron control of yours and just enjoy life."

His laughter faded away. "Maybe you should follow the same advice." *And you should stay with me. Just for the night.* "Are you always on guard?" Sullivan asked her.

Her dimples flashed, but her smile wasn't real. "You tell me. You lived in my world for a few months. Is it really the kind of place where you can let down your guard?"

He'd joined the CIA and worked in the Special Activities Division, or SAD, as the group was called. He'd been undercover, working to make a difference, desperately trying to collect needed intelligence in a hostile country—only that case had gone to hell, fast. Friends had become enemies, and he'd found himself on the run.

Then…captured.

Tortured.

Left for dead.

"You can let your guard down with me, Celia. Trust me, just for this night," he told her. Because now he could see the edge of fear that she'd been working so hard to conceal at his office. And...she was pale. Shadows were under her eyes, shadows that even the careful application of makeup couldn't hide.

She needed rest. She needed safety.

I want her to need me.

"Just for the night," Celia said. "Only that."

He actually shook his head because he hadn't thought she'd agree, but— "You'll stay with me?"

"Just for the night," she said again. "Come morning, I have plans."

She pulled away from him and headed toward his hallway. "Which one is the guest room?"

It took a moment for her question to register. She'd never been in his house before, so she didn't know her way around. They'd been married, but...he hadn't brought her to his home. He hadn't introduced her to his family. He'd said his *I do* part to her, then taken a mission almost the next day. He'd been shipped out of the country. She'd been scheduled to follow him two days later.

But...everything had changed.

"The third door," he said. "On the left."

She looked back. "That better not turn out to be your bedroom there, Marine. Because trusting you to give me a place to crash tonight is *not* the same thing as trusting you in bed."

If only.

"My bedroom is the first door." Had his voice been too gruff? Maybe. The thought of her in his bed had made him sound too rough.

She turned away.

He called out, "But feel free to go in there. Because you can trust me on this…if you go to my room, I will give us both what we need."

If she'd give him the chance, he'd give her everything. Anything she wanted.

"Don't hold your breath on that one," Celia threw back at him. Then she vanished down the hallway.

His breath expelled on a long rush. *I've got you in my house, baby. That's step one…*

"YOU LOST CELIA JAMES?"

Porter Vance winced as he heard the rage, transmitted so very clearly over the phone. "Look, boss, the woman is CIA. It's not like she isn't trained to—"

"*You're* ex-CIA. You're supposed to understand her moves. You're supposed to find her and eliminate her. End of story."

Porter glanced around the busy intersection. The parking garage was behind him—the garage that contained Celia's abandoned vehicle. "You were right, you know," he said, trying to distract the boss. "She did go to see Sullivan McGuire. That's where I found her. I just parked myself right outside McGuire Securities and she damn near came running out of the business and straight at me. I trailed her, had her in the parking garage on Forty-Seventh Street and then…" He cleared his throat.

"Then you lost her. A woman that I paid you ten thousand dollars to eliminate."

Right. He hadn't exactly gotten the money yet. It was one of those pay-on-delivery deals. So far, he hadn't delivered a dead Celia James. "I'll get her. Listen, I'm already back at McGuire Securities. She'll show here again. If she doesn't, I'll just use Sullivan to get her. She's still tied to him. He can be the bait. When she knows I've got him, she'll come running to me."

Laughter carried across the line. "Sullivan isn't easy prey. None of the McGuires are...but especially not *him*."

There was something in the boss's voice...

"Do you think I didn't try to eliminate him? Do you honestly think I didn't do my best to kill that guy when I had the chance?"

"I—"

"Your usefulness is at an end."

It took a moment for those cold words to sink in.

And another minute to realize...

I've been shot.

Because the bullet had been so quiet as it found its mark. There was no bang. No boom. Just a faint whistle as it cut through the air and sank into Porter's chest.

And then the pain came, burning slowly through his heart.

He looked down. It was dark there, too dark for him to see clearly but—

My shirt is wet. I'm bleeding.

He still had the phone in his hand. Still had it pressed to his ear. But his legs were crumpling and Porter knew...the boss had called him so that he'd be distracted. The boss had already known he'd failed at his mission.

And the boss didn't accept failure.

He was watching me. He called... He was going to kill me, no matter what I told him. Maybe because he'd just been another loose end.

Just like Celia.

The phone fell from his fingers and he crashed onto the concrete.

Chapter Three

"Will you marry me, Celia?"

She lay in bed, the covers pulled up to her chin, and the past wouldn't stop haunting her.

"Don't tease, Sully. When you say that to a woman, she might just take you up on the offer." They'd been in Vegas. Bright lights. Slot machines. Parties that didn't stop.

The champagne hadn't stopped, either.

But she hadn't been drunk. She couldn't pretend that she had. Sully…

"I'm not teasing." His handsome face had been dead serious. That wonderful square jaw of his had been hard with determination. His green gaze had seemed to see straight into her soul. *"I want to be with you, C. Tonight and always. Marry me?"*

Her hold tightened on the covers. There were no rings on her fingers—not any rings at all. But he'd given her one that night. When they'd pulled up at that little chapel. When she'd been almost delirious with happiness. When she hadn't been able to stop smiling.

"I love you." Her words, to him. She should have known, even then, that it wouldn't work. Because Sullivan hadn't told her that he loved her. He'd held that

part back. He'd kissed her wildly. Made love to her endlessly that night. But…

But did he ever love me?

She wasn't sure that he had.

And now she was in his home. In his spare bedroom. And she couldn't stop thinking about *him*.

"This isn't working." The sound of her own voice was jarring, but maybe she needed to be jarred. Because for her to just agree to stay with him—how wrong was that? She knew exactly how bad the guy was for her. She'd gone to his office because—yes, she actually had planned to use him. He had connections in Mexico, and she'd intended to call in her favor when she slipped over the border. She hadn't planned to wind up in Sullivan's bed.

Celia dressed as quickly as she could. As soon as she was gone, her first order of business would be finding new clothes. Maybe changing her hair again. Red was actually her natural color, but by the time she cleared the border, she intended to be a brunette. Maybe a brunette with green eyes? It'd be easy to pick up some contacts and then she'd nearly be a new person.

Again.

She tiptoed into the hallway. Celia figured she'd been in the guest room for nearly an hour, maybe two, tossing and turning and replaying her past too many times. Sullivan would be asleep by now, and she'd sneak out of his house as quickly and easily as she'd slipped in. But maybe she'd leave the guy a note, telling him that he really needed to install a few new security measures. The setup was good, but *not* good enough and—

"Celia."

She froze in front of his open bedroom door. He'd

spotted her. It wasn't pitch-black in the hallway. Light spilled in from the den, illuminating the narrow corridor. She turned her head and stepped toward his room, her movements still soundless. She started to speak.

"Celia, don't go."

Words froze in her throat.

He sounded so desperate. When had Sullivan ever been desperate? She inched closer, her chest seeming to burn, and then—

Moonlight spilled through his blinds, revealing his form in that big, sprawling bed. Sullivan's muscular chest was bare, and the sheets were tangled around his hips. He was rolling a bit in the bed, and his eyes were *closed.*

Surprise held her motionless.

Sullivan had picked up a few habits since they'd last been together. It seemed that he now talked in his sleep. And he dreamed about…her.

A low warmth bloomed in her belly.

She found herself stepping toward him. The floor creaked beneath her feet. Celia froze, but it was too late.

So much for being quiet.

Sullivan instantly shot up in bed.

"Sully—"

In an instant he had his hands on her. She could have escaped his hold. Could have fought and had *him* tumbling back, but she didn't. He caught her in his arms and pinned her between his body and the door frame.

"Celia?" His hands slid over her. "What is it? What's happening?"

Oh, just the usual. I was sneaking away in the middle of the night. She wet her lips and tried to figure out a nice excuse that might work. And one that just might not make her seem like the coward she was.

He wasn't holding her prisoner any longer, not now that recognition and consciousness had hit him fully. In fact, he'd backed up a bit so that his body wasn't touching hers at all. But he was still there, a strong, immovable object in her path, and the heat from his body seemed to wrap around her. Her hand lifted and her fingers slid over his chest.

She hadn't meant to touch him...had she?

He called for me in his sleep.

Her fingers trailed over his chest, and she felt the raised marks on his skin. "You didn't have these scars before." She knew she was touching scars. In her business, you could always recognize them. Carefully now, she slid her hand down and felt more scars along his ribs. Another near his stomach. Another—

His hand locked around her wrist. "Be careful just how far you go." In the darkened room, his eyes glittered at her.

She swallowed the lump in her throat. "Did you get those scars when you were captured?" The last mission he'd worked with the CIA. The mission that had changed *everything*.

Traitors had been revealed. Loyalties had been tested. And when the blood and dust finally cleared, he'd left her.

And she'd picked up the pieces and carried on.

"My captors wanted information." His voice was a hard growl, but his fingers were lightly stroking the inside of her wrist. Could he feel her skyrocketing pulse? "They were real interested in learning everything they could about the Special Activities Division."

"I didn't betray you." Hadn't she told him that before? When she'd finally gotten him on the phone after that brutal mission. He'd refused to see her when she tried to visit him at the hospital. Mac had gruffly turned her away, but she'd finally gotten Sullivan on the phone and—

It's over, Celia.

Her eyes closed. Her cheeks burned. "Why couldn't you have trusted me?"

"Because I'd spent seven days in a hellhole. They'd sliced me open. They'd nearly killed me—again and again—and all the while, they kept telling me things that only *you* should know. They told me you'd been playing me, from the very beginning. That you'd sent me out there, knowing they'd capture me. That you weren't on that transport with me because you were keeping your cover in place. That everything that happened to me…it was because of you."

Pain hit her so much harder than she'd anticipated. So hard it stole her breath and left her gasping. "I didn't… I wouldn't! I'd never—*not to you!*" How could he have thought, even for a moment, that she'd done that to him? That she'd married him one day then betrayed him the next?

"I was in hell, C. *Hell.* Barely alive when Mac pulled me out."

"I know," she rasped. "I was there. Who do you think drove the getaway jeep?" But he should know that. Mac had said—

"What?" Stunned surprise was in his voice.

"I was there. Don't act like Mac didn't tell you. I know he did." She'd been there, and she'd seen the blood on him, but she hadn't been given the chance to fully take stock of all his injuries. She'd been too busy driving hell fast to get them to safety. Then the transport chopper had whisked him away and she'd stood below, watching the dust and sand billow around him. There hadn't been enough room for her and Mac on that chopper. So she'd backed away and let Mac stay with his brother.

And when she'd finally gotten back to him...

It's over, Celia. She tried to slam the door on that memory before it hurt her even more.

"Mac told me...he said that you used intel to find me...that you helped...but hell, no, he never said you were there." Sullivan sounded stunned.

"I was there." And she'd heard his words so clearly as she'd driven that jeep. *It was...Celia. Never trust... her.* "I didn't give up on you. I wouldn't have." Even if he'd given up on her. She fought to keep her emotions under control. She had to get away from him. Staying had been a definite mistake. But she couldn't stop herself from saying, "You were a marine, first and foremost. You should have known that you can't trust your captors. They always try to make you turn on the people you *should* be trusting." It was a basic rule of survival. Never trust them.

"They knew so many things about you," Sullivan said. "About us. Things I'd only told *you.*"

They were lying. "I need to leave." This wasn't working. In fact, she felt as if she were about to splinter apart. "Get out of my way and let me go."

He didn't move. "You were running from me, weren't you? Trying to slip away in the dark? You were going to vanish without saying good-bye."

Her chin notched up. Could he see that little movement? "No, I wasn't just going to vanish," she said flatly. "I was strongly thinking about leaving you a note first."

And then he was touching her. Sullivan put his hands on her shoulders and pushed her back against that door frame once more. His heat scorched her. "A note?" His voice was strangled. *"A note?"*

"Let me go." Or he'd find out just how strong she was.

"I can't. I tried that before, but you came back, and now we're both in trouble." Then his head lowered toward hers. She expected a kiss. Hard. Angry. Passionate. She wasn't going to respond to him. She wasn't.

But his mouth didn't crash down onto hers.

Instead, his lips…feathered over her neck. Over the pulse that raced so frantically, for him. He kissed her skin lightly, tenderly, moving in a sensual trail along the column of her neck.

He remembered.

Even after all the time that had passed, he still remembered how much she'd enjoyed it when he kissed her there. How the passion had spiraled inside her from such a tender touch.

A moan built in her throat and slipped free before she could hold it back.

"I love that sound," he whispered against her. "I missed it."

Her eyes had squeezed shut. She wondered how the world had gotten so out of control. Once, she'd nearly had everything she wanted. Now…everything had been ripped away. Tears stung her lashes, but she'd never let those tears fall.

She couldn't.

"Celia, I want you."

Wanting had never been their problem.

I want him so much right now that I'm shaking.

But taking him wasn't an option. Was it?

His hands slid down her arms, moving closer to her elbows, and she felt the edge of his fingertips skim over the curve of her breasts. She sucked in a sharp breath. "Sully..."

"Do you know how many times you've been in my dreams?"

Her eyes opened. She blinked the moisture away. "You were dreaming about me tonight. I heard you." His call had stopped her.

"And that's why you didn't run away? Why you came to me?"

No, she hadn't been going to him. She'd just wanted to make sure he was all right. "I thought you were calling out to me."

"I've called out to you a hundred times, but this is the first time you've heard me."

His words didn't make sense to her. "Sully..."

"I love it when you say my name like that."

"I can't." *Can't be with you. Can't do this.* "Goodbye." Then, yes, she jerked from his arms and pretty much ran from that room. She—

His phone was ringing. A loud, hard music beat that followed her.

She paused, escape so close but...*no calls this late are ever a good sign.* She looked back in time to see a light flash on—Sullivan had turned on his lamp.

Sullivan grabbed his phone from the nightstand,

yanking it off the charger. "Sullivan." The light from the lamp spilled around him.

Naked. The man is totally naked.

She'd just had that long talk with a naked man. No wonder he'd grabbed her wrist when she'd been searching for his scars. She'd almost touched something a whole lot bigger than a scar.

"What? In front of our building? Hell, no, that can't be... Listen, more is going on here. It's..." His gaze cut toward her. "Celia is with me," he said. "She was chased tonight. She thinks some bozo followed her from our office. Yeah, yeah..." His hold tightened on the phone. "My gut says there is a connection, too. I'll be right down there. I want to see the guy."

She inched closer to him. As soon as he lowered the phone, Celia demanded, "What happened?"

"That was Mac. A man was killed right in front of McGuire Securities, shot in the heart. Mac is down there now because a cop buddy tipped him off."

Her breath came a little faster. "You don't buy that the guy's death is a coincidence, do you?"

"After what went down with you tonight? Hell, no, I don't. I want you to see the body. *I* want to see him."

She shook her head. "I told you already, I didn't get a look at the guy after me tonight."

"No, but that doesn't mean you don't know him. It wouldn't be the first time someone in the agency decided to turn traitor."

"I heard his voice." And she hadn't recognized it.

"And I've heard you adopt nearly a dozen accents at will. Voices can be disguised. I want to see this guy. Once we get an up-close look at him, we'll know more."

She cleared her throat. "And I'd, um, really appreciate it if you'd cover up."

He glanced down at himself and swore. Then he grabbed a sheet and wrapped it around his hips. "Happy now?"

"Not really." She edged a bit closer to him. "But I'm going with you. Have they already transferred the body?"

"Mac says they're working on that now. But don't worry, I've got a friend who will give us access at the medical examiner's office."

She knew exactly how well connected the McGuire family was in Austin. "If it is the guy who was after me," Celia said, her mind spinning, "then how'd he wind up dead?"

Sullivan just stared back at her, and she could almost hear his suspicions.

"It wasn't me," she snapped. "I didn't kill him."

"Celia—"

"But why would you believe me, right?" She turned away. "Forget it. *I'll* call Mac. He can take me to the body. You just stay here."

"You don't need my brother's help. You have me."

She glanced back at him. *No, I don't.*

"And I never said I thought you'd killed anyone. But you haven't told me why the man was gunning for you."

I don't know why. I just know that he's been coming after me. My home wasn't safe, so I had to run, fast. And I ran to you.

A move that had been a serious mistake.

"I'm trying to figure all this out," Sullivan said. "Maybe the dead man was just the flunky doing the dirty work and someone else is out there pulling the strings."

Her lips pressed together. She had the same suspicion that he did. Maybe the guy's boss had gotten fed up with his failure.

"Perhaps his employer didn't like to hear that you'd slipped away." Sullivan was dressing now, yanking on jeans and a T-shirt. "Maybe that made him so angry that he decided to take out that frustration on someone."

And he'd killed a man? Unfortunately, she knew just how often events like this occurred. That knowledge was one of the reasons she was ready to escape the dark world she'd lived in for so long.

A woman could only handle so much death and despair before they started to choke the life from her.

HE'D CALLED THE authorities and anonymously left a tip about the body's location. If he hadn't, it would have been dawn before Porter's body was discovered. He hadn't wanted to waste that much time.

Celia James was off the grid. He needed to get her back in the game ASAP. And a dead body pretty much dropped at her ex-lover's business? That should snag her attention.

Especially since I think Sullivan is helping Celia once more.

But it wasn't Sullivan McGuire who raced to the scene when the blue lights first appeared on Austin Street. It was Sullivan's older brother, Mac. A foe just as dangerous.

From the shadows, he watched as Mac talked with the cops, acting as if he was old friends with them. Probably because he was. The McGuires had gotten in deep with the cops while trying to unmask their parents' killers.

And you still haven't found them, have you?

He smiled at that thought. *What would you do, Mac, if you knew I was right there when your parents were shot? I'm across the street from you right now. So close, and you haven't got a clue...*

And Sullivan...blind Sullivan...he'd been in the same room with the guy before. He'd worked missions with Sullivan, and the guy had been completely in the dark.

Porter's body was being loaded up now. He'd been zipped up and was being placed in a van for transport to the coroner's office. Mac headed back to his car, seemingly leaving the scene.

This can't be it.

The guy wasn't just going to walk away. But...wait, Mac *had* called someone before. He'd seen him place the call. Had Mac phoned Sullivan?

And when the medical examiner's van pulled away from the scene, he saw Mac leave in his vehicle and tail that van.

Ah...*going after the body.* That made sense. Mac would try to ID the fellow. And as the watcher shifted position, he realized, *I bet Sullivan will go after the body, too.*

His plan was working. He just needed to trail behind, carefully, and see what happened next. Celia would show herself soon enough, and then she'd be the one loaded into the back of the medical examiner's van.

THE MEDICAL EXAMINER'S office was cold. Icy. From the corner of his eye, Sullivan saw Celia shiver. He wanted to wrap his arms around her, but he doubted she'd ap-

preciate that gesture, so…he shrugged out of his coat
and put it around her shoulders.

She glanced over at him, her eyebrows shooting up.

"You were cold," he said simply.

Her fingers caught the coat. "Thank you."

He offered her a smile. "I brought you to a morgue,
C. It's not like I took you out on some fancy date. I
should—"

"We've never gone on a fancy date."

Her words gave him pause. Then he realized…hell,
she was right. They'd worked missions. They'd rid-
den out hard and desperate adrenaline highs together.
They'd shared passionate nights that were permanently
singed in his memory.

But I never took the woman out on a real date?

He would never dig himself out of the hole he'd dug.
"I'm sorry," Sullivan said gruffly. "If I could go back
in time, there are about a million things I'd do differ-
ently with you."

Her gaze cut away from him.

"Celia…about our marriage…" It was definitely past
time he cleared up a few issues there. "You need to
know why I proposed."

She laughed. The bitter laugh. The *not* Celia laugh.
"You were drunk. We'd both worked too many cases.
We were both—"

"You said you loved me."

"No." Her voice was hard. Cold.

And something inside him died. *She didn't love me?
She—*

"We are not doing this here. We are not talking about
our past, about my feelings for you, in a morgue! It's
dark, you snuck me in here like we were robbers, and

the place smells. This isn't where we have that conversation, got it?"

He cleared his throat. "I, um, got it." But his lips were quirking. How had he forgotten her wonderful bite? Damn, but he could fall for her again so easily.

The doors to the morgue swung open. A gurney was pushed inside by a whistling man who seemed totally oblivious of their presence.

Sullivan had a quick déjà vu moment. He'd flipped on his own lights and found Celia just waiting for him.

But then the man pushing the gurney glanced over at them and offered a broad smile, and Sullivan realized this wasn't some county employee.

"What in the hell?" Sullivan demanded. "Mac?"

His brother shrugged. "Figured you'd be waiting inside. I told the ME to take a little break." He pushed the gurney forward and paused to pull on a pair of gloves. "We are so screwing with the chain of evidence here, so don't touch him, okay? Just look at the body, nothing more."

The chain of evidence? Yeah, they were messing with it, all right. Because they weren't supposed to be there, but…when Mac lowered the zipper and Celia gave a sharp, indrawn breath, Sullivan knew that his instincts had been dead-on.

"You recognize him," Sullivan said.

"Hi, Celia," Mac murmured. "Good to see you again…"

She inched closer to the body, but she made no move to touch the dead man. "His hair should be blond, not black. But yes, yes, I know him." She looked up at Sullivan. "I trained him, right after you left. He was my next assignment."

Because Celia was a handler. She brought in the new agents. Trained them. Guided them.

"Porter Vance," she said softly. "He can't be the man who tried to kill me. He had no reason to come after me!"

"He appears to have been staking out McGuire Securities…" Mac said.

"Just like the guy who followed me earlier," Celia murmured.

"And he had a gun," Mac added. "It was found on scene, so I think it's safe to say the fellow wasn't just hanging around for some friendly little chat." Mac's voice was curt. His green eyes were solemn as he stared back at her, and his face was tense.

Celia glanced over at Sullivan. "You think he was there to kill me. That he was waiting for me to show again?" Her gaze slid back to Mac. "That's what you both think?"

"I don't think he was there selling Girl Scout cookies," Mac drawled.

Sullivan forced his back teeth to unclench. "He was lying in wait, Celia." It was the only thing that made sense to him. "You gave him the slip before, so he went back to McGuire Securities. Maybe he thought I'd lead him to you."

"But someone took Porter out instead," Mac said. "So either someone was protecting you, Celia, or someone shut this guy up so he couldn't reveal anything about who wanted you dead." He paused just a moment. "I realize it's been a while since Sully and I have been in the business, so I don't know…just how many enemies have you made lately?"

She'd paled as she stared at the dead man. Sullivan

studied the guy. Porter Vance appeared to be in his thirties, maybe late twenties. He had short hair, a muscular build and a bullet hole in his chest.

"I didn't think Porter was my enemy," Celia said softly. "He had no reason to want me dead. He was... he was one of the good guys." Her right hand lifted and she rubbed her temple. "At least, I thought he was."

Mac glanced over at Sullivan. "One shot, straight through the heart. I talked with the forensics team on scene. Based on the angle of entry and the bullet used, they think it was a sniper shot, probably from the building directly across the street. Porter probably never saw the attack coming." He inclined his head. "A smashed burner phone was found beneath the body. No ID was on the fellow, but like I said before, he was armed. The cops took his gun into evidence." Then he glanced at his watch. "Our five minutes are nearly up. We need to clear out of here, now." He zipped the bag back up.

"Porter," Celia said his name again. "This just doesn't make sense to me. He left the CIA a year ago. There's no reason for him to come after me!"

But he was there.

And he'd tried to kill her that night.

"Porter was always good with voices and accents," Celia muttered as she kept rubbing her temple. "Even better than me. I should have remembered that. He was one of the chameleons. He could become anyone on command." Her lashes lowered. "Just like me."

"Okay...again..." Mac cleared his throat and glanced over his shoulder. "Our five minutes are about up. I promised we'd be out of here. Our presence can't exactly be widely known, unless you want to explain to all the authorities just who Celia is."

No, he didn't intend to explain her to anyone. They'd sneaked in the back door and his contact had let him in. Only one person had seen Celia so far. Others would be arriving soon, so it was definitely time to go.

"We have a starting point now," Sullivan told Celia as he caught her elbow and steered her toward the door. "We start with him and we work back. We can figure this out." They were in the hallway now, and Mac was following close behind them.

"There's no *we* in this thing," Celia said. She squared her shoulders. "Your part is done. I obviously made a mistake contacting you. Don't you see that? There was a dead body dropped—almost literally—on your doorstep." She shook her head. "I should have just emailed you the information about your parents and not tried to work a deal."

"Uh, our parents?" Mac demanded. "Just what information do you have on them, Celia?"

Her gaze cut to him. "I know why your mother entered the Witness Protection Program. I know who she was before she changed names and moved across the country. I know the real reason she was running."

Mac took an aggressive step forward. "And that reason would be?"

Celia looked back at Sullivan.

I haven't opened the envelope yet. He'd waited because he wanted to share that information when his family was all together. And because he'd been too tangled up in her. "I was calling a family meeting in the morning," he explained quietly. "Things got a little...out of control, so I didn't get to call you."

"Right, *out of control*." Mac nodded. "I can see that. Dead bodies can lead to a loss of control."

Celia was hurrying down the hallway.

"So can sexy ghosts from your past," Mac added.

After shooting a glare at his brother, Sullivan took off after her. He'd only taken a few steps when Mac grabbed his arm. "Maybe you need to let her go."

"Are you kidding me?" Sullivan gaped at him. "You're the one who told me I made a mistake! You're—"

"I'm the one who saw how much you hurt her before. And I'm the one who doesn't want to see her in pain again. If you aren't serious about her, you need to just back off. She's got enough to deal with now as it is."

An enemy—one killing in the shadows. "She won't even tell me why she's being targeted. It's like she doesn't trust me."

Mac laughed. "Well, I guess that means you know how she felt before, right? Sucks, doesn't it? When someone turns on you?"

He heard the clatter of her heels. She was at the end of the hallway. A few more moments, and Celia would be outside.

But we came in my car. It's not like she'll hot-wire it and leave me.

Hell. She would.

He shoved his brother aside and rushed after her.

She opened the door. Darkness waited.

"Celia!" Sullivan yelled. "Don't—"

There was a whistle of sound, then a *thunk*. Wood flew into the air—splintering away from the door—even as Celia dove back inside the building. She hit the floor before he could reach her. Sullivan was pretty sure that his heart stopped when she slammed into the ground.

The bullet didn't hit her. The bullet didn't hit her.

He grabbed her arms and yanked her away from the still-open door. He held her close, his grip probably too tight, but he didn't care, and he backed down the hall-way as fast as he could.

"What in the hell was that?" Mac snarled.

"That…" Celia huffed out a hard breath. Her body was tense against Sullivan's. "That was someone who wants me dead. And that bullet would have hit me if Sully hadn't called my name."

And in that last instant, she'd turned back. She'd moved back toward him. The bullet had missed her head and hit the door.

Too close. Too close.

"This is a county facility!" Mac's grating voice seemed to echo around them. "To attack here…this guy is freaking insane."

Insane…or just very, very determined to take out his target.

And now Sullivan realized just why Porter had been killed and left at McGuire Securities. "The shooter knew we'd come to look at the body. He wanted to draw you out so he could—"

"Try to kill me?" Celia finished. She glanced up at Sullivan, her dark lashes making her blue eyes appear even brighter. "Yes, I figured that out, too. Right after the bullet nearly lodged in my head."

It was hard to breathe. *She can't die.* "You're not run-ning from me," Sullivan rasped.

Mac was on his phone. Probably getting all his cop buddies ready to search the scene out there. The shooter had missed, though, and Sullivan was betting he wasn't just going to sit around while the authorities closed in. No, he'd flee, for the moment.

And then come back for another attack.

"You're not running," Sullivan said again. "You're going to tell me exactly what's going on. Why you're on some nut job's hit list… And then *we* are going to stop him." He'd let her down once before. He'd be damned if he did it again.

Chapter Four

The McGuire ranch.

Celia shivered a bit as Sullivan's car headed down the winding drive that led to the main ranch. She'd never been out to the ranch. Never met any of Sullivan's family—well, except for Mac. Mac knew plenty of her secrets.

But after the shooting, Sullivan had insisted she head out to the ranch. And after her discovery about Porter's identity and that near bullet to the head, she'd needed a safe haven.

Havens didn't get much safer than the McGuire ranch.

She knew all about the dark history of that ranch. Years ago, Sullivan and his brothers had all left home—they'd gone out, trying to save the world, in their own ways.

Grant McGuire, the eldest brother, had been a lethal Army Ranger. Davis and Brodie—the twins—had both excelled as Navy SEALs. Mac…he'd been Delta Force, as cold and deadly as a man could be. Then Sullivan, the youngest of the brothers, had signed up to be a marine.

She'd tapped into their files during her time at the CIA. She'd read accounts of their dangerous missions.

She'd been impressed—and a little awed—by all that they'd accomplished.

At the CIA, she'd actually been the one to suggest recruiting both Mac and Sullivan. Their exploits had caught her attention. She'd been the one to bring Sullivan into the nightmare... *It was my fault he was taken.*

Her fingers twisted in her lap. Yes, she'd been the one to do all the digging into Sullivan's life. She'd been the one to first put him on the CIA's radar.

It started with me.

They drew closer to the ranch. The sun had risen and she easily saw all the vehicles parked there. The whole family had obviously gathered for this meeting.

They're not here for me. I'm just the tagalong. They're all gathered to learn about the past.

Sullivan was going to share the information she'd given to him about his mother. The McGuires would continue their search for justice.

While I hide.

Oh, how the mighty had fallen.

She exhaled slowly and peered up at the house. It had been rebuilt, rather extensively, by Brodie and Davis. She really knew far too much about the McGuire family. But learning about them...it had been almost a compulsion for her.

Because of Sullivan.

While Sullivan and his brothers were out protecting the world, evil had come to the ranch. Sullivan's mother and father had been gunned down in their own home, and Ava—the baby of the family—had been forced to bear the brunt of the tragedy. For years, rumors had swirled that Ava had even been involved in their deaths.

She hadn't been.

She'd been a victim.

There are so many victims.

Sullivan braked the vehicle near the main house. He killed the engine and turned his attention toward her.

"Thanks for giving me a place to stay," Celia said softly. "I won't be here long. I just need to pull some intel together and then I'll be—"

"I've already told you." His voice was a rough growl that made goose bumps rise on her skin. The rather good kind of goose bumps. "You're not running from me again."

I didn't run before.

Her gaze slid from his and headed toward the house once more. A man had just come out. Like Sullivan, he was tall, with dark hair and broad shoulders. "What are you going to tell them about me?"

"What do you want me to tell them?"

Her index finger tapped against the side of the door. "Do they know you were married to me?"

"No."

That hurt. But she wouldn't let him know that he'd just ripped into her heart. She forced a smile to her lips and turned toward him. "Of course they don't. It was really just a brief thing. A mistake easily forgotten."

His eyes narrowed.

"I don't think they need to know anything about our past." Maybe her words came too quickly, but she was suddenly desperate to get out of that car and put some distance between them. "Just tell them I'm a client. I can even pay you, if you want. Make it legit so you don't have to lie to your family."

"Celia…"

She shoved open her door and bolted from the vehicle. Mac had followed a bit behind them, and she heard the approach of his car. She was pretty grateful for his timely arrival. Mac had always been a friend to her.

She could really use a friend right now.

Sullivan slammed his door and hurried to her side. She stiffened her spine and glanced up at him with raised eyebrows. All in all, it had been one heck of a night, and the morning wasn't looking much better for her.

He never told them about the marriage. In case there had been any doubt, now she knew with certainty—he really hadn't cared about her.

"While you talk to your family, I just need a quiet place to make a phone call." She'd picked up a burner phone before they'd left the city. The cops—and Mac—had searched for the shooter, but he'd been long gone. She'd had to watch from the shadows while that search was conducted. She hadn't wanted to talk with the cops. That would just have been a complication she didn't need.

That shooting had been too close for comfort. *Another step forward, and I would have been gone.*

So maybe her night hadn't been as bad as it *could* have been.

"I want you with me."

The dark-haired man on the porch had been joined by another guy—a guy who looked exactly like him.

The twins. And they were both staring at her a bit suspiciously. Wonderful. If they knew that she had a man gunning for her—literally—she was sure they'd look even less welcoming.

Hello, there. My name's Celia. And I just brought death to your door. Oh, yes, they'd love her.

She just knew how to make a killer first impression.

Sullivan's hand reached for hers. Instinctively, she stepped back.

Pain flashed on his face.

Join the club, buddy.

"Celia?" Sullivan whispered. "What's wrong?"

She started to bite her lip but then thought—*why?* There was no need to hold back any longer. She had nothing to lose. "Oh, let me see… I just found out that the man I married decided I was so beneath him that he never bothered to tell his family about our wedding. I mean I get it," she snapped, anger pulsing through her. "You thought I was part of the group that set you up. I wasn't. I went in to save your ungrateful butt, but you wouldn't listen to me."

A car braked behind her. She looked back and saw Mac.

She didn't calm down. "Mac knew the truth. He never thought I was some terrible double agent out to kill you." Her heart was about to burst out of her chest. "Why could he trust me?"

Mac was climbing from his car now and closing in.

"Why could he," she pushed, "but not you?"

"Because I was a fool."

That answer just wasn't good enough. She looked back toward the porch. At his brothers. The family she was supposed to just meet with a fake smile. "I can't do this." Not anymore. Wasn't that why she was getting out of the game? Leaving the CIA? Because she was just *done*. "I'm going to the guesthouse." She spun on her heel.

"You…know where it is?"

She laughed and glanced over her shoulder. "Hi,

there," she said with a little wave at Sullivan. "I'm CIA, remember?" Well, *ex*-CIA. "It wasn't exactly hard to research your family and home. So, yes, I know about the guesthouse. And I'm heading there." Not into the fire of his home with his family. "When you're done… hell, don't come to me, okay?" She turned and focused on Mac. "After your family talk, will *you* come and get me?" Mac owed her. She'd helped him *and* his bride-to-be, Elizabeth. And that case—well, it had been the final straw for her.

"What's going on?" Mac wanted to know.

She could only shake her head. She'd just been pushed too far. Too hard. Her life was hanging in the balance, and Sullivan—

Will the pain ever stop?

Sullivan reached out and locked his fingers around her arm. She froze. Her frantic gaze met Mac's.

His jaw hardened. "Let her go, Sully," Mac ordered.

"You want to stay out of this," Sullivan warned him. "This is between me and Celia."

"No, it isn't. Because she's my friend. She has been, for a long time."

She kept her expression schooled to show no emotion.

"Let her go," Mac said again. Then, voice lower, "Sully, can't you see that you're hurting her?"

And instantly, Sullivan let her go. She marched forward, moving almost woodenly. She'd gotten maps of the property before. She knew where the guesthouse was located. But, despite her words to Sullivan, she didn't head there. Instead, she walked toward the bluff that overlooked the nearby lake.

One step. Then another.

She didn't look back at Sullivan.

SULLIVAN COULDN'T TAKE his eyes off Celia. "I didn't mean to hurt her."

But he had. Her eyes had swum with tears. He didn't think that he'd ever seen Celia cry, but she'd just come very, very close.

Mac moved directly into his path, blocking Sullivan's view of Celia. "I don't know what in the hell is going on between you two…"

Neither did Sullivan. He knew what he wanted, though. Her.

"The family is waiting," Mac said. "Give Celia time alone. Give her space."

She'd had space from him—for years.

But he nodded grimly and turned back toward the main house. Brodie and Davis were both there, glowering. They did that a lot, so their expressions weren't particularly surprising. No one spoke until Sullivan reached the porch steps.

"Want to tell us," Brodie asked quietly, "just who that pretty redhead is?"

"A client," Sullivan replied, voice curt. That was the story Celia had said to give, but…*but she flinched when I told her my family never knew about the marriage.* He hadn't told them because talking about Celia had just hurt too much.

From the corner of his eye, he saw the swift glance that Mac gave him, but his brother didn't call him a liar.

"And why is your client…I mean, *our* client," Brodie amended, "walking around the ranch on her own?"

"Because Celia needed a safe place to crash," Mac quickly told him. "And we knew she'd be safe here."

Unable to help himself, Sullivan's gaze once more sought out Celia. The sun was hitting her red hair, bringing out the fire there. She was so achingly beautiful to him. Even more than she'd been years before.

Would he ever look at her and not crave?

No.

Sullivan cleared his throat and tried to focus on his brothers. "I've got news on our mother."

"The rest of the family is waiting inside," Brodie said. "I gathered them all when I got the call from Mac."

Davis was silent. Silent and staring after Celia. There was curiosity in his expression and…suspicion.

"You got a problem?" Sullivan snapped at his brother.

Davis slowly turned his head toward Sullivan. "She seems familiar to me."

"I don't know why she would. I doubt you've ever met." But…uncertainty stirred though him. Many SAD operatives came from military backgrounds. Only Mac knew that he'd committed to that unit. Secrecy had been required, but…

What if Davis was involved with SAD, too? What if Sullivan wasn't the only one keeping secrets?

"Ava and the others are waiting inside," Brodie said. "Don't you think they've waited long enough?"

Sullivan nodded and climbed up the steps. But at the threshold to the ranch house, he hesitated and glanced over his shoulder. Celia had paced toward the bluff. The wind tossed her hair.

I have waited long enough for the thing I want most.

CELIA PULLED OUT her burner phone. She dialed the contact number for her ex-boss, her fingers moving quickly, without hesitation. She'd have to make the call quick because she knew exactly what sort of technology was out there. She couldn't risk someone triangulating the signal from the phone and coming after her.

But she also needed answers.

The phone was answered on the second ring.

"You've got the wrong number," a gruff voice said instantly.

"No," she replied, "I don't."

"Celia?"

"Hello, Ronald." Ronald Worth had been her supervisor at the agency from the first moment she walked through those gleaming doors. He'd weathered many storms with her and she'd certainly never expected this, not from him. "Want to tell me why I'm on the kill list?"

"Celia, where are you?" A heated intensity filled his words. She could picture him in her mind. He'd be in his office, hunched behind his desk, his brow furrowed as he stroked his chin.

"I'm on the run—where else would I be? I mean, when another agent comes gunning for me, it certainly becomes obvious that I'm not exactly on the team's roster any longer."

And if she was being targeted by her own agency, there was only one man who could have ordered that hit. The man she was speaking with right now.

"You aren't on any kill list!" Ronald blasted. "Celia, you said you wanted out, so I started the paperwork for you. New name, new place. You know how the deal works."

Yes, she did. She also knew how things worked when agents were being eliminated and not retired. "I didn't sell secrets. I never turned on anyone."

"Celia, I swear…we aren't after you!"

"Then why is Porter Vance hunting me?"

Silence.

She only had a few more minutes. There was no time to waste with silence. "I've known for a while that something was going on," she continued, her voice stark. "My computer files were hacked. My home—I could tell when someone had broken in." And she'd tried to figure out who was after her. But then things had changed... Mac had called her in to help him on the case in North Dakota, and Sullivan had come back into her life.

And my life imploded.

"I'm being targeted by my own team. After all my years of sacrifice. After all the work I did for you... *why*?" She deserved an answer.

"I'm on your side," Ronald said. "Believe me. Trust me."

She laughed.

"We have to meet, Celia. There are things going on that you don't understand. When you hooked up with the McGuires again, you set off a chain reaction..."

"And you knew all about me hooking up with them?" That would explain Porter's presence at McGuire Securities. Ronald had sent him after her. And Porter had just waited to attack, like the good killer he was.

Is that all any of us are? Good killers?

"I found out something...dammit, I wanted to tell you in person," Ronald groused. "But you didn't come back to the office."

No, she hadn't. Because she'd realized she was being hunted. In their business, when the Agency turned on you, you ran.

A TV show had been made about an agent who was betrayed by his agency. There was a reason that show had been called *Burn Notice*. When the agency decided to target you, then you truly were burned.

"You're still tied to him."

She had no idea what he meant. "This call is over."

"No, wait! Listen, *listen*! You aren't being targeted by the agency. You're being targeted because of your connection to Sullivan McGuire."

She hesitated. It was a trick. It had to be. All signs pointed to the threat coming from the CIA, but…

Maybe Porter was at McGuire Securities because of Sullivan?

No, no, that—

"I didn't want to say this on the phone, but—you're still married to him, Celia."

That wasn't possible. She'd signed papers. Talked to a judge and—

"The divorce wasn't legit. You're still his wife. The man has powerful enemies. You *know* that. Enemies that would do anything to control him. To stop his investigation into his parents' murder. They're trying to send a message to him by hurting you. That's why you've been targeted. That's why your files were hacked. Yeah, yeah, I found out about all that—not because I'm the one doing it, but because I'm trying to protect you."

"This call is over," she said again, because too much time had passed. She didn't want to give away her location.

"If Porter Vance is after you, I didn't send him! He's a free agent now. He's—"

"Dead," she said flatly.

"What?"

"Goodbye, Ronald."

"Celia, wait, you need—"

She hung up. Right now she had no idea what she needed.

SULLIVAN OPENED THE white envelope Celia had given to him. He took out the papers inside and unfolded them.

Around him, his family waited. His brothers and the women they loved.

His sister, Ava, stood a few feet away, with her husband, Mark Montgomery, at her side.

They'd all been waiting so long to unravel the past.

And all Sullivan could think about in that moment was Celia. *I keep hurting her.*

"Damn, man," Mac snapped. "Cut the suspense and just tell us. Why did Mom go into the Witness Protection Program? What happened to her?"

He looked at the pages before him. "It's her death certificate." His eyes narrowed. "The woman she'd been before...they said she was dead. There was never going to be any going back for her." Which was damn odd. Normally, a person in Witness Protection would go back to testify in a trial or—

"She had to get away," Ava said. "She was running when she came here."

They all knew that already.

"Then she met Dad." Grant's voice was solemn. "She never seemed scared to me. My whole life, Mom just seemed...happy."

"She was." Sullivan would never believe otherwise. He'd seen the love and joy in his mother's eyes. He moved the death certificate and focused on the next form that Celia had given him.

A police report. Very old, from the looks of it. Not a

copy. Hell, an original? How had she gotten her hands on that? "Mom saw a murder," he said. No, not a murder, Sullivan realized as he read the paperwork. "An execution. She witnessed a white male in his early twenties walk up and put a gun to the back of her boyfriend's head. The attacker fired one shot, and her boyfriend fell right there." He didn't share the other parts, not right then, but the police reports covered the fact that blood spatter had been all over their mother. That she'd been hysterical at the scene. "According to her statement, the killer said if she talked, he'd come back and shoot her."

And she had been shot, years later. Killed in her own home.

"She talked," Grant said.

Obviously. "It says, 'I won't be afraid.'" He was thumbing through the small stack of papers now. "That's in her handwriting. She wrote out her statement and signed it. She wasn't going to be afraid. She wanted that man brought to justice. A white male with golden eyes. Six foot two. Two hundred pounds." He read the description, aware that his voice had gone flat. All those details were there, stark but not cold—they couldn't be cold when they were written in his mother's hand.

Mac cleared his throat. "She always told us how important it was to help others."

"Especially those who were weaker," Grant added. "Mom never was the type to stand by and let anyone else suffer."

Sullivan's head lifted. He glanced around the room and saw that silent tears had slid down Ava's cheeks.

"There's more, isn't there?" Ava asked, catching his gaze. "Tell us everything now, Sullivan. That's why we're all here."

His gaze swept over them. Grant's wife, Scarlett, was at his side. Their hands were linked. Sullivan stared at their hands for a moment. Grant and Scarlett hadn't been through an easy time. It had taken Grant years to win a place at her side again. If Grant had given up, his brother would have been lost. Sullivan knew that with certainty.

Over the years, Sullivan had carried secrets for Scarlett. He hadn't told his brother about the baby she'd lost because he hadn't wanted to hurt Grant. But those secrets—they *had* hurt. Because Grant had wanted to know everything about Scarlett. He'd wanted to be there for her, through the good and the bad.

Now they were together.

And Grant was frowning at him. "Sully? What is it?"

He shook his head, and his gaze kept sliding over the group. Ava and Mark, Grant and Scarlett, Mac and his pretty Elizabeth. They were all so settled now.

Even the twins had left their wild times behind. Brodie had his hand wrapped around Jennifer's shoulder. Ah, Jennifer...now, there was another woman who understood all about secrets. She'd been hiding the truth about herself from Brodie from the moment that they first met. But when danger had closed in on her, she'd turned to Brodie. She'd trusted him fully.

And Brodie had been willing to walk through hell to keep her safe.

Even Davis and his new wife, Jamie...they'd had to battle a dark past. Jamie had also been in Witness Protection—it was through her that they'd first learned about their mother. But Davis hadn't cared at all about Jamie's past. In fact, he'd been determined to battle the demons that haunted her.

"Secrets," Sullivan muttered. "That's what's been in my way all along."

Grant stepped toward him. "What aren't you telling us?"

He looked back down at the papers. "The cops thought they were after a professional hitter. They figured he'd been hired just to kill Mom's boyfriend. The boyfriend—Henry Jones—was a marine, just back from deployment."

And he remembered right then the way his mother had looked when she first saw him in his uniform. Her lips had trembled. She'd hugged him so tightly.

He had to force his fingers to stay loose around those papers. It took all his strength not to crumple them right then and there. "The marine was gunned right down and Mom was just collateral damage." *The hell she was.* "She wasn't a target, so the gunman let her go. But she went to the authorities. She didn't let fear stop her."

"Did they ever catch the guy?" Jennifer wanted to know. Yes, that would be Jennifer. Wanting to make sure that justice had been served.

"It doesn't say that they did." He'd ask Celia if she knew. "But it does say…the cops suspected this guy was tied to other crimes. Other military personnel who'd been killed." *Executed.* "She was sent away because they believed she would be murdered because she'd come forward. They wanted her to be protected at all costs."

So she'd left her life behind. Gone to Texas.

And started a family there.

A family that hadn't known about her secrets. But… *Dad knew.*

He must have known.

"This doesn't make sense to me," Ava said. "Mom

was shot *first*. The men who came after them were trying to make Dad talk, not her. They killed her outright. If those men were here because of her, then what secrets did they think our father knew?" She surged forward. "I remember what he said at the end. Those words have haunted me for years—'I'll never tell you. No matter what you do, I'll never tell you.'" Her voice had gone hoarse with pain. "If the men who killed them were here because of Mom's past, then why would they be trying to make Dad talk? It doesn't make sense, it—"

"He was her handler," Sullivan said, revealing the very last bit of information that Celia had provided in that envelope.

Ava stilled. "What?"

"Mom and Dad didn't meet by chance. When she entered the Witness Protection Program, he was the one who was protecting her. He was the one who was supposed to give her a new start and then, once she was settled, walk away."

"What the hell?" Davis demanded, his expression shocked. "You're saying Dad was law enforcement? I thought—he was always a rancher."

Not always. "I'm not saying it." He gave the papers to his brother. "It's what Celia found out."

Davis blinked. "Back to her, huh? I thought she was a client."

Mac thrust back his shoulders. "A client who helped us. This whole family owes her more than we can ever repay."

Elizabeth gave a quick nod. "I certainly do. If it weren't for Celia, I'd still be running from my past."

Instead, she had a future. Mac had a future.

What do I have?

Papers tied to his bloody past.

"If this Celia might know more, then she needs to come in here," Davis said. His gaze held Sullivan's. "Bring her in with the family."

He wanted to do it, more than anything else. But she'd asked to be kept separate. No…she'd asked after he'd admitted that his family didn't know about her.

Tell them I'm a client.

He glanced toward the door. Was she still at the bluff? That was his favorite spot, and his chest felt tight as he imagined her there.

She had no reason in the world to help him, yet she'd brought him all this information on his family. Why? He had to know.

He turned for the door.

"Bring her in," Davis called again. "Don't you think it's past time we all met her?"

Something about the way Davis said that… Sullivan looked back.

Grant had moved to Davis's side. Grant. The eldest brother. The one who'd worked so hard to hold them all together after they buried their parents.

Grant was staring at him with suspicious eyes. "More secrets, Sully?"

Dammit… "Yes."

"Secrets can destroy you, if you let them," Grant said.

He wasn't in the mood to be destroyed.

He yanked open the door and marched back outside. His gaze swept the area, and, sure enough, Celia was still near the bluff. Her hair was blowing in the faint breeze. The sun warmed her skin, and as he hurried toward her, she turned to face him.

He saw the fear flash across her delicate features. She tried to school her expression, but it was too late.

"What's wrong?" Sullivan demanded instantly as his muscles hardened. He scanned the area, searching for danger, but no one else was there. Just him.

Just her.

Surely she wasn't afraid of him, was she?

Her right hand gripped the burner phone she'd purchased.

"Did you find out something else?" Sullivan asked her.

Celia's lips parted, but then she shook her head. "Nothing that can help us."

"You checked in with your supervisor at the agency, didn't you?" He remembered the guy. Ronald Worth. A by-the-book fellow who'd believed in running a tight ship. Until that ship exploded in his face.

"He says that I'm not on any agent termination list. Ronald swears the threat isn't coming from the agency."

"Then who's targeting you?"

She turned back to face the lake. "It's really beautiful. I mean, I knew the lake was here. It was on the mapping schematics I retrieved, but seeing it in person is something else entirely."

"You got schematics of the ranch property?"

She nodded. "I knew the one thing you wanted most was to find out who killed your parents. And I wanted to give that to you. So I dug...and I bartered and I traded my way to information." She tipped back her head and closed her eyes. "Sometimes, I feel like I know your world so well, but then other times, I realize how much of a stranger you are to me."

She was confusing him. Typical Celia. She'd always been a puzzle he couldn't figure out.

"Why would you want to help me?"

Her lips curved into a smile. "That's something you'll have to figure out on your own."

"Celia…" He heard a door slam. Sullivan glanced over his shoulder and saw that Davis had followed him outside. Seriously, his brother needed to back off. Jaw locking, Sullivan focused on Celia again. Her eyes were still closed, as if she'd shut out the world.

Or maybe just him.

"Do you know my brother Davis?"

"No."

"Are you sure, Celia? He thinks you look familiar to him."

And her eyes opened. She cocked her head as she studied him. "Are you asking if I tried to recruit your brother?"

"Yes."

She shook her head. "I've never met Davis. Just you and Mac. You're the only two McGuires I know."

He could practically feel his brother closing in on him. "Well, you're about to meet Davis. You're about to meet them all."

"No, I told you, I'd stay in the guesthouse and—"

"Are you ever bringing her inside, Sully?" Davis asked as he closed in on them.

Celia blinked and—just that fast—her expression was a perfect blank. Almost like a doll's mask. He didn't like that. He wanted to see her emotions, the good and the bad. Sullivan didn't want Celia to ever hide from him again.

He moved his body, taking up a protective position

in front of her. If she didn't want to face his family, he'd make sure they backed off until she was ready for them.

"You have answers that we need, ma'am," Davis said, his voice softer, gentler. Never let it be said that Davis didn't know how to manipulate and charm in order to get what he wanted. Because gentle? That was the last thing Davis actually was. "So why don't you come inside so we can all talk?"

"She doesn't want to come inside," Sullivan gritted out. "I'm taking her to the guesthouse. I'll discuss the situation more with Celia when we're alone and see what she—"

"Why does that happen?" Davis asked, cutting him off.

Guarded now, Sullivan said, "What?"

"When you say her name, your face changes. So does your voice."

Hell. Davis always had been far too observant.

Davis put his hands on his hips and rocked back on his heels. "You're not a client, are you?"

Celia stepped around Sullivan. "If Sully told you I'm a client, then that's exactly what I am."

Davis smiled. It wasn't an overly friendly sight. Typical Davis. "I've seen you before."

"No," Celia said with certainty. "You haven't. We've never met."

Davis lifted one dark eyebrow. "I never said we'd met. Just that I'd seen you before." He cocked his head as his gaze swept over her. "But your hair was a different color then. Darker, almost black, if I remember correctly."

Sullivan's guts knotted. "Davis..." With that growl, he tried to warn his brother to shut the hell up.

Davis decided to ignore his warning. "I first saw

your photo when I helped Sullivan move into his place. He didn't want to stay here, you see, too many bad memories." He glanced around the ranch. "For a while, all anyone saw was the blood and the death, so I understood that he wanted to leave."

Celia's expression gave nothing away.

"He had a framed photo of you." Davis shook his head. "Crazy thing is…I could have sworn you two were in some kind of chapel."

"You never said a word to me," Sullivan snapped. If the guy had seen the photo, why not question him?

Davis just shrugged. "I figured if you wanted me to know, you'd tell me. But you never did. The years passed, and instead of talking to me, you kept your secrets." He advanced toward Sullivan. "And you started to change. You shut yourself down. I can still remember when you'd laugh freely. When you'd look at the world without suspicion in your eyes." His hand clapped down on Sullivan's shoulder. "With every day that passed, you just pulled away more and more." His hold tightened. "Are you coming back now? Since *she's* here, are you coming back?"

And Sullivan didn't know what the hell he was supposed to say.

Chapter Five

He had her picture.

Celia was pretty much floored by that revelation. A man wouldn't keep a woman's picture, not unless she mattered, right? And she did vaguely remember someone snapping a photo of them at the chapel in Vegas. She'd been so excited then, nearly delirious with happiness for the first time in her life, so she hadn't even stopped to wonder what happened to that image.

Now she knew. Sullivan had kept it.

He stood toe-to-toe with his brother. There was so much tension in the air. She wanted to back away from them, but she couldn't. Celia felt glued to Sullivan's side. No, more than that—she felt protective. It was obvious Davis realized Sullivan had been keeping secrets, but he didn't know the hell Sullivan had endured when he was taken captive. Sullivan had shouldered that burden.

She cleared her throat, wanting to draw Davis's attention away from Sullivan. "I'm Celia James," she said, and offered her hand.

His head turned toward her. His eyes were just as green and just as hard as Sullivan's. "Are you?" His hand curled around hers and she felt the hard press of his calluses against her skin. "Or are you Celia McGuire?"

According to Ronald, I am Celia McGuire. But he had to be wrong. And she wasn't about to talk about that news, not right now. That particular bombshell would wait to be dropped—once she found out whether or not it was even true.

"Celia James," she said again, flatly. "Sullivan and I are divorced." *Are we?* She pulled her hand away from his. "And I am a client. Sullivan agreed to help me. It was one of those I-scratch-your-back—"

"You-scratch-mine deals," Davis finished as his lips quirked. "Right." He paused. "I'm supposed to believe that's the reason you delivered all that intel to him? Because you wanted to pay for his security services?"

"Well…" She slanted a quick sideways glance at Sullivan. The guy appeared to have frozen—or turned to stone. His expression was hard and deadly…and a bit scary. She was afraid that he'd be unleashing on his brother any moment, and that couldn't happen. "McGuire Securities does have a top-notch reputation," Celia replied coolly. "If you want the best, you have to pay for it. By any means necessary."

Davis didn't appear convinced. "And just how is it that you came into possession of such hard-to-acquire material? Because my family has been digging for years, and we couldn't unearth that particular intel."

"I knew where to look," she said carelessly, as if all the hours and bribes and deals she'd made to uncover the past had been easy. A real walk in the park on a Sunday afternoon.

Bull. It had taken blood, sweat and some serious pay-offs to get that information. But she'd been determined.

She hadn't intended to stop, not until she gave Sullivan what he needed. Because she'd thought that maybe then her guilt would end.

"You knew where to look…" Davis laughed. "I sure get the feeling there is a whole lot more to you than meets the eye."

She knew the other McGuires would grill her when she walked into that house. But she'd wear her mask. She'd control the information she revealed to them. There was no need for them to know—

"It was a chapel," Sullivan said, his voice deep and rumbling. "And I still have that picture of her."

What? Her gaze flew to him.

Sullivan's glittering stare was locked on her. "If you'd looked inside my nightstand drawer, you would have found it, Celia."

She shook her head.

"I guess I had a hard time letting go." His hand rose and his fingers skimmed down her cheek. "I tried. You think I don't know how damaged I am? When the chips were down, I was the one who turned on you."

He wasn't saying these things to her. He couldn't be.

"I didn't deserve you. I woke up in that hospital, and I knew that truth. I had been ready to believe the worst of you, when I should have been the one protecting you with every breath that I had."

"Sullivan?"

He looked at his brother. Davis was watching them with an avid gaze. "I married her," Sullivan said to him. "She divorced my fool self. There, happy?"

You're still married to him. Ronald's words rang in her ears.

"And you're right, bro, I did change," Sullivan continued. "Because every single day that passed, I missed her. I wanted her. But she was in the wind and I couldn't find her, not at first. I tried at the agency, but they stone-walled me."

"Uh, the agency?" Davis asked.

But Sullivan just kept going. "I didn't know that Mac had managed to make contact with her—hell, when he first told me about her, that she was going to help us out with that mess that nearly destroyed Elizabeth, I think I went a little crazy."

Her cheeks flashed hot, then ice-cold.

"She's not just a client," Sullivan said as his fingers stroked her cheek once more. "She's always been so much more."

"What are you doing?" Celia whispered to him. "Stop!"

But it was too late.

"I won't ever deny you again," Sullivan swore. "I'll prove that you can trust me."

This wasn't happening.

Frantic, she glanced at Davis. A faint smile curved his lips. A rather satisfied smile. Had he deliberately been pushing Sullivan?

Davis turned away. Took a step. Then stopped. "You talk in your sleep, Sully."

Yes, he did. She'd learned that fact for herself.

"I heard you call for her once. It was easy to put the pieces together after that." Davis looked over his shoulder. "I'll take care of the folks inside. You two need to talk this out before you see the others. If you want to tell the rest of them, do it. For my two cents...you should. But if you want to keep your secrets well, hell, it sure seems like this family was built on them, doesn't it?" Then he walked away.

Celia didn't speak, mostly because she was trying to figure out what to say. Sullivan's hand had fallen away from her cheek, and she felt strangely cold without his touch.

But then, she'd felt a bit cold without him for a very long time.

Don't make the same mistakes. Don't give in to the need. But it was so hard. Especially with him standing right there and—

"You kept my picture?" She hadn't meant to blurt out that question.

He nodded.

"You were the one who told me to walk away." As if she'd ever forget that phone call. "You, Sully, not me."

"You think I don't know what a mistake I made? I was half out of my mind with painkillers. They'd sliced me open in that pit. I thought I was going to die there, and yeah, it was in that hell that I made my mistake. It was there I turned on *you*." He heaved out a breath. "I believed them when they said you'd set me up. They knew so much about my family—things I'd only told you. They knew, C, and rage took over. I wanted—"

He looked away.

"You wanted me to suffer." She wrapped her arms around her stomach and backed up.

"No." His gaze flew right back to her. "I just wanted my life back. I wanted to feel like my heart hadn't been ripped apart. Thinking you'd betrayed me? It gutted me. I was broken. Not by those jerks and their torture, but by what I thought you'd done. I couldn't live like that. I had to get away."

From me.

She focused on breathing, nice and slow.

"Mac told me that you helped him. I didn't know you were driving the damn getaway car—not until you told me. I didn't know you walked into hell for me."

Her lips trembled a bit as she told him, "My boss didn't authorize a retrieval mission for you. It was believed that you were part of the compromised group."

"What?"

Ah, so she had managed to surprise him.

"I was informed you were one of the traitors. That you'd turned on us. Retrieval wasn't an option." Ronald had told her that with sympathy in his voice. "I was boarding the plane to rendezvous with you when my boss gave me the news. The mission had gone to hell. You'd turned. Most of the team members who'd been on-site with you were dead." She'd grabbed the railing beside her and held on tight, not wanting Ronald to see that her legs had nearly collapsed beneath her. "I didn't follow his orders. I contacted Mac instead. We got you out."

He yanked a hand through his hair. "Because you never gave up on me."

"Because it was my fault you'd been taken." Why hide anymore? Davis had gone back into the house. It was just the two of them in that moment, alone on that bluff. No one could hear their secrets. "I was the one who recruited you. I was the one who gave you initial training. I was the one who should've had your back." *Because I was the one who loved you.* "Traitor or not, I was going to find you. You deserved that from me."

His hand fell. "And you deserved a hell of a lot more from me."

"We moved too fast back then," she said, the memories stirring within her. "We barely knew each other. When the chips were down, what more could we expect?"

He stepped closer to her. "More. Expect one hell of a lot more from me this time." His arms wrapped around her and he pulled her close.

She should step away. She should stop him.

Instead, Celia rose onto her toes. She locked her hands around his shoulders, and when his head lowered toward her, she kissed him.

MAC WAS WAITING for Davis just inside the house. When he saw Davis's expression, he demanded, "What did you do?" Trust Davis to go meddling.

Davis shut the door. "You and Sully...did you really think I didn't know what the hell was going on? He vanished for weeks, and when he came back, he was as pale as a ghost. I knew my brother had been hurt." He rolled back his shoulders. "I just respected him enough not to beat him while he was down and demand answers."

"You think you have those answers now?" Mac kept his voice low. Davis might be in the know, but the rest of the family wasn't, not yet.

"I have some answers, but definitely not all. I knew when I saw them together that she was the one who tied him in knots. His obsession, come to life."

Mac exhaled. "Davis, it's not that easy. You don't know her..."

"She's Celia James. I just shook her hand."

Mac glared at the guy. Davis put his palms up. "Look, I know what matters, okay? I know that Sully lights up when he's near her."

But did he know how much pain Sully had brought her before? How much pain Sully had brought himself? "She's already got a dead body in her wake. Danger follows her." Mac liked Celia. He respected her. But that didn't mean he wasn't aware of the risk that she presented—to Sullivan and to them all. "That dead body that was found outside McGuire Securities last night? Celia knew the guy. Sully and I think he was trying to kill her."

A faint furrow appeared between Davis's eyebrows, the only sign of his concern. "Yet he wound up dead." A brief hesitation. "By her hand?"

"Celia said she didn't kill him."

"Do you believe her?"

"I want to." He truly did. But he couldn't trust her with his family's lives. "But I haven't ever been that close to her."

"Not like Sully," Davis murmured. "He got close enough to marry her…"

But he still didn't fully trust her. And that had been their downfall.

"Sully mentioned the agency a few moments ago," Davis said.

Mac hid his surprise. Davis was obviously probing, but Mac just stared back at his brother.

"If overseas work was involved, and I'll assume it was with Sullivan's background…" Davis cocked his head to the right "…then the agency, I'm guessing, is… CIA?"

"If you say so."

Davis grunted. "You *and* Sully, huh? Because you know her well, too. Was she your handler?"

Mac shrugged.

Davis's eyes hardened. "You never told me you were an operative."

"I don't remember you asking." Mac rubbed his jaw, feeling the scrape of stubble there. He considered stone-walling his brother, but decided that enough was damn enough. "Someone had to watch Sully's back."

"I think that's what Celia's doing."

No, he rather thought Celia and Sully were doing something else entirely. Especially if he knew his brother...

"But now that I know we're dealing with the CIA," Davis added, "I know which contacts to use in order to check her out."

Right. Because Davis would never accept Celia at face value. He never accepted anyone at face value. Their whole family had trust issues.

"Let's just see what my sources have to say about her..."

"Your sources?" Mac pushed. Since when did Davis have sources at the CIA?

Davis smiled at him. "You think you and Sully were the only ones approached by the CIA? Get in line, bro. I didn't take them up on the offer, but that doesn't mean my friends didn't."

Hell. He'd wondered about that... Davis and Brodie had both been SEALs, and SEALs would have made perfect candidates for the CIA's Special Activities Division. With their elite training, they would have been perfect agent picks for the covert operations.

"Give me thirty minutes," Davis said with a nod, "and I'll know everything I need to know about Celia James..."

"Good luck with that," Mac told him. *Because you'll need it.*

Thirty minutes wouldn't be nearly long enough to explore the mystery that was Celia. Sully could have easily told the guy that fact.

CELIA WAS IN his arms. She was kissing him. She tasted sweeter than candy, better than wine, and he never wanted to let her go.

And I won't.

Not this time.

Sullivan pulled her closer. Kissed her deeper. He loved it when she gave that faint moan for him. He could feel the tips of her breasts pushing against him. Perfect breasts. They'd always fit just right in his hands. He wanted to strip her. To taste every delectable inch of her body.

When the pleasure swept over her, Celia was so beautiful.

She's always beautiful.

His hands slid down her back. Moved to the curve of her hips. She had such a fine—

Celia pushed against him.

Jaw locking, Sullivan eased back, but he didn't release his hold on her.

"Tell me what you want from me." Her voice had gone husky with desire.

What he wanted? Easy. Everything. But he said, "From now on, no secrets."

Her eyelashes flickered.

"I won't keep any secrets from you," he promised her. "So what I want right now, more than anything… is you. I want to take you someplace private, where I don't have to worry about my family intruding on us. I want to strip you, and I want to drive you wild."

That plan seemed simple enough to him.

"But what do *you* want?" Sullivan asked her. "Tell me, and I'll make it happen."

Her gaze searched his. The desire was plain to see in her stare. Her cheeks had flushed and her lips were red, slightly swollen, from his mouth. Sexy as all hell.

"I want you," she said slowly. "I don't want any hesitations. I want us, alone, and I want to let go of every fear that I've ever had."

Yes.

He caught her hand in his and pretty much started pulling her toward the guesthouse.

Only...

A glance toward the main ranch house showed him that Mac was on the porch. The guy jumped off the steps and headed toward him.

No, no, no. His brother could not really have timing that bad. It just couldn't be possible. "See..." Sullivan sighed. "There's the family, intruding."

Mac kept marching toward them. The guy was totally ignoring Sullivan's get-away glare. "They want to meet her," Mac called.

And I want to keep her all to myself. That equaled a problem in his book.

"She brought them answers," Mac continued as he sauntered closer. "Well, answers and more questions... They're all waiting inside for her."

So much for Davis taking care of them. Just where had his other brother gone?

Celia bit her lower lip. A shudder of need rushed

through him. He wanted to have that lip against his mouth again. He wanted to taste her, and if she wanted to bite him...*feel free, baby*.

The sex between them had always been intense. Wild.

Hot.

His arousal shoved against the front of his jeans, and the last thing he wanted was a sit-down with his family. He'd been away from Celia too long. She'd just admitted that she wanted to be with him, too.

Now...this?

Fate was so cruel. Terribly, twistedly cruel.

"I don't have any more answers to give them," Celia said. "Everything that I had...I gave that to Sully. There wasn't any more for me to find on your mother. I looked. I searched. But I couldn't find more. I think there was another file on the man who shot her boyfriend. She went back in for a sit-down with the local cops, but that file was destroyed in a fire. And the cops she talked with back then? They both died in a shoot-out a few months later. So if she ever officially said anything else about the man who executed Henry Jones, no record exists of that testimony."

"Come inside," Mac said with a slow nod. "It's time, Celia."

Time? A swift glance at Mac showed that his expression had turned very solemn. Sullivan realized this wasn't just about the past—it was about the present that Mac knew Sullivan wanted with Celia.

She nodded. "Fine. We'll be right behind you."

Mac turned and headed back to the house.

Celia watched him in silence, and she made no move

to follow. Sullivan started to feel…nervous, and that sure wasn't something he was used to experiencing.

"I'm scared," she finally admitted.

Nothing she could have confessed would have shocked him more.

"What if they don't…what if they don't like me?"

His jaw nearly hit the ground at that whispered question. Then he laughed.

Celia blushed furiously when she saw his expression.

"Oh, baby, no, I'm sorry." He pulled her close once more. If he had his way, she'd always be close to him. "I wasn't laughing at you." He'd never do that. "I was laughing because…you've faced down killers. International terrorists. And you're worried about what my family thinks of you?"

"Yes." Still flushing, she held his gaze. "I am."

She shouldn't be. "I'm just hoping they don't say something that sends you running," he said honestly. "They can be overwhelming." To say the least.

"I've never had a family, Sullivan. You know I was raised in the foster system."

Yes, he remembered her telling him that. And he remembered thinking, *I'll be your family, baby*. He still wanted to offer her a family. A home. All that she'd ever dreamed of.

"I was pretty much on my own for as long as I can remember." She cast a quick glance toward the house. "There were no big holidays. No family gatherings. No barbecues in the summer. A crowd like that one in there—all the emotions—it just…what if I say the wrong thing?"

"You won't." He was dead certain. "Elizabeth is already eternally grateful to you. Mac is ready to slay any dragon that appears…and you have me."

"Do I?"

"Yes." *For as long as you want me.* "We've got this."

She smiled and her dimples flashed. He actually felt his heart stop at the sight of those dimples. It was a real smile from her. Not cold or taunting. Not a fake stretch of her lips. Her dimples winked. Her eyes gleamed.

In that instant, she was once again the woman he'd married.

"Let's do this," Celia said. Her fingers twined with his. They headed toward the house. They didn't speak again as they climbed the porch steps and walked inside.

But as soon as they crossed the threshold, every bit of conversation in the house died. All eyes turned on them.

Not so subtly, Sullivan moved closer to Celia. If anyone so much as looked sideways at her…

Ava rushed forward. She shoved Sullivan to the side and threw her arms around Celia. "Thank you," Sullivan heard his sister gasp out.

Over Ava's shoulder, Celia stared at Sullivan with wide eyes. *What do I do?* She mouthed those words to him, looking rather like a gorgeous deer in the headlights.

But before Sullivan could say anything, Ava was talking again. She pulled back a bit but didn't let Celia go. "This is a huge break for us. Knowing more about our mother *and* our father—it's a game changer!" She shook her head. "I don't know how you got that intel, but thank you. I am in your debt and I will do anything—"

"No." Celia's voice was quiet, but very firm. "You don't owe me anything, I promise you that."

Ava finally let Celia go. Her husband, Mark, who

had a habit of staying protectively close to Ava, came to her side.

Celia squared her shoulders and peered at the assembled crowd, and it truly was quite a big group. Sullivan looked at them all, trying to see them from a stranger's perspective. He and his brothers all looked alike—dark hair, green eyes. Tall and strong. Ava—she had long, dark hair and the McGuire eyes—but she was delicate. Physically, anyway. Inside, the woman had the heart of a lion.

The other women there were all beauties in their own way. Beauties and true forces to be reckoned with. They'd each had a time battling to save the men they loved. Nothing had stopped them in their fight.

Jennifer was sleek and polished. Scarlett was glowing, her hair hanging over her shoulder in a braid. Elizabeth was wearing jeans and a loose T-shirt. Her smile for Celia was warm and welcoming. And Dr. Jamie, the vet who'd married Davis, brushed off her hands—she'd probably been out working with the animals earlier—made her way to Celia and offered her hand. "It's a pleasure to meet you."

Celia took her hand. She still looked a bit overwhelmed, but she didn't appear ready to bolt. "And it's nice to finally meet all of you."

Did the others note that little slip of *finally*? He was betting some of them did. Celia seemed to catch herself, and then she turned a horrified glance on Sullivan.

He just smiled. "Celia isn't a client."

She still had her spine ramrod straight. Her expression had turned back to that calm mask. She had—

"She's the woman I owe my life to."

Celia shook her head.

But he nodded. "So, yeah, Ava, the family is in her debt. We all owe her." He caught Celia's fingers in his and brought them to his lips. He kissed her knuckles, not caring at all that others would see the move. He *wanted* them to see it. Celia was his, and he was more than ready to fight for her. "But no one owes her more than I do."

"CELIA JAMES IS at the McGuire ranch." After delivering that message, his caller hung up the phone.

The ranch. He should have known. It seemed oddly fitting, as if the journey had come full circle.

Such a bloody start in that place. He'd thought that he was ending a nightmare when he left that ranch. He hadn't realized that the McGuire children would be as much of a nuisance as their parents.

They'd just kept digging.

Why hadn't they let the past die? They could have all moved on. All had a chance at happiness.

But no…they just hadn't stopped. And the trail of bodies had lengthened as the past was unraveled.

Now more would die. The body count would keep coming. It would be tragic. One of those tales that people read about and shook their heads and muttered sadly about what a loss it had all been.

The attack would need to look like an accident, of course. There would be less suspicion that way. A fire would work. Maybe a few well-placed bombs. He knew all about planting explosives. You just had to set your device in the right spot.

And if he moved carefully enough, he could make that happen. He could create a big blaze that would take out the McGuire ranch…and those unlucky enough to be caught inside.

Maybe some would escape. He'd have to be ready for them. Eventually, he'd get them all. It was time to end this story. Time to stop sweating and worrying that the secrets from his past would be uncovered.

He had a job to do, and he'd do it.

The key…the key would be Celia. Celia James. All the intel he'd gathered on her indicated that she'd always been so good at following orders.

Except when it came to Sullivan McGuire.

But everyone had to have a weakness…and for Celia, Sullivan was that weakness.

So does that mean you're his weakness, too?

He was about to find out.

Chapter Six

She pretty much ran into the guesthouse. As soon as Sullivan shut the door behind her, Celia exhaled on a rush of relief before she spun to face him.

Sullivan leaned back against the door. "Was it really that bad?"

No, it hadn't been bad at all. His family had been welcoming. Kind. They'd opened their home and been so *grateful* as they talked to her.

Now that she considered things more...maybe it had been bad. Maybe it had been hell. *Because I wanted to belong there with them.* "You made them think we're still involved."

He shrugged.

And then he yanked his dark T-shirt over his head and tossed it to the floor.

"Sullivan!" His name emerged way huskier than she'd intended. She swallowed and tried again. "What are you doing?"

He quirked an eyebrow at her. "Really, baby? I'm stripping."

He was. His hands were on his belt.

"Why?"

He'd unhooked his belt. "Because I'm going to make love to you."

Her heart pounded against her chest. "Your family—"

"They're not going to bother us. I told them you were up for most of the night. A true story, by the way. And that you needed to crash." He hadn't lowered the zipper. Not yet. He walked to her, those jeans hugging his lean hips. His six-pack abs tempted her far too much. "You can crash with me."

She put up her hands and wound up touching his warm, strong muscles.

"You said you wanted me," he reminded her.

Celia didn't need that reminder. "I never stopped." Did he think that just because they'd been miles apart, he hadn't been in her mind? Her dreams? There had been plenty of fantasies that left her aching for him.

"Baby, I'm pretty sure I'll go insane if I'm not with you now." His eyes darkened as he stared at her. "It's been too long."

Her breath hitched. "But what happens tomorrow?" Were they just going to walk away after this? One night and then goodbye?

"Whatever you want to happen." His head bent as he pulled her toward him. His lips feathered over her neck. Right in that spot that she loved. "Anything you want."

He was what she wanted, and she wouldn't pretend otherwise. Her hands slid over him, moving across those faint scars, but then she pushed against him. There was something she needed to do.

Instantly, he stilled. "Celia?" His head lifted.

She smiled up at him. "I missed you, Sully."

His face softened.

She pressed a kiss to the scar near his heart. He sucked in a sharp breath.

"Baby..."

"Did you miss me?" She kissed another scar, moving down his body. She wanted to kiss every wound that he had. She wished she could take away the pain. Make the past better—for them both.

But she couldn't go back.

Instead, maybe they could go forward, together.

"I missed you more than you'll ever know." His words were rough, almost guttural, and the emotion in them had a surge of warmth spreading through her.

She'd never wanted another man the way she desired him.

Sullivan pushed her to the edge—and beyond.

She kissed another scar. Her knees hit the floor before him as she tried to get closer. The scars—there were so many of them and—

"No." In a flash, he'd lifted her up into his arms. "If you touch me anymore like that, I'm done." His voice made her shiver. "I can't go slowly this time. I have to be in you. I *need* you." He kissed her as he carried her through the house. Deep and hard and hungry, his mouth took hers. She loved his kiss. Celia ached for him.

In moments, they were in a bedroom. They fought with her clothes as they both tried to toss them away. Then she was in just her bra and panties.

He ditched his shoes and dropped his jeans beside the bed. He stood there for an instant, staring at her.

She certainly looked her fill at him. He was heavily aroused, a big, hulking form near the bed. His eyes were so very dark now, the green almost completely gone. A faint red stained his cheeks as he stared at her and asked, "How did you become even more beautiful?"

He'd always made her feel beautiful, when they were in bed together and when they weren't. She lifted her arms toward him.

He touched her, and she was surprised to see that his fingers were shaking. "Sully?"

"I want you so much." His hand fisted. "I don't think I can hold on to my control much longer. I should seduce you, caress every inch of you…"

She rose next to him. Kissed his neck. Licked along the line of his racing pulse. Then she bit him, a light, sensual nip. "You can do all of that," Celia whispered to him, "next time." Her hands slid over his back. "But this time, I don't want to wait, either. I just want you."

He kissed her. Not gently. Not tentatively. Instead, he took her mouth with a wild need that she eagerly met.

His hands slid down her body. He pushed her legs apart and then he was touching her. Sliding his long, broad fingers over her sensitive core. She arched against him even as her nails scraped lightly over his arms. She wasn't looking for seduction. She wanted the wild ride that came with him. The pleasure that swept her away from everything else.

But he'd bent over her and now he took her breast in his mouth. Licking, kissing, driving her crazy even as his wicked fingers kept working the center of her need. Her muscles locked and her breath heaved out. *"Sullivan."*

He moved between her legs. She felt the broad shaft of his arousal pressing against her and she pushed her hips toward him.

"Protection." His hands locked around her hips. "Baby, I'm sorry, I didn't bring anything—"

"I'm covered and I'm clean." She didn't want to stop.

His gaze held hers. "I'm clean, too."

Then it would be this way. Flesh to flesh. The way it had been the night they married. The night so much had changed.

Still holding her stare, he sank into her. The pleasure wasn't easy then. *Easy* didn't apply at all. It was as if a volcano went off inside her, and all the desire that she'd held back for so long just exploded. Their bodies moved in perfect tune, a fast, hard rhythm. The bed was squeaking, she was panting and every glide of his body had her wanting more.

Wanting everything.

Deeper. Harder. Faster.

They rolled across the bed and suddenly she was on top of him. His hands locked around her hips as he lifted her, again and again, and the pleasure slammed into her. She could only gasp out his name and hold on tight as the release consumed her.

But Sullivan wasn't done. His grip was steely on her as he surged into her, deeper and ever stronger. She fell down against his chest, kissing him, and he rolled them across the bed once more, maneuvering so that he was deep, so very deep in her core.

When his release hit him, she felt the warmth deep inside and it set her off again, aftershocks that had her shivering and holding tightly to him.

And when it was over, when her heart wasn't racing in her chest any longer, she lifted her lashes and stared into his eyes.

Part of her had wondered if it would still be as good

with him. Maybe she'd turned their past into something more than it had actually been.

But…no.

It was still as good. No, it was even better.

"I missed you," Sullivan confessed as he turned to curl his body around hers.

Her hand lifted and pressed over his heart. *And I missed you.*

How was she supposed to walk away from him again?

THE SUNLIGHT FELL onto the bed, sliding over the red of Celia's hair and turning her skin an even warmer gold.

Sullivan studied her for a moment, his gaze slowly trailing over her face. Her eyes were closed, her full lips parted in the faintest of smiles. Part of him—such a big part—wanted to just stay there with her. To forget everything else.

But…

But someone was trying to kill Celia, and that *wasn't* going down when he was near. He leaned forward and pressed a soft kiss to her temple, and then, moving as quietly as he could, he eased from the bed. Sullivan grabbed his clothes and slipped into the hallway.

He dressed quickly, then left the guesthouse, making sure to secure the place first. The sun seemed too bright outside and every step that he took away from Celia felt wrong.

But he needed to work. He was going to get his brothers to call in every single favor they were owed. Someone had to know something about the person after Celia. Because if it wasn't a hitter from the agency, then just who wanted her dead?

When he strode back into the main house, he saw that the group had disassembled. Only Mac was still there—Mac and Davis. Mac turned toward him and asked, "Did Celia get settled?"

"Ah, yeah, I got her settled right in." He cleared his throat. "She's sleeping now. She didn't get much sleep last night—not with us spending so much time trying to figure out where that shooter had gone." After firing at the medical examiner's office, the fellow had vanished without a trace.

Davis grunted. "Mac was bringing me up to speed on all that happened."

Sullivan lifted an eyebrow. He was sure Davis had been learning plenty. Sullivan crossed his hands over his chest and studied Davis. Of all the brothers, he'd always thought he, Mac and Davis were the most alike—not big on trust, and far too well acquainted with suspicion. "You think I don't know what you did?" Sullivan asked him. "I know, because it's exactly what I would have done, too."

Davis didn't move from his position on the couch. He sprawled there, looking as if he didn't have a care in the world.

"You dug into her background, didn't you?" Sullivan guessed. "Probably as soon as you left us on that bluff."

Davis rolled one shoulder in a careless shrug. "Is it so wrong that I wanted to know a bit about the woman you married?"

Sullivan's back teeth ground together. "We don't need to make her any more of a target, so I'm hoping you used *some* discretion when you started prying."

"Monroe Blake."

The name was familiar, but...

"We were SEALs together, and I happen to know that he joined the Special Activities Division a while back." Davis inclined his head toward Sullivan while Mac just watched in silence. "I called Monroe because I wanted someone else's take on your lady. No offense, but you're not exactly unbiased in this situation."

"I sure as hell hope you can trust the guy…"

"I saved Monroe's hide a time or ten, so he owed me."

Owing someone didn't equal trust.

"And he saved me," Davis added quietly. "When he should have just hauled butt and gotten out of there. He walked through the fire for me." His voice was flat. "So, yes, I trust him."

Sullivan's shoulders relaxed a bit at that revelation. "And what did he have to say?"

"A guy named Ronald Worth is in charge of the division."

Yeah, he already knew that. Ronald had been there during Sullivan's unfortunate employment. All hell had broken loose, and he'd rather thought that Ronald would go down with the ship. He hadn't. Obviously, it paid to have friends in high places.

"According to Monroe, Ronald had been grooming your Celia to be his replacement. She was the shining protégée who was supposed to take over when he retired."

Your Celia. He wanted her to be his again.

"Only Celia seems to be gone out on some kind of mission right now, or at least, that's what good old Ronald is telling the others."

"And your contact didn't have any qualms about

sharing this information with you?" Suspicion pushed inside him.

"I didn't ask for her location. I didn't ask him to disclose any top-secret intel. I just asked Monroe for his take on your Celia."

Sullivan waited.

Davis stared back at him.

The guy loved to push buttons. Brothers. They could be such damn pains. "And that take was…?" Not that it mattered. He knew Celia.

"Dedicated. Brutally smart. And willing to go to any extremes to protect her team." Davis scratched his chin. "Though there were some rumors swirling about her when my buddy first joined the division. She'd gone in, risking her life, in order to retrieve an agent suspected of turning on the group. Seems she walked straight into hell."

Sullivan's gaze cut to Mac. "I thought she just drove the getaway car," he gritted out.

Mac shrugged. "Not quite. She was there with me, every step of the way, helping me to battle the men who had you. She's the one who begged you to live when we found you lying so still in that pit, and Celia was the one—standing right there—who heard you say that she was the enemy. That she couldn't be trusted and you never wanted to see her again."

He could hear his own heart pounding. Every breath became painful. "I loved her." He rasped out those words. They were hard to say because he'd held them in for so long. But it was past time for him to admit the truth.

"I fell for her," Sullivan continued quietly. "Hard and way too fast. Love wasn't supposed to be like that.

I wasn't supposed to think about her every moment. I wasn't supposed to need her that much."

A frown had pulled Mac's eyebrows down low.

"I saw Mom and Dad. They loved each other. It wasn't dark and frantic. Their love was steady. Strong." The way he'd thought love should be. "I was out of control with Celia. I hardly recognized myself at all. I couldn't let her go—I wanted to tie her to me in any and every way possible." It had been that way from the beginning. Hell, he hadn't even joined the CIA out of some big desire to help his country. He'd done it *for her*. To be close to Celia.

"So you married her," Mac murmured.

He nodded. "Trust wasn't easy for me. Not with our parents' deaths and then…so much was happening. We weren't getting anywhere with the investigation and I—" He expelled a rough breath. "There were double agents in our group. I was set up. Taken down. My location was known as soon as I stepped foot off that plane. They knew so much about me…"

His gaze slid from Mac to Davis. "About all of you. They taunted me. Said that they'd take me out with a bullet at the end, just the way my parents had gone out. But first, they wanted information. Intel on covert missions I'd worked, that *you'd* all worked. They planned to use me in order to get to all of you."

Davis sighed. "And you thought Celia was the one who'd served you up to them."

"She was supposed to be on that plane with me, but at the last minute the plans were altered. Instead of traveling over with me then, she was coming two days later." Though now he was so grateful for that change.

Because if she'd been taken, too...*would Celia be dead?*
"And the other agents—the ones who'd turned—they'd
been working with her far longer than I had. She was
close to them. They told me...my captors said everything she'd done was part of a setup. Even marrying me
was just a ruse so that I'd trust her and be ready to follow any order she gave. Like a lamb to the slaughter."

"And you believed them?" Davis asked quietly.

"Not at first. But when you go days without food or
water and the jerks start slicing you open and they keep
playing videos...recordings of Celia talking about her
plans... Hell, at first, I knew those recordings had to be
fake. I knew it. I knew her!" His hands had fisted. "But
I went a little crazy after a while. When I was sure no
one was coming for me, it got harder to think straight. I
was so angry. At the captors. At myself. I wasn't going
to turn, no matter what they said, so I had to use that
rage to help me stay alive."

Mac rose and came toward him. "You know that's
part of the interrogation techniques they use. They want
to break you down. Because when you give up your
hope, you have nothing left."

Celia was my hope. "I needed her too much," he said
again. "I realized that in the pit. The way I felt for her—
it scared even me. I didn't think it was normal. I wasn't
normal. And when I got out, I still had so much anger in
me." Now he would confess his darkest shame. "I was
afraid I'd hurt her. I had to send her away from me."

"What?" Davis demanded, voice sharp. "Sullivan,
hell, no, you—"

"You didn't see me back then. I stayed away. I
thought..." He swallowed the lump in his throat. "I

thought they'd succeeded, you see. That they had broken my mind. I was too dark. Too dangerous. The way I felt about Celia…it wasn't safe for me to be near her." Because love could become a dark and twisted obsession. And if he'd ever hurt her…

"Post-traumatic stress," Mac said. "Damn, man, I didn't know it had gotten that bad. You should have told me…"

More like post-traumatic hell. "I crawled my way back." Moment by moment. "But yeah, Davis, to get back to what you said before about me calling for her… I talk in my sleep. I call out for her. I have night terrors and flashbacks and sometimes I wonder if it will ever end." He drew in a shuddering breath. "But I've tried living without her, and it sucks." No other way to describe it. "The need is still there. The yearning for her. Only her. I thought it would go away. It didn't. But *I* have control back. I'm not going to that dark place, ever again. I can be the man she needs."

Mac locked his hand around Sullivan's shoulder. "You should have told me this stuff."

"We all were going through enough…with our parents and Ava." For a while, he'd worried that Ava might hurt herself, too. She'd been in so much pain. "I was just trying to make it through the days and nights." His brothers had said they'd seen him withdrawing. It had been true. He'd had to withdraw in order to survive.

Sullivan shook his head. "That's it. My screwed-up, twisted past." He inclined his head toward a watchful Davis. "I want to be better, for her. I want to be the man she deserves now. She came to me for help, and you can damn well bet that is exactly what I'll give her." He'd give her everything he had.

"So you trust her...completely?"

"Yes." Said with no hesitation. "So even if your contact—"

"Monroe said that he'd only trust a few people to watch his back, and Celia would be at the top of his list."

Sullivan nodded. "And does he know who is after her? Have they recently worked any missions that put a target on her?"

Mac's hand tightened on his shoulder. "Celia didn't tell you that?"

"Celia hasn't told me much at all about her work with the government." Probably because she was protecting the other agents. "She just said she was getting out."

Davis sighed. "If we're going to help her, she'll have to open up about her past, too. You think she'll do that?"

He wasn't sure. And he wasn't going to push her too hard. "She'll share what she can." To him, it was as simple as that. "She'll—"

His phone rang. Frowning, Sullivan pulled the phone from his back pocket. *Unknown caller.* He started to just ignore the call, but a tightness in his gut made him answer. "Sullivan."

"McGuire..." a man's voice drawled. "The deadly ex-marine. It's been too long."

"Who in the hell is this?"

"You aren't doing Celia any favors by staying close to her."

He listened carefully to the caller's voice. Arrogant tone. Faint drawl.

"Do you remember me?" the voice pushed. "Once upon a time, you worked under my command."

The voice finally clicked for him. "Ronald Worth."

He saw surprise flash on Davis's face.

"Celia wouldn't listen to reason, so I hope you will," Ronald said.

It was no surprise that the guy had managed to get his number. The fellow no doubt had plenty of strings he could pull. Accessing a private number would be all too easy for a man like him.

"We need to meet," Ronald said bluntly. "Just the two of us. There's a lot you don't know about, and I don't exactly feel comfortable sharing over the phone."

"Because you think someone could be listening in?"

Ronald laughed. "I don't trust anyone these days. Friends can turn on you in a blink. So can family. But that's a lesson you already learned, isn't it?"

His brothers moved closer as Sullivan swiped the button on his phone to turn on the speaker. "Why do you just want to meet with me?" Sullivan asked. "Why not Celia?"

"Celia has already thrown away her career for you," Ronald said. "Do you really want her to lose her life, too?"

His fingers tightened around that phone. "Did you just threaten her?"

"No, son, I'm the one working desperately to keep her safe. She's got hunters on her trail because she doesn't have agency protection any longer, not officially. What she has…that's me. That woman has been like a daughter to me, and the last thing I want is to see her dead."

"That's the last thing I want, too."

"Then maybe you shouldn't have pushed her to go digging into the past."

Sullivan frowned at that response. He hadn't asked Celia to—

"Now the target isn't just on the McGuires. It's on her."

Suspicion gnawed at Sullivan's gut. There was just something about the guy's voice. "You know who killed our parents, don't you?"

"I know you shouldn't have pulled Celia into this mess."

"You bastard..." Had that man known the truth all along? *"Tell me."*

Fury was marked on Davis's face, too, a fury that matched Sullivan's. If Ronald Worth knew who'd killed their parents, why would he have kept silent for so long? Why not come forward?

"You have no idea the players who are involved in this game," Ronald stated flatly.

"It's not a game. It's our lives."

More laughter. "You think that by keeping Celia at the ranch, you're keeping her safe?"

Ice slid through Sullivan's veins. "How do you know I'm at the ranch?" But hell... "You triangulated the signal, didn't you? Is *that* why you called? To find out where I was?" And he'd just given up the fact that Celia was with him. He should have known—

"I'm not the threat," Ronald snapped. "I'm the one trying to help. Now if you want to learn more, you'll meet me. Just you. Slip away and leave Celia with your brothers. They can keep guard. Come to see me, and I'll tell you everything I know."

"You'll tell me who's after Celia?"

"I'll tell you the names of the men who killed your parents."

Go, Davis mouthed.

Mac nodded grimly.

"Where?" A flat demand from Sullivan.

Ronald rattled off the address.

And that ice just got thicker in Sullivan's veins. "You're already down in Austin?" Where another ex-agent had been killed just hours before? No way was that a coincidence.

"I've been trailing Celia. I lost contact with her after she left North Dakota. She has to come in, before it's too late."

Sullivan was starting to think it already was too late.

"Can you meet me in two hours?" Ronald pressed.

"Yeah, I'll be there."

"Good. Remember, come alone. You're not going to want anyone else to hear this…"

Did the guy think he was a fool?

The call ended.

Sullivan stared at his brothers.

"All right…" Mac sighed. "So what's our plan of attack?"

Chapter Seven

She was alone in the bed. Celia knew she was alone even before she cracked open her eyes. She felt cold, and she knew that Sullivan had left her.

Slowly, she stretched, aware of a few aches and pains in all the right places. She was naked and the sheet slid over her skin as she sat up. The sun still shone brightly through the window, so she knew a lot of time hadn't passed.

I didn't mean to fall asleep. I never fall asleep that way...not with someone so close to me.

But she'd felt safe in Sullivan's arms, and it had seemed so very natural to just close her eyes and drift away.

And just where had Sullivan *drifted* away to? She rose from the bed, pulling the sheet with her. "Sullivan?" Celia called, but he didn't answer her, and it only took a few moments to realize that he'd left the guesthouse. Pursing her lips, she went back to the bedroom. She eyed her clothes, scattered on the floor, then moved to the closet. A search through the boxes in there revealed some old jeans and a T-shirt. Very close to her size, a little too tight in the rear, but they'd work. She figured the clothes must belong to Ava or Jamie.

Now to find some shoes…

A few minutes later, she'd pulled a pair of tennis shoes out from beneath the bed. Those shoes would be so much better than her heels. She'd have to remember to thank those ladies later for the items they'd left behind.

Dressed, she hurried toward the front of the guest-house. She'd go out, find Sullivan and then…then she had to figure out her next step. She certainly wasn't going to sit back and hide at the ranch. Hiding wasn't her style. Never had been. She'd contact Ronald again and figure out if he was telling the truth about the agency. Maybe…could another traitor have infiltrated their unit? The same way a traitor had gotten inside when Sullivan was taken before?

It was possible, even with all the vigorous screenings that were in place. Some people were so very good at lying.

She opened the door. Hurried outside. She'd turned toward the main house when she saw Sullivan and Mac heading in the direction of the cars. For an instant, she stilled.

No, he wasn't just planning to leave without telling her. Was he?

But Sullivan didn't glance her way. He jumped into the car, his movements too quick and tense. Mac followed, riding shotgun.

Those men needed to think again. She wasn't the left-behind type.

Her pace picked up until she was nearly running. Her instincts were screaming at her.

Sullivan cranked the car.

Oh, no, you don't.

She put herself in front of the vehicle, blocking his path.

Instantly, the engine died and Sullivan jumped from the car. "Celia!" Her name sounded like an angry snarl. Funny, earlier it had sounded like a caress. But that had been when they were in bed together, and obviously those moments had been fleeting. "What in the hell are you doing?" he asked.

"Getting your attention," she answered immediately as she braced her legs apart. "You didn't seem to notice my approach, so before you went roaring out of here, I thought I'd stop you."

"You jumped in front of the car!"

She smiled at him. "There was no jumping. Just stepping."

"I could have run over you!"

"No."

He gaped at her.

She glared back. "Where are you going?"

Sullivan glanced over his shoulder, looking toward Mac. Mac had climbed out of the car and was watching them with a tense expression.

"I have a meeting," Sullivan said, his voice still gruff. "It shouldn't take too long. I didn't want to disturb you, because I knew you had to be dead on your feet."

As if he wasn't? "Who's this meeting with?"

His lips thinned. A total sign he didn't want to tell her.

"Sullivan?" she prompted.

His hands curled around her shoulders.

As if a little touch from him was going to distract her. "No secrets, remember?"

He swallowed and his Adam's apple clicked. "I remember."

And that's why you were trying to sneak away? The guy had a whole lot to learn about *not* keeping secrets.

"I was told to come alone," he said.

Mac was shotgun. That hardly qualified as alone. She lifted one eyebrow and tried not to tap her foot as she waited.

"Ronald Worth."

Her jaw almost dropped. "My boss? You're going to meet my boss?" Or rather, her ex-boss. Celia's stomach knotted. "Why?" And why wouldn't she be included in that meeting?

"Because he knows who killed my parents. The guy called me. Set up a meeting." He looked at his watch. "I'm supposed to be there—alone—in the next hour."

This wasn't right. And it was making zero sense to her. "How would he know who killed your parents?" When she'd first started digging into Sullivan's past, it had been Ronald who told her there was nothing to find. He'd been the one to say she had to stay out of that old investigation.

Not our area. He'd said that curtly. And yes, she knew the CIA didn't normally get involved in domestic situations—their targets were more internationally focused, and the Special Activities Division had certainly been targeting international groups who were hostile to the US. So much counterterrorism work had been going on with her unit, but...

But I know how the government works. One agency scratches the back of another. She'd wanted to pull in help from other agencies to unravel the mystery of the McGuire murders.

Ronald hadn't helped her. In fact, he'd ordered her to stand down. Only now he was calling up Sullivan? She didn't like that setup. Not at all.

"He gave me the meeting location," Sullivan said. She realized he hadn't answered her question. Probably because he didn't have an answer for her. "The guy is down here, in Austin. Did you know that?"

No, she didn't. "I don't trust him." It hurt to say those words, but they were the truth. "He shouldn't have contacted you."

"He said you wouldn't listen. That he'd tried to warn you, but you kept digging." Sullivan tilted his head as he studied her. "You were digging for me, weren't you?"

Obviously. "You needed closure. It was the only thing you ever seemed to really want—the truth about your parents."

He shook his head. "That's not all I want."

Her gaze slid to Mac, then back to Sullivan. "Why weren't you taking me with you?"

"Because I don't trust the guy, either. I think it's some kind of trap. Maybe a straight setup. And I didn't want you put at risk."

She didn't deny that it could be a trap. With Porter dead and Ronald already on the scene, suspicion was heavy within her.

"Mac will watch my back," Sullivan said. "He'll be there to—"

"Ronald never goes into the field alone. He always has backup, too." Only she was usually that backup. Until she'd started branching out more in the last year.

Making her plan to leave the agency behind. "You need me."

"I need you *safe*."

She shook her head. "I'm not the type to sit on the sidelines. You know that about me."

"Yes."

Resolutely, Celia nodded. "Then it's settled. Mac and I will both be your backup."

He didn't move.

So she just went around him and headed for the back of the vehicle. But before she could reach for the door, he'd raced after her. Sullivan caught her wrist in his hand. "I'm fine with any risk that comes my way," Sullivan said gruffly. "But I am not fine with risking you."

Sweet. But… "I'm not yours to risk, Sully. I'm my own person. I make my own decisions."

"You were hunting to find the truth about my parents—*that's* what put the target on your back, Celia. That's what Ronald said. I did this to you."

"Have you noticed," she murmured, "that you and I play the blame game? I thought it was my fault you were taken, that I should have seen the enemy sooner. And now you… You're trying to put any threat I face on your own shoulders." She shook her head. "We've got to stop that. Let go. Bad things happen in this world." She could hate them. She could rage against them, but they happened. "Maybe we should just focus on *stopping* those bad things now."

He didn't let her go. "I don't want anything bad happening to you."

She stepped closer to him. Her body brushed against his. "Then maybe you should watch my back while I watch yours." Because she wasn't letting him go out to this meeting without her. She knew Ronald. She'd seen him in the field plenty of times.

He could be absolutely deadly.

If the agency did turn on me, it would have been from Ronald's order.

"What if..." His voice lowered as his head dipped toward her. "What if I'm the bad thing that happens to you?"

She didn't understand that, not at all. "Sully?"

"You are too good for me. I've always known that." His fingers caressed the inside of her wrist, moving lightly over her pulse and sending a shiver sliding over her. "Letting you go isn't possible for me. I'll try to be the man you need. I swear, I will."

He was the only man she wanted. Just as he was. "Sully—"

A car horn honked. Loudly. Celia actually jumped, and then her head whipped around. Mac was back in the vehicle and currently blasting away on the horn. He lowered the driver's-side window, leaned across the seat and called out, "Look, I get that the two of you are really into each other—good for you. Fantastic. I was always rooting for you guys. But we have a rather dangerous man waiting for a rendezvous, and I'd really like to see how this damn scene plays out with him." His jaw hardened. "If he knows who killed our parents, the guy *will* be talking to us. One way or another."

It wasn't as if Ronald would just give in to a threat, even a threat that came from the mighty McGuires. But he might talk to her.

Or he might shoot her.

They'd find out, soon enough.

She pulled her wrist from Sullivan's hold. "Time to go."

He swore.

AN ABANDONED WAREHOUSE wasn't exactly a prime meeting spot...unless you were looking for a place to run some shady deal.

No eyes, no ears...no one around for miles.

Sullivan braked the car in front of the warehouse. He'd already dropped Mac off—a good distance back so the guy wouldn't be seen—and he knew his brother would be moving into position. Sullivan hadn't wanted to arrive with Mac in the seat next to him. After all, there was no sense tipping Ronald off to Mac's presence just yet. So he'd taken precautions and made sure to drop off his brother in a secure area.

One that would be hard for Ronald to see from that warehouse.

But Celia had stayed with him. Determined, fierce Celia.

"Are you ready?" she asked him now.

Hell, no, he wasn't ready. He would be *ready* if she was far away, maybe behind half a dozen guards, but Celia wasn't the hiding type. She'd been trained as a fighter, and that was just who she was, straight to her core.

If he tried to push her to the side...no, that couldn't happen. He had to respect what she could do. They'd stand together, and both of them would be stronger for it.

He saw her check the gun he'd given her. Her movements were quick, practiced.

"Ready," Sullivan replied, his voice quiet. There were a dozen other things he'd rather have said to her, but this wasn't the time. It sure wasn't the place.

Later, he'd tell her how he felt. Later, they'd figure this thing out between them.

We can make it work. He'd do anything to make it work between them.

They exited the vehicle and stayed low as they made their way inside the warehouse. The door was unlocked, no doubt courtesy of the welcome wagon that was Ronald. When they pushed on that door, it squeaked open slowly. The interior of the place was dim, dust-filled. Light spilled in from the busted windows on the right and overhead. Sullivan made sure not to step on the broken glass as he made his way forward. He kept his gun in his hand, kept his body alert and waited for the danger to show itself.

"I thought I said to come alone..."

Hello, danger.

Ronald Worth walked through the doorway on the right. He had his hands up, apparently showing that he wasn't armed. Just because the guy wasn't flashing a weapon, it didn't mean he wasn't dangerous.

"I thought you wanted to see me," Celia said, her voice incredibly calm. "So I figured you wouldn't mind if I tagged along."

Ronald Worth was in his early sixties, or at least that was what Sullivan had heard. The guy was damn deceptive in person. He was fit, his hair was still a dark black and his light brown eyes had faint lines near their corners.

Ronald's gaze slid from Sullivan's gun to the one

held easily in Celia's hand. "Are you really pointing that thing at me?"

"Yes," she said flatly. "I really am."

He made a faint rumble of disappointment. "After all we've been through together? Come on now, Celia, I made you into the woman you are."

"No, I did that myself. You were just my boss."

Sullivan kept his weapon aimed at the guy as he stepped forward. "You said you had information on my family."

A faint smile curved Ronald's mouth. "I figured you'd bring her along. I mean, even though I said come alone—that was probably like waving a red flag in front of your face, right? You decided I had to be the threat in this game, so you came running, with Celia at your side." He dropped his hands. "Since that worked so well, it's time to leave."

What?

Ronald's smile tightened. "Come, Celia. I'll have you with a new assignment by dusk. You can slip right back into the fold. No one ever needs to know about this little defection—"

"It's not a defection," Celia fired right back. "I told you after the assignment in North Dakota went sour—I'm done. I've had enough and I want out."

Ronald sighed. "Are you still upset about that presidential hopeful? Look, I was told he was the man to watch. Our job was to get close and look for skeletons in his closet. You found plenty of those. I don't see where the problem was."

"There are skeletons in everyone's closet," Sullivan murmured. "Just like I'm betting there are plenty in yours."

His words drew Ronald's gaze back to him.

"I don't remember saying you should lower your hands," Sullivan snapped at him.

Ronald's gaze hardened a bit. "You're not actually barking orders at me."

"Uh, yeah, I am." He raised his weapon. "Hands *up*."

Ronald lifted his hands. "I have a car out back, Celia. We need to leave."

She took a step closer to her ex-boss. "I'm not leaving Sullivan."

Anger flashed across Ronald's face. "Not that again. Look, so you're still married to him. We can fix that mistake. No problem."

Still married—

Sullivan's gaze cut to Celia.

"The guy is dragging you down," Ronald continued, his voice roughening. "You don't want to be a target like he is. You don't want to get caught in the hell that's coming."

But Celia's expression never wavered. "Why don't you tell me about that hell? Tell us both. You seem to have been holding back on me for quite a while. According to Sullivan, you know who killed his parents."

The guy gave the faintest of nods.

"Who killed them?" Sullivan demanded.

Ronald's eyebrows rose. "It was all in the family."

What in the hell was that supposed to mean?

"Crimes like that, they can be personal. They can be—"

"Stop it," Celia blasted. "You're just jerking us around! His brothers didn't kill them! None of them were even in the country when his parents were murdered!"

"Ava was in the country," Ronald murmured. "Always wondered…just what did she see? So much more than she said, I bet. Only she knew how to keep quiet, not like her mother."

Sullivan lunged forward. He grabbed Ronald and shoved him up against the nearest wall and he put the gun under the man's chin. "Not Ava. I won't believe your lies!"

"Look at him," Ronald said, and he didn't sound even a little scared. Instead, his words vibrated with fury. "Look at what he's doing, Celia! Is this really the man you want to throw your life away for?"

He's pushing my buttons. Playing a game with me.

Celia grabbed Sullivan's shoulder. He let her pull him back.

"Ava didn't kill them," Celia said flatly. "And just so you know, I *won't* pull Sullivan back next time."

Surprise rippled through Sullivan. Celia truly did have his back. *And I'll have hers.*

"Because I think you've been lying to me, Ronald," she added. "You stonewalled my investigation, didn't you? And you worked so hard to get this little face-to-face meeting…was it because you wanted to get close to me?" Her words were calm, eerily so. "Are you trying to kill me?"

"No." The one word seemed torn from her boss. "I'm trying to keep you alive. You stirred up a hornet's nest. You should have left it alone. They all should have. Now I want you out of this mess before it's too late—"

"Who killed them?" Sullivan roared.

Celia stepped in his path. "Sully, let me—"

Ronald grabbed her. He yanked Celia back against him, and in that quick instant, the guy had a knife at her throat.

"Drop your gun, Celia," Ronald ordered her.

She didn't drop it.

Sullivan took aim at the other man. "I will put a bullet in your head." They should be clear on that. "Let her go, *now*."

"I need to walk out of here with Celia," Ronald rasped. "We'll go, and you won't follow."

Sullivan shook his head. "I will follow wherever she goes." Celia still had her gun, and he *knew* she'd be making a move soon.

"I was following orders back then," Ronald said, his words barely more than a whisper. "I didn't pull the trigger. I want you both to know that."

Then he dropped the knife and whirled Celia around to face him. His hands closed tightly around her shoulders.

She pressed her gun to his chest.

"I didn't pull the trigger," he told her, voice desperate. "But it's all coming back on *me*. I wanted you to stop digging into the past. Dammit, as soon as you recruited him, I knew it was a mistake. So I—"

"You were the one who set up Sullivan," she said, her voice hoarse. "You were the one who sold out him and the others agents on that mission. *You* were the one behind it all?"

His jaw locked. "I didn't know you'd married him. Not until later. And when I told you that we couldn't go in after him on a retrieval mission, you should have just listened to me! This could all have been over! You could have been safe! I would have been safe!"

She shook her head. "I think it is over now. For you."

Ronald was there when my parents were killed. "You SOB," Sullivan snarled. "Why?"

"I didn't have a choice," Ronald rasped. "There was too much to lose. And I... He held the power. Back then, and now."

"Don't give me that," Celia said. "You're the director of the Special Activities—"

"And how do you think I got that job?" Disgust tightened his face. "I sold my soul long ago. He got rid of the enemies in my path, and I turned a blind eye when necessary."

The knife had clattered to the dirty floor near them.

"You came here to kill us both, didn't you?" Celia asked. "You're still turning a blind eye, aren't you? Protecting yourself, no matter who else you hurt."

His eyes closed. "I was going to lead you out, and that would be the end for you. Sullivan wasn't going to escape, either."

Lead you out...

"You are dead," Ronald continued, and he actually sounded sad. "You just don't know it. I'm sorry, Celia... really sorry this had to end like this for you..."

Then Sullivan saw a glint from the corner of his eye. He'd been in the battlefield before and seen a glint just like that. *Off a sniper's rifle.*

"Celia!" He roared her name even as he leaped toward her. He grabbed her arm and slammed to the floor with her.

He heard the thud of impact. There was no mistaking the sound a bullet made when it sank into flesh. Once you heard that hard thud, you never forgot it.

Not Celia. Not Celia.

He was on top of her, shielding her body with his own. But Ronald Worth had no shield. And the bullet that *would* have gone into Celia just seconds before had lodged in Ronald's chest.

As Sullivan looked up and watched him, Ronald put a hand to his chest. His legs gave way. The bullet must have gone straight through him, tearing through his organs, because a trail of blood followed him as he slid down that dirty wall, marking a deadly path.

"Celia," Sullivan whispered. She was so still beneath him.

"I'm okay." Her voice was a faint breath of sound. "Get Mac on the line. He needs to know a shooter is out there. We need to warn him."

Celia had told him that Ronald always had backup with him. And that backup was ready to kill.

He eased off her, making sure not to present a target. They were both well away from all the windows now.

That's why Ronald grabbed Celia. To make her a target. Sullivan would bet the SOB had said that if he couldn't get Celia to walk out with him, then he'd pull her into the line of fire.

But I got her out.

"C-Celia…" Ronald rasped her name. "Help me."

Sullivan put his phone to his ear. He knew his brother would have turned his phone to vibrate. Mac wouldn't risk having a ringtone give away his presence. Before the first ring could even finish…

"What the hell is going down in there, Sully?" Mac demanded.

"A sniper is in the area. He just tried to take out Celia, but he hit Worth instead." One glance and he knew… "The guy isn't going to be living much longer. I need you to call your cop buddies and get a team out here. Now."

Before the sniper slipped away.

A ghost who disappeared in the wind.

"Stay alert," Sullivan ordered him.

Celia was creeping toward Ronald.

Sullivan slammed down his phone and grabbed her hand. *"Don't."*

"He's dying," she whispered back to him.

"And he was ready for *you* to die." He pulled her closer to the nearest wall. He needed to get out there and hunt that shooter. "You can't help him, Celia. You know that."

Her hand brushed over his cheek. Sullivan stilled.

"I can," she said. "I will."

"Celia—"

"Go after the shooter. I've got this."

Then she crawled away, heading back toward Ronald. The other man was gasping now as he tried to clumsily put his own hands over the gaping wound in his chest.

The man could still be a threat. He'd been working covert operations for years. Celia had to know just how dangerous the fellow still was. The knife was far too close to Ronald.

Celia kicked the knife away. Then she put her hands over Ronald's. "Look at me."

Sullivan barely heard her voice.

"It's okay, Ronald. You're not alone."

And Sullivan knew just how Celia planned to help the man who'd been ready to kill her.

She wasn't going to let Ronald die alone.

Slowly, Sullivan slipped from the room.

Chapter Eight

His blood soaked her fingers. It was warm, slick, and the flow wouldn't stop.

She'd pulled Ronald down onto the dirty floor. His head was in her lap. Her hands were over his chest.

"Celia…"

"Save your strength. Help will come soon." She'd heard Sullivan tell Mac to call the cops. Any minute they'd be hearing the wail of sirens. "You'll be all right."

His laughter was little more than a rasp. "You know… that isn't…true."

Yes, she did. She also knew that when a man was dying in your arms, you said what you could to comfort him.

Even if he'd just tried to kill you.

"I'm…sorry." Ronald seemed to force out those words.

"Shh…" She didn't want to hear his apologies. She didn't want to open the floodgate on the pain inside her. She needed to be strong now.

"Always…respected you…saw so much…in you…"

She pushed down harder on the wound. So much blood. If Sullivan hadn't grabbed her, she'd be the one bleeding out on that dirty floor. She'd be the one struggling for each breath.

And Ronald would have been the one to send her to her death.

She stared into his eyes. Dark, deep and pain-filled. She tried to smile for him.

"Celia…" He did smile for her. "You're usually… a better liar…"

And he was usually a better man. "Why?" She wanted to know before it was too late.

"Because you were…destroying me."

She shook her head but never let up the pressure on his wound. "I wasn't. I never did anything to you."

"Past…tied up…a weight that's been pulling me… for so long…"

She stared into his eyes. His breath was coming in slower pants. "How were you connected to Sullivan's mother? Were you—were you the man who killed her boyfriend?"

His bloodstained fingers lifted toward her cheek.

"Talk to me, Ronald." *You don't have time to waste.*

"I'm…sorry."

"Then tell me what you can." She still didn't hear the shriek of sirens. "What was your connection?"

"Her boyfriend…was a target…"

Her breath expelled in a rush. "A government target?"

"Only doing my…job." His eyelashes began to sag closed. "Hired…assassin. We didn't…didn't kill the woman. Let her go… She should never…never have been…there… She…recognized him…knew killer… F-family…"

His eyes had closed. His breath was so hard, so—

There was no sound.

No more hard breaths. No more rasping voice struggling to speak.

She swallowed. "Ronald?"

He didn't answer her. Her left hand slid up his neck and searched for his pulse. Her bloody fingers lingered against his skin, but there was no pulse to feel.

"Goodbye, Ronald," she whispered. She remembered the first time they'd met. His firm handshake when he'd welcomed her into his office. Her knees had been knocking together, but she'd refused to show him her fear. She'd promised him she could handle any job the agency threw her way. She'd been so eager to prove herself.

Carefully, she slipped from beneath him. Celia lowered his head to the floor.

She'd thought she knew him. She'd thought wrong.

Celia wiped her bloody hands on her jeans, then picked up her weapon again. She went after Sullivan.

HE HEARD THE roar of a motorcycle. The distinct sound of the engine couldn't be mistaken, and Sullivan bounded around the corner of the warehouse. A good fifty feet away, he saw the man on the motorcycle— a guy wearing a heavy black leather coat and a dark helmet. There appeared to be a heavy gear bag of sorts strapped to his back.

Not a gear bag. A weapon bag. Sullivan would bet the guy's sniper rifle was in that bag.

"Stop!" Sullivan yelled.

The guy didn't stop. He shot forward on the motorcycle.

Mac leaped from the shadows, his gun up, and fired at the guy on that motorcycle.

The bullets slammed into the bike's body and the rider nearly lost control. But then he revved the engine once more and took off, even as Mac kept firing at him. The guy crouched low on the bike and was vanishing as Mac and Sullivan raced after him.

Hell, no, we won't catch him on foot.

Sullivan spun around. "Go stay with Celia!" he called to Mac. "I'm going after that jerk." Because if that guy got away, they'd be back to square one. No way. No damn way could that happen. He ran back to his car, jumped inside and twisted the key.

The engine sputtered, not starting instantly.

He stiffened.

The car was just tuned up last week. It should have started right away.

His head whipped up. Through the glass of his window, he saw Celia run out of the warehouse. He threw open the door and lunged out of the car. "Back, Celia!" he bellowed at her. "Get back—"

There wasn't enough time for him to get to her. The car exploded behind him, sending a blast of fire rushing right at him. He saw the terror on Celia's face—that one instant seemed to be frozen in time. Her mouth was open, as if she was screaming.

Was she calling his name? He couldn't tell for sure. He couldn't hear her. The blast was too loud, deafening.

But Sullivan could see the terror in her eyes. Her gaze had gone wide, her blue eyes never bigger than they were in that desperate moment.

He'd told her to get back.

She was still rushing forward.

And the fire seemed to surround them both.

HE BRAKED THE motorcycle when he heard the explosion. Through the visor of his helmet, he glanced back and saw the dark cloud of smoke rising into the air.

It had been pathetically easy to predict the moves of the McGuires. Of *course* they would give chase. Of course they'd think they were the unstoppable force who could follow him and save the day.

Like father...like sons.

So while Sullivan had been kept distracted by Ronald, he'd put his little surprise in place. Then he'd waited, giving Sullivan and his brother—because, sure, he'd known Sullivan would have a tagalong with him—a chance to spot him. After all, they couldn't give chase unless they'd actually seen him.

Now the chase was over. For the McGuires, at least.

The smoke kept drifting in the air. In the distance, he heard the wail of sirens. The local authorities, finally coming to the rescue. Only who was left to rescue?

He turned back around. He'd have to go off-road to avoid the cop cars. Easy enough to do. He'd lie low for a bit. Maybe even take refuge at an old cabin he'd enjoyed once before.

And when it was clear, he'd just slip right out of town and get back to the life that waited for him.

But before he left, he'd make sure that the McGuire ranch burned to the ground...a final end to that dark chapter of his life.

No more mistakes.

His fingers curled around the handlebars and he drove away.

"SULLIVAN!"

She heard the cry distantly, a muted call.

"Celia!"

Her eyes opened. She sucked in a deep breath and nearly choked on the smoke. Her breath came out in a coughing spree as Celia realized where she was.

Not on the ground. She'd reached Sullivan. Their bodies were tangled together, as if they'd been tossed by the explosion. They'd landed together, but he was beneath her, and he wasn't moving.

Just as Ronald hadn't moved.

"No." Her voice was so weak. "Sully?"

"Celia! Sullivan!" That cry wasn't so muted now. It was Mac's desperate bellow. He was racing toward them.

Sullivan's face was cut. Dark ash and dirt covered his features. Her hands flew over him, frantic, as she searched for wounds. "Sully, please, talk to me."

Her fingers pressed to his throat. When she felt his pulse, her whole body shuddered. He was alive. "He's okay!" Her voice was too weak to carry over to Mac, so she tried again. "Sully is breathing! His pulse is strong." She cleared her throat, pushing back the lump that had risen there as she managed to shout, "He's alive!"

Sullivan's eyes opened. Bleary, but aware.

His car kept burning, sending that smoke billowing up into the air. He'd escaped, just in time. They both had.

"Celia?"

She threw her arms around him and held on as tightly as she could. "You're alive," she said, her voice catching.

His arms rose and locked around her. He held her in a strong grip. Strong, unbreakable Sullivan. Just what would she have done if he'd burned in that car?

The air was heavy with the scent of the blaze. She

could hear the crackle of the flames. She knew the shooter had set that bomb. Ronald wouldn't have had the time to do it.

And Ronald didn't tell me about it. Even as she'd been trying to comfort him in his last moments, he hadn't tried to warn her that death was waiting. Had he known? Had he just not cared?

"You weren't supposed to leave this meeting alive," she whispered. She held him even tighter. "You're a target, Sullivan. Someone is gunning for you." Someone with powerful connections.

Footsteps pounded toward them. "That was too damn close," Mac said, his breath huffing out. "When I heard the explosion, hell, Sully, I thought you were still in the car!"

Sullivan pulled back from Celia, but he didn't let her go. "The ignition sputtered." A muscle flexed in his jaw. "I've heard that same sound before, in the Middle East. The engine sputtered when I was on a mission there…" He coughed, and then rasped, "Back then, I had about five seconds to get the hell out of my jeep before it exploded."

Five seconds.

Five seconds to live.

Five seconds to die.

She shuddered against him and finally, finally heard the sound of sirens.

CELIA DIDN'T NORMALLY spend a whole lot of time in police stations. When she was with the agency, she'd worked her own brand of law enforcement, and it hadn't entailed sitting in a police interrogation room while she was the one being grilled.

But when the cops had rushed to the warehouse and discovered both a burning car and a dead body…she knew that she wouldn't be going anyplace soon. Sure, Sullivan and Mac might have a relationship with the local cops, but she was an unknown.

A potentially deadly threat.

Celia stared at her reflection in the one-way mirror. Her hand lifted as she brushed back her hair. She didn't look completely like hell. Maybe forty percent? Thirty percent like hell? Her fingers rubbed at the soot on her cheek. Her nose scrunched up as she realized she still smelled like fire.

And she still had blood on her jeans.

The door opened and a tall, broad-shouldered African-American man entered the room. He was dressed casually, with a badge clipped to his waist.

"Ms. James…" He pulled out the chair across from her and sat down. He sighed, looked absolutely less than thrilled as he stared at her, then drummed his fingers on the tabletop. "We have a problem."

She had a lot of problems right now, so the guy needed to narrow things down a bit.

"I'm Police Captain Ben Howard," he said, his voice not friendly and not threatening. Just flat. "And I have some questions for you." After that announcement, he just waited.

So she asked, "Um, what are those questions?"

His dark eyes scanned her face. "This is the part where you're supposed to ask for a lawyer."

"I don't want a lawyer." She didn't want to draw anyone else into this mess. "I haven't committed any crimes, so I don't need one."

"You were found at the scene of—hell, I don't even

know what," Ben muttered. "An unidentified male was shot, a bomb was placed in Sullivan McGuire's vehicle and—"

"The dead man isn't unidentified. I knew him quite well." That news probably wasn't going to help her in the suspicion department. "But he was CIA, and if I start talking about him, the talk won't get very far."

He stared back at her. "CIA." Then she was pretty sure he swore under his breath and she caught the mutter of, "Things can never be easy with the McGuires..."

She considered the matter again—as she'd been doing the whole time she was waiting in the interrogation room. "I don't think he was acting under government orders. In fact, I think he was tied to the deaths of Sullivan's parents years ago." Though there was no *thinking* about it. Ronald had confessed. She knew of his involvement with one hundred percent certainty.

Years ago, two men had slipped onto the McGuire ranch and committed those murders. Ronald Worth had been one of those men. And the mysterious shooter? She thought he had been the second man.

The captain stared back at her. "Just how do you fit into this mess?"

"I was CIA, too," she said.

He closed his eyes.

She waited. He didn't open them again.

Her gaze slid to that one-way mirror. Just who was in there, watching them?

"How long will it be," Ben asked, still with his eyes closed, "before federal agents swarm in here and tell me they're taking over my case?"

"I don't think the CIA is aware of what's been happening down here. The the victim you found, he was acting outside his parameters with the agency."

Ben's eyes snapped open. "A rogue agent?"

She swallowed. "So it would seem." Only he hadn't been acting alone. They had to find the shooter.

Before he went after the McGuires.

Her shoulders straightened as she focused on Ben. "You've been talking with Sullivan." She had no doubt about that. "I'm sure he told you what happened." As much as Sullivan could tell him. "I don't see what other information I could provide—" She broke off and folded her hands on the table. "Most of my past is classified."

"Then give me the name of someone at the CIA who can verify what you've told me."

She nodded and rattled off a phone number for him. He wrote it down on a pad beside him. She waited a beat, then said, "Ask for Alexandra Sanchez." Because Agent Sanchez had been a fixture at the agency for as long as Celia could remember. She'd been the supervisor of the Special Activities Division before being promoted up the chain of command. Sanchez would have to be informed of Ronald's death…and his betrayals.

There's going to be a housecleaning at the agency.

"Agent Sanchez can verify my identity for you," Celia said. "But when you call her—"

"Her group is going to swarm and whisk you away, right?"

They'd try.

He rose but didn't leave the little room. Instead, Ben put his hands on the table and leaned toward her. "Are the McGuires in danger?"

She held his gaze. "I believe that they are." Until that shooter was caught, none of the McGuires should sleep too deeply. "A hunter is out there. He's trying to tie up loose ends."

Like Sullivan.

Like me.

"You don't have a name for me? Not a face?"

She shook her head. "I never saw the shooter."

"But you were with the victim when he died, right? Did he have any famous last words?"

She didn't look away from his stare. "Nothing that can help you."

He snatched up the notebook. "I'm going to make that call."

She nodded. When the door shut behind him, she didn't move from that uncomfortable chair. But she did remember...

Only doing my...job. Ronald's last words were replaying through her mind. *We didn't...didn't kill the woman. Let her go... She should never...never have been...there... She...recognized him...knew killer... F-family...*

In the end, it kept coming back to that. *Family.* Just who had made the McGuire family into a target?

"THEY'RE NOT LETTING Celia go," Mac said as he marched out of the police station.

The sun was setting in the city, a red glow that spread across the sky. That glow looked far too much like blood for Sullivan's taste.

"What in the hell do you mean," Sullivan demanded, "they aren't letting her go? They have to! They aren't charging her with anything—"

"They can't even confirm her identity right now." Mac closed in on him and kept his voice low. "Look, my buddy Ben is working the case. He's doing everything possible, but this thing is a nightmare. With Celia's ties to the agency, with Ronald's dead body…hell, you know it's a mess."

"She can't stay in interrogation forever!"

Mac looked away.

Oh, hell, *no*, Sullivan knew he wasn't going to like this.

"They've moved her to a cell," Mac said.

"No." He shook his head. "Celia doesn't belong—"

"Protective custody, okay? That's what Ben is calling it right now. He's trying to figure things out. Seems Celia gave him the name for some lady at the CIA. When he called her, she demanded that he keep Celia secure until she could arrive. And *that's* all he'd tell me. Ben clammed up after that, and I knew he'd already been pushed too far." Mac glanced up at the police station. "We need to go home for the night, man. Check on the family. Try to figure out our next move."

His next move *wasn't* going to be ditching Celia. Ever since they arrived at that police station, he'd been fighting to see her. "I'm not leaving."

"You can't do anything today. The CIA boss they called in should be here tomorrow and—"

"And how do we know that she can be trusted? How do we know that someone won't swoop in here with federal ID and take Celia—then kill her? We can't trust anyone right now. You know that."

Mac focused on him. "We can trust each other. Mc-Guires always stick together."

Yes, they did. And if what Ronald had said was true…if he was still married to Celia… "She's a Mc-Guire, too."

Mac didn't have a comeback for that.

"Would you leave Elizabeth?" Sullivan pressed. "Just walk away while she was locked up and a killer could be closing in on her?"

"There are cops all around Celia. She's—"

"We know cops can go bad." They had personal experience with a cop going rogue. A cop they'd wrongly trusted for years. "Yeah, we have some friends in there, but we both know friendship doesn't always stand up against money or threats. With the right leverage, anyone can turn."

"You can't break the woman out!"

And I can't leave her.

Mac whistled. "Sully, look, you're covered in soot and blood and you smell like a fire. At least just go home and shower. I'll keep watch and make sure she's not transferred out, okay? She won't leave that building, and I know that's what you're afraid of."

Sullivan's back teeth had clenched.

"You're worried the CIA will whisk her away and you won't see her again," Mac added.

"I can't lose her." He knew his voice sounded ragged, but there wasn't much he could do about that tone.

"You won't. I told you, I'll stand watch, I'll—"

But Sullivan had stalked around his brother. He was marching up those steps and heading into the police station.

Mac grabbed his arm and leaned in close. "Sully, don't do anything stupid."

He wouldn't make a promise he couldn't keep. "I'm not leaving until I see her."

Mac searched his face, then gave a grim nod. "Guess it's like that…"

"Yeah, it's like that." And anyone who got in his way would regret it. He stormed back inside the station and cut a path straight to Ben's narrow office. He didn't bother knocking—he just shoved that door wide-open and demanded, "I want to see my wife."

Ben had his phone pressed to his ear. He stared at Sullivan a moment and said, "I understand the full seriousness of the situation. You have my word, the witness will be handled." He swiped a hand over his sweating forehead. "Three, yes, that sounds good."

Sullivan didn't move from that doorway. The last time he'd seen Celia, she was in the back of a patrol car. He'd argued like hell at that scene, but the cops hadn't listened to him. When a dead body was close, they had a tendency to overreact a bit.

"Right. Yes, yes, I understand," Ben said into the phone. "I'll see you then." He hung up the phone and rose. "When a door is shut, Sullivan, it usually means people should stay the hell out."

"My...wife," Sullivan snarled. "You've had her here for hours. She didn't get to speak to an attorney—"

"I brought that up to her. Said most folks asked for one," Ben said as he maneuvered around his desk. "She refused. I *wanted* her to call in a lawyer, but she wouldn't."

A growl built in Sullivan's throat. "You also can't keep her here indefinitely." He was aware of footsteps behind him. Sullivan glanced over his shoulder and saw Mac heading toward him.

"It's for her protection," Ben muttered.

Sullivan's gaze snapped right back to him. "Bull. In your cell, she's a sitting duck for whatever trouble comes her way." He advanced on Ben. "The dead man today? He was CIA. How do you know that the next killer who comes calling won't also be flashing CIA identification? Would you just turn her over to any bozo with a government ID?"

Ben squared his shoulders. "It's not my call to make."

"I want to see her. *Now.*"

Ben raised one eyebrow. "You're giving me orders now?"

Sullivan opened his mouth to reply.

"We all need to calm the hell down," Mac said from behind him.

Since when was Mac the one to give advice on being *calm*?

"We're on the same team here," Mac added. "We all want justice."

Ben nodded. "That's why I wear the badge."

"You put her in a cage," Sullivan said. He hated that thought. Was Celia scared? Was she wondering why he hadn't gotten her out of there? Did she think he'd just walked away?

"I gave her protection. The woman wasn't exactly sharing a lot with me. I got that she was CIA, and then I pretty much got stonewalled because she didn't think I had clearance to learn anything else." Ben huffed out a breath. "I called the number she gave me, all right? *They're* the ones who said to keep an eye on her. Want to know what I was just told about the woman you're claiming is your wife?"

He didn't need to know anything else. He already—

"She's a dangerous threat to security," Ben blasted. "A woman who should be monitored at all times. I walked in there, saw her and thought, *no way is that lady a killer.* But the CIA—the *CIA*—just told me otherwise! And they have someone coming to collect her tomorrow. The sooner she's out of my hands, the better."

Someone is coming to collect her...no, no. "That can't happen. You can't trust them!"

Ben just stared back at him with a troubled gaze. "Then what else am I supposed to do?"

Ben was a good cop, he knew that. The captain had worked with Mac plenty of times and Sullivan had been right there with them. But...

"Are you asking me to go against the CIA?" Ben's voice was soft.

"I'm asking you to let me see my wife." That was all he'd say.

"Come on, Ben," Mac added, voice cajoling. "Five minutes. What will it hurt? If she's locked up, she's certainly no threat to anyone."

Sullivan's whole body was tense. The seconds ticked by and then...

"Five minutes," Ben agreed, "but you McGuires had better not do anything to make me regret this decision."

Chapter Nine

Celia's cell was in the back of the police station, far away from anyone else. There was a toilet to her right. A sink waited close beside it. One saggy cot was pushed near the back wall of the cell.

She wasn't on that cot. Celia was busy pacing. They'd taken her clothes—claiming they were evidence. With all the blood on them, they probably were. Now she was wearing prison gray, and the clothes scratched against her skin with every step she took.

She heard the clang of one of the doors opening and stilled. She'd heard that same clang when they brought her back there earlier. Was a guard returning? Her growling stomach reminded her that she hadn't eaten...

All day.

So maybe someone was bringing her food.

Footsteps came toward her. She strained, listening. Not just one person. Two. Her heartbeat quickened a bit and—

Captain Ben Howard appeared.

She gave him a grim smile. "Got more questions for me?" *And maybe a sandwich?*

"Not this time," Ben said. He stepped aside. "Five minutes."

Sullivan. Sullivan was there.

Celia leaped toward those bars. Her fingers wrapped around them and she held on tight. The smile on her face almost hurt, it was so wide. "Sully!"

His fingers wrapped around hers.

"I'll be back," Ben said. Then his footsteps shuffled away.

She didn't look after him. Her gaze was glued to Sullivan's face. "You still have some ash on you," she whispered. His hair was tousled, his gaze dark and tumultuous, and he'd never looked sexier to her than he did in that moment.

If only they weren't separated by bars.

"You shouldn't be in here," he said, his voice gruff. "I'll get you out—"

"No, you won't, but it's rather sweet of you to say."

"Celia?"

"I'm a woman with no past. I can't even give the cops my Social Security number. And a dead man's blood was all over me." She shook her head. "There's no way I'm going anyplace soon, not until the CIA comes for me."

He stepped closer to the bars. "You know you can't trust them! Why did you tell Ben to contact the agency?"

"Because there are some people there I can trust." She had to believe that, despite what had gone down in that warehouse.

"Ronald and Porter," he gritted out. "Two men from the agency tried to kill you."

"That's why I told Ben to contact Alexandra Sanchez. She was Ronald's boss. If there are others in the CIA—men and women like them who are going to turn and kill—then she has to know about the risk." She leaned toward him. "Alexandra will come and take me into custody. I figure she'll be here by tomorrow morning."

"And I won't see you again."

No, he probably wouldn't. "Not until all this is cleared up." Until the powers that be decided her fate.

"You can't just be taken!"

She didn't want to talk about what might happen to her. "You and your family—you need to dig more into the life of your mother's ex-boyfriend. Ronald said he was the target. His death started this whole chain reaction."

"That twisted joker also said I needed to look to my family for the killer." A muscle jerked in his jaw. "That isn't happening. I trust them all."

She shook her head. "You trust the ones you know, but…what about the ones you don't know? What about the family your mother left behind? Ronald told me that your mother recognized the man who killed Henry Jones. She knew him."

His eyes glinted. "If she knew him, she would have just said the guy's identity—she would have just told the cops who he was."

Maybe. Maybe not. "She went back to see the cops a second time, remember? I told you there was a fire, and all evidence from that meeting was lost. Maybe she *did* tell them the guy's identity…"

"And someone made sure that testimony was destroyed?"

A man like Ronald Worth would've had the power to make the evidence disappear. *Is that why he was angry with me for digging? Was he afraid I'd find some link to that truth? And his involvement?*

"Family." The one word was heavy as it slipped from Celia. "That's what this keeps coming back to, every single time. You have got to find out more about your mother's family."

"There isn't anyone left there," he said. "I already ran the files. She had an older brother, but he was killed in a car accident just before she gave up her life there. Hell, that was probably one of the reasons she was so eager to walk away. There was nothing else left for her there."

She wasn't so certain. "Dig. You'd be surprised at the skeletons you might find."

The captain had said they had five minutes. How much time had passed? "Do me a favor?"

"I'd do anything for you."

In that instant, she believed he meant those words. Her heart ached. "Kiss me."

There was just enough room between those bars. He could kiss her once more.

It would be a kiss goodbye.

Sullivan instantly leaned toward her. His lips brushed against hers, and then that kiss deepened. She hated the bars. If only she could touch him fully. Savor him.

Why had fate been working against them from the very beginning?

She gave herself fully to that kiss, trying to forget everything else in that moment but him. She'd always loved his taste. Loved the way his lips pressed to hers. Her heart galloped in her chest and she pressed ever closer to him. She'd never wanted anyone else more than she wanted her Sully.

The familiar clang reached her ears, and Celia knew the captain was coming back.

She pulled her lips away from Sullivan's. "I'll miss you," she said.

"That *wasn't* goodbye."

Arguing with him would serve no purpose. Her gaze slid over him, memorizing his face. "Keep your guard up, Sully."

He took a step away from the bars. "And keep your trust in *me*, Celia. I won't let you down."

She made herself keep smiling as Ben appeared and led Sullivan away. Her shoulders remained straight, her back upright, and then...

He was gone.

A tear leaked down her cheek.

Sullivan had finally done it. He'd made her cry for him.

No, for what could have been.

"WHAT IN THE hell are you going to do?" Mac demanded as he glared at Sullivan. "Sit on a stakeout at the police station all night?"

Sullivan crossed his arms, leaned back against the brick wall and kept his eyes glued on the station across the street. "They'll take her out the back."

"What are you even talking about?"

"I'll need a ride," Sullivan said, thinking this through. "Preferably a car that won't ignite when I crank it."

Mac coughed. "Yes, right, that goes without saying."

"They'll take her during the night."

"Sully?"

"I know how they work." After all, he'd worked with them before. "Ben was talking to the agency when I went into his office." The guy had been sweating bullets. "He said three. Had to be 3 a.m. That's the time they're coming. And when they get her, I'll be right behind them."

"You're really going up against the CIA? Do you know how crazy that sounds?"

For Celia, he'd go up against anything. "Ronald Worth was there when our parents were murdered."

"Yeah, and now *he's* dead. The family is champing at the bit to talk to you and find out what the hell went down."

"The shooter got away." His eyes narrowed. "Ronald Worth took a bullet to his chest. But before he died, he told Celia that Mom's ex-boyfriend was his target. Target," he repeated. "That's the term you give an assignment." His gut had clenched. "The shooter is tied up with the agency, too—I'd bet my life on it." So much more made sense for him now. "*That's* why I was taken years ago. They kept talking about my family—but it was just because they were trying to see what I knew before they killed me."

"What about the Witness Protection Program?" Mac wanted to know. "They're the ones we need to grill. If Dad was working with them, if that is how he first met Mom—"

"There is no *if* to it." Their father had been so much more than he realized.

"Then maybe their deaths were tied to another case that he worked. Dad's last words were, 'I'll never tell you. No matter what you do. I'll never tell.'" Those words had haunted them all. "Maybe it was someone else's identity he was protecting. Maybe he died trying to keep one of his charges safe." Mac started to pace. "What we need is access to all his old case files."

As if those were just going to be turned over to them. Not without the right leverage, they weren't.

"Go back to the ranch," Sullivan said. "Check in with the others. Pull in every contact we've got. Plenty of people owe us favors. Let's start calling them in."

Mac paused. "And you're going to just stay out here on your own? I mean, could you make yourself any more of a target?"

Yes, he could. "Go back to the ranch," Sullivan said again. "I'm good here."

"No, what you are is obsessed. You need to watch yourself. Celia will—"

"Celia is my priority now." And the second those words were out of his mouth, he realized just how true they were. It wasn't about solving the mystery of his bloody past. For him…Celia was what mattered. Keeping her safe. Making sure she didn't vanish from his life.

Mac gave a low whistle. "Like that?"

"Like that," he agreed.

Mac's stare measured him. "Then how about I get that ride for you…you know…the one that doesn't explode when you turn the ignition?"

SHE ACTUALLY SLEPT. True testimony to just how exhausted she was. But when Celia heard the clang of metal, her eyelids flew open and she jerked up on the cot. It was so dark in that holding area.

Too dark.

There had been a faint light shining when she closed her eyes, but now there was nothing. The whole area was pitch-black.

Footsteps shuffled toward her.

"Don't be afraid…"

That voice—it was the police captain's voice. Ben.

"You're being transferred, ma'am." A bright light shone in her eyes, and she lifted her hand, trying to shield her gaze. "It's for your own protection."

She'd heard two sets of footsteps coming her way. Celia rose slowly from the cot as the cell door was unlocked. "Who's giving the orders for the transfer?"

"I am."

She couldn't make out the second person's form, but she knew that voice.

"You asked for me specifically," Alexandra Sanchez said, "so you got me. You'll come with me tonight, and you'll tell me exactly what happened to Ronald Worth."

Celia had expected to capture the lady's attention.

Now, if only she could be sure that Alexandra wasn't about to lead her off to a slaughter.

As for what had happened to Ronald… "He died." That was what had happened. "Though quite a few interesting twists and turns happened before his death."

"I'm sure they did," Alexandra murmured.

"Do you already have the body?" Celia asked. Because she knew Alexandra would want her own team reviewing Ronald's remains.

"Yes."

The light was still shining in Celia's eyes, and it was annoying the crap out of her. She moved forward and felt someone grab her hands.

"Sorry," Ben said. "But I'm going to need to cuff you for transfer."

Her gut clenched. "Hardly seems like standard procedure."

"None of this is standard," Ben said. "But the order to move you came down from the governor himself…"

"We're old friends," Alexandra revealed. "He was happy to assist me in this matter."

Celia was sure the guy had been only too happy to help the CIA. *Scratch my back…*

"He swore you'd be safe," Ben added. "That's the only reason this transfer is happening."

Right. Because if you couldn't trust the CIA, who could you trust? "I assume you're also retrieving Porter Vance's remains?" Celia asked as the cuffs were snapped around her wrists.

"Yes, when the helpful captain here told me about the body that was recently found near McGuire Securities, I investigated and realized the victim had been… one of ours."

Had been. The emphasis there was a telling one.

"We'll want to compare the injuries that the two men possess." Alexandra's voice was mild. Her footsteps tapped away as they left the holding area. "At this point, it would appear a sniper took them both out. We'll know soon if it was the same weapon, and from the weapon we can find the killer."

That made sense. Many snipers had signature bullets that they enjoyed using to mark their prey.

She was led out of holding and to a back door. It was still so dark. But when that door opened, she saw the alley behind the station.

A black SUV idled near the curb.

"You swear she's not in danger?" Ben asked. His hand was curled around her elbow.

Alexandra Sanchez turned back toward him. Now

that they were outside and the starlight fell down on them, Celia could just make out Alexandra's profile. The woman's hair was pulled back and twisted at the nape of her neck. She wore a long skirt and a loose top. "I give you my word, Captain. I absolutely mean Celia James no harm."

Then Alexandra strode toward the SUV. She opened the back door and waited.

Celia could feel the captain's concern. It was almost touching. "Don't worry about me," she said to him. "I can take care of myself."

"Cuffed?"

She smiled. "You learn a lot as a government agent." Including how to get out of cuffs very, very quickly. "When Sullivan comes back tomorrow—" and she had no doubt that he'd return for her "—tell him it...it still isn't goodbye." Eventually, she'd find a way back to him.

Then Celia turned and headed for the waiting SUV. She climbed into the back. Alexandra followed her and the door swung closed.

"Get us away from this place, Monroe," Alexandra instructed.

The driver waited just a beat then accelerated, taking them away from the station. The silence in the SUV was thick and far too heavy, as it seemed to weigh down on Celia.

Finally...

"I didn't know," Alexandra said quietly. "I assure you, Agent James, I had no idea that Ronald Worth had gone bad. When we had that—that *issue*—years ago, there was never any suspicion that he'd been involved. Now that I know the truth, I've already issued a full investigation into his life. Agents are searching his home even now."

"That issue." Celia nodded as she repeated those words. "You mean when Sullivan McGuire was betrayed and three other agents were killed? When we realized we had a mole in our group?" Not just one mole, though. Another that they hadn't seen. Ronald.

"Yes." Alexandra's voice had hardened. "That issue. If any intelligence had pointed to his involvement, Ronald would have been dealt with immediately."

Celia glanced down at her cuffs. The SUV had just moved beneath a streetlight, and the metal gleamed.

"He was involved in the murder of Sullivan McGuire's parents," Celia said.

A delicate pause. "I'm looking into that."

Celia glanced up. "Look harder."

"Who was the shooter, Celia? Who took out Ronald?"

Her fingers flexed within the cuffs. "I didn't see him."

"But you were with Ronald when he died. Did he tell you who was working with him?"

"No." Her voice was curt. "Where are we going?"

"A safe house. I'm not transferring you out of the area just yet…"

Her shoulders brushed back against the seat. "Because you're too busy doing housecleaning at the agency?"

"Every case Ronald ever worked will have to be reviewed. Every member of his team—past and present units—will need to undergo a thorough investigation. If he sent Porter down here on an execution mission for you, then that means he could have been using other agents to do his dirty work, too. Everyone who has been working with Ronald is under suspicion."

Celia understood exactly what was happening. "A nightmare."

"And it's just beginning." Alexandra exhaled heavily. "I don't know how deep this goes. I don't know who in that unit is loyal to the organization or who was just a puppet on a string for Ronald. Every single person must be vetted."

"Where do I come in?" Celia asked. Part of her was afraid to find out.

"You're dangerous," Alexandra said flatly.

Some days. True.

"You're obviously a threat. Ronald thought you knew something that would incriminate either him or the shooter he'd been working with. And that fact means you're valuable. Valuable *alive*."

"So I am in protective custody," Celia murmured. Her gaze slid toward the front of the SUV. The driver appeared to be completely focused on the road, but she knew he would be closely monitoring their conversation.

"He's been vetted," Alexandra said. "And because of his personal connection to the McGuires, I thought Monroe could be of assistance to me. This tangled web is closing around them, after all."

Monroe. The name clicked for Celia. She'd recruited Monroe Blake herself. An ex-SEAL, the guy had been a perfect candidate for the Special Activities Division. Tough, fearless and with a drive that had impressed everyone in the unit, Monroe had fit right in with the team.

Monroe braked the SUV at a red light. "I know Davis," he said, his rumbling voice carrying back to them. "He's a good man, and when Alexandra briefed me on what was happening, I volunteered to haul butt down here to help."

It was great that he said that, but Celia was past the point of taking anyone at their word.

"It hurts, doesn't it?" Alexandra asked her. "When you look around and realize that everyone else could be as good a liar as you are."

She'd been trained to lie by the agency. "Covers were a natural part of this business. Turning on your team-mate wasn't."

The light changed and Monroe accelerated.

"The shooter needs to be brought in alive," Alexandra said. "I'll personally handle his interrogation. He'll tell me just how deep this thing goes."

"It's not like he's just going to offer himself up for capture," Celia pointed out. If Alexandra thought so, she was living in a dream world.

"No, he won't." Alexandra paused a beat. "That's where you'll come in. Let's just see how eager he really is for you to be eliminated from the picture."

Ah, now it made sense. Celia fully understood just why she'd been whisked out of that jail cell by the most powerful woman in the CIA.

It wasn't about being kept safe.

It was about being used as bait.

SULLIVAN WAITED UNTIL all the lights were off in the little house at the end of Juniper Drive. He kept his vehicle well hidden, and he stayed in the shadows of the old trees that lined the street. There'd been a flurry of activity in that little house before, but all was silent now.

Celia was in that house. He'd seen her go in.

She hadn't come out.

He checked his weapon. It sure was getting ever harder to tell the good guys from the bad in this little game. He wasn't going to take any chances. He would be getting Celia out of there. Until she was back at his side, he felt as if he couldn't draw a deep enough breath. Fear gnawed at him. He knew both of them were in the sights of a killer.

Together, they'd be the stronger team.

He slipped toward the house. He'd studied the exterior for a while, looking for the best spot to gain entrance, and right now…he went to the side window. A quick swipe of his knife and he'd cut the screen. Would the house be wired with an alarm?

If so, then when he lifted that window, everyone inside would know he was there, but…

But he hadn't seen any signs of an alarm. The house had been taken at short notice, so he wasn't thinking that full precautions had been implemented, not yet.

Sucking in a deep breath, he reached for the lock on that window. Breaking it wasn't hard, and then he just pushed that window right on up…

No alarm shrieked and his breath slid past his lips.

SHE HEARD THE creak of the old wooden floor. Celia hadn't been asleep in that little bed; her mind had been too busy spinning. But when she heard that creak, her eyes strained to see in the darkness and she reached under the mattress, searching for the knife she'd insisted on getting before Alexandra left her.

I won't stay unarmed.

Alexandra had slipped her the knife before she

walked away. She'd also gotten rid of the cuffs, a very good thing.

There were no more creaks. Only a heavy silence, but Celia was sure someone was closing in on her. Moving closer and—

A hand pressed to her mouth. Rough, hard, strong. She swung up with her knife.

"Baby, try not to cut anything vital."

That rough whisper belonged to Sullivan. She stilled instantly, the knife probably far too close to his throat.

"Good, I appreciate that restraint," he muttered.

She dropped the knife and threw her arms around him. Celia yanked Sullivan down on the bed with her as her heart galloped in her chest.

"Knew you were in here, smelled the sweet flowers as soon as I opened the window," he rasped, his breath blowing lightly over her ear.

She smelled like flowers? No way, she probably smelled like a jail cell. She was even still wearing her prison gray! Alexandra had promised to bring her new clothes come morning, but—

The lights flashed on.

She blinked, trying to adjust to the sudden brightness.

"Get the hell away from her," a hard male voice snarled.

Sullivan tensed against her. "I'm guessing there was an alarm set to go off when I opened that window, after all." But he didn't sound particularly concerned. Very slowly, he eased away from her. "Must've been a silent alarm."

"Drop your weapon." That was Monroe barking the

orders, because he was the guard who'd been left to make sure she stayed alive.

And didn't escape. Not until Alexandra came up with a full plan, anyway. *A plan to use me.*

"The thing is," Sullivan drawled, "I'd rather not be unarmed."

Monroe glared at him. "Look, fellow, this isn't a debate, it's—"

A man came up behind Monroe, moving fast, a dark shadow that rushed into the room. Monroe sensed the threat too late and whirled.

But a heavy fist drove into his jaw and Monroe fell back, slamming into the floor. Before he could lurch to his feet, Sullivan had his gun aimed at the guy's head.

"Sullivan, stop!" Celia leaped toward them. "You don't need another enemy!"

Monroe wiped away the blood that dripped from his mouth. "I recognize that hook…" His gaze slid toward the man who'd sneaked up behind him. "It's been a long time, Davis."

Her gaze swung between them.

Davis gave Monroe a grim smile.

"You know this joker, Davis?" Sullivan demanded. He didn't lower his gun. And he still looked enraged.

"His name's Monroe," Davis offered. "And he saved my hide a time or two."

"And you saved mine." Monroe slanted a glance Sullivan's way. "Sure didn't expect you to find her so fast."

"I never lost her." Finally, his weapon lowered. "And you need to do a better job of checking for tails. I'm not the only one who could have followed you back to this place."

Monroe flushed. "I did check for tails. You're just… good." That admission was grudging.

"Right. I'm good. So good that I'm about to walk right out that door with Celia." Sullivan caught her hand in his and threaded their fingers. "Come on, baby, let's go."

He stepped forward.

And Monroe moved into their path. "Sorry." He rubbed his jaw. "But that can't happen."

"The hell it can't. You aren't keeping Celia here! You don't get to hold her against her will!" Sullivan blasted. "You don't—"

"He's not," Celia said quietly, cutting through his words.

Sullivan's head whipped toward her. "What?"

"I'm not here against my will. I'm here because I wanted to be."

The poor guy still looked confused.

"Monroe is an agent with the Special Activities Division. He's working for a woman named Alexandra Sanchez. For all intents and purposes, she *is* SAD now." She pushed back her hair. "She's the one who got me out of the police station, and she's the one tracking the shooter."

Davis swore.

Right. So Davis had obviously figured out where this was going, and, based on the darkening of Sullivan's face, he knew, too.

"The shooter wants me dead," Celia said. "So I'm going to be the bait to draw him out."

It was odd. She'd never seen Sullivan's eyes go quite that glacial before. Fury was supposed to be hot and burning, but his—his gaze was ice cold.

"Out," Sullivan growled.

Her eyebrows rose.

"Davis...take your buddy Monroe and get out," Sullivan ordered, his voice far too quiet. "My wife and I need to have a little chat."

She flinched. *Wife.* That one word got beneath her skin.

"Uh, wife?" Davis seemed to focus on that word, too. "I mean, I know it's been a busy twenty-four hours and all, but did I miss something? Celia said you were divorced—"

"She's my wife." His hand tightened on hers. "She's *mine*, and I want to talk to her, alone, right now."

"You aren't going to change my mind," Celia said.

He didn't reply.

But Monroe and Davis headed for the door. She glared at them. Just because Sullivan said jump, it didn't mean everyone had to leap so high. He was just a man. An angry, coldly enraged man.

The door closed behind Davis and Monroe. Jeez, so much for Monroe being her protection. *Way to abandon me in the face of danger!*

But they were gone, and she was suddenly alone with a very different Sullivan. She'd never seen him quite this way before, and for an instant, she hesitated.

Chapter Ten

"No," Sullivan said instantly. "That can't happen. It can't."

"I—"

He pulled her closer to him. "You can't be afraid of me." But he was seeing the fear in her eyes as she gazed up at him. "Anything but that. I will *never* hurt you."

Her breath whispered out.

She was wearing a gray prison uniform. Her hair was pushed away from her face and her eyes—those big blue wonderful eyes—drifted slowly over his face.

"How well do we know each other?" Celia asked him.

"No one knows me better," he said flatly. "Not my brothers. Not my sister. You know me, inside and out. I haven't hidden my dark spots from you. You're the only one who has ever seen me just as I am." And that was why he couldn't bear her fear. He needed Celia to accept all of him.

Just as he would accept all of her.

"Then you should know," she said, "that I have to do this."

"There's no need for you to be put at risk!"

Her smile was bittersweet, those dimples almost

painful to see. "We don't have this man's face. Not his name. He's got a cover firmly in place, one he has hidden behind for years. But he's come after me. He thinks I know something—he must believe I uncovered something that can expose him when I was digging for you." She gave a little shrug. "As long as he believes that, then we have an advantage. He has to keep coming for me, and when he does, we can be ready for him."

"Celia—"

"He's a ghost now. One that has haunted you and your family for far too long. I'm going to stop him."

He absorbed that. "I don't want to change you."

Her lips parted.

"Because I happen to think you're pretty damn perfect just as you are."

The fear was gone from her eyes. He couldn't decipher the emotion that had replaced it.

"I'm not about forcing you to hide, because you're right, that's not you." He brought her hand to his mouth and pressed a kiss to her knuckles. "But I will be at your side. You're not being the bait when it's my family at the center of this mess. He wants me dead, too. That bomb was in my car. You and me, Celia. Together. We'll go after him together or not at all."

Her gaze fell to her hand, cradled so close to his lips. "I always feel…warmth when you touch me."

He felt a whole lot more than just warmth when he touched her.

"Sometimes I wouldn't even realize I was cold, and then you'd be there." Her lashes lifted. "I like it when you're near. I like it when you touch me."

His brother was right outside that door. The other

guy—Monroe—was no doubt trying to eavesdrop and figure out what move Sullivan would be making next.

And the move he wanted to make? Getting Celia into the bed that waited just a few feet away.

Not here.

"We're leaving," he said as he cleared his throat. "Your new guard can come with us. Davis backs him up, and if you think he's on our side…" He let those words trail away.

"I don't have any reason to doubt him. Or Alexandra."

That wasn't exactly a ringing endorsement, but Davis had seemed sure of the fellow.

"The guard can come with us. Only him, no one else." Because he wasn't ready to put his trust in Alexandra. "The ranch is a hell of a lot safer than this place. I'll take you there, and then we're not going to be bait." He gave her a grim smile. "We're going to be the hunters."

ALEXANDRA SANCHEZ RODE the elevator up to her suite. It had truly been one hell of a day. This scandal was going to nearly destroy the Special Activities Division. Ronald Worth had certainly made a mess of things.

The elevator dinged and the doors opened. She'd used a special card to access this floor, and she clutched that key card now as she headed into the hallway. The lush carpeting swallowed her footsteps.

At least Celia James was settled for the night. Monroe would keep a close watch on her. He was a good man, and one of the newer recruits. More important, he was a man she knew personally. She'd been involved in

Monroe's life for years. She could vouch for him, and she knew that Monroe would not let her down.

The hallway was dead silent. At this hour of the night, most folks were already asleep. She wanted to crash herself, but there was too much work to do before she could fall into bed.

Too much.

Retirement was starting to look pretty good to her.

Alexandra opened the door to her suite. She hurried inside.

She'd taken five steps before she realized she wasn't alone.

He'd been as still as a statue, so she hadn't even noticed him. Or maybe—maybe it had just been far too long since she was actually in the field. She'd lost her killer instinct.

Before she could flee back into the hallway, he managed to grab her. His arm locked around her neck and he yanked her up against his body, holding her tightly.

"You are so easy to predict," he said, his voice rough and his breath blowing against her ear. "Ronald told me that you always believed in doing things first-class. Once I realized you'd been called in, it took me no time to figure out which hotel you'd be in." He laughed. "And a little bribe to the desk clerk got me your suite number."

He was cutting off her air supply. She kicked back, but he moved, easily avoiding her defensive maneuver. She tried to slam back with her elbow, but he just laughed again.

"Oh, now, come on, you can do better than that. Or have you gotten soft…sitting behind that big fancy desk for all those years?"

She wasn't soft. She twisted hard and managed to break free of him.

But he kept her purse. And her weapon.

In a flash, he had that weapon pointed right at her.

He smiled. "You don't usually remember the ones who do the dirty work, do you? I spent a lifetime doing that dirty work...so much time. That blood will never come off my hands."

"You haven't worked for me," Alexandra said definitely. Though there was something very familiar about him. Her gaze swept over him and lingered on his eyes.

Her heart beat even faster.

He just shrugged. "These days, I'm really more of a free agent."

She inched back. She could grab the nearby lamp and use it as a weapon.

"I know you talked to Celia. I know you *took* Celia from the police station. Because, see, when I slipped in to finish her off, she was gone." He sounded angry. Maybe she could use that anger against him. "Just what did she say to you?"

He thinks Celia knows who he is. She'd let him keep believing that. "Celia stayed with Ronald until he died." She gave her own grim smile. "You know how it is when death is so near. People always want to unburden their souls." He wasn't supposed to be here. She wasn't the bait. Celia was. Only...

He couldn't find Celia, so he came after me.

She should have stayed at that little safe house with Celia and Monroe.

"He confessed?" the man demanded.

Alexandra hesitated. He'd come here without a mask.

He'd stepped right into the light to show his face to her. She knew what that meant.

He doesn't intend to let me leave this room alive.

But she wasn't going down without a fight.

"What do you think Ronald did?" Her chin jutted into the air. She'd spent her life fighting to make the world a better place, and yes, sometimes she'd gotten her hands dirty and sometimes she'd done things that didn't make her proud.

But she'd never been a coward and she'd never, ever backed down from a fight.

You think I'm easy prey? Think again.

"I think he didn't have a long time to live, not after my bullet ripped into his chest."

"He lived long enough," she allowed.

She hated his smile. Alexandra inched a bit closer to the nightstand. *He is familiar. Too familiar.* Those eyes…even his smile… For an instant, grief burned through her.

"You're going to tell me where Celia is."

"You're going to give yourself up," she said in the next instant. "Because you have no idea what kind of enemy I am. You have no—"

He shot her. The bullet tore out of the gun—her own weapon—and slammed right into her chest.

She looked down, truly shocked for an instant. The blood was already pumping from her wound. Alexandra grabbed for the bedcovers as she slid to the floor.

He stalked closer to her. He grabbed her hair and yanked her head back. Then he put the gun right between her eyes.

"I don't care who you are," he said. "I don't care what kind of power you *think* you have."

He'd missed her heart. It was still beating. Painfully, so very fast. But beating. "I...know..." Alexandra tried to say. *I know who you are.* Too late, she understood.

"That's right, you know. And you *will* tell me where she is. Celia and Sullivan McGuire won't destroy me. I'll destroy everything and everyone around them before that happens."

"BEFORE WE LEAVE, I have to check in with Alexandra," Monroe said. "There's no way I'm letting Celia walk out of this place without official approval."

Celia slanted a quick glance toward Sullivan.

"By the book," Davis muttered. "Still play that way, huh, Monroe?"

"There's nothing wrong with that!" Monroe snapped. He had his phone pressed to his ear. "I happen to respect my boss, and until she gives the all clear—" He broke off, frowning. "The call went to voice mail."

A shiver slid over Celia's skin.

Monroe dialed again. "Look, I know where she's staying. I'll just call Alexandra's room directly." But his words held an edge now, and Celia could feel his worry.

Alexandra wouldn't ignore his calls. Not with everything going on.

Davis stepped toward him. "Where is she?"

"The Wattley Hotel. She told me that she always stays there when she's in town."

Celia's breath caught. "And Ronald would know that! He might have told the shooter..." It made sense. He could have told the shooter all about the habits of those in power at the agency.

Learn everyone's weaknesses.

And if the guy knew Alexandra Sanchez was in town...

"She's not answering," Monroe said. The edge in his voice had gotten worse.

Maybe she can't answer.

Celia and Sullivan were already running for the door. "Call the desk clerk!" Celia yelled. "Make him get someone up to her room!"

Because she was worried the shooter had already gone after another target.

"You just missed a call, Alexandra," he said as he picked up her phone and stared at the screen. "Monroe Blake. I'm guessing that's one of your agents, hmm? Is he the one guarding Celia?"

Every breath was a struggle. Her hands pressed to her chest. He hadn't hit her heart, but she was bleeding so much.

Is this the way Ronald felt, at the end?

"Alexandra! Look at me!" he snarled.

Her gaze jerked to him.

"Is Monroe the agent guarding Celia?"

She glared at him. She wasn't going to give up Monroe or Celia to this killer.

"He is, isn't he?" He smirked at her. "We're going to call Monroe back. You're going to tell him that there has been a change of plans. He has to bring Celia to you."

"No." She had to keep Monroe away from the killer. Monroe—he was her responsibility. She'd promised his mother that she'd always look after him. *I can't let this man get Monroe. I can't fail Susan that way!*

"Yes. You're going to do it, or else I will make you suffer every single moment until I finally put a bullet in your head and put you out of your misery."

"Won't...call..." She wouldn't do it. No matter what, she'd protect Monroe. And where was the help? He'd just shot her—surely someone had heard the noise! There had been no silencer on the gun, but...

Maybe no one else is on the floor. I paid for privacy.

Unfortunately, she'd gotten it.

"I'm dialing," he murmured. And he had pushed the button to return Monroe's call.

She prepared to scream. To give Monroe a warning—

But someone pounded on her door.

Someone did hear the shot!

"What the hell?" the man next to her muttered. And he ended the call. He kept the phone in his grip as he headed for the door.

His attention wasn't on her now. So she crawled back, moving toward the lamp.

"Mrs. Smith?" a voice called out as a knock sounded at her door again.

Mrs. Smith. What an obvious alias, but she'd always enjoyed using it. So simple. Why waste time with an elaborate cover when a simple name change did the trick?

She tried to clear her throat so she could call out, but only a whisper escaped from her lips.

The man who'd shot her was right at that door. In another moment, he'd be yanking it open. The hotel employee out there—the poor fellow—would find himself facing off against a killer and probably dying.

She threw her body against the lamp. It wove and crashed down, shattering.

"Mrs. Smith!" The cry of her pretend name was nearly frantic now. "We're coming in! And I've got a crew with me, we're—"

The shooter opened fire, blasting right through the door.

"GOVERNMENT AGENT!" MONROE BARKED when they got to the Wattley Hotel and found chaos waiting for them on Alexandra's floor. "Get the hell *back*!"

And the crowd did. They were on the top floor, they'd just left the elevator…and Celia could already see the blood.

There were some uniformed cops on the scene, but they looked shaky. One cop—a young woman with dark hair—had her hands pressed to the bloody shoulder of a fellow who appeared to be the desk clerk. Or maybe the concierge. He was wearing a well pressed hotel uniform and a name tag. *Justin.*

"What happened here?" Monroe demanded. "Where's—"

A gurney burst out of the suite up ahead. Celia's breath caught when she saw the form on that gurney. Alexandra Sanchez had never looked more vulnerable. Her face was chalk white, her body shuddering. And the blood—

Alexandra's eyes darted around the scene as her gurney was pushed toward the elevator, and her frantic stare locked on Celia and Monroe. "Not…here…" she gasped. "He's…watching…get away!"

Sullivan's hands closed around Celia's shoulders.

"The guy just came out of that room, shooting!" Justin's voice rose. "He was crazy. Just—just firing and then running straight for the elevator!"

If the shooter had been in the elevator, then maybe he'd been picked up on video surveillance. Maybe they could get the guy!

Monroe hurried to Alexandra's side. "I'll stay with you. It's going to be—"

"Get...her...out..." Alexandra ordered, her voice far too weak. "He could still...be here... Get...away...both of you...away! Leave...me."

The EMTs pushed her into the elevator and they all hurried to follow. Their group closed in around Alexandra and the EMTs as the elevator rushed down to the ground floor. "Tell us...who was he? What did the guy look like?"

Monroe's face had turned to stone as he stared at Alexandra.

Alexandra's stare drifted between Sullivan and Monroe.

"Please, Alexandra, stay with us." Celia could feel the other woman slipping away. She caught her hand and squeezed. "You saw him. Describe the shooter. What did he look like?" Celia held tight to Alexandra. "Please, tell us." Alexandra was the key and—

"H-him..." Alexandra whispered. Then her eyes closed.

THE AMBULANCE ROARED away with a scream of its sirens. Celia stood in the shadows of the hotel building, her arms crossed over her chest and her gaze on that ambulance.

Sullivan approached her slowly. "Celia?"

"There's so much blood and death. Sometimes I feel like it's all I know."

More wounded—Justin and a security guard—were loaded into the back of the second ambulance.

"One day," she said, voice soft, "it would be nice not to worry about a killer. Not to think about attacks or danger."

The second ambulance pulled away.

"But that day won't be today," she added.

He put his hands on her shoulders and pulled her back against him. "The hotel staff members are going to be all right." He'd checked out their wounds. Superficial. The shooter hadn't been trying to kill them.

He'd just wanted them out of his way.

But Alexandra…she was a different matter. They'd have to see just how much of a fighter she could truly be.

"Is your brother checking the security footage?" Celia asked.

"Yes." And Alexandra's last whispered word kept replaying in his head. What had she meant, the shooter looked like him?

"I've been looking at every face. Checking out every person I see. He knows me, but I don't know him. Hardly seems fair."

No, it didn't seem fair. Nothing about this mess did.

The hotel doors slid open and Davis hurried out. One look at his grim expression and Sullivan knew he hadn't recovered any usable footage.

"The guy is good," Davis said.

Monroe was right behind him.

"He disabled the security feed before he went up to

the suite. There's no sign of him on the videos. Nothing at all we can use."

Monroe expelled a frustrated breath. "And the hotel staff couldn't identify him. When he started shooting, they ducked. They never even got a look at his face."

"You need to follow the ambulance," Celia said. "She's defenseless now——"

"I've already got a call in to the CIA," Monroe said. "A whole team will be swarming soon."

"But she doesn't trust a team," Celia insisted. "She trusts you. She's still alive, and we need to make sure she stays that way."

His hands were clenched at his sides. "She gave me an order. I'm supposed to stay with you."

Sullivan's shoulder brushed against hers. He needed to be close to her. Her words were haunting him. *There's so much blood and death. Sometimes I feel like it's all I know.* "I'm with Celia," he said flatly. "You need to follow that ambulance and take care of Alexandra. Right now she's the only one who can identify the killer. As soon as she's stable, she can give us the guy's full description and we can find him." His lips thinned. "We just have to make sure that she does wake up. We can't risk him going after her again."

"That's why she needs you," Celia insisted to Monroe.

Davis had his phone out. "And that's why I'm calling in Mac. I want him at that hospital, too. The more people we have that we can trust on scene, the better."

Monroe's eyes glittered. "You're asking me to go against orders."

"Sometimes you have to," Celia said, "in order to do what's right."

Like when she'd gone against Ronald to save him. She hadn't known the guy was a twisted jerk at the time...

She'd just been doing right by me.

Monroe gave a ragged sigh. "You're going back to the McGuire ranch?"

Celia's gaze cut to Sullivan.

"Yes," he said. "She'll be with me." They both needed to crash and regroup before they started their hunt. "I'll guard her, you can count on it. I'll always have her back."

Just as she would have his. He knew that with utter certainty.

IT HAD WORKED, just as he'd planned. By attacking Alexandra, he'd managed to draw Celia right out into the open again.

He stared at their little group. Did they truly think they were safe in the shadows? He'd spotted them the minute they pulled up. The CIA was ridiculously predictable with their black SUVs. Whether abroad or at home, those vehicles truly screamed *look at me*.

The group was separating. Again, something else he'd anticipated. Alexandra—tough agent that she was—had still been clinging to life when she was loaded into that ambulance. Someone would follow her to the hospital. They'd probably stalk around and try to keep her safe.

There was no point in keeping the dead safe. She wouldn't survive until dawn. Her wounds were too grave. She wouldn't be talking about him to anyone else.

So he could move on to his main target.

The McGuires...he figured they'd be going back to the ranch now. Just what he wanted.

So fitting. They thought they were safe out there. So well protected behind their security measures. They couldn't be more wrong. He knew that ranch too well.

After all, he'd been there before. Many times. He'd even killed there.

The ranch is my hunting ground.

They wouldn't see him coming.

But plenty of people would see the flames he left behind.

THE HOSPITAL WAS a scene of total chaos. Monroe Blake had burst through the ER doors just moments before, following the gurney that held Alexandra Sanchez.

At the CIA, Alexandra had always been revered. Respected. And feared. No one had ever gotten close to her there. But—

I share a past with her. As long as he could remember, Alexandra had been in his life. She and his mother had been friends. Always close through the years. And when his mother died, it had been Alexandra who took him in. She'd encouraged him to become a SEAL. She'd brought him into the CIA and the Special Activities Division.

To the rest of the world, he acted as just another agent when he was near her. But...

Alexandra is my family.

And he was afraid she was slipping away from him.

Desperate, he reached out and grabbed her hand. Why had he never noticed just how fragile Alexandra was? She'd always seemed larger than life.

Until now.

"Sir, you need to step back," one of the doctors said. "We have to get her in the OR now."

He didn't want to step back. "Alex..."

Her lashes lifted. Her dark eyes met his. Still alive. Still fighting.

"You should…go…" she whispered. "Told you…"

And he'd ignored orders, for the first time in his life. "You need me."

Tears gleamed in her gaze. He'd never seen her cry before.

"S-sorry…" Alexandra said. The docs and nurses were pushing her gurney toward the OR, and Monroe was running right with them. "Should have… protected…"

Why in the world would she be apologizing to him?

"He's…always…been looking…" Each breath she took was a painful rasp. "Always…searching…never thought he'd…find…"

"Who, Alexandra? Who did he find? Celia? Sullivan?"

"Y-you…"

A doctor grabbed his arm and pulled Monroe back.

Alexandra's gaze lingered on his. He could see her fight to keep her eyes open. "Go…stay with…McGuires…*family…*"

She was giving him another order. Protect the McGuire family. "I want to stay with you."

She gave a sharp shake of her head. *"Family!"*

She was his family. She was—

The OR doors burst open as the doctors took her inside.

THEY'D JUST PULLED onto the ranch's property when Sullivan's phone rang. He lifted it to his ear even as he kept one hand wrapped tightly around the wheel. "Sullivan."

"She's in surgery." Monroe's voice was ragged. "As soon as I know anything, I'll call you."

"Stay with her—"

"Alexandra kept saying for me to come to you! That's her order...*and I'm here because I can't leave her.*"

There was such pain in the agent's voice. *This is personal.*

"She's all the family I've got," Monroe muttered.

Family. It could come in all shapes and sizes, and Sullivan knew the bonds weren't just about blood. "Mac is coming to the hospital. He'll help you, in any way you need."

"What I need..." Now Monroe's voice hardened. "What we all need is for this SOB to be stopped. He can't get away from us. He doesn't get to kill and walk."

"No," Sullivan agreed. "He doesn't."

He ended the call and drove the vehicle forward. He didn't head for the main house, though. Instead, he drove them toward the guesthouse.

Her pain-filled sigh almost hurt to hear. "I'm the one who got her down here. I'm the one who thought she'd be able to help me—help *us*. Alexandra kept SAD going for so long. With Ronald dead, I knew she'd come back to investigate and keep everyone on track. Now..."

Now if she died, the whole unit would fall apart.

He couldn't help wondering...had that been the shooter's goal? Just how much was really at play in this deadly game?

"I respect her," Celia said. "And she deserves so much more than that pain-filled death."

The headlights cut through the darkness and fell on the guesthouse. He braked and killed the engine, but neither one of them made a move to leave the vehicle.

"I keep thinking about what she said," Celia whispered. "When we asked her to describe the man, she said—"

"She said he looked like me," Sullivan continued. Those words had stunned him.

"Maybe Ronald wasn't lying."

His eyes narrowed in the darkness as he strained to make out her expression.

"He said we needed to look to the family. We haven't done that, Sullivan."

"My brothers—"

"I'm not talking about Grant or Davis. Not Mac, not Brodie. Not you."

He waited.

"You didn't know that your father worked Witness Protection. Maybe there's more you don't know about him, too. Maybe…do you think it's possible you could have family members out there that you don't know about?"

His heart felt as if it were encased in ice. "You're saying my father might have another son."

"I'm saying Alexandra stared right at you—she used the last bit of her strength to tell you the killer's description. And Ronald—what did he have to lose? At the end, he said it was family. All this time, I think you've been searching too far away for the killer. I'm wondering if, all along, he's been closer than you realized."

As close as blood.

He shoved open his door and headed around to her side of the vehicle. Before he could open that door, Celia was already rising. His hand brushed against her back. They were safe at the ranch. As safe as it was possible to be, and there, he could let down his guard.

"I needed to be close to you," Sullivan confessed.

Her hands rose and pressed to his chest.

"When I thought that you were going to be taken from me…" His jaw ached because he'd clenched it so hard. "Nothing else mattered to me. Finding you. Getting you back—that was it."

"Let's go inside," Celia said.

Right. Inside.

But…

She took a few steps away from him, heading toward the guesthouse.

He stared after her. The stars were glittering overhead. There was no smoke from a car bomb. No scent of blood and death.

It was just them.

"Do you think we're still married?" Sullivan asked, his voice gruff.

She paused and gave a faint, sad laugh. "It's kind of funny…but to tell you the truth, I always felt like we still were."

She had to be careful what she said. Did the woman realize how close she was pushing him to the edge?

Over that edge?

"Even when we were apart, I still felt connected to you. No matter what I did, no matter how many times I told myself to let go, you were still there." She turned toward him. "Why couldn't I let go?"

He stalked toward her. Sullivan lifted his hand and brushed back the hair that blew over her cheek. Before, they'd been all about passion and need.

But desire alone—it didn't survive that long. It didn't last for years.

"I want you to make love to me," Celia said.

Love. For him, that was exactly what it was. The reason he hadn't ever been able to let her go. He'd been far too caught up in Celia from the beginning.

His Celia.

"Always," he said, and Sullivan leaned down. His lips brushed over hers. He didn't push. Didn't consume. He just savored her. If he could have frozen one moment in time, it would be the moment when he kissed her. When he tasted her lips and a surge of warmth filled him.

His eyes were closed and her soft body pressed to his.

"Come inside," Celia said.

As if he needed another invitation.

He followed her in and stopped to secure the guesthouse. He put his shoulders back against the door and stared at her as she stood in a pool of light. There were so many things he wanted to know about her. The past hadn't gotten in their way before. He'd been too focused on the moment, the present with her.

But now he wanted more.

He wanted to secure a future with her.

"I—I need to shower first," Celia said. Then she touched the prison garb she still wore. "And this has got to go."

She turned on her heel and headed down the hallway. A few seconds later, he heard the roar of water in the shower.

He started to follow, already yanking up his shirt.

The floor creaked a bit beneath his feet. By the time he reached the bathroom, Sullivan was already naked.

So was Celia. Naked and under the spray of the shower. Her back was to him, so he had a perfect view of her graceful back and her truly inspiring hips and rear. Such perfect curves.

Steam drifted lazily in the air.

Celia glanced over her shoulder at him, and she smiled.

There was something about that smile. It froze him a moment, then made his heart beat in a double-time rhythm.

"Come closer," she urged him. Nothing had ever tempted him more.

As soon as he saw the doctor, Monroe knew she was gone.

The doctor's face was grim as he approached. Monroe stood. Mac and Davis McGuire were at his sides.

"The damage was too extensive," the doctor told him quietly. "I'm sorry, but she's gone…"

Davis put his hand on Monroe's shoulder, squeezing tightly.

And Monroe lost the last member of his family.

You bastard. I will find you. I will make you pay.

Chapter Eleven

The water pounded down on her, washing away the terror of the day. She forgot about fire and death and being caged behind bars.

She looked into Sullivan's eyes and she couldn't look away. She didn't want to look away.

The water was warm on her skin. The steam had filled the air around her.

And she wanted him.

Celia turned fully toward Sullivan, exposing her body to him. She felt no shyness. With him, she never had. She wanted him to see all of her.

Still married?

In her heart, they always had been. She'd never been able to give him up. She'd always been willing to take any risk, for him.

Her gaze dipped down and she saw that he was more than turned on for her. Good.

Her smile stretched.

Sullivan could always take her away—to a world of only pleasure. A world that consisted of only them.

She needed to be taken right then. Taken so far away.

He stepped into the shower with her. The water poured over them both and her hand lifted, sliding over his skin. He bent to kiss her, a hot, openmouthed kiss that only fanned the flames of her desire for him.

Her hands slid over his body. She wanted to touch every bit of him. His scars still hurt her—she hated to think of him suffering—and she bent to kiss them as the water slid over her back. She stroked his aroused flesh. Celia loved his strength and that raw power, but when he gave a deep, rumbling growl in his throat…

She just stroked him all the more.

"Celia."

She'd always enjoyed playing games with him. Seeing how far he could be pushed. How far he could push her.

Sullivan caught her hands. He pushed her back against the cold tile wall of the shower. She gasped at the contact, and then he kissed her. Deep. Hard. The way she liked.

He freed her wrists and his hands curled around her hips. He lifted her up, holding her right there, and his mouth still took hers even as he positioned his body at her core.

He drove into her. Her legs wrapped around him.

Pleasure.

Desire.

More.

He withdrew, then thrust into her. The water made their bodies so slick. Her breasts pressed to his chest. Her nipples ached for him. Her whole body ached.

Thrust.

Withdraw.

Her hands weren't against the tile any longer. She was holding tightly to his shoulders, and her nails were sinking into his skin.

Every movement of his hips sent him sliding right over the center of her need. Her climax was rising, building and building...

He kissed a heated path down her neck, and she lost it.

Celia screamed when her climax hit.

And Sullivan...let go. She felt his control splinter as he thrust hard, deep, again and again, and it was fabulous.

No fear.

No regrets.

Only pleasure.

His body stiffened. He drove into her once more and she saw the pleasure wash across his face. For an instant, his green eyes seemed to go blind with that surge of release.

Their breaths heaved out. The water kept spraying down on them.

Her legs slid—rather limply—away from his hips. She felt like falling into a little puddle right there. Her body was sated and her mind had finally stopped spinning.

She blinked the water out of her eyes—surely just water from the shower and nothing more—and stared up into Sullivan's gaze.

I love you.

She wanted to say those words so badly.

But then he kissed her. Such a sweet, tender kiss.

A few moments later, he turned off the water. Very carefully, he dried her with a towel, then yanked that same towel roughly over his body. When she stepped out of the shower, he lifted her into his arms.

She didn't need him to carry her. She'd never needed

anyone to do that. But she liked being in his arms, so she relaxed her body against his. Her arms curled around his neck.

Soon they were in the bedroom. He lowered her onto the mattress. Turned off the lights. Then they slid under the covers together.

Exhaustion pulled at her. She just wanted to close her eyes and drift away, but at the same time, she wanted to stay exactly where she was. Awake and aware with Sullivan. She felt as if a clock were on, the time running away too quickly. She needed to reach out to him—

So she did. Celia put her head on Sullivan's chest, right over his heart so she could feel and hear that steady beat. His arm wrapped around her back and he held her there.

Warm and safe.

"There's so much I want to know about you..."

She smiled at the rumble of his voice. "Ask me anything." Her answer was soft. Sleep pulled at her.

"Where were you born, Celia?"

"A town called Jackson, Mississippi." She hadn't been back there, not in so long. Would it still be the same if she returned? Would she still smell the magnolias drifting in the wind?

"What happened to your family?"

Pain tried to pull at her, but she pushed it away. "My father died in an accident at work. At the sawmill." She wouldn't think of that horror—a horror that had scarred a child. "I was seven. My mother never got over it." She'd turned to a bottle to escape the pain. Booze. Pain pills. Whatever she could get her hands on. "She...she was in a car crash when I was thirteen."

A one-car accident on a lonely stretch of road.

Strangely enough, when Celia had gone back years later to read that accident report, she'd learned there was no alcohol or drugs found in her mother's system that night.

But she'd gone off the road and driven straight into that telephone pole. Not stopping, not even trying to brake...

"What was foster care like?"

She thought of that for a moment. Her eyes drifted closed. "Lonely." She didn't even think of filtering her words. With him, why should she? "I was never part of a family. Not really. Always just the girl looking through the glass at the others." Wondering what it would be like to belong.

To be loved.

Was it any wonder she'd been such perfect pickings for Ronald? With no one to notice when she disappeared, she'd slipped right away into a life that...

Was full of secrets.

Lies.

"It was hard for me to make friends. To really connect with anyone." Why? Maybe because she'd been afraid.

Afraid they won't like me, not really. Not when they see who I truly am.

Afraid I'd lose them. Afraid if I cared, it would hurt more.

She'd stopped being afraid with him.

His steady heartbeat reassured her.

"You connected with me."

Even as her breath evened out, Celia smiled. "Yes."

"Why?"

"Because you've always been different." His heartbeat drummed beneath her. And very slowly, Celia slipped into sleep.

SULLIVAN KEPT STROKING her hair. He felt the exact moment when Celia gave in to sleep. "You've always been different, too."

Special.

He stared up at that dark ceiling and he tried to figure out just what he'd need to do in order to keep Celia in his arms forever.

Just as his eyes began to close, his phone rang, vibrating lightly on the nearby nightstand. His hand reached out and he grabbed it, answering it before Celia could wake. "Sullivan…"

There was a pause and then, "She didn't make it," Davis said softly.

Hell. Another victim. Another loss.

Another sin the killer *would* atone for, one way or another.

AFTER HE ENDED the call, Davis walked through the hospital. People brushed by him, nurses and doctors intent on their patients. They hardly gave him a second glance.

That was just one of the things he didn't like about these places. They were so busy. It was incredibly easy for someone to slip in and get close to a vulnerable patient.

He rounded the corner and saw Monroe Blake sitting in one of the waiting room chairs. Monroe's shoulders were slumped and he'd put his fists against his eyes, seemingly propping up his sagging head. The guy was taking Alexandra's death hard, so very hard, and Davis wished there was something he could do for him.

Monroe was a good man. Davis could still remember the smell of blood and death that had been around them on their missions. Monroe had never hesitated. He'd never backed away from any mission.

He'd also never looked beaten.

Until now.

Davis paced toward him.

Monroe stiffened and glanced up at him. His golden eyes swept over Davis, then slid away. "I've been informed," he said, his lips twisting, "by the new authority at the Special Activities Division that I'm supposed to be standing down on this case. With Alexandra gone, my involvement is over."

Davis sat next to the guy. "I figured that call would be coming in, sooner or later." He'd hoped for a bit later.

"Because I knew where she was, right?" Monroe sighed. "That puts me on their suspect list. Some pencil pusher back in the office—a guy who has never seen fieldwork—figures that I just turned on Alexandra and let her die."

"You didn't."

"No," Monroe said grimly, "I didn't. I respected the hell out of that woman. I would *never* hurt her." He held Davis's stare. "Ronald Worth would have known her habits. *He's* the one who told the killer where she was."

Yes, Davis rather suspected that had been the case.

"They're sending in a team. This mess is a huge embarrassment for SAD. They want me on a plane back home, and they said they have *people* who'll be taking over the investigation."

People Davis wouldn't trust. He didn't know them. "What are you going to do?"

"I don't have much choice!" Monroe fired back. "I

was given orders. Stand down." His lips twisted. "And stay the hell away from the McGuires. Apparently, your family is seen as some kind of major threat right now."

Davis made a noncommittal sound. "What do you think will happen to Celia?" That was a question that had to be answered. He already knew Sullivan wasn't just going to let Celia be taken into government custody. Hadn't they all learned that lesson already?

"They want her back." Monroe's voice was gruff. "Everyone sure as hell seems to think that Celia can identify this guy, but I heard her talking with Alexandra. Celia was adamant that she didn't know his identity."

Davis watched a nurse bustle by in the hallway. She appeared frantic to get to her patient. "Sometimes," he said slowly, "you have to make a choice." He rose.

"Davis?"

"You have to decide which orders you are going to follow…and which ones you're just going to forget."

Monroe shook his head. "You act like I have some kind of choice here. I'm not a free agent. I'm a government employee. Do you know what they'll do to me if I go off on my own?"

Davis shrugged. "Oh, yeah, I have a pretty good idea. I mean, Celia went off on her own, didn't she? Then all of a sudden she had folks gunning for her. Strange, isn't it? That the folks in authority up there aren't scrambling to solve this case? Instead, they're too busy covering their own backs. They want this case erased, not closed. It's an embarrassment. You know what went down, so I'm suspecting that when you get back to that fancy office—you know, the one that hides all the bloodshed—they'll probably ship you off on an immediate new assignment. You'll go overseas, and you won't come back until everything about this case is nothing more than a memory."

Monroe rose. "Alexandra deserved better than that." Emotion cracked in his voice and grief darkened his eyes.

"Because she was your mentor, right? The woman who pulled you into the group?"

"She knew my mother," Monroe said as his chin notched up. "Alexandra was always looking out for me. My whole life, she was there for me."

Davis hadn't realized the connection was so personal. "Then I am especially sorry," he said quietly, "for the loss you're suffering." He gave a slow nod. "And if you should decide you want to fight for justice for her…then maybe you should come and join a family that understands that battle."

He turned and took a step away.

"You're telling me…what? To throw away my job with the Special Activities Division? To turn my back on them?"

Davis glanced over his shoulder. "Actually, I'm saying let's give this thing twenty-four hours. We've got a killer out there, one who is champing at the bit. The plan that Alexandra had—to draw him out into the open— it's not bad. It can work. We just need the right team in place."

Monroe's hand rubbed over his jaw. "And this team?"

"You want to join it?"

Monroe's gold eyes gleamed. He seemed to consider that offer for a very long time. Davis just waited.

Then Monroe nodded.

"Then welcome to the family," Davis murmured.

Monroe swallowed. "Alexandra...before she died, she told me to protect your family. To stay with the McGuires." He nodded. "And I will. I swear, I will."

"CELIA..."

Her eyes opened. The faintest streaks of light drifted through the window.

"Not...her..."

She pushed up in the bed. She was pretty much sprawled on top of Sullivan, and she winced, ready to apologize, when she realized—

His eyes were still closed. He was talking in his sleep again. Saying her name.

She eased a bit away from him as her gaze swept over him.

"Let me go!" Sullivan suddenly yelled out.

Celia jerked back.

"Have to get...Celia!"

"Sully?" she whispered as she reached out to him. "It's okay, I'm right—"

"Have to make...her pay..."

There was such fury in his words.

Pain knifed through her, but her fingers gently stroked his shoulder. *I've paid more than you know.* For crimes that hadn't even been her own. "It's okay," she said again, keeping her voice soft.

"Celia..."

Her hand stilled. There hadn't been fury in that one word. There had been longing.

Her eyes stung.

"Love," he whispered. His hands had fisted around the covers. "Love...Celia..."

She almost fell out of the bed. One moment he was

raging against her, and the next—declaring his love? Not possible, of course. Sullivan was just trapped in some twisted nightmare. She needed to wake him up. He didn't love her.

Did he?

Her hand curled around his shoulder and she lightly shook him.

He jerked beneath her touch and grabbed for her. In a flash, he had rolled her beneath him and pinned her hands on either side of her head.

And this is why you don't wake up a person in the middle of a nightmare...especially if that person is a tough ex-marine...

"Hi, there," Celia whispered softly. "Remember me?" She offered him a gentle smile when he blinked blearily down at her. "I'll take that as a yes."

"Celia." He immediately released her and sat up in bed. "Baby, I'm sorry, I was—"

"Dreaming."

"Reliving hell."

She sat up, too, grabbing for the sheet to cover her chest. "That hell you were reliving...you called my name."

He climbed from the bed. He turned on the light and dressed, his movements jerky as he yanked on a pair of jeans. Then he stilled, pausing near the side of the bed as his gaze lingered on her. "I usually call your name in my sleep."

Because you still blame me? Or because you love me? She licked her lips. "Want to talk about what happens?"

"I'm back in that pit. They're slicing me open and I can't get away."

Yes, definitely the stuff of nightmares. "I'm sorry."

"They're telling me that you're involved. That you sold me out."

She didn't move.

"And then..." He expelled a rough breath. "Then it changes and gets all twisted. Because they're saying they are going to hurt *you*. That they're going to kill you, and I know I can't let that happen."

"They...threatened me?" He'd never told her that before.

Sullivan shook his head. "That just happens in my dreams. My worst nightmares." He edged even closer to the bed, and his hand curled under her jaw. "Because that *is* my worst fear, you see. Something happening to you."

"Why?" She needed him to say the words. While he was awake. Fully aware. Staring into her eyes. After everything that had happened between them, she had to hear those precious words.

"Because I love you. More than anything else. And I can't lose you."

She leaped from the bed. Celia wrapped her arms around him and held on as tightly as she could. "I love you," she whispered.

His hands locked around her. The grip almost too tight. "Celia?"

"I love you. I never stopped loving you." Though she'd tried. But the emotion had lingered within her and when they'd been pushed back together, it had flared to life again, stronger, deeper than ever before. "Why do you think I took so many risks? Why do you think I worked so hard to unearth the truth about your past?"

She eased back a bit and stared up at his face. She'd never seen that expression in Sullivan's eyes before.

Hope. So much hope. Enough to break her heart.

"I wanted to give you the one thing you wanted most…because I loved you so much."

But Sullivan shook his head. "*You're* the thing that matters most. It's you, I just realized the truth too late."

"It's not too late." Not for them. Not for what could be. "It's not."

"You're too damn good for me," he gritted out. "I made so many mistakes…"

"We can start again. We *have* started again." She smiled up at him and laughed. "We can do anything."

His gaze swept slowly over her face. "I missed that sound. So much."

Her laughter faded away.

"Your laugh is the most beautiful sound I've ever heard. Just the memory of it got me through too many dark nights."

"You don't need a memory any longer," she said, her heart feeling as if it were about to burst right out of her chest. "You have me. We can make everything work. Together, we can do this. We'll stop the killer. We'll put the past to rest and we'll have the future that we want."

Together…

His head lowered and she leaned eagerly forward, wanting to feel the crush of his lips against hers. Their lips nearly touched. She could nearly taste him.

And someone was pounding on the door. Knocking so hard. Totally and completely ruining the moment.

"My brothers," Sullivan growled. "They must have seen me turn on the light. I swear, they all have the worst damn timing."

She laughed again, unable to help herself. She just felt happy, even if they had been interrupted. *He loves me.* "It's okay. I'm not going anywhere, Sullivan. We have nothing but time." She eased away from him. "Go answer the door. I'll get dressed." The smile just wouldn't stay off her lips. *He loves me. He loves me!*

But Sullivan didn't move. "I want the danger over. I want to find the shooter and make sure he's locked away so that he can't hurt anyone again." His fingers slid down her cheek. "You're in this mess because of me."

No, she was involved because of the choices she'd made.

"There's something else you should know..." His voice had deepened. "A call came through while you slept. I'm sorry, baby, but Alexandra didn't make it."

For an instant, she couldn't breathe. Pain knifed through her, so sharp and deep.

"We *will* get the bastard."

Celia gave a grim nod. *He has to pay. For all the lives he's destroyed. He must pay!*

The pounding grew more insistent.

"Dammit..." His fingers fell away. "Let me go find out what the hell is going on out there..."

She watched him walk away. Sullivan. *Her* Sullivan.

At the bedroom door, he paused and looked back. "I meant what I said before, Celia. Only I should have given you those words long ago. I love you."

Then he headed out.

For an instant, she just stood there. Then she wiped away the tear that had fallen down her cheek. *Alexandra.* The grief wanted to pound through her, consume her, but she couldn't let it. Not now.

She squared her shoulders. Took a deep breath. Pushed past the pain.

I'm so sorry, Alexandra.

Her eyes kept burning as she hurried toward the closet. When would the death stop? The fear? How much longer would it go on?

Celia dressed quickly, pulling a pair of old jeans and a shirt from the closet. Then she shoved up the skirt on the bed. She'd seen another pair of tennis shoes under the bed the other day. Those shoes had to be more comfortable than the ones she'd been given at the police station. She snagged the shoes from under the bed, put them on and then—

Something else was under the bed.

Frowning, she eased down a bit more as her eyes narrowed. She could see the glowing digits of a clock beneath the bed.

That clock hadn't been there before.

Why would a clock be under the bed? The question pierced through the grief she felt.

And her heart stopped. No, that wasn't a clock. Goose bumps immediately rose on her arms.

The digits on that device were counting down so quickly. A small box, with wires coming out the top and those numbers flashing on the top...

A bomb. Dear God. It's a bomb. Hidden under the bed, where no one should have seen it, not until it was too late.

Terror exploded within her.

SULLIVAN YANKED OPEN the guesthouse door. "Seriously, *stop* that damn pounding!"

Davis didn't look particularly concerned about his

snarl. His brother just raised his eyebrows. "So sorry, bro. Didn't mean to disturb your beauty sleep with the little matter of a life-and-death situation. My bad."

Behind him, Monroe Blake grunted.

Sullivan leaned against the door frame. "Give me ten minutes, and then Celia and I will meet you up at the—"

"Run!"

His head snapped back at Celia's shout. He glanced over his shoulder.

"Get out!" she said as she rushed toward him.

"What the hell?" Davis demanded.

"There's a bomb under the bed!"

No, that wasn't possible. They had the best security imaginable—

She grabbed his arm and yanked Sullivan out of the door.

Monroe and Davis were already running up ahead.

"It had five minutes left on the timer," Celia panted out. "Five minutes!"

If his brother hadn't come pounding on the door, they'd still be in the guesthouse. In the bedroom. They'd be—dead?

They ran toward the bluff, but halfway there, Sullivan stopped.

Celia was still holding his arm, so she staggered to a stop, too.

"Sullivan!" Her eyes were so wide. "You didn't see that thing—it is going to destroy that guesthouse! We have to get away."

But his mind was whirling. "Someone got on our property." He didn't doubt Celia's words, not for an instant. He was never going to doubt her again. "If he got to the guesthouse, he could've gotten to the main house, too." His gaze flew toward the main house.

"Brodie's in there," Davis yelled. "Jennifer and Jamie—*they're inside!*"

Horror washed through Sullivan and he tore off after his brother, rushing as fast as he could for the main house. Maybe there wasn't just one bomb. Maybe the killer had placed more around the ranch.

Five minutes. That wasn't long enough. He had to get his family to safety.

Five minutes. Five damn minutes.

Celia was racing to keep up with him. Davis and Monroe were both hurtling toward the main ranch house.

Home. Family. Life. He'd been tied to this place for so long. It couldn't go up in flames like this. He couldn't let it happen.

How did he get in? How did he get past all our security?

Davis didn't stop at the door to the ranch house. He kicked the thing in and roared, *"Jamie! Jamie!"* There was terror in his voice as he bellowed his wife's name.

Sullivan bounded into the house after him.

"What's wrong?" Brodie demanded as he rushed out of the hallway. Jennifer was at his side, her hand clutching her robe. "What's happening?"

"Get out of the house!" Sullivan yelled at them.

Davis had run in search of his wife.

"There's a bomb in the guesthouse," Celia shouted. "There could be one here, too. We have to go!"

And Davis was running back. He had Jamie in his arms, holding her tight. She looked stunned and scared and—

"Is anyone else in the house?" Monroe demanded.

They were all rushing for the door.

"No one else," Brodie yelled as he pushed Jennifer in front of him. "Just us."

How much time had passed? How much damn time?

They were outside now. Running fast and frantically toward the bluff. Part of Sullivan was waiting for the heat of the blast to wash over him. And another part of him…he feared that bullets would rip out and hit him. This would be the perfect time to attack. While they ran. While there was no cover and—

Boom.

The blast shook the earth all around them and flames rushed into the sky.

And those flames were blazing when the first shot was fired.

Chapter Twelve

"Get down!" Sullivan bellowed. It was just as he'd feared. The guy who'd set that bomb was close by, waiting to pick off any survivors.

Now they were all out in the open, with no weapons, sitting ducks for the killer who waited in the woods.

Brodie grabbed Jennifer and yanked her behind the branches of the sprawling tree.

Davis curled his body around Jamie, and they hit the ground, staying as low as they could for cover.

Monroe was right beside Sullivan, and they were both hurrying to reach Celia. That first shot had lodged in a tree just inches away from her head. The second shot could come at any moment.

Celia spun toward Sullivan. Her eyes were wild, frantic, and she lunged toward him, her arms outstretched as if she could reach him.

He saw the bullet hit her. Time seemed to slow down as the blood soaked her shirt. The boom of the gunfire was distant. Everything was distant.

Celia was calling his name.

He grabbed for her, held her tight. "Baby, no!" He fell to the ground, covering her with his body because there was nowhere else to go. Staying low was their best chance of survival.

She trembled beneath him.

His heart shattered.

But then—

Gunfire. Blasting. Not gunfire that had been aimed at them, but...

His head turned. Monroe had drawn his gun and was firing into the trees—right at the spot where the shooter must have been hiding. The direction and the angle were right based on Celia's wound.

That bastard shot her!

And now Davis had joined Monroe in the gun battle. Hell, yes, both men were armed and firing—giving the others cover so they could run for better protection.

"Stables!" Brodie snarled.

Right. It seemed as though there would be less of a chance that the stables would be wired to blow, but, hell, Sullivan didn't know for certain. He just had to get Celia out of the line of fire.

He scooped her up into his arms. Davis and Monroe blasted out their shots, moving with Sullivan and shielding the group as best they could.

"Hold on, Celia," Sullivan urged her. "Baby, you're going to be okay."

Then they were rushing into the stables. The smell of fresh hay permeated the air, and the horses neighed nervously.

Davis yanked the big doors closed behind him.

And Sullivan gently lowered Celia to the ground.

"I'm okay," she said. She even tried to smile up at him. "It's just a flesh wound."

They'd promised not to lie to each other again. But

he stared into her beautiful eyes and said, "Just a flesh wound. Nothing to slow you down."

Then, carefully, he pulled back her shirt.

His breath expelled in a rush as he examined her. And relief nearly made him dizzy. It *was* a flesh wound. One that was bleeding far too much, but nothing vital had been hit.

"Mark will see the flames," Brodie said. He and Jennifer were close by. "His men will notice the smoke, and they'll come running."

Yes, Sullivan knew that was true. Mark Montgomery was their closest neighbor. And Ava—she'd be with her husband when he rushed over to investigate the flames.

Would the shooter be waiting for them, too?

"Call them," Sullivan ordered curtly. "They can't come here blindly!" He didn't want his sister walking into an ambush.

Davis already had his phone out.

"I'm okay," Celia said to him once more.

His hand sank into her hair and he leaned close to her. He kissed her then—deep, hard and fast. "If you hadn't been, I would have gone insane." A simple fact. He needed her to function. When he'd seen the blood, fear and fury nearly maddened him—

I need Celia.

Behind him, he heard Monroe talking into his phone, too. The cavalry would be coming—local cops, government officials. Hell, maybe all of them. But the shooter was always two steps ahead...

"He's going to vanish again," Celia said quietly. Her face had paled, but her eyes burned with her usual fierce passion. "If we don't stop him, he'll vanish...and come back again."

He knew she was right.

Celia locked her jaw and started to rise.

Sullivan pushed her right back down. "Hell, no, baby. *Hell, no.*"

"But I can—"

"You can fight the world, I know it. But this time, for me...*don't.*" Because she was already wounded. And she was *his* world. He couldn't stand any additional risks to her. "Stay here. I know this land. I can find him."

"How the hell did he even get on our property?" Brodie wanted to know. "We installed the security system—there is no way he could just have snuck past our safeguards without setting off an alarm."

It would seem the guy was just as familiar with the land as they were.

And once more, he thought of what Ronald had said... "Family," he whispered.

"What in the hell does that mean?" Monroe snapped, his eyes gleaming. "Look, I get that you all are tight, but there is one very skilled killer out there. He's taken out trained agents, and now he has us pinned down. For all we know, these stables could be set to blow any minute. Maybe we didn't escape into them...maybe he deliberately corralled us in here. Maybe he's just waiting. No timer this time, but a bomb *he* sets to explode."

The bastard could be planning anything.

Sullivan's gaze slid back to Celia. Gently, he brushed back her hair. He had to keep her safe. He had to protect Celia and the rest of his family.

"We need dogs," Celia said. Her breath seemed to come faster, harder. "Bomb-sniffing dogs to search the entire ranch."

Yes, the whole place would have to be checked. There could be more deadly surprises just waiting for them. Maybe that was what the SOB wanted.

To see them all burn.

Then he plans to shoot any survivors. He wants to take us all out.

"What in the hell did we miss?" Sullivan demanded. Who was this killer? A man who'd been after their family for so long. A man who seemed determined to destroy the McGuires.

He could still hear the crackle of flames coming from the guesthouse.

The hunter out there wanted to see them burn. Maybe Monroe was right. Maybe the jerk had corralled them all into the stables. *The better to kill us off?*

Too bad. None of them would be dying.

He knew he had a choice to make. He could go out there and hunt the shooter. Track him down. He could leave Celia inside with his brothers while he searched.

I don't want to leave her. She needs me.

He needed her.

Yeah, he could hunt or…

I can work with my family. Together, the way we've always done things. No one would be left behind. They'd all be safe. His gaze jerked around the stables. The horses were neighing louder, shifting in their stalls.

"Get the saddles," he ordered. "Because we're getting the hell out of here." Moving targets were so much harder to hit.

And we won't just wait for an attack.

THEY'D ESCAPED THE BOMB. Celia had gotten them out of that guesthouse. Then the whole damn group of them had come racing across the ranch. He'd fired, desperately, because he'd needed to stop Celia.

But he hadn't.

I missed again.

He'd wanted her heart. He hadn't gotten it. She'd survived. The woman was so much harder to kill than he'd anticipated.

Now they were in those stables. Hunkering down. No doubt planning their next move. He hadn't put a bomb in the main house—he hadn't been able to get close enough before. There hadn't been any time.

So I went for Celia. I knew she thought she was safe in that little guesthouse.

She was wrong.

I've been too soft. I should have attacked them all sooner.

They'd be calling in backup. The rest of the family would swarm. They'd close ranks. It would just keep going and going…

Unless no one was left.

He pulled out the detonator from his pack.

No, he hadn't been able to get to that main house.

But he had been able to plant explosives in the stables. Just in case. He'd always believed in having a contingency plan in place.

He stared at those closed doors of the stables. For a moment, the past swam before him. He and Ronald had hidden in those stables. They'd waited until they thought it was a good time to make contact. He'd gone in. The rage had taken over.

I fired before I even thought about it. My finger squeezed the trigger, and she was just gone.

There was one thing that he'd regretted—and that had been her death.

Stop it. Focus. It's you or them. You or them!

He pressed the button to detonate, and when the stables exploded...

He could have sworn he heard his sister scream. But then, he'd been hearing her scream in his dreams for years. Some sins really did stay with you.

No matter how hard you tried to bury the past.

SULLIVAN HELD TIGHT to Celia, keeping a firm grip around her body as the horses bolted away from the blaze. They'd barely cleared the back of the stables when the place erupted, raining fire and chunks of debris down around them. The horses were going nearly wild now, so desperate to escape from that heat.

He didn't head back toward the front of the ranch, or to the main house. Instead, Sullivan and the others surged into the line of trees. That would be their cover. Their protection.

The horses' hooves pounded over the earth. He risked a glance back over his shoulder, and he saw the flames shooting into the sky.

Just another few moments, and they would have been dead. Celia. His brothers. Jennifer. Jamie...

All dead.

It has to stop.

Fury twisted within him. No one attacked his family like this. No one came to their home and tried to destroy them.

His horse surged forward even faster. He controlled the animal easily even as he pulled Celia closer to him.

He directed the horse to the right. He was going

to the main road, but by a different path than the one Davis and Brodie would take with their wives. Sullivan had wanted the family to separate—that way they wouldn't present an easy target in case the shooter found them again.

They would be safe and—

Someone raced out of the brush. A man who appeared to be little more than a shadow. He lifted his gun and fired.

But Sullivan had already leaped from the horse. He'd taken Celia with him and he rolled, twisting his body so she was protected and he hit the ground first. The impact knocked the breath from his body.

A shot rang out. One, two—

He looked up and saw Monroe take a hit in the stomach. Monroe's gun fell from his hand and he rolled off his horse. The horse galloped into the darkness, rushing away.

Monroe groaned and began to rise from the ground.

And the man aimed his gun right at Monroe's head. "This wasn't even your fight."

"Stop!" Celia cried. She'd leaped off Sullivan and, even with her wound, she was rushing toward the shooter. "Just…*stop!*"

He immediately swung the gun toward her.

And Sullivan's world seemed to end.

DAVIS HEARD THE thunder of the gunfire, rising even above the flames. He drew back on his horse's reins.

Brodie stopped beside him.

Jennifer and Jamie were close, edging their mares toward them.

Davis's head turned. "Northeast," he said. His blood had iced. Two shots had been fired.

He was supposed to keep going to the main road. To safety.

But no way was he leaving his brother now. He turned his horse. Everyone did, as if on cue. And they took off, riding fast, so fast.

Is this what it was like for my father? In those last moments, when a masked shooter aimed at my mother? When she was taken from him?

Sullivan rose slowly. "Don't."

The flames were still raging in the distance. The horses were long gone. And the gun was too close.

But the shooter hasn't fired. Not yet.

Sullivan put his hands up and walked forward. "It's my family, right? We're the ones you've always been after. *Family.* The McGuires. I'm the one you want to kill." He stepped in front of Celia.

"No, Sully," she said, her voice desperate.

"Me," he said, "not her." He made sure his body fully blocked hers. This guy would not hurt Celia again, not without going through him first.

Monroe groaned and tried to push himself to a sitting position.

The shooter still hadn't fired.

Where are Davis and Brodie? Did they hear the shots? Or had the flames been too loud?

"Just like your father," the shooter snarled. "Always trying to play the hero."

"My father was a good man," Sullivan said simply. "And I'm not playing anything." He had his hands up.

"You want to shoot someone? Fine, do it. Shoot me, but not her. She never did anything to you. *Not her.*"

"She set this nightmare into motion again! She should never have gone digging—"

"She did it for me." Because Celia loved him, and he—he would do anything for her. *Even take a bullet.*

Sullivan stared at the man before him. The guy had a mask over his face. The two men who'd come for his mother and father that long-ago night—they'd worn masks, too. Ava had seen those masks. "You killed my parents," he said.

Laughter. "And I'll be killing you, just like I did them."

"Sully, no." Celia's hands pulled against him. "Stop it! Not for me. *Not for me!*"

Didn't she get it? Everything that he did, it was for her. He'd protect her with his last breath. He'd give anything and everything for her.

"Two lovers," the guy snarled. "You thought you'd get to be happy, didn't you? Just like *her.*"

And Sullivan knew the shooter was talking about his mother.

"She rode away with her lover, became someone new, but I never forgot. Or forgave. I *never* stopped." He took a step toward them. "She wasn't safe here. I snuck in, I got to her…the same way I got to you." That hard laughter came again. "I know this land damn better than you all do. I spent so long watching, waiting, thinking I'd find what I'd lost."

No wonder the guy had been able to sneak onto the property. He'd probably mapped out the whole area long ago.

"She wouldn't tell me. Your father...*he wouldn't tell me.*"

"What do you want to know?" Sullivan rasped. "What was worth killing them for?"

"Family!" And it was a roar. A scream that cut through the night. "I wanted *my* family! Your father hid them from me. Took them...and I wanted them back!"

"Witness Protection," Celia cried out from behind Sullivan. "That's what this is about—they were hidden..."

"And I wanted them back!" His yell. "My woman. *My* child. But I didn't get them...and guess what? You won't get your family, either..."

He was squeezing the trigger. But Sullivan could hear the pounding of horses' hooves. He knew his family was coming. *I've always got them.*

Sullivan grabbed Celia and they flew toward the shelter of the nearest tree as gunfire erupted.

Gunfire from the shooter's weapon.

And gunfire...

"No one hurts my family," Davis snarled.

Gunfire from Davis's weapon.

Sullivan looked up. Davis still had his gun aimed at the masked man.

The shooter was on the ground.

Sullivan's shoulder throbbed and burned. He knew the masked man's bullet had hit him, but he didn't care about the wound. He was alive. Celia was alive. His family—*we're safe.*

"Sullivan?" Celia's fingers slid over his cheek.

His precious Celia.

"You're bleeding," she whispered.

So was she. They'd both earned new wounds from this night.

Davis jumped off his horse and closed in on the killer—on the man who'd taken so much from them. But he would *not* take any more.

"Doesn't even hurt," Sullivan said to her. He rose, pulling her with him, and he kept his arm around her.

Brodie had leaped off his horse, too, and Sullivan saw that Jennifer had already grabbed the shooter's weapon. She held it aimed at the prone man, her body tense.

"It's over," Sullivan said. "You're not hurting us anymore."

The fallen man just laughed. He rolled over, still wearing that mask. "The house is going to blow next," he said. "I've planted my bombs—you'll lose everything. All gone…in a puff of smoke."

Was he bluffing?

But…it didn't matter. "I'll lose nothing," Sullivan said. Blood dripped down his left arm. "Bricks and wood. The home will be rebuilt." It was the people who mattered.

Brodie leaned forward and ripped the mask off the guy's face.

Sullivan and Celia crept closer. Sullivan expected to see a stranger staring back at him.

He didn't.

He heard Celia's sharply indrawn breath.

The man's face was older, sharper, but…Sullivan had seen him before. In a very old photograph.

A photograph of his mother's brother.

No, no way…he wouldn't kill his own sister!

"I told her not to go…to the cops…" he rasped.

"When I shot that boy...I told her...I *warned* her, but she turned on me. *Me.*"

A dull ringing filled Sullivan's ears. He stared at that man—*family*—and he'd never wanted to kill anyone more.

"Thought when Celia started digging..." The guy swiped his hand over his face and then his hand dropped to the ground beside him. "Thought she'd find out... that *I* was the one my sister identified all those years ago...that I was the one she ran from..."

A killer, intimately close.

Too close.

"Faked my death...Uncle Sam helped...I was killing for him..." He laughed. And his hand...it was sliding toward his boot. Sullivan's eyes narrowed.

"But then I learned what McGuire had done, what he'd taken...not just my sister...*everything!*" And his hand slid into his boot. Sullivan knew he was going to pull up a weapon, a gun or a knife, and Sullivan yelled a warning—

But Davis didn't need a warning. Davis didn't even need to fire. Neither did Jennifer. Because Monroe had managed to drag himself up. And Monroe took aim at the killer. The bullet blasted from Monroe's gun before anyone else could even move.

One bullet.

The killer fell back—*their uncle.* He tumbled into the dirt. His breath rasped out in a sick, rough gurgle, and Sullivan knew the bullet had found its mark. That was the last gasp of a dying man.

He bent next to the fallen man. The guy's eyes were still open—wide, desperate, a dark gold. A gold that Sullivan had seen before. Now he knew why Celia had gasped. She'd never seen the picture of his uncle. She hadn't recognized the guy from a photograph. She'd recognized his distinctive eyes.

Him.

When Sullivan had asked Alexandra to identify the shooter, she'd just said that the guy looked like... *"Him."*

At the time, Sullivan had thought that the man must somehow look like him. But despite their blood connection, his uncle didn't resemble Sullivan at all.

Instead, his golden eyes looked exactly like Monroe Blake's. Exactly like the man who'd just killed him.

The golden eyes closed.

No one moved. Everyone stood there, staring at the dead man.

Past and present merged.

Grief twisted through Sullivan as he thought of all he'd lost.

Then...

Celia slipped closer. Her hand curled around his. "It's going to be okay," she said softly. "I promise. Everything will be okay..."

His fingers squeezed hers. The threat was finally over. Finally.

Sirens screamed in the distance.

Justice had come to the McGuire ranch.

Epilogue

The fires were out. The body was gone.

There were no more bombs. No more shooters lurking in the woods.

The ghosts from the past were gone.

There was just…family. And that family had gathered together at McGuire Securities, a somber meeting as they closed this final chapter.

Sullivan sat on the couch, his hands entwined with Celia's. They'd both been taken to the hospital. Patched up. Stitched. Released.

The cops had been there, interviewing them, asking questions that never seemed to end. Then the government had taken over. Agents in their fancy suits who were interested in containing the story.

After all, there were some secrets that weren't supposed to be shared.

Like the fact that their uncle—he'd been a trained assassin for the government. He'd spent years working with Ronald Worth, being the guy's attack dog. When Ronald needed a target eliminated, their uncle had been the man he called for the job.

After quite a few closed-door meetings with the CIA agents who'd swooped in, Celia had come to Sullivan to share what she'd learned. Apparently, Ronald had kept a secret file in his home office—a file that detailed all of their uncle's assignments for him. Once the powers that be at the agency had learned of his deception, Ronald's home was turned upside down. And all his secrets had been discovered.

Along with the truth about dear old Uncle Jeremiah.

Sullivan's mother had only mentioned him a few times. Her older brother. The soldier who'd survived battle but wound up dead at home. Sullivan had seen a picture of him, once. *Jeremiah.* He'd had dark hair and a wide smile.

Celia cleared her throat. "My contacts in the government have said that there will be no further inquiries on this investigation. As far as they're concerned, the case is closed."

The case. The McGuire legacy of pain and death. Now—over.

"He was a killer," Grant said, pushing back his shoulders. His voice was grim. "But he was her *brother.* Mom's own brother...he pulled the trigger."

Sullivan's gaze slid to his sister, Ava. He could never imagine hurting her. Would *never* do anything to so much as mar her skin. Tears glistened in Ava's eyes, and he hated that sight.

Davis was beside their sister. Ava's husband was to her right. Mark kept tenderly rubbing her shoulder.

"Every family has secrets," Celia said quietly, "and yours is certainly no exception."

No, theirs was the extreme.

"Your father...he helped your mother in many ways. It seems that she needed to make someone else disappear. Someone else that she feared Jeremiah might hurt.

It was never official. From what I've been able to learn, there was no record of this woman entering the Witness Protection Program."

All eyes were on her.

"Susan Salenger," she said quietly. "She was Jeremiah's lover over thirty years ago. His lover and your mother's best friend. When your mother saw what her brother had done, what he'd become, she knew that she had to get away from Jeremiah. She also knew that she had to protect her friend."

"But—but I thought Mom's brother was *dead*." Ava shook her head. "He was killed in a car accident. That was the story—"

"I'm afraid that's all it was. A story." Celia's voice was gentle. "Your uncle Jeremiah was working with Ronald. When it looked as though Jeremiah would be exposed, Ronald stepped in and tried to cover for the guy. After all, who looks for a dead man?"

Ava shivered.

"Ronald got rid of your mother's most damning evidence and Jeremiah…he got rid of the cops who'd heard her testimony. He ordered the hit on Henry, and then he made sure no one would connect the dots back to him…or Jeremiah."

Grant swore. "The guy was a damn monster."

Yes, he had been.

"Maybe your mother never bought the story of his death," Celia continued. "After all, she faked her own death, too, so maybe she suspected he was still out there all along."

"One death for another…" Grant shook his head. "And I never knew. She hid this all from us behind a wide smile."

Sullivan would never forget his mother's beautiful smile.

Silence lingered in the room until Ava said, "Jeremiah finally tracked down our mother, with Ronald's help."

Celia's voice was so quiet. "He wanted information from her. Or rather, from your father."

"He said…our dad said he'd never tell…" Ava's voice broke a bit.

"And he never did," Sullivan said.

"No." Celia shook her head. "He didn't. He never revealed what had become of Susan Salenger. He never told Jeremiah where she'd been taken. Who she'd become."

Grant surged to his feet. "Why the hell did she matter so much? Matter enough that Jeremiah killed his own sister?"

"She mattered…" Celia glanced at Sullivan, then continued. "Because she was pregnant. Ronald kept a file on Jeremiah, and in it he'd written that Jeremiah spent years looking for his child. Before Susan vanished, she was eight months pregnant. She had a baby, and Jeremiah wanted his son."

"Hell." Grant raked a hand over his face. "It was all about family."

In Jeremiah's twisted world, it had been. "I think the bastard wanted to punish Mom for betraying him—both for going to the cops after he told her to keep quiet, and then for taking Susan away…"

"Susan." Ava glanced around the room. Then her gaze focused on Celia. "Do we know what happened to her? What happened to her baby?"

There was a faint knock at the door.

Sullivan glanced at his watch. *Just in time.*

The door opened. Monroe Blake stood there. The faint lines near his eyes had deepened and the man appeared far too pale. He'd been in the hospital, but Sullivan knew he'd fought to get out early.

From all accounts, Monroe had always been a fighter.

"Sorry," Monroe said as he looked around. His golden eyes were wary. "I got a call from Celia telling me to be here."

Because Sullivan had asked her to make that call.

"Come in," Sullivan said. "You're just in time."

But Monroe didn't move. "No," he said. "I don't belong here. I just—I came to say how sorry I am. I came to say—"

"You didn't know he was your father," Sullivan interrupted. "Not until it was too late."

If possible, Monroe became even paler. "I'm nothing like him," he rasped.

Sullivan nodded. "No, I don't think you are."

Monroe stared at them all, his eyes tortured.

Celia had already told Sullivan what had happened to Susan. She'd become Katie Blake, and she'd given birth to a son.

Monroe.

A man who'd grown up and become a SEAL. A man who had—because fate was twisted and mysterious—saved Davis McGuire's life in battle, just as he, in turn, had been saved.

A man who was family, even though he hadn't realized it.

"I don't belong here," Monroe said. Shame flashed on his face.

Sullivan rose and went to his side. "Yes, you do."

And it was time they all let go of the pain from the past. It was time the McGuires looked to the future.

To hope.

"Welcome to the family…"

CELIA'S STOMACH WAS in knots. She'd been given the all clear from the agency. No one was coming after her—there were no more secrets she had to keep. She was…free.

Sullivan and his family were making peace with the past, and they were fully embracing Monroe. Poor, shell-shocked Monroe. The guy had killed his own father in order to save Sullivan.

She owed him. They all owed Monroe. She was sure the debt would be repaid.

They were back at the ranch. At the bluff that overlooked the lake. The water was still, and it reflected the sun, throwing the bright light back at her. But she didn't mind that light. After being in the darkness for so long, she found it nice.

"Are you hiding?"

She didn't tense at Sullivan's voice. After all, she'd known that he was coming. Deep inside, she'd always known they'd come together again.

Known. Hoped. Same thing.

She turned her head and found his gaze on her. Celia smiled at him. She barely even felt the pull of her stitches. Her new scar was nothing compared to what she could have lost.

Sullivan. And every hope she'd ever had.

"Not hiding," she said. "Just enjoying the sunset."

He reached for her hand. He was so warm and strong. And he was—

Kneeling.

"Sully?"

He had a ring in his fingers. "Will you marry me?"

"We…I…I think we are married." That part of Ronald's story had proven true. She just hadn't been able to tell Sully sooner because of—

He smiled up at her. "Then will you promise me forever, Celia? Because that's what I want. Forever, with you."

She couldn't speak.

His smile dimmed. "I've made mistakes. I know I've made so many, baby, but I swear, *you* are my world. I will do anything and everything to make you happy, I will—"

"I love you," Celia said.

His eyes darkened.

"And you've always had my forever." He'd had every part of her.

He slid the ring onto her finger. It was a perfect fit, and the diamond gleamed in the light. "You've always had my heart," he said gruffly. His fingers curled around hers. "Right here, it's been in the palm of your hand all along. You own me, Celia. Body and soul, and there is nothing I would not do for you."

Her own heart was pounding far too fast.

"I will love you forever," he promised her.

And she knew it was true. She could see that love on his face, in his eyes. And when he kissed her…she could feel it.

Forever.

The past was over, and their future waited.

* * * * *

MILLS & BOON®

INTRIGUE
Romantic Suspense

A SEDUCTIVE COMBINATION OF DANGER AND DESIRE

A sneak peek at next month's titles...

In stores from 5th May 2016:

- **Deep Secrets** – Beverly Long *and*
  APB: Baby – Julie Miller
- **Warrior Son** – Rita Herron *and*
  Armoured Attraction – Janie Crouch
- **Colorado Crime Scene** – Cindi Myers *and*
  Native Born – Jenna Kernan

Romantic Suspense

- **Cavanaugh Cold Case** – Marie Ferrarella
- **A Baby for Agent Colton** – Jennifer Morey

Available at WHSmith, Tesco, Asda, Eason, Amazon and Apple

Just can't wait?
Buy our books online a month before they hit the shops!
visit www.millsandboon.co.uk

These books are also available in eBook format!

MILLS & BOON®

The Irresistible Greeks Collection!

2 FREE BOOKS!

You'll find yourself swept off to the Mediterranean with this collection of seductive Greek heartthrobs. Order today and get two free books!

Order yours at
www.millsandboon.co.uk/irresistiblegreeks

0516_IG

MILLS & BOON®

Mills & Boon have been at the heart of romance since 1908… and while the fashions may have changed, one thing remains the same: from pulse-pounding passion to the gentlest caress, we're always known how to bring romance alive.

Now, we're delighted to present you with these irresistible illustrations, inspired by the vintage glamour of our covers. So indulge your wildest dreams and unleash your imagination as we present the most iconic Mills & Boon moments of the last century.

Visit **www.millsandboon.co.uk/ArtofRomance** to order yours!

0516_AOR

MILLS & BOON®

The Billionaires Collection!

2 FREE BOOKS!

This fabulous 6 book collection features stories from some of our talented writers. Feel the temperature rise with our ultra-sexy and powerful billionaires. Don't miss this great offer – buy the collection today to get two books free!

Order yours at
www.millsandboon.co.uk/billionaires

0516_BR

MILLS & BOON®

Why shop at millsandboon.co.uk?

Each year, thousands of romance readers find their perfect read at millsandboon.co.uk. That's because we're passionate about bringing you the very best romantic fiction. Here are some of the advantages of shopping at www.millsandboon.co.uk:

* **Get new books first**—you'll be able to buy your favourite books one month before they hit the shops

* **Get exclusive discounts**—you'll also be able to buy our specially created monthly collections, with up to 50% off the RRP

* **Find your favourite authors**—latest news, interviews and new releases for all your favourite authors and series on our website, plus ideas for what to try next

* **Join in**—once you've bought your favourite books, don't forget to register with us to rate, review and join in the discussions

Visit **www.millsandboon.co.uk** for all this and more today!

MILLS_WEB